Praise for the novels of Jo McNally

Barefoot on a Starlit Night

"A fun read."

—*Harlequin Junkie*

"Filled with tension and raw emotion, *Barefoot on a Starlit Night* is sure to please readers of contemporary romance."

—*New York Journal of Books*

"If you are looking for a feel-good book with romance, laughs, and a guaranteed HEA with an author who writes with a practiced hand, then look no further than this book!"

—*The Lit Bitch*

Stealing Kisses in the Snow

"Readers will be charmed by this sweet, no-nonsense Christmas romance full of genuine emotion." —*Publishers Weekly*

Slow Dancing at Sunrise

"With witty characters and only a small amount of drama, *Slow Dancing at Sunrise* is an entertaining and charming story that will appeal to readers of small-town romances."

—*Harlequin Junkie*

**Also available from
Jo McNally
and HQN**

Slow Dancing at Sunrise
Stealing Kisses in the Snow
Sweet Nothings by Moonlight (ebook novella)
Barefoot on a Starlit Night

For a complete list of titles available from Jo McNally,
please visit jomcnallyromance.com.

JO McNALLY

Love Blooms

HQN

HQN

Recycling programs
for this product may
not exist in your area.

ISBN-13: 978-1-335-94933-2

Love Blooms

Copyright © 2021 by Jo McNally

This edition published by arrangement with Harlequin Books S.A.

For questions and comments about the quality of this book,
please contact us at CustomerService@Harlequin.com.

HQN
22 Adelaide St. West, 40th Floor
Toronto, Ontario M5H 4E3, Canada
www.Harlequin.com

Printed in Spain

Dedicated to the memory of one of the original classy,
sassy ladies in my life.
We love and miss you, Aunt Shirley.

Acknowledgments

I loved this runaway bride story idea from the moment it came to me, but it was trickier to write than I'd anticipated. For one thing, I wrote it in 2020, so...you know...nothing was easy. And writing a story about a guy who chases after the woman he loves is a bit of a high-wire act. I needed to be sure Owen never came across as anything other than a good man who truly wanted to be worthy of Lucy's love again.

I had some help pulling that off, so many thanks to editor Anna J. Stewart for helping me frame the story properly before I got started, and of course to my editor at HQN, Michele Bidelspach, for her wise guidance. And a huge thank-you to the constant and invaluable member of my writing team: my agent, Veronica Park at Fuse Literary, who always tells it like it is and has my back no matter what. And most of all, thanks and so much love to my very own cinnamon roll hero—my husband of twenty-five years, John.

I dedicated this book to my aunt Shirley, who was one of the women who inspired the bawdy senior book club in Rendezvous Falls. We sadly lost Shirley in January at the age of ninety. She was a feisty, independent, always stylish inspiration right to the end. Her final words to me via a family video call from the hospital were a command to "keep writing those books!"

And I promised her I would.

CHAPTER ONE

LUCY HIGGINS WAS supposed to be having fun.

Everyone *around* her certainly was. The noisy bar was full of women—her friends, relatives and relatives-to-be. All drinking and laughing, singing and dancing. It was a whirling kaleidoscope of noise and frantic activity that Lucy wanted no part of. But she couldn't leave.

It was *her* party.

At least, it was a party *for* her. About her.

Hooray... Lucy's getting married tomorrow...

She drained her wineglass and gestured to the bartender, one of the few males in the room, for more. Everyone here knew she was the bride, mainly because of the white baseball cap she wore with cheap netting sticking out the back and the word *BRIDE* emblazoned on the front. The bartender, an older gentleman, gave her a wry smile as he refilled the glass.

"Drinking away your wedding jitters?"

She nodded, just to be polite, but didn't answer. She'd passed *jitters* a few hours ago, and was headed straight down the road to Panic City.

Was ditching your own wedding a crime? Would the cops come after her if she just packed up and left Greensboro tonight? Would anyone even notice? Would they care more about *why* she left than the inconvenience and rumors her absence would cause?

She stared into the shimmering white wine in her glass and sighed. Her future in-laws would care very much. At least about the inconvenience. Definitely about the rumors. They were the ones who'd coughed up the money for this circus...er...wedding. Who would even eat all that food if Lucy never walked down the aisle? Her parents would be mortified, which would serve them both right.

They were the main reason she was having a meltdown at her own damn bachelorette party.

Owen would care. Hopefully. He *was* the groom after all. But...how *much would he care*? And for how long? Sure, he'd be surprised. Maybe momentarily pissed off. But would he actually *care*? Sometimes it seemed like he came back from Afghanistan a totally different man. Or maybe her fiancé had always been rigidly aligned with following the rules and she'd just chalked it up to him being...reserved. She'd jokingly called him her calm in the storm when they'd met. Maybe his love of having a plan just *seemed* like calm to her, because her own life had always felt so chaotic. Maybe she'd never known him at all.

Maybe she was actually losing her mind right now. She stared into the wine even harder, hoping that—like a liquid crystal ball—it would reveal the answers she so desperately needed. It did not. All she knew for sure was the thought of walking down the aisle tomorrow morning made her palms go clammy and her heart start racing. Tripping. Running. Like *she* should be doing...

Her older sister, Kris, threw herself onto the barstool next to Lucy and plunked her empty beer glass onto the bar.

"Barkeep," Kris shouted, "Ah'm runnin' dry!" The alcohol was making her sister's North Carolina accent sharper than ever. "I haven't danced this much since last year's Appalachia festival. Your friend Nikki is a *beast*! She hasn't been off that dance floor in an hour, and she's older than I am. I don't know how she does it." Kris paused for a breath, her smile fading. "Wait. You look like you're getting ready for a wake. What's up?"

"Did you know about Mom and Dad?" Lucy couldn't hold in the hurt any longer. She had to know if she was the only one who'd been duped all these years.

Kris's hesitation, along with the way her gaze bounced everywhere in the bar but never quite landed on Lucy's face, was all she needed to know.

"Oh, my God." Lucy drained her wine again. "Y'all are frickin' unbelievable. What else have I missed? Are you and Kevin breaking up, too? Does *anyone* actually love each other in this family?"

Kris pulled her dark blond hair up off her neck and blew out a long breath. "First of all—no, Kevin and I are *not* divorcing, so you just keep those words outta your mouth. What exactly do you *think* you know about Mom and Dad?"

"I know they're only waiting until after my wedding to get divorced. And that Mom is having an affair with some guy."

Just saying those words out loud felt like a betrayal of everything she'd ever known. Her happy family with her loving parents at the helm—even if life at home hadn't always been sunny and bright. Dad was an auto mechanic, and there always seemed to be money woes. Some periods felt downright desperate. When Kris was sick they'd moved from their doublewide in the mountains to a tiny brick ranch closer to Greensboro and the doctors who were treating her leukemia. Then Dad's mom got sick and her parents were juggling their time between Kris and Grandma. It was a lot of pressure on a family, sure, but the one constant throughout her parents' partnership was their teamwork. The high school sweethearts always managed to make things work. Until now.

When Lucy overheard them talking last night, she thought they were pranking her. That they'd heard her come back inside and were playing a twisted, unintentionally cruel joke. But the longer she'd listened, the more real it became.

She flinched when the DJ started playing "It's Raining Men." The bar went wild with female screeches and applause. But Kris and Lucy were in their own little bubble of sorrow at the bar, staring each other down like a scene from one of those police drama interrogations.

Kris swallowed hard. "They *told* you that?"

"No." Lucy shook her head. "I heard them arguing yesterday afternoon, before we came to the hotel." The wedding was set to happen in a historic chapel in High Point, not far from Greensboro. The Coopers had decided on the location, just like they'd decided everything else about this wedding. "Mom and Dad thought I'd left… I mean, I *did* leave, but I forgot my list of what I needed to pick up. I went back in the house, and…" Her eyes closed. She was relying on lists a lot these days. Planning the wedding to happen so quickly after Owen's discharge may not have been the best idea. He seemed to be having a hard time acclimating to civilian life. To a life with her. She understood if he felt overwhelmed. She did, too. Hence, order. Lists. One day at a time.

But when she went back in the house and heard raised

voices on the back deck, she'd stopped feeling like anything was in order. She'd hardly known her parents to
argue…*ever*. The open window allowed her to hear every
harshly whispered word.

…*can't wait until this wedding is over, Tom, so we can
end this farce…*

…*you're so eager to be with your lover, just go…*

…*be stupid. We can't ruin Lucy's day. But by next
week…*

…*don't tell me, Marsha. Tell my lawyer…*

…*supposed to intimidate me? Your lawyer is your idiot
cousin…*

…*at least I can trust her, which is more than I can say
about you…*

…*didn't start, Tom. I hope Lucy has better taste in husbands than I did…*

"Oh, shit…" Kris grabbed Lucy's hands in hers. "You're
crying! Come with me." Lucy blindly followed her sister
out the back door of the bar to the dimly lit parking lot.
Kris dabbed at Lucy's face with a wad of tissues. "Stop
crying, honey. It's gonna be fine."

"It's *not* going to be fine, Kris. Our *parents* are *divorcing*. Mom's cheating on Dad. How could she do that? How
could they hide this from us?" Kris's gaze dropped, and
Lucy pounced. "You knew, didn't you? And you didn't
tell me? How can you protect Mom when she…"

"It wasn't just Mom, okay? It's complicated. You need
to get back to your party, Luce, before people notice.
Things have been bad with them for a while. You just
didn't want to see it."

Lucy swatted Kris's hand away. "I didn't see it because
you all *lied to me*." Lucy's voice rose, her hands gestur-

ing wildly. "You were going to let Dad walk me down the aisle and sit with Mom in the front row and you *knew* it was all going to be an act. I'm starting my wedding with a *lie*, Kris."

"That lie has nothing to do with you and Owen. Tomorrow is still *your* day, Lucy. Come back inside…"

Lucy stomped away, marching across the parking lot with no destination in mind other than *away*. That was the one word that kept scrolling through her thoughts. *Away*. She heard Kris go back inside, propelled by a labored sigh. *Good*. She couldn't look at anyone in her family right now without feeling betrayed. She walked all the way to the back row of cars and stared off into the swampy stand of trees behind the parking lot. Behind her, the door to the bar opened and closed again. Light footsteps headed her way.

"What's goin' on?" Lucy's posture softened at the soft, no-nonsense voice of Nikki Taggart. Her maid of honor. Her best friend. Hopefully, someone who'd never lied to her. The possibility made her spin on her heel to face her, gulping back tears.

"Did *you* know? Did you know my parents' marriage is a sham?"

"Hand to God, I did not." Nikki, with her short dark hair and darker eyes, gestured from her chest to the sky. "Kris just filled me in, but I'm still fuzzy on the details. Something about your mom cheating? I'm so sorry."

Nikki opened her arms and Lucy didn't hesitate to walk into the embrace. They stood there in the back of the dark parking lot. Nikki didn't say a word, just held Lucy tight. They could hear the music from the party, still going strong. Eventually her tears subsided enough for Lucy to gasp out a few words.

"They're only…together…for the wedding…" She pulled in a steadying breath. "They're breaking up as soon as it's over. They weren't even going to tell me…" She wiped her face with the back of her hand, bumping her white BRIDE hat in the process. She snatched it off angrily and held it up. "This whole weekend is just people pretending to be something they're not. I wanted to get married barefoot on Grandfather Mountain, in that little hollow in the pines where the azaleas grow and you can see the Blue Ridge going on forever. But no. Owen's parents insisted on this fancy wedding in High Point, so all *their* friends and business associates can come." She swished the hat back and forth in anger. "It feels like someone else's wedding. Owen and I are supposed to starting our new life together, and I'm not sure I even know who he is right now. Who *I* am. What we're doing. And my parents are divorcing!"

"Okay," Nikki said. "Let's take a step back. I know you were blindsided by your parents' news, but don't weave their mistakes into *your* relationship. You and Owen have got *years* invested in this. He waited when you moved to Boone to care for your grandmother. You waited while he did his Army thing. And you love each other, right?" Lucy didn't answer, and Nikki folded her arms on her chest. *"Right?"*

Lucy stared up at the stars, her chest constricting. When she and Owen met at that noisy beachside bar, she'd teased him for being the strong silent type. But there was something in that strength, all solid frame and broad shoulders. Something in his silence, too. He'd seemed so at home in his own skin. So willing to let the world spin wildly around him without actually affecting him in any way. His golden eyes felt like a safety net to her. He made her feel okay about everything.

Lucy dug the toe of her shoe into the gravel parking lot. She was so tired. She'd been pushed and pulled a hundred different directions lately by Owen's parents. Faye and Edward Cooper were a force of nature unto themselves. Faye had her name on the children's wing of a hospital. Edward spent three days a week at the country club, where he owned his own golf cart and was president of the men's club.

Once Faye accepted the fact that Owen, her only child, had chosen Lucy, with her lowly Appalachian roots, Faye made it clear that she would single-handedly ensure this wedding would be one scripted for the society pages. She'd even browbeaten Lucy into a frothy, cotillion excuse for a wedding dress that seemed to engulf her petite frame every time she tried it on. Faye was paying for it, so Lucy felt she couldn't argue. But she couldn't lie to herself anymore. She hated the dress. In fact, she pretty much hated everything about this wedding.

"I can't do this."

"Do what?"

"Get married."

Saying it aloud was like a death sentence, or a stay of execution, or maybe a little of both. Silence hung between the two women. The only sounds were muffled party music and a swamp full of frogs singing their nighttime serenade. With a stoic sigh, Nikki led Lucy to someone's pickup truck and lowered the tailgate, slapping it to let Lucy know she was supposed to join her. They sat for a moment before Nikki finally spoke.

"My job as your maid of honor is to make sure all your pre-wedding needs are met. And if you're telling me there's a good reason for you to back out—to back out the *night before the wedding*—then I've got you. You know that's how we roll."

It was true. Nikki was a successful restaurant chef and caterer in Raleigh. She was also a down-to-earth woman who knew who she was, what she wanted and how to get it. She was able to mingle with Raleigh's politicians and college presidents without losing her sense of self or putting on airs. Lucy was envious of Nikki's confidence in every choice she made. Maybe it was the age difference—Nikki was thirty-six, and Lucy was barely thirty. Nikki had grown up with a nomad of a father, who dragged her and her older brother all over the country chasing pipe dreams. That experience had left Nikki craving reality and roots over wishes and dreams.

Nikki reached over and plucked the white hat from Lucy's hands. "But first, you need to convince me this isn't a massive case of cold feet. What's happening with your parents sucks. But you're not marrying your parents. You're marrying that strong, dependable, arguably too good to be true all-American hero, Owen Cooper. You and I have known each other what—almost four years?" Lucy nodded. "The whole time, you've been dreamboating over this guy of yours. Why are you even *thinking* of ditching him now? Did he do something stupid? Do I have to go beat him up? 'Cause you know I'll do it."

"I told you he's been…different." Lucy shrugged. "Quieter than usual. He hardly ever laughs anymore…" His laughter was one of the first things she'd fallen in love with when they met at the beach. He seemed to always be surprised and amused by her. Not in a *you're weird* way, but in a genuinely affectionate way. He told her she made him laugh like no one else ever had. "I can't get him to express an opinion on *anything since he got back.* He just goes along with whatever his mother says. I mean, the guy *hates* crowds, and he didn't even blink when Faye said we're having three hundred guests."

Nikki turned the white cap in her hands with a frown. "Have you tried talking to him? Did something…bad… worse than the usual, happen to him on this deployment?"

Lucy swung her legs back and forth under the tailgate.

"I've tried talking. He keeps saying things will be fine after the wedding. When I cornered him before the rehearsal tonight, he said that we just have to—" she formed air quotes with her fingers "—'get through it' and then we can start our lives. He looks at marrying me as something he has to *get through*, Nikki. I can't get him to talk about anything that happened on his last deployment. He just says it was tougher than the first, but he's fine. That's all he says, over and over. 'It was tough, but I'm fine. It was tough, but I'm fine.' Like if he says it often enough he might actually believe it. But I sure as hell don't."

There was a beat of silence.

"Do you still love him?" Nikki asked softly.

Wasn't that The Question?

For the first time in a long time, Lucy forced herself to look directly at it. Did. She. Love. Owen? Impossible to say for certain, at least in that moment. Which was terrifying. She loved how she used to feel with Owen. Protected. Happy. Simple. That was the operative word. Simple.

Life was *simple* with him. Uncomplicated. Whether it

was gathering with friends or making love together, everything just…worked. But was that *love*?

Lucy threw her hands up. "I *thought* I did… I think I do…but what if this is a horrible mistake? What if I have no idea what love even is? What if we end up just pretending for decades like my parents? Tolerating each other until we hate each other? What if he never snaps out of this robotic mood of his? What if I'm only marrying him because he's a safe choice? I said *yes* years ago. What if we're strangers now?" She slid off the tailgate and started pacing back and forth. "We've put our relationship on hold more than once. Maybe that's a sign. Maybe I'll wake up someday and regret everything. Will I become my mother? Worse, oh God, what if I become *his*?"

Nikki hopped off the tailgate and stepped in front of Lucy, taking her by the upper arms and giving her a gentle shake. "Slow the What-if Train down a few notches, kiddo, before you hyperventilate. I can't decide if this freak-out is you being prudent or you being irrational." She turned Lucy around and they walked around the parking lot perimeter. "When's the last time you ate?"

Lucy scowled in thought. "Breakfast?"

Nikki nodded. "And how much have you had to drink?"

"A…few glasses of wine. Plus a shot of something blue."

"Lovely." Nikki grimaced. "I'm taking you home, but first we're stopping at Popeye's for some fried chicken to soak up that booze. In the morning, after a good night's sleep, *then* you can make your final decision." Nikki pulled out her keys and pushed a button to unlock her shiny blue convertible, tossing the white cap onto the back seat. "If you decide to marry this guy, which is what we've been planning for weeks, then I will make sure you're at the church and headed down that aisle as scheduled." They both got into the car, and Nikki started the engine, which rumbled to life like an angry tiger being disturbed from sleep. "And if you decide you absolutely *don't* want to marry the guy you've been engaged to for years, then…" Nikki pulled out of the parking lot and hit the gas, sending Lucy's *Bride* hat flying out of the back seat and floating away in the warm night air.

"Well, if you *don't* want to do this, I'll help you make a run for it." She said it as casually as if she was telling Lucy she'd buy doughnuts. But Lucy knew Nikki meant it. Instead of making her sad or anxious, the idea of an escape plan loosened something around her heart. It felt like… She blinked away tears and stared out the passenger side so Nikki wouldn't see.

It felt like hope. Plus a little bit of nausea.

CHAPTER TWO

OF ALL THE contingencies Owen Cooper had prepared for on his wedding day, having his bride's best friend hand him a *Dear Owen* letter at the church was nowhere on the list. Nikki Taggart looked almost pleased with herself when she did it, too. She hadn't done anything more than give the slightest of crooked half smiles, but he should have known it meant trouble. He should have been at least somewhat prepared for the bombshell he found inside the envelope. After eight years in the Army, *bombshell* wasn't a word he used loosely. But at that moment, as he stood there in the church vestibule wearing his tuxedo, boutonniere in place…well, it was hard to imagine even a roadside IED could shake him up more than this.

Lucy had left him. *Left. Him.* On their goddamn wedding day! He closed his eyes and willed his heart rate to slow. Flying off the handle would accomplish nothing. Every problem had a solution. He'd learned long ago not to complain about anything to his father or grandfather unless he also presented a solution. Same thing in the Army. Never bitch about a plan unless you had a better one. He blew out a long, slow breath, reprocessing the past few weeks to figure out where it all went wrong.

He knew Lucy had been uptight. His dad said all brides became bridezillas as the wedding got closer, so he'd dutifully dismissed Lucy's heavy sighs and restlessness as just normal bride stuff. She was the one with the max pressure, putting this together with his mom. Lord knew that couldn't have been easy. Mom could be a real bulldozer when she wanted to have her own way. Which was always.

Sure, he'd been surprised to get home after his discharge to learn that hundreds of people were coming to this thing. Lucy always talked about keeping their wedding small. But she must have agreed to it. If that's what she wanted, he figured he could handle it for one day. Dad said the wedding was always about the bride anyway. Owen's role was to show up and smile.

But Lucy kept asking his opinion on stuff. Did he like the flowers? Did he like the menu? Did he like the idea of a pink champagne-flavored cake? It almost felt like a test. One he was destined to fail. He wanted her to pick whatever *she* wanted. Seemed like the only possible right answer. Lucy hadn't had the easiest of childhoods, and if she'd decided she wanted this big, fantasy wedding instead of barefoot on a mountaintop, it was fine with him. Him telling her he didn't care what flavor of cake she picked didn't mean he didn't care about *her*.

She'd mentioned more than once in her emails during his final months in Afghanistan that things weren't her "style," but she'd ordered all this stuff, so it was too late to change it now. Unless, of course, she just walked away. Away from everyone. Away from him.

One of the things he loved most about Lucy was her free spirit. Her quick laugh and willingness to try some new adventure, from kitesurfing to ziplining. She'd upended his world when they met. She was a sparkling counterbalance to his rigidly controlled life. His sunshine surprise. Unpredictable. But this? For her to just…leave.

She was the kindest person he'd ever met, so how could she do this?

How had he missed the signs? Had she given him any? Had he been too far into his own head to notice? Lucy had been tense since his return. Restless. He'd brushed off her concerns more than once, so he could hardly say she hadn't tried to talk. But damn…just a few months ago he'd been freezing his ass off in the Hindu Kush mountains,. He'd rolled out of his bunk more than once, in the supposed safety of their own camp, with enemy shells landing just yards away. Men *died*. And a few weeks later he was back in the States, listening to conversations about linen tablecloths vs. lace ones. It felt like mental whiplash, so…he'd tuned it out. Tuned *her* out.

And she'd definitely noticed. There were times it seemed she was more worried about him than she was about the wedding. She wanted to know why he was quieter than usual. *Did something happen overseas? Do you want to talk about it? Are you really okay?* He kept saying he was fine, but she didn't believe it any more than he did. He kept changing the subject, not wanting his experiences to darken Lucy's big day.

But now the big day was here. And Lucy wasn't.

Maybe he'd been gone too damn long. They met right before his second deployment to the Middle East. By the time he got back and proposed, she was helping take care of her sick grandmother. They decided to wait to get married—it didn't make sense for her to be stuck on some base, sitting alone. And she'd *agreed*. Just like everything else with Lucy, it was easy. Uncomplicated.

He looked down at her note, crumpled in his too tight grip. There was nothing easy or uncomplicated about *this*.

Guests were arriving. The pastor was standing a few feet away, watching Owen in wary silence. He'd probably done enough of these things to recognize trouble when he saw it. And this was way beyond trouble. In Army lingo, this was FUBAR. Fucked Up Beyond All Recognition.

Owen muttered a few curses under his breath. This wasn't the time to try understanding why it happened. It happened—was actively *happening*–and he had to deal with it. He'd have to tell everyone to go home. Call the caterer and deal with the food. Worst of all…he'd have to break the news to his mother.

A piercing howl of female fury echoed down the hall-way from the rooms where the rest of the bridal party was still getting ready. He could check one thing off his to-do list. His mother definitely knew.

LUCY STARED AT the drugstore shopping bag sitting on the dresser in her tiny hotel room in Pennsylvania. The stop at the strip plaza drugstore near the hotel had been impul-sive, and now she was doubting a few of her choices. But if she wanted to be a new person, she needed to do new things. Was hot pink a good hair color for her? There was only one way to find out. But first…the scissors.

Fifteen minutes later, the hotel trash bin was filled with six-inch-long locks of discarded tawny blond hair. The choppy shoulder-length layers she'd hacked into existence made her laugh. She stared into the mirror, running her fingers through what felt like someone else's hair. Some-one else's life. Before she had time to second-guess her-self, she grabbed the box of hair dye and got busy.

When she was done, the woman staring back at her in the mirror left her speechless. The color had taken differently in spots, probably due to the fact that she had no idea what she was doing. It was a softer rose gold in some areas, with intense spikes of hot pink in others. It was… fun, like an anime character. Or a more grown-up version of the Sparkle Pony Princess doll she'd played with as a kid. It made her smile. It made her feel fun. Lighter. Free. And—armed with the six-pack of mango-flavored hard seltzer she'd picked up at the store—it made her feel brave enough to turn her phone on and deal with the debris she'd left in her wake. She put the phone on speaker and chugged the seltzer faster as each voice mail played. If there was such a thing as a runaway bride bingo card, she would have ticked off all the squares and won.

Her parents, distressed. *Don't throw your life away because of us.*

Her sister, awed. *Damn girl, I didn't know you were serious. You're gonna be the talk of this town for years.*

Her bridesmaids together on someone's speaker, sounding like a chicken coop full of agitated hens.

What happened? Did you catch him screwing around?

Did you meet someone else?

Did you find out something awful about Owen?

Ohmygod, like this one story I saw on Dateline *about this guy in Houston. It turned out he had a collection of human teeth….*

Next was Faye Cooper, voice dripping with rage. She was a drama queen on a good day. And this would not have been a good day for her. *After all we did… I tried to tell Owen years ago…do you know how much seventeen swan-shaped ice sculptures cost?*

Nikki Taggart, amused. *I'm not saying I intentionally*

waited until they were all at the church to deliver your notes, but I'm not saying I didn't...

And then there was Owen. Urgent. Confused. *Send a text to let me know you're safe. For the love of God, tell me why.* A long, tension-filled pause. *What happened? Was it me? What can I do?*

But then he pivoted to more practical matters, as always. *I'm sure it's no surprise that my parents are unhappy. I don't know what to tell them. His voice broke.* His obvious confusion and hurt made her doubt herself. She tossed the phone on the nightstand and turned on the television. Maybe another can of seltzer would help. Maybe another ancient episode of *Law and Order* would make her feel less like a criminal.

Maybe she should drive back to Greensboro in the morning. Explain herself to everyone. They deserved that much, right? She looked up and caught her reflection in the mirror. The chopped pink hair made her look younger than she felt. Her grandmother had always called her an *old soul*. She didn't look like an old soul now. She looked like a spunky anime character with a solid dose of She-Ra. She grinned at her reflection. The would-be wife was gone now. And she wasn't coming back.

Goodbye, Lucy. Hello, Princess Sparkle Pony Mc-DoesntCare, the Wild Woman of the North.

Lucy had driven all the way to southern Pennsylvania. In Nikki's blue convertible. As she drove, she'd alternated between laughing out loud at her reflection in the rearview mirror, and crying in horror at what she'd just done. Whenever the tears threatened to blur her vision and make her a danger to the other drivers, she'd force another laugh. It had made for a wild and exhausting journey.

Technically she didn't leave Owen at the altar. There's no way it would have gotten that far. But Nikki's voice mail made it sound like it had been pretty damn close. She'd left several notes for her friend to deliver. Her parents. His parents. Her sister. She'd spent most of last night packing and writing notes.

True to her word, Nikki had been all in when Lucy called her at five in the morning.

"I can't do it," Lucy had blurted out.

"Uh…" Nikki cleared her throat. She'd obviously been sound asleep. "You're gonna need to be more specific…"

"I can't do this." Her words came in a rush. "It would feel like marrying a stranger. It wouldn't be fair—not to Owen…not to me. *I* feel like a stranger. I don't know who I am… I'm a mess! How can I marry him like this? I don't know if I'm in love… Or what love is… Or marriage. It's not fair to Owen. I can't…"

"Okay." Nikki had been wide-awake by that point. "Inhale, sweetie. Hold it. Then exhale. Are you really telling me you're canceling the wedding? The wedding that takes place in…six hours?"

"I can't do it." As jumbled as her emotions were, that was the one sentence that repeated itself in her head, over and over again. "I need to leave. I need to go. I can't do it."

It was Nikki's idea for Lucy to head north. In the convertible. Nikki referred to the Mustang as her therapy. She drove a hybrid SUV for her everyday travels. Lucy, on the other hand, drove a vintage Volkswagen Beetle she'd inherited from her grandmother. It was the one thing Owen had shown actual emotion over since his return. He'd taken one horrified look at the balding tires and insisted she get them replaced. Like he thought she had some magical money tree in the backyard. As if his parents had been paying her much more than minimum wage at Cooper Landscaping. The VW got her around town. How bad could it be?

But Nikki had put her foot down, saying Lucy needed to leave Buttercup—her grandmother's name for the old car—in North Carolina. At least for now.

Nikki sounded like Owen about the car. So logical. "Lord knows your old Bug won't make that trip. If you decide to stay there a while, we'll figure out something. I'll fly up or whatever. I promise driving my convertible will be good for your soul. You'll feel like a *Thelma and Louise* badass." Nikki had given her a wink. "Just don't go driving off any cliffs with it."

As she'd driven, thankful for the warm June sunshine on her face, she realized this was one of the very few times in her life she'd been truly on her own. Certainly the farthest away she'd been from home, other than a few vacation trips. She'd gone from her childhood home to college, where she'd shared a dorm room with Alice Nasmith, one of her stunned bridesmaids. She'd lived alone for a while in Wilmington, but she'd met Owen there and, even though he was back and forth between her apartment and Fort Bragg, she'd never felt alone. They emailed and texted constantly, even when he was deployed.

Then her grandmother had fallen ill agaun right after he'd returned from that deployment—his second, but the first since they'd met. They'd bounced between Grandma's place up in the mountains and Fort Bragg in Fayetteville for a year, and then he was gone again. This time he'd left her with a ring on her finger. After Grandma lost her long battle with cancer, Lucy moved in with her parents, going to work for *Owen's* parents at Cooper Landscaping and finding herself ensnared in the supercharged Cooper family dynamics.

If she'd gone through with the wedding, she'd have been living with Owen in the apartment he'd found in Greensboro, having *never* lived her own life. She'd never dated anyone else seriously, at least not since high school. She'd never discovered what she was or wasn't capable of on her own.

Sometime later, Lucy woke with a jolt, sitting up and blinking at the television's glow. She hadn't been out too long, because the *Law and Order* episode playing was still from the Lennie Briscoe years. Pink-haired Princess Sparkle Pony blinked back at her from the mirror on the wall. She wasn't sure what she'd dreamed about, but her only thought was that she needed to let Owen know she was okay. She'd never responded to his calls or texts. But even Princess Sparkle Pony didn't have the guts to call him directly. A text was the coward's way out, but she wasn't prepared for anything more.

I'm okay.

It was well after midnight, but his reply was instant.

Thank Christ.

That was such an Owen thing to do. He cared about people. He cared about her. She tapped her screen.

I'm sorry. I didn't know what else to do.

She watched the dots floating on the screen. They

started and stopped a few times, and she thought he might be sending a long message. But in the end, he just sent one impossible request.

I love you. Help me understand.

First, she'd have to understand it herself. She could imagine him distractedly running his fingers through his hair, still short from his military cut. His square jaw would be flexing, the cords in his neck tight with worry. Owen wasn't a bad man. She'd loved him. She may *still* love him. And she'd hurt him.

I'm so, so sorry. Maybe someday I can explain. For now I need time to think.

There was a long pause before he replied with a request.

Can you tell me where you are?

She pulled back, blowing out a low breath. She felt a shadow of the same panic she'd felt before she'd bolted.

Let me figure some things out on my own first.

More bubbles floated up and down.

At least check in once in a while?

She felt a pinch in her chest. There was no reason to refuse him.

I will. Good night.

Dropping her phone on the faded polyester bedspread, she stared at her reflection in the mirror until she heard the dun-DUN of another episode beginning. She turned off the television and the lights. Tomorrow she'd be in Rendezvous Falls, New York. Nikki's brother and grandmother lived there. They knew nothing about Lucy other than she was Nikki's friend and needed a place to stay. They had no expectations of her.

In Rendezvous Falls, she could be whoever she wanted to be.

Pink hair and all.

CHAPTER THREE

CONNIE PHELPS WAS in a particularly foul mood. Hell, plenty of people in Rendezvous Falls would say she'd been in a particularly foul mood for years now. But today's mood was exceptionally, particularly, ultra foul. She tossed an armful of long-stemmed pink roses onto her worktable and scowled at them. Three times she'd tried to gather them into a cylindrical bundle tied with ribbon to put in the front window. And three times her trembling right hand had betrayed her just as she had the ribbon gathered into a pretty bow.

She reached for one of dozens of vases on the back shelf. The minty green one would look nice with the pink, and was narrow enough that the roses would stand tall without being tied. It would still looked summery. A workable compromise.

Connie *despised* compromises.

She managed to get the June bride's window display for Rendezvous Blooms Flower Shop finished without any more compromises. And without breaking or dropping anything. *Yay, Connie.* She draped the pink lace backdrop over the back wall of the display. Then she tossed around giant knots of tule and glittery silvery fabric. The buckets of colorful roses, hydrangeas and lilies looked festive and bridal without requiring a lot of effort on her part.

She unlocked the front door—she was getting good

at using her left hand on bad days like this—and steeled herself for another day at the business she'd started thirty years ago. A business she was determined not to lose. But things were getting grim. Grimmer than her mood.

The brass bell above the front door tinkled as her first customer of the day came in. Cecile Manning, decked out in pink as always, her blond curls tucked under a ball cap, smiled brightly.

"Good morning, Connie! The window display looks great, but you know me and pink, right?"

"I think *everyone* knows you and pink are in a committed relationship." Connie wiped her left hand on her apron. "As far as this being a good morning, I guess that remains to be seen. What's with the hat?"

Cecile reached up and touched the cap—which was an uncharacteristic green instead of pink—with a grimace. "Ugh. It's Charlie's. I'm on my way to Suzy's for a trim, so I just stuffed my hair under the hat until I get there." She looked around the shop. "I saw your window when I walked by and thought I'd say hi. How are you?"

"You mean, have I dropped anything lately? Only a box and a few flowers. But the day's young yet." Connie's right hand began to tremor again, and she slid it into the pocket of her work apron. But not before Cecile noticed.

"Connie, you really need to hire someone to help you. Or, you know, break down and accept some help from your friends." She gave Connie her sternest look, but Cecile was such a bubbly, the-sun-will-come-out-tomorrow sort that she could never really look stern. "I'd be glad to help in the mornings."

"I'm fine." Connie moved behind the counter. "I don't need charity, and I can't afford to pay someone."

"You realize those two statements completely oppose each other, right? If you really can't afford hiring someone, then you *need* volunteers."

Her friend was right and they both knew it. They also both knew Connie would never admit it. Cecile tossed her hands up in exasperation.

"Okay, if you won't take volunteers, then maybe if you hire someone you'd be able to do more business to cover the expense? Didn't your doctor say stress and exhaustion were bad for you?"

"Whatever. Are you gonna buy something or are you just here to jaw at me?"

Cecile watched her for a long moment, then her shoulders sagged. "Fine. Give me a half dozen of those purple tulips. I'll take them to Suzy's salon."

Connie went to the refrigerated case and pulled out the container of tulips. Hopefully this latest onset of tremors would subside, as others had over the past year. The flare-ups were scary, but sometimes they went away. If not, she'd have to call Dr. Osgood and discuss the change in medication he'd suggested.

Back at the counter, she plucked out six stems and grabbed a length of polka dot cellophane to wrap them in. But she couldn't do *everything* one-handed. Tulips could be fragile, and just as she raised them upright her right hand shook sharply, sending one grape-colored petal floating down.

"Well, *shit*."

She turned for the display case, but Cecile stopped her, picking up the wrapped bundle.

"It's okay. It's just a little gift to put on Suzy's reception desk." She slid a bill across the counter. "They look lovely."

"Don't patronize me, Cecile. You know I hate that."

"Oh, for God's sake, you hate everything these days. Stop being so ornery, or you'll take the Town Grump award away from Iris Taggart. And you're too young to take her crown."

Iris Taggart was the owner of the Taggart Inn, although the inn was mostly being run by Iris's grandson, Logan, and his new wife, Piper, these days. Iris had a reputation for being a tough businesswoman…or just *tough*, period. The octogenarian was a longtime leader of the community business association and several festival committees.

"Too young? I'm almost seventy!"

"Exactly." Cecile accepted her change. "Iris is over eighty."

"Humph." Connie sniffed. "At least Iris's family supports her business instead of taking it away."

As much as Connie hated self-pity, she knew that sounded petulant. Maybe she really was becoming the Curmudgeon of Rendezvous Falls. Part of her didn't care. To hell with what people thought. But one increasingly insistent part of her was growing tired of being unhappy. Cecile put one hand on her hip.

"You know damn well Iris's grandkids tried to get her to *sell* that place for years. She just refused to do it. Nikki pushed the hardest, but once Logan came back to town and fell for the new manager, it made sense for him and Piper to take over." Cecile adjusted her ball cap again, and several strands of curly hair escaped. There were a few bits of gray among the artificial gold. "Is David still pressuring you to move in with him and what's-her-name up in Syracuse?"

And just like that, the sourness took over again. Connie slammed shut the cash drawer at the register. "Haven't you heard? There's a brand-new plan. For once, my daughter-in-law and I agree on something." The trembling in her hand grew more pronounced, and she pushed it back into her pocket. "Specifically, that she and I living under the same roof would be a disaster. Her solution is for them to move me into an assisted living complex near them in Syracuse."

Cecile's mouth dropped open. "Assisted living? Isn't that for people who can't wipe their own undercarriages?"

"Exactly! Just because Susan wants to use the lake house, I'm supposed to move into some studio apartment somewhere I've never lived and have my meals spoon-fed? I don't think so." That her son was even considering his wife's suggestion was enough to make Connie's stomach do somersaults. Thinking about it was *not* a good start to her day. She gave Cecile a pointed look. "Don't you have a hair appointment to get to?"

Unoffended, her friend just chuckled. "I'm going, I'm going. I can see I poked the bear one too many times." She turned back at the door. "But let's be real. Between the online florists taking your business and you turning down any jobs you're afraid you can't handle, your business is down. You can't take care of that house alone for much longer, especially those overgrown bushes taking over the front of it. If you want to prove to your son that you don't need assisted living, you might have to break down and accept some help from friends." She winked. "We won't tell him, I promise."

Connie waved her off, but once she was alone again, she couldn't stop thinking Cecile might be right. The pandemic a year ago had canceled almost every event on her calendar, leaving the business in the red for the first time since she'd opened. Her Parkinson's tremors had gotten worse over the winter, and word was getting around that she couldn't handle the intricate arrangements she used to be known for. Lately she'd been declining any event with more than a few items. She = couldn't take a chance of dropping someone's centerpiece half an hour before their wedding reception began. Or worse…ruining the bridal bouquet. The thought made her shudder.

Or was that just another Parkinson's tremor? Damn it all.

"MAYBE IF LUCY stared into her coffee cup a little longer while waiting for her breakfast at the Taggart Inn, she'd be able to figure out what to do next. She jumped when she heard a small voice next to her.

"Miss Lucy, can I walk with you again today?"

Six-year-old Lily Montgomery had her hands clasped in an adorable—and obvious—plea.

"That's up to your mom, sweetie." Lucy smiled at the adorable girl with all her golden curls.

"Her mom says no." Piper Montgomery Taggart set Lucy's breakfast in front of her and cast a stern look at her daughter. "You're going shopping with your grandmother, remember? So dial down the cute quotient, and stop pestering the guests."

Lily shrugged with a gap-toothed grin and skipped off to a new adventure. Lucy had been at the inn less than a week, and already knew the little girl rarely stood still more than a minute.

"She's welcome to come with me if she wants." Lucy smiled up at Piper. "I'm getting bored with just my own thoughts rattling around my head." Lucy looked at her overladen plate of blueberry pancakes and laughed. "Then again, I'm not sure I'll even be *able* to walk after eating this. Y'all are gonna force me to buy a new wardrobe if you keep this up."

Piper, petite and blond like her daughter, gave her a teasing grin. "You're too skinny anyway. A few pounds won't hurt you one bit. Any more thoughts on what's next for you?"

"Why? Do you need my room? I can…"

"Relax. You're Nikki's best friend, and Nikki is my new sister-in-law, which means you have a room here as long as you need it." She winked. "And no, you're not putting us out, so stow your Southern charm or Southern guilt or whatever it is. You're part of the family."

"What exactly did Nikki tell you?"

Lucy had been keeping a pretty low profile since arriving at the inn on Sunday. She'd slept most of the first few days, worn out from the drive and emotionally drained from…everything. Or maybe she'd been hiding. Yeah… she'd definitely been hiding.

Piper folded her arms. "Nikki said you needed a fresh start in a new place. Something about a wedding that didn't happen? I asked if you were running from the law, and she assured me you were not."

Lucy chuckled. "Definitely not." But she wouldn't be surprised if Owen's mother had some private investigator looking to find her so they could sue her to recoup the expenses of a canceled wedding. She'd already received an email from Faye, threatening legal action over the bills. "And yes, there was an almost-wedding. I don't want to be your charity case, Piper. I know I need to find a job. And a place to stay."

"You already have a place to stay. Take all the time you need to rest and regroup." She winked and walked toward the kitchen. "But first, eat your pancakes before they get cold."

A few hours later, Lucy was walking up Main Street in Rendezvous Falls. It was sunny, but there was a slight chill to the air. The Finger Lakes were definitely *not* North Carolina. Things were just starting to bloom here, while Carolina already had its spring, followed by pollen season, and was now headed into the steam heat of summer. Here in New York, she could tell the trees hadn't been leafed out that long.

The flower baskets hanging from the old-style lampposts hadn't filled out completely, but they added another layer of color in this town. Rendezvous Falls was famous for its wildly painted Victorian houses. Lucy knew that because signs proclaimed it everywhere. The brochure in her room at the Taggart Inn told her all about it, too. Apparently, it was a big deal—big enough to bring in tourists from all over to see them. And the buildings *were* pretty, especially closer to the center of town. Blues, pinks, yellows, greens…and that was just on one house. To add to the charm, Main Street was lined with flowering trees. The lampposts were festooned with red, white and blue buntings. It was Americana on overload, but…it worked.

The ornamented houses were offset somewhat by the low, stone buildings on the campus of Brady College, which hugged the shore of Seneca Lake at the base of the hill Rendezvous Falls was on. Above the town, acres of vineyards and trees marched up to the blue sky. Lucy walked along, smiling at people passing by. Up ahead was a flower shop, Rendezvous Blooms. It brought happy memories every time she saw it. Lucy had worked in her aunt's flower shop during high school, and she'd *loved* it.

This shop was similar, located on Main Street, with a large mullioned window filled with flowers. The display had changed today. It was all about June brides. *Of course.* It was a pretty basic setup, with a drape of pink lace and big knots of white tule behind buckets of flowers. It said "wedding" as a theme, but didn't have much *wow* factor.

Through the window, she could see a customer standing at the counter, talking to an older woman on the other side of the counter who did *not* look happy. In fact, neither of them looked happy. There was a sparse bridal bouquet on the counter between them. It was none of her business, but…she opened the door and walked in anyway.

The shop was small and tidy inside, if a bit dated. A variety of baskets and vases were stacked on shelves in a center display unit. A cooler lined the far wall, full of flowers and a few pre-made arrangements for customers who needed a last minute I-forgot-our-anniversary bouquet. There was a wide doorway leading to what looked like a bright and spacious workroom in back.

"This is exactly what we agreed on, Melissa," the older woman was saying. "Pink roses and white calla lilies. Pink ribbon. The bridesmaids will have pink rosebud bundles. I'll have those together in time for tonight." Her voice grew more firm. "You signed off on the quote, which included a description."

"I *told* my mother we should have ordered the flowers in Rochester. I mean, I *sent* you a picture, Connie." Melissa's voice was hard. "There are supposed to be cascading rosebuds and ribbons, remember? With the little seed pearls on them?"

Connie looked to be in her sixties or seventies, and Lucy could see she was stressed. She kept tucking one hand in her pocket, and it was trembling. Connie's head had a barely noticeable shake to it. One of Owen's uncles had Parkinson's disease, and Lucy was quite sure Connie had the same neurological disorder. One with no cure. She was probably just covering the front counter for the actual florist. And she was being ambushed by this bossy bride, threatening to call her father who, of course, was a "very important man."

Before Lucy took even a minute to think about what she was doing, she embraced her pink-haired Princess Sparkle Pony and jumped into the conversation.

"Melissa, I know just what you're describing—you want the ones like Princess Marcella carried in April at that royal wedding in Europe, right? I don't think it'll be a problem. There are pink roses in the window display we can use, and…" Lucy leaned to the side to look through the doorway to the workroom. There was a long ribbon rack on the back wall. "We have plenty of beads and ribbon back there."

The older woman, Connie, went rigid with displeasure. "I beg your pardon, but who…"

"I'm the…uh…new assistant." She winked at Connie. "Or I *could* be." Owen always said she was impulsive… why not go with it? Without waiting for an answer, she turned back to Melissa. "What time do you absolutely need the flowers by?"

The bride-to-be narrowed her eyes, assessing Lucy, but finally replied. "My brother is supposed to pick them up at five to bring to the church." She cast a malevolent gaze at Connie. "Since the florist doesn't deliver."

Connie started to protest. "I told you my delivery guy is sick…"

Lucy glanced at her watch. "We can make that happen. Dow you mind if I get started?" Connie just stared. Yeah, Lucy was surprised, too. But she was eager to work with flowers again, so she decided silence was permission. She headed into the workroom. The pickings were a little slim, but there were several rolls of pink ribbon, and she found a box of white seed pearl beads on a shelf, along with a couple of glue guns. She started cutting lengths of ribbon, laying them out side by side on the long porcelain-top table.

She heard Melissa leave, and Connie stormed into the workroom with a thunderstruck expression. "I don't know who you are or what the hell you think you're doing, but I want you out of this shop right now." She pointed toward the front door.

Lucy had to talk fast. After all, she'd promised Piper she wasn't a criminal, so she didn't want to end up being arrested the same day. She kept cutting lengths of ribbon as she spoke.

"Look, you need these flowers done in a few hours, and I can make that happen for you. I know exactly what the bride was talking about and how to do it. We can just glue the beads onto the ribbon and it will have the same effect. Why don't you put the bouquet in the cooler for now so it stays fresh. I'll grab some of those roses from the window display. Or do you have buds…?" She looked at the more utilitarian refrigerated unit that took up one wall back here. "Oh, there they are. Is the owner of the shop going to have time to put the bridal party bouquets together? Are the boutonnieres done?"

"I *am* the owner, you lunatic. Now get *out*."

Lucy tried to keep her expression neutral. She also tried not to look at Connie's shaking hand. And failed. She knew it as soon as she saw a flash of embarrassment cloud Connie's eyes.

"Oh…well…that's great." Lucy gave her an encouraging smile. "We can do this together, then."

"Get. Out." Connie reached for the cell phone sitting on the work counter along the wall by the door.

"No…wait…"

Then a new voice joined them. "What in the world is going on back here? Connie, are you…?" A woman walked in and came to an abrupt halt. She was Connie's age—maybe a bit younger—but far more upbeat and… fluffy. Her hair was butter yellow, falling in tight, shining curls to her shoulders. She wore pink jeans and a slightly lighter pink pullover. She stared at Lucy with wide eyes, then smiled brightly at Connie. "Wait, did you hire an assistant while I was getting my hair done?"

Lucy and Connie answered in the same breath, but Connie said *no* while Lucy said *maybe*.

The woman's brows lowered in confusion. "Let's start at the beginning. I'm Connie's friend, Cecile Manning. And you are?"

"I'm Lucy Higgins." Lucy put on her most cheerful expression. *Think positive.* "I was here while Connie was dealing with a difficult bride-to-be, and I jumped in to help. I have experience with flowers and I could use a job, so…"

Cecile clapped her hands. "That's perfect! Connie needs an assistant!"

"No, Connie does *not* need an assistant." Connie put her hands on her hips. "Now if you two will *both* leave, I have a lot of work to do."

"Connie," Lucy said, trying not to look desperate, "I'm sorry for barging in the way I did. I can be…impulsive." *Especially lately.* "But I really *can* help you give the bride what she wants. I don't expect you to pay me for this, since I volunteered myself." She took a steadying breath. "I am good with flowers, and…well, you'd be doing me a favor. And frankly…" She looked at the clock on the wall, then started gluing beads on the ribbons randomly. "Time is racing by and you have a bridal party expecting flowers with cascading beaded ribbons by five. You really want to fire me now?"

"How can I fire you? I didn't even h—"

Cecile answered over her. "No, she does *not* want to fire you." Connie started to object again, but Cecile raised her hand and continued, talking directly to Connie. "This girl is fate. You know damn well you need the help."

Connie's face was red. "I wouldn't *need* her help if she hadn't told my customer that we could do what the bride wanted!"

Cecile, who Lucy was liking more and more as the conversation went on, folded her arms and stared right back at Connie, unflinching.

"Excuse me if I'm wrong, but isn't giving the customers what they want the whole point of your business?"

Connie stammered, but Cecile talked over her again. "And look at this cute young thing with her pink hair and all her sass. I think Lucy Higgins is exactly what you need, and she's here exactly when you need her."

"Were you in on this, Cecile?" Connie demanded. "Did you and those book club busybodies come up with this? Leave it to you to find someone with pink hair to do your dirty work."

The atmosphere in the room took a turn toward testy, and Lucy put down the glue gun. She may have carried this ploy too far.

"Connie…" Lucy started. "Gosh, I don't even know your last name. This isn't a setup, I swear. I'm new in town and I need a job and my aunt taught me to do flower arrangements, so I really *do* know what I'm doing. Please give me a chance. Let me help you with this wedding order today, and then you can decide whether you want to hire me. Deal?"

Connie looked from Cecile's broad smile back to Lucy.

"How new to town are you? Who do you know here?"

Lucy knew how small towns operated—who you knew could determine a lot of things.

"I'm staying at the Taggart Inn. The Taggarts are related to my best friend."

"Who's your best friend?" The question felt like an interrogation. Lucy crossed her fingers in hopes that people here remembered Nikki fondly.

"Nikki Taggart. Iris's granddaughter."

Cecile's smile brightened even more. "Oh my gosh, I remember Nikki! She's Logan's sister. She was here for the wedding. Remember, Connie?"

Connie hadn't moved, but there was something… softer…about her stance. But not to her voice.

"Of course I remember. I'm not daft. She's a banker in Fresno, right?"

Lucy laughed at the attempt to trip her up. "She's a chef in Raleigh, as I'm sure you know. You can check out my story with the Taggarts, but I'm telling the truth." Cecile had said Lucy had *sass* as if that was a good thing, so she went with it. She looked up at the clock again, holding the glue gun in the air. It was heavy, and she wondered how Connie managed it with only one steady hand. "We should get busy on this order, don't you think?"

Connie hesitated, then went to the cooler to pull out a bucket of tight pink rosebuds. She set it on the opposite end of the table, then reached for her shears.

"Phelps."

Lucy looked up at her in confusion. "I'm sorry?"

Connie kept her eyes on the stems she was cutting. "My last name. It's Phelps."

Cecile turned to go, waving as she did.

"You two play nice and have fun, okay?"

CHAPTER FOUR

OWEN COOPER WAS DRUNK. That didn't stop him from pouring himself another glass of whiskey. He was on the small balcony of the two-bedroom apartment that was intended to be where he and Lucy would start their new life together.

He'd spent a few nights out here on the balcony over the past week, listening to the music rising up from the bars in downtown Greensboro. It was the hip and happening area of the city, or so his cousin had said when she sent him the lease to sign. She'd done the looking while he was wrapping up his obligation to the Army.

His mother had had a fit when he enlisted after two years of college, but the Coopers had a long history of military service. Owen was proud to be able to do his part as well as pay off his own college loans without relying on his parents. It was a good plan.

He and Lucy had agreed to wait on marriage until he was out of the military. It was a practical plan. They'd both agreed. He figured he'd come home, marry his girl and start a life together. He'd take over his dad's landscaping and nursery business. Lucy would go to work at the nursery. Hell, she'd already started working there after her grandmother passed away. He'd even promised her she could set up a flower arranging counter in the nursery because it was all she talked about. It was a good plan. Until it wasn't.

He took another sip of whiskey. This line of thinking felt painfully familiar and exceedingly pointless. He'd gone through it a hundred different times, in a hundred different ways. Putting himself through the drills, ignoring the pain, torturing himself because hey—no pain no gain, right? Just as he'd been trained.

His time in the military taught him to anticipate roadblocks, but he sure as hell never anticipated arriving at the church on his wedding day to discover his bride had fled. Not just changed her mind. *She'd run away.* From her entire life. From her family obligations. From her obligations to *his* family. From…him. He took another sip of his drink, relishing the sharp burn as it went down.

He couldn't seem to stop hearing her voice in his head, repeating those questions before everything went toes up. She started after him as soon as he came home in April. *Did something happen? Are you okay?* What did "okay" even mean? He was more okay than the guys who came back in body bags. More okay than Katherine McCabe, sitting in a VA rehab center trying to adjust to life without her left leg. So…yeah, he *was* okay. Technically. But Lucy wasn't happy with that answer. It was too late for better answers now. She was gone.

He was worried sick about her. Was she safe? Was she living out of her car? Or more correctly, Nikki Taggart's car? Was this an I-have-to-find-myself road trip that she'd return from in a few days? Or was she gone for good? She'd texted him on what should have been their wedding night. She told him she was sorry. She told him she was safe. Insinuated that he'd be fine without her. All in a string of texts, like that was all the effort he was worth.

Lucy threw a grenade right into his life, then acted like it was no big deal. Sure, she'd apologized, but for what exactly? *Oh, sorry I just cost your parents seventy grand. Sorry you signed that lease for an apartment. Sorry about humiliating you in front of your pals. Sorry about breaking your heart…*

Owen drained the glass, refilling it and scowling when the bottle went dry in the process. Good thing he'd restocked that afternoon. He'd been living on takeout food and booze since she left. There was a sharp rap on the apartment door, sending him stumbling to his feet. Some dim part of his brain grasped at the possibility it was Lucy. That she'd come back. But no, that was male laughter in the hall. He opened the door and nearly got stampeded by his buddies from Fort Bragg. He'd forgotten they were coming. What day was it, anyway?

Pete Lamphear was first, carrying a case of beer. Joe Callaway followed with shopping bags full of chips and junk food. Marcus Jones brought up the rear, carrying a brown paper bag from the nearest liquor store. Owen wanted to tell them to get lost, but what the hell. He didn't exactly have anything better to do.

Before long, Owen was even *more* drunk. So were his pals. He'd already told them they were spending the night, because nobody was in any condition to drive. Wasn't like he had to check with a wife for permission. He didn't have a wife.

"Fu-u-u-ck." He groaned, wincing at the wound he'd just picked open. Again.

"And there it is!" Pete raised his beer as if in victory,

then twisted his arm to squint at his watch. "Who had an hour and a half in the 'Coop Finally Loses It' Pool?"

Marcus crunched a mouthful of corn chips, sputtering crumbs everywhere as he pumped his fist. "I had eighty minutes! I knew my man wouldn't crack that easy."

"What?" Owen was having a hard time following the conversation, and wasn't sure if it was the booze or his so-called friends.

The guys ignored him. Joe pointed at Pete. "You only gave him *thirty*, you low-faith bastard. At least I gave him an hour."

Owen slammed the whiskey bottle down on the table, making glasses rattle. "What in the ever-loving hell are you idiots talking about?"

Pete was sprawled on the floor, his head propped against a chair, chip crumbs scattered on his shirt like snow. "We took bets on how long it would take for you to crack and tell us what's goin' on. That delayed-detonation f-bomb sure sounded like a crack to me."

"Agreed." Marcus nodded. "'Cause this?" He held up Owen's empty whiskey bottle. "This ain't gonna do it, man. So enjoy tonight, because it's time for you to dry out."

He stared at his friends. His comrades in arms. They'd shared a lot of laughs. And they'd seen some shit in the mountains outside of Kabul. Pete and Joe were career Army, in it until retirement. Marcus had two years left, then he was headed home to Alabama.

Owen shook his head, trying to clear the whiskey fog. "I'm not *cracking*. I'm fine." The three men stared, wordless. He ran his fingers through his hair. "Look, I'm not saying it was fun to get stood up at my own damn wedding. But it's better than getting dumped *after* the wedding, right?"

"You ready to talk about it?"

"Nope."

Joe's head tipped to the side. "Ready to hit the bars and find someone new?"

"What? No!" Owen shook his head emphatically. His filter failed him. "I still love Lucy."

Marcus started to chuckle, his voice deep. "And there you have it. I *told* you he wasn't over her." He gave Owen a hard look. "You want her back, after all this?"

No sense denying what he'd already blurted out.

"Yes. Damn it. YES. We had a life planned. We have a home." Well, okay, it was a rental. "I'm gonna take over the business. She's going to work there. We'll get a nice, new house someday." He scrubbed his hands over his face. He was reciting a plan that no longer existed. "She panicked. It happens. But once I get her back here, then we'll be good to go. Reschedule the wedding…" His mother would not be pleased, but that was *her* problem. He suspected Mom's overbearing ways were a big reason why Lucy seemed so detached from the wedding plans to start with. "After we're married, we'll start the life we had planned." He felt another pinch of guilt. Lucy hadn't given much input on those plans. He'd assumed her silence meant agreement. Another mistake.

"So how are you going to convince her to come back? Do you know where she *is*?"

"I've got a hunch. I think she's in New York. Upstate, not the city. Lucy's sister said Nikki handed Lucy the keys to her Mustang. Nikki Taggart went to her brother's wedding up there a while ago." He'd called Nikki a few times, but she'd been uncooperative. "I'll plead my case in person with Nikki if I have to, which will be good practice for groveling to Lucy."

Joe snorted out a laugh. "Sounds like good practice for your whole married life, my friend. Apologizing is Job Number One for husbands...trust me, I know." His laughter faded. "But if you don't know why she left, how will you know what to apologize for? What if she's still pissed off at you? What if she tells you to go to hell?"

Owen stared at the coffee table, unable to answer. This was a mission he hadn't trained for.

"Here you go!" Pete crowed, holding up his phone. *"Ten Guaranteed Ways to Get a Lady's Attention.* It's from an app my brother tipped me off to—Dr. Find-Love. The guy has a podcast on how to pick up ladies at bars, how to woo a woman you're serious about, how to dump a woman you're *not* serious about, and shit like that. And there's even a phone app."

"Yeah, right." Owen grimaced. "Just what I need—cyberdating advice from some sleazeball named Dr. Find-Love. You know what we called blowhards like that in Kabul—*oxygen thieves.* Sounds like a con."

"No, man," Pete answered, handing Owen the phone. "The guy's got a PhD or something."

"Emphasis on the *or something,*" Joe muttered.

Pete didn't break his stride. "He's legit! He writes books and stuff. I'm telling you, his ideas work. How do you think I got Holly to fall for me?"

Owen glanced at the app, then dismissed it, asking which professional basketball team had the best odds to win the upcoming championship game. The guys went along with the change of subject, and they talked and laughed for another hour or so before everyone claimed a bed or a sofa for the night. But Owen couldn't sleep. He kept thinking about that stupid app Pete showed him.

He quietly grabbed his tablet from the kitchen and went back to his room. Dr. Find-Love—clearly not his real name—smiled back at him from the screen with gleaming blond hair and a toothy smile. Owen scrolled through a long list of testimonials. The guy did seem legit. And for just $1.99 per month, Owen could subscribe to Dr. Find-Love's newsletter and app. He scrolled through the sample tabs, and one caught his eye.

Screwed Up and Lost Her? How to Grovel Successfully.

He knew there was still too much whiskey in his system to be shopping online, but damn. If he could pull up a blueprint for what to do to get Lucy to come back home, it could save him from wasting time, or from making things even worse. He didn't give himself time to rethink it. One click on the app store and he became an official member of the "Lucky Guy Club." He ignored the quiet voice of reason in his head, telling him the whole thing felt sleazy. As he opened the app, he felt more hopeful than he had since the morning his mother started screaming about the abruptly canceled wedding.

He had a plan now. He was going to find Lucy. He was going to follow this groveling checklist and win her back. Then they'd come home to Greensboro and start their life together. He looked at the top of the screen.

Guaranteed Results!

It was a done deal.

LUCY SLAPPED AT her phone, swearing at the alarm she couldn't turn off. She was still disoriented most mornings when she woke to find herself in room 12 at the Taggart Inn in Rendezvous Falls. She blinked a few times after silencing the phone, then stretched and sat up. It was a pretty room, with soft yellow walls and cornflower blue curtains at the long windows. The queen-size bed was tucked into the corner at an angle, covered with a pastel quilt. There was an antique writing table in front of one window, and a large mahogany dresser on another wall, opposite the small private bath and equally small walk-in closet.

Piper Taggart, the manager of the inn, had explained that this room was one of three larger corner rooms they tried to keep available for long-term guests like her. These were the rooms with the most closet space and small sitting areas to relax. In room 12, on the third floor, that meant an overstuffed armchair and ottoman in one corner, near the tall windows. There was a flat-screen TV on the wall near the chair, and Lucy had spent most of her evenings staring at reruns of 1990s sitcoms on a streaming service.

She showered and dressed, pinning her hair back in a messy pink twist. It wasn't easy to pin it up as short as it was now. The pink was already beginning to fade, but there was still enough to make her look like little Princess Sparkle Pony. Eventually it would be gone. Eventually she'd have to deal with the mess she'd left in North Carolina. Eventually she'd have to deal with Owen. She frowned into the mirror. The pink dye was her hourglass—slowly running out until her time was up.

It was Thursday, so she'd be working at the flower shop today. As long as Connie hadn't changed her mind again. It had been touch and go since Lucy helped complete the wedding order for the angry young bride last week. She'd volunteered to make some updated arrangements for the cooler display, and they'd sold well that weekend. Connie paid her a percentage. Pocket money, but it helped. Connie had an order for a dinner party at some fancy home on the shore of Seneca Lake. She'd let Lucy create three tall table arrangements.

Lucy kept the blossoms heaviest on the bottom eight inches, then spray painted some curly willow branches with metallic blue paint she'd found in the workroom. Connie had a trio of blue china bowls on her shelves that helped keep the low profile intact. The tall narrow sticks added drama to the arrangements, but still allowed guests to see each other for dinner conversation. Mrs. Hudson declared them "divine" when she and her grandson, Mark, stopped to pick them up.

On Tuesday, Lucy had asked Connie point-blank for a job. She couldn't stay at the inn much longer without one, and she wasn't ready to go back home. She'd go stir crazy without something to keep her mind off the wreckage she'd left behind in North Carolina.

After a lot of hemming and hawing and repeated declarations that *I don't need help*, Connie agreed that Lucy could work at the shop part-time. She'd help with inventory on Wednesdays, when fresh flowers arrived for weekend orders, and then she'd work five hours a day through the weekend. But Connie fixed her with a hard look before she left that day, telling her that this was strictly probationary and "might not last." Not exactly reassuring. But Lucy knew she was skilled with arrangements. Better than Connie in some ways…certainly more contemporary with her designs. She slipped into her comfortable canvas sneakers and braced her foot on the edge of the bed to tie the laces.

It wasn't fair to say she was *better* than Connie. It was Connie's shop, and the arrangements she'd seen were nicely done. Technically perfect. They were just a little... dated. Lucy could show her more modern displays to appeal to a younger clientele, and maybe even tackle the shop window to give it some pizzazz. Lucy wouldn't be staying here forever, but working at the flower shop could work out for both her *and* Connie if she played her cards right.

She was just sitting down at her usual breakfast table by the window in when Piper Taggart asked her The Big Question as she filled Lucy's coffee mug.

"So what are your long-term plans?"

Lucy straightened. "Why? Do you need my room? I can look for..."

"Don't be silly," Piper said, shaking her head. "You have room 12 as long as you need it. Even if I *wasn't* terrified to refuse my sister-in-law Nikki, I'd never make you leave. I just wondered... I know you broke up with your fiancé, but what made you leave the entire state of North Carolina? Did he do something that bad?" Piper started to laugh. "And oh my God, I'm giving you an interrogation before you've had a chance to eat breakfast! I'm sorry."

Lucy had been admiring the Taggarts' restraint since her arrival. Maybe they didn't know all the juicy details. She smiled. "You've been holding in all those questions since I got here, haven't you?"

"And you have no idea how hard that's been!" Piper laughed again, glancing around. It was after nine on a weekday, so the inn was quiet and the dining room empty.

"But seriously, you don't owe anyone, especially me, any explanations. Nikki doesn't ask for many favors, so we didn't hesitate to say yes."

"Nikki's an independent one, for sure," Lucy agreed.

"She and Logan didn't have the easiest childhood, with their mom gone and their dad moving them all over the country chasing his big dreams. Logan's my hardworking gentle giant, and Nikki…" Piper hesitated. "Well, I've only known her a couple of years, but Nikki is so *fierce* about everything she does."

"*Fierce* is a good word for Nik."

Lucy remembered Nikki talking about how her brother had unexpectedly settled in Rendezvous Falls to run their grandmother's inn after a lifetime of globe-hopping from one oil rig to another. These days he lived in a fanciful pink Victorian house right next door to the Taggart Inn with previously widowed Piper and her two children. As surprised as she'd been at Logan's life change, Nikki said she loved her new sister-in-law. And she adored being Aunt Nik to Piper's children, Ethan and Lily.

"I only ask the questions because I want to be sure you're okay. If you need anything, or ever want to talk or go have a drink or anything, just say the word." Her smile brightened. "I'll stop talking now and get your breakfast. Today's special is our Greek omelet, if that's okay."

Lucy nodded, and found herself blinking back tears as she watched Piper, petite and trim, walk away. She'd kept to herself since her arrival, not engaging much with other guests. It wasn't as if she was vacationing here. The flower shop had kept her busy, but other than that, she'd hardly spoken to a soul. At least, not in person.

Her phone and her social media accounts had blown up.

Seemed everyone in Greensboro wanted an explanation, from friends and family like Kris to opposite-of-friends like Faye Cooper. Her parents begged her to reconsider leaving and to forgive them for not being honest about what was happening between them.

Dad called and they'd had a long talk. He insisted the divorce wasn't all her mother's fault. The fight Lucy overheard was a fluke. He'd forgiven her mother. Mom called, too, but Lucy hadn't answered. She wasn't ready to have that conversation. Mom's voice mails were an endless cycle of apologies and explanations that she and Dad would always be friends, but they'd fallen out of love. Lucy did not find that very reassuring—hearing how people could just fall out of love the same way kids fell out of trees.

But it hadn't just been her parent's divorce. They were simply the final straw in a long line of disappointments.

Nikki had packed up more of her clothes from Lucy's parents' house and shipped them to her, with a note telling her to take as much time and as little bullshit as needed for her sanity. And Owen had called. And texted. And DM'd. He didn't understand, which was fair. Kinda hard to explain what she didn't fully understand herself. She needed more time. Or was she just avoiding the inevitable? For someone who hated confrontation, she'd created the fodder for an awful lot of it.

With every day that passed, Lucy realized Owen wasn't the only reason she'd run, either. She missed the man she'd fallen in love with, and when he came home all cold and silent, it was just one more thing that knocked her off balance. He was so determined to follow the life path his parents had set for him. She just wasn't sure anymore that she could go down that path with him. But as mad as she'd been about Owen shutting down emotionally when he returned from deployment, she knew she was doing the same thing in return.

Piper returned with a breakfast platter, and Lucy thought she might stay and ask all of those burning questions she had. Instead, she said she had to make sure room 3 was ready for a guest arriving shortly, leaving Lucy alone in the dining room. And surprisingly disappointed. Maybe that was a good sign. Maybe she was ready to start talking—and thinking—about what came next. Because right now she had no clue. As angry and hurt as she was by her parents, Owen's parents and Owen himself…running away wasn't going to solve a damn thing.

After eating more of the giant omelet than she thought she would, Lucy put her dishes and silverware on the tray on the sideboard. Time to go see what kind of mood Connie would be in. Defensive and belligerent, as she'd been most of the time? Or reluctantly attentive, as she'd been on Sunday when Lucy was putting those dinner party arrangements together?

Lucy grabbed her bag from her chair and headed out to the hallway toward the front door. Logan Taggart, easily a foot taller than his petite bride, Piper, and looking every inch like the former oil rig worker he was, was checking in a guest at the desk.

A prickling sensation swept under her skin as she got closer, heading for the front doors. The man had his back to her. An olive green military duffel sat at his feet. His hair was in a near-military cut. It was an all-too-familiar chestnut brown.

"Lucy!" Piper rushed up behind her, breathless. "I'm

glad I caught you. This is your phone, right? You left it on the table and I…" Piper stopped. She followed Lucy's gaze down the hall to the front desk and back. "What's wrong?"

The man at the desk had frozen as soon as Piper called Lucy's name. He turned. It seemed like he was moving in slow motion, or maybe it was her brain moving slowly, trying so hard to understand how this could be happening. Then he was facing her, his golden eyes wide. His name fell out of her mouth in a startled breath.

"Owen?"

He moved toward her, and she backed up in a panic. That confrontation she'd been avoiding was now standing in front of her. *Action, meet consequences.* Piper jumped in front of her, facing down Owen with her finger waving in the air.

"Stop right there, buster," she said. Piper was only a few inches over five feet tall, but there was a fierce mama bear strength in her stance. Owen stopped abruptly, rocking back on his heels. He nodded toward Lucy, his jaw tight.

"That's my fiancée."

"Not anymore." Lucy shook her head so forcefully that her hair started to fly free from the clips. How could he still call her that after she'd left him at the altar? His eyes were darker and more solemn than she'd ever seen.

There was a rush of movement, and her view of Owen was blocked. Piper had been replaced between them by her husband Logan. The moment's intensity ramped up exponentially.

"You need to take a step back, pal." Logan's voice was low and calm, but it was the type of calm that came before a storm. A *violent* storm. "In fact, you need to step right on out of here."

Logan was bigger than Owen. He was every inch the clichéd mountain of a man, making his pairing with petite Piper even cuter. But Owen was a soldier fresh off deployment to one of the most dangerous places in the world. The two men glared at each other in the hallway, chests beginning to swell in posturing aggression. This wouldn't end well for *anyone* if she didn't snap out of her stupor and do something.

"Logan..." She put her hand on his bicep and stepped to his side, feeling the rock-hard muscles pulsing beneath his shirt. Owen's eyes narrowed even further when she left her hand on Logan's arm, but she ignored it. "It's okay, Logan. Owen and I...well... I wasn't expecting him, but I'm *not* afraid of him." She should have known he'd find her eventually. She gave Owen a firm look. "Stand down, soldier. Logan and Piper own this place. He's Nikki's brother. I'm assuming *she's* how you knew how to find me?" It was a disappointing thought.

Neither man budged. Finally Piper Taggart let out a loud sigh and moved between Owen and her husband. She stared back and forth between both men. "Okay, I'm officially declaring this testosterone competition a tie. No winners. No losers. It's over. Let's all step into the library where we won't be scaring any guests who might wander downstairs. We don't need people posting online reviews mentioning some fight they saw happening..." Pipers eyes narrowed dangerously. "In. The. Lobby."

The men continued their glaring contest for another beat, then Owen stepped back, holding his hands up. "I'm not looking for trouble."

Lucy rolled her eyes. Typical Owen. Those words should have been emblazoned across his forehead like a warning, because Owen was *never* looking for trouble. Or conflict. Or even an uncomfortable conversation.

It wasn't like she wanted him to punch Logan Taggart in the lobby or anything, but there was something infuriating about the way he backed down. Maybe it was the way his eyes had shuttered, closing himself off from displaying any emotion at all. Then again, he'd be an idiot to want her after what she'd done.

She cleared her throat. "What exactly *are* you looking for, Owen? Why are you here?"

Piper grabbed Owen's elbow in one hand and Lucy's in the other, steering them toward a nearby doorway.

"Like I said, let's move this conversation to the library." Her voice dropped to a whispered hiss. "The Millers are coming down the stairs!"

CHAPTER FIVE

OWEN HAD STARTED to follow Lucy and Piper into the library when Logan Taggart stopped him with a firm hand on his shoulder. He knew the weight of that hand was intentional on Logan's part, to emphasize his five-inch-height advantage. Owen bit back his irritation. He could drop this guy with a fist to his solar plexus and a sleeper hold from behind until he lost consciousness. But he wasn't in the mountains of Afghanistan anymore. He didn't need to size up everyone he met and determine how fast he could render them unconscious. Old habits died hard. He waited for Logan to make the next move.

"I don't know everything about the wedding-that-wasn't," Logan said quietly. "But one thing I *do* know is that my sister would *never* have sent you here without giving me a heads-up first."

"Nikki didn't send me. I figured it out." It wasn't that hard after Lucy's sister told him Lucy had borrowed her best friend's car for her runaway caper. "I meant what I said. I'm not here for trouble. I just want my fiancée to come back home."

Logan's eyes narrowed. "And if she says no?"

Owen's chest tightened, choking his lungs for a moment. He *loved* Lucy. Failure wasn't an option here. They had a life waiting for them in North Carolina. Jobs. Families. Sure, Lucy had panicked, but she was going to get over it. If not…the unknown rose before him like a dark cloud. Lucy *had* to come back. Nothing worked in his life if she didn't. He took a steadying breath, quelling his own rising panic.

"I'm not going to force her to come with me, for Chrissakes. But… I have to at least *try* to get her back. Right?"

Logan stared hard into Owen's eyes for a moment. "I don't know. Do you?"

Owen looked into the library, where Lucy and Piper were talking. Lucy, naturally, was fussing with a vase of flowers on a side table. That woman couldn't stay away from anything that blossomed. Maybe that's why she'd dyed her hair pink, like a rose. She'd cut it, too. At the rehearsal dinner, his mother had commented that Lucy's hair was finally long enough for a *proper updo*, whatever that was. Lucy had stiffened when Mom said that, which Owen didn't understand. He was pretty sure it had been a compliment. He could just imagine what his mother would say about this pink shoulder-length hair. But…the look fit Lucy somehow. It matched the soft blush she used to get when she laughed. When was the last time he'd seen her laugh? When was the last time he'd tried to *make* her laugh?

Logan's voice lost its edge. His grip on Owen's shoulder eased. "Are you here because you feel obligated?" The question sounded more curious than accusing. "Because you don't want to let her have the final word?"

Owen shook his head sharply. "That's not it."

"Do you love her?"

In the library, Piper plucked a stemmed flower from the vase and shook it at Lucy, playacting something and mentioning someone named Connie. As if she'd read his thoughts, Lucy held up her hands playfully and…laughed.

The sound cut through him like a sharp knife. He'd been home almost two months, and he didn't think he'd heard that sound once. And he hadn't even noticed. He closed his eyes and took a breath, pushing down the feelings of remorse. No time for regrets now. Once he had Lucy back home in North Carolina, they'd figure out how to laugh more. How to talk more. How to find that lighthearted feeling he used to have around her. He'd lost it somewhere in the mountains of Afghanistan, but surely Lucy could help him find it again.

She turned and looked toward the doorway, raising a brow in curiosity. Her expression was cool. But not frightened. The way she'd jumped back in the hallway had nearly broken him. The thought that she might *fear* him…it gutted him. She tipped her head to the side, as if examining some puzzle she couldn't solve. He could work with curiosity. It was at least interest. That was better than hatred. With interest, he could make her laugh again. Hopefully make her love him again. A low chuckle snapped him out of his head and back to reality.

"Oh, man, you've got it bad." Logan slapped his hand on Owen's shoulder, but now it was a friendly guy-bro gesture. "I'm going to enjoy watching this."

LUCY COULDN'T INTERPRET Owen's expression as he stood in the doorway. Logan said something she couldn't hear, and Owen paled, swallowing hard. Was he…was he *nervous*? She pressed her lips together tightly. If so, that would be the first actual emotion she'd seen on his face since his return from deployment. There was a time when she'd been concerned and tried to get him to open up to her. A time when she'd loved him. Her chin rose. But that time was over. She'd tried. She'd failed. She'd run. *No going back, girl.*

"Did Nikki...?" she started to ask, and he shook his head, stepping into the library.

"Of course not. She's the Thelma to your Louise. Told me to go screw myself when I pressed her for information."

"Then how...?"

He shrugged, stopping a good ten feet away from her, as if afraid to spook her.

"Your sister said you'd taken Nikki's convertible." His eyes softened. "A smart move, by the way. Your deathtrap would never have made it here."

"My Buttercup is a classic." Her grandmother had named it, and the name stuck.

"It's a rolling wreck." He shook his head. "I don't know what you were thinking, trying to keep that thing on the road."

"It's not like I always had a man around for advice." She sniffed. Maybe it wasn't fair to jab at him about his deployment but the fact was, he *hadn't* been there for her. Not even when he'd returned.

He opened his mouth to answer, his eyes narrowing, but Logan muttered something behind him. It sounded like something about *not taking the bait.* Owen's shoulders rose and fell with a heavy sigh before he finally spoke.

"My point is that once I knew you had Nikki's car, I remembered you writing me about her brother's wedding in New York." He glanced over his shoulder at Logan. "I did a little digging and figured she might have sent you his way."

"A little digging? You found me in Rendezvous Falls

after Nikki mentioned the entire state of *New York* a year ago?"

He gave a one-shouldered shrug. "It didn't hurt that there's a business right here with Nikki's last name on it." He gestured around the room.

"Owen…" She sighed. "I told you I needed time. And *space*." She gestured between them. "This is not space."

"It's been almost two weeks, Luce. I gave you time. You wouldn't talk to me, so I didn't have a lot of choice. I had to find you. Did you really think I was going to let you dump me on our wedding day and not try to find out what happened?"

"*Let* me?" She stepped toward him, surprising them both with her vehemence. "I didn't need your damn permission to leave. It may not have fit within your mother's precious social etiquette rules, but I'm allowed to change my mind about marrying you." She glanced at her watch. *Damn it.* As much as Connie liked to bitch about not needing Lucy's help, she'd also complain if Lucy was late. "Look, I have to go. And that's what you should do, too. Go home and live your life at Cooper Landscaping and Nurseries of Greensboro." There was a spark of panic… or maybe sorrow?…in his eyes. More emotion. Maybe she wasn't being completely fair here. She *was* the one who took off on him without warning. Her voice softened. "I'm sorry for what happened. For *how* it happened. But why would you even *want* me back?" She waved her hand in front of her. "You know what? Never mind. I really do have to go."

"You won't even give me the courtesy of explaining *why*? You don't think I deserve that much?" The gravel in his voice was somewhere between anger and pleading.

Then it hardened. "For God's sake, Lucy, just tell me what the hell happened. Is there someone else?"

"What? No! I'd never..." And she wouldn't have. But by not giving him answers, she understood how he could imagine the worst. She'd completely forgotten Piper and Logan were still in the room until Piper spoke quietly.

"I know this is none of my business," she started, "but sometimes a simple conversation is a good place to start when there's a...disagreement...between two people." She flashed a quick smile at her husband. "Right, honey? You're both out of sorts right now. Owen, you just drove overnight to get here. Lucy, he caught you completely by surprise, and you have someplace to be..." She glanced at Owen. "And no, I won't be telling *you* anything about that. All I'm saying is that you both should catch your breaths and try to work things out when you're calmer..."

Logan walked over to his wife, dropping an arm over her shoulders. "My bride is a hopeless romantic. Don't let yourselves feel pressured..."

Lucy and Owen gave their answers at the same time.

"Not happening."

"Sounds great."

Piper looked deflated, but resigned. She turned toward Lucy. "Do you want us to make him stay somewhere else? There's an old hotel up on Route 12."

As tempting as it was to scream *yes!* so she could avoid dealing with him until she was ready—as if that would ever happen—Lucy shook her head. She'd caught the way Piper emphasized the word *old* and figured she was saying the hotel was less than ideal. She wasn't looking to punish Owen.

"No. He has every right to rent a room here for the night."

Logan tugged on Piper's shoulders. "We'll leave you two alone."

Lucy started past Owen, eager to follow the Taggarts out of the room. Owen reached for her as she went by.

"Lucy, please…"

She closed her eyes tightly, trying to ignore the familiar warmth of his touch. The way it reminded her of hot summer nights on the Outer Banks, the two of them walking for hours on the beach in the moonlight. Sneaking into the condo he'd rented with his buddies, tiptoeing down the hall to his room. Her giggling as he hung a sock on the doorknob, as if that would really stop his rowdy Army pals from hassling them if they woke up. But the guys tended to drink themselves into a solid sleep that week. Giving her and Owen privacy to get to know each other. Which reminded her that she didn't know him at all anymore. Or herself, for that matter.

She stepped back, and he released her immediately. It made sense that he wanted to talk. The money she'd cost his family. The embarrassment for everyone. The way she'd just vanished on them all. She took a deep breath.

"I owe you an explanation. I'm sure I owe your parents thousands of dollars." She looked at him and did her best to smile. "I know I shocked everyone. Hell, I shocked myself. But I had to do it, Owen. I don't know if I can explain it, but I just… I couldn't stay there another minute." She swallowed hard, surprised at the swell of emotion inside her. She'd been stuffing all of this away for a time when she felt like she could deal with it, but it looked as though

her emotions, just like her fiancé—her *former* fiancé—
had other plans.

"Lucy, I don't understand…"

Something snapped inside her, lancing across her heart
like a sword's edge. His words were calm and totally rea-
sonable. But they unleashed something that made her
throat tighten dangerously. Still…she tried to hold it in.
She was afraid she might split apart like hammered gran-
ite, leaving nothing but pebbles and dust.

"*You* need to understand?" She glared at him, holding
on to the last vestige of self-control. "What about all the
things that *I* need to understand? Oh, that's right…" She
snapped her fingers in front of his face and he flinched.
"… Lucy just goes along, whether she *understands* or
not, right? Good ole Lucy. Everyone can depend on *her*
to understand."

Owen didn't answer, just stared at her in obvious confusion. Her anger faded as fast as it had arrived. She wasn't
being fair to him. He'd come here to try to salvage things,
and it was hard to hate the man for that.

She thought about their happier days together. Like
the Friday night they'd met at that beachside restaurant
near Wilmington five years ago. They'd literally run into
each other near the bar—she'd spilled her beer all over the
dark T-shirt he'd been wearing with his swim trunks. Her
profuse apologies mingled with her embarrassed laughter somehow inspired him to order her a replacement beer
and invite her to join him and his Army buddies at a table
overlooking the beach. That whole weekend had seemed
charmed. They'd laughed, talked, walked the beach in
the moonlight and just before sunrise Sunday morning,

they'd made love in the back of his old Ford Bronco. It was hands-down the best sex she'd ever had, before or since.

The corner of his mouth twitched. "If I didn't know better, I'd say you're almost smiling at me."

She lifted one shoulder and let it fall. "Just thinking about Topsail Beach."

He nodded, his mouth still slanted. He'd barely cracked a smile since his return from Afghanistan.

"That was one fine night, Lucy Higgins."

He might be hiding the grin, but he couldn't hide the flash of heat that crept into his voice when he said *one fine night*. He was right. They'd really had something back then. But it was over. She raised her chin.

"It was. But it was a long time ago." She smiled sadly. "I'm sorry, Owen. I shouldn't have acted so shocked at your arrival. You deserve an explanation, but…clearly I'm still figuring a lot of it out myself." Her smile faded. "The wedding, your family, my family, the job, us… I felt completely disconnected from all of it. I'm not angry with you, but… I don't see a future for us with all of that to deal with."

He didn't react, other than a quick flicker of emotion. He'd become very good at hiding his feelings. A muscle ticked slowly in his cheek. His pallor was grayer than usual. His eyes shuttered. Holding all of that…*stuff*…inside was taking a toll. But she couldn't dump the man and then try to fix whatever had broken inside of him. It wouldn't be fair to either of them.

"So," he finally said, "just like that, huh? You pronounce us over with no explanation, and I'm supposed to just…walk away?" The words should have carried hurt and anger, but instead, his voice was completely flat.

"Well, I've already walked—or run—away, haven't I?" She kept her voice gentle. Despite his emotionless tone, she knew that somewhere deep inside this had to hurt, if only his pride. "You should go home and live the life you've planned."

"*You* were the life I planned, damn it. How am I supposed to follow the plan without you as part of it?" The words were whip sharp and hot. His emotions hadn't vanished completely. There was only one problem.

"Are you angry about the *plan* being messed up or about losing *me*?"

His eyebrows shot up in unison with his mouth dropping open. "What's *that* supposed to mean?"

She sighed and moved to walk past him again, not speaking until she reached the door and turned. Her mind grasped the reality of it as the words tumbled out.

"It means I was right to leave. The little box in your future labeled *Lucy* isn't going to be there anymore, and you're more freaked out about the empty box than losing what used to be in it." She put her hand on her chest. "*Me*. Admit it, Owen. All you care about is the change in plans. But you'll figure that out. Back in Greensboro."

Her hand was on the doorknob before he finally attempted to deny what she'd said.

"I can't go back without you…"

She turned. "You *can*. And you should. No one would blame you. I humiliated you. I left you at the altar. I—"

He held up his hand. "I was there, remember? And still… I'm here. I can't leave without at least *trying* to make us work again." He hesitated. "I mean, if you really insist, I'll go. I'm not here to harass you. But please, Luce. Give me a chance. I won't… I'll *try* not to pressure you.

Give me a few weeks. Give me a month." He brightened. "Give me a month, Lucy. Let's try to figure out what happened and how to fix it. If after a month of me around you still don't want…us, then I promise I'll leave you alone."

"What about the business? What will your family think about you taking off for a month?"

He shrugged. "My cousin Lori has a handle on things. They've done it without me for years, so one more month won't hurt anything. And frankly, a month without Mom pestering me about what's happening with us sounds pretty good to me. Give me a month. No wedding to worry about. Just us."

Lucy was tempted. Being in the same room with Owen reminded her of how good they'd been. Once. But he had a job waiting in Greensboro. A future she wasn't ready to join him in. "I think I've blown *us* up for good, don't you? You're a grown man and can stay wherever you want, but I'm pretty sure *us* wasn't good for me, and it's time for *me* to matter."

He wasn't the only reason she'd left North Carolina, but she had to resolve *all* the reasons before she could trust herself to love again. She deserved that much.

Owen took a step forward, his voice soft. "I couldn't agree more…with the last part, I mean. You do matter. Just say it's okay for me to try to prove how much you matter to *me*. I screwed up. I get that. Give me a chance to fix things."

Her shoulders dropped in defeat. The man loved to have a plan, even if it was a hopeless one. "If you want to bang your head on that wall for a month, go for it. I won't stop you, but I don't see you changing my mind."

She wondered why, if that were true, she didn't just

tell him to leave? He said he would if she wanted. But he was begging for permission to stay. For a month—such an arbitrary period of time. She opened the door, barely hearing his reply.

"And yet you're giving me a chance..."

Considering that she'd had her own epiphany about him caring for the plan more than he cared for her just half a minute ago, she couldn't expect him to see the truth yet. He'd leave Rendezvous Falls once he did. So giving him a month didn't mean anything.

It would be a gentler let-down than her walking away from their wedding. It was the least she could do for the poor guy.

CHAPTER SIX

OWEN'S ROOM WAS spacious—a corner room on the first floor of the Taggart Inn, where there were only a few guest rooms. He tossed his duffel on the end of the king-size mahogany four-poster. A little formal for his taste, but his mother would love it. Luckily, she'd never see it. Only four people in Greensboro knew exactly where he was, and only one was a relative. His cousin, Lori, had heard only the barest of details. She was more than happy to keep running the nursery, just as she had been for the past three years.

Pete, Joe and Marcus knew all about his plan. They'd enthusiastically helped him pore over Dr. Find-Love's website, even though he kept telling them he shouldn't need gimmicks to win back his own damn fiancée.

Lucy had been such a trooper during his deployments, staying busy caring for her grandmother and working for his parents at Cooper Landscaping and Nurseries. The only time she'd protested was when he'd taken that last extension. It was only an extra year, so she'd surprised him when she asked to wait one more time for him.

"Everyone keeps telling me to *wait*. How much longer am I supposed to wait for my life to actually, finally *happen* for Christ's sake?"

They'd worked it out, or so he'd thought. She hadn't been thrilled, but she'd agreed on the plan. Not that he'd given her much choice—it was pretty much a done deal. But after that he'd be home for good, and hopefully ready for phase two of his life plan—taking over the family business. And getting married, of course.

His parents had already brought Lucy into the nursery to work, so she'd have an extra year to learn about the business that would be theirs someday. That was a good thing for both of them, seeing as he didn't know much about the new nursery setup Dad and Lori had expanded into. It was a perfect job for a woman who loved plants and flowers, but Lucy hadn't sounded all that enthusiastic whenever he'd talked to her from Afghanistan.

Owen stretched out on the bed with a long, loud groan. He hadn't slept in over twenty-four hours, and he'd driven seven hundred miles. He was used to long, sleepless stretches in Afghanistan, but that didn't mean his body didn't work better with rest.

He was missing something in this whole situation with Lucy, but he couldn't put his finger on what exactly. Her sister told him about their parents' breakup, but why punish *him* for something *they* screwed up? His eyes closed. He just needed a nap to get the cobwebs out of his head and come up with a plan that would win her over.

If he got *really* desperate, he could always pull up the newest app on his phone and take a few groveling cues from Dr. Find-Love. The thought made him cringe inside. It was a ridiculous app, but he was in uncharted territory right now, so he'd take help wherever he could find it. He still hoped it would never come to that.

CONNIE SIGNED THE delivery receipt and thanked Rupert Knowles for carrying the boxes full of cut flowers all the way back to the workroom. Technically, his brown uniform dictated he only bring boxes as far as the front door. But Rupert had been delivering her weekly flower shipment for over a decade now, and he insisted he didn't mind the extra steps. She repaid his kindness with the occasional container of fresh-baked snickerdoodle cookies…his favorite.

After Rupert accepted a long-stemmed red rose to take home to his wife and headed out to finish his route, Connie glanced at the clock and frowned. She shouldn't be surprised if Lucy Higgins had gotten bored with her part-time job at the flower shop already. Connie kept telling Cecile that Lucy was bound to quit. The woman was on the run or something…she hadn't really said who or what from. A modern gal like Lucy, with her pink hair and endless nervous energy, was hardly destined to stay in quiet little Rendezvous Falls for long.

Connie gathered up an armful of yellow roses, most of them still tightly budded. She took them to the deep work sink and snipped just a little from the bottom of each stem so they'd soak up water and food more efficiently. Then she plopped them one by one into the water at the bottom of the tall plastic buckets in the storage cooler. She started on the pink roses next.

It may not be surprising that Lucy Higgins had bailed on her, but it was oddly disappointing. Lucy's enthusiasm and could be annoying, but over the past week, Connie had been able to go home without feeling totally worn out. Her energy was usually shot by Saturday afternoons, after the wedding or party orders were finished and *before* she started the altar arrangements she put together every week for the local churches. Those standing orders for the churches helped keep the place afloat, but for the past few years she'd been doing them with her last gasp of energy and creativity.

With Lucy's help, though, not only had Connie felt more rested, she'd also had to concede that Lucy had some real talent with flowers. Some of her ideas were a little too…out there…for Connie's traditional tastes, but the customers seemed happy. And this past Monday was the first time Father Joe Brennan had *ever* stopped by to comment on altar flowers.

"I won't lie, Connie love. I checked the receipt to be sure they came from your shop." The Irish-born priest had given her a wink. "It's the first time I've seen a three-foot-tall flower arrangement on the altar, but 'twas lovely. And colorful, too. Rather youthful lookin', I thought." His soft accent made *th*'s sound like *t*'s, so the word came out sounding like *taut*. The priest knew everything that happened in Rendezvous Falls, sometimes seemingly before they happened, so surely he'd heard she had a young assistant. She also knew that whatever details the priest *didn't* know tortured him, so she didn't respond other than thanking him for stopping.

She gathered up the miniature sunflowers and started snipping the stems. It was just as well she didn't admit she had someone working for her, since it seemed that was no longer the case. Everyone would just have to be satisfied with Connie's sturdy, if predictable, floral arrangements now that Lucy had clearly flown the coop…

The shop door swung open so fast the brass bell above it just let out one angry *clang* instead of tinkling lightly. Connie almost dropped the whole bundle of sunflowers. She'd barely turned when Lucy rushed into the back room.

"Oh my God, I'm *so* sorry I'm late, Connie. I know I promised to be here to meet the delivery, but something—" she looked away, then back again "—some*one* surprised me and I had to deal with it...*him*."

So it *was* a man she'd been hiding from. Not that Connie cared. The girl wouldn't stay in this town, regardless of why she'd showed up. But just because Connie didn't care didn't mean she was heartless.

"Are you...are you safe?" She caught the surprise in Lucy's eyes and checked herself. That sounded dangerously close to caring. Connie's carefully crafted don't-give-a-damn attitude was slipping. She cleared her throat. "I don't want some wild-haired drug dealer showing up in the shop and causing trouble."

The corner of Lucy's mouth lifted. "Do I look like the type of woman who'd date a wild-haired drug dealer?"

"Well," Connie huffed. "You've got that pink hair, and you said you went to a tattoo studio last week, so..."

Lucy laughed as she grabbed some lilies and put them in fresh water. "So pink hair and a tattoo make me a drug dealer's moll? Besides, I decided to wait on the tattoo. That's a big commitment. *But lots* of people have tattoos and dyed hair, these days. Look at Evie from the Spot Diner right across the street."

Connie didn't answer right away. She'd known Evie and her husband, Mark Hudson, since Evie's parents had taken over the diner from old man Hudson when Evie was just a baby. And yes, Evie had always been a free spirit, to put it mildly. The girl was in her thirties, and still sported a brightly colored streak in her dark hair. And she did have tattoos—morning glories wrapped around her leg, and a flock of swallows swirled around her arm and up her neck.

"That's different" Connie insisted. "Evie got those when she was in her rebellious youth."

"Umm…it was Evie who introduced me to Kat at Indigo Ink…" Lucy put her hand on her hip and arched one eyebrow. "Where Evie was adding more ink to her back."

Connie turned away and dropped the sunflowers into their container in the cooler. "Let me put it this way…tattoos and crazy hair may not mean drugs and gangs, but people in drug gangs often have tattoos and crazy hair." She wasn't sure what her point was, but it silenced Lucy for a moment. A very brief moment. She was pretty sure she heard her whispering *"Wow."* Best to get this conversation back on track. "You never answered my actual question, you know."

She turned to find Lucy pulling fronds of various ferns and greenery from a box.

"Which one? The one about me being safe or the one about a drug lord ransacking your flower shop?" Lord, this young lady had sass to spare. She also had a disarming smile, which she flashed at Connie after setting the greenery in the cooler. "Yes, I'm safe. At least physically. And no, my ex is not a drug dealer."

"But you *were* hiding from him."

Lucy took a deep breath, and her forehead furrowed. "I don't know if *hiding* is the right word, but… I didn't tell him where I was."

"If he's your ex, he doesn't need to know where you are. Unless…do you have children together?"

"No." Lucy moved the box of black-eyed Susans near the sink and started snipping the ends of the stems like Connie had been doing. "But…he didn't become my ex until…" She paused, staring blankly into the sink. "Until I didn't show up for our wedding a few weeks ago."

"No…" Connie breathed out the word in shock. Sure, Lucy had sass, but she hadn't seemed unstable. To leave a guy waiting at the church? "You didn't really… you left him at the *altar*?"

Lucy started snipping away sharply, making Connie worry about the girl's fingers. Those scissors were razor sharp.

"Technically, I don't think he ever made it to the altar."

Connie had never heard of that happening outside of some soap opera. "Was it a big wedding? Or should I say was it *supposed* to be a big wedding?"

Lucy sucked a corner of her mouth, puckering her face. And avoiding Connie's gaze. She plunked the yellow flowers into the container and marched to the cooler. She didn't reply until she'd put them inside and grabbed the large box of carnations, returning to the sink.

"Obnoxiously big," she finally said, separating the flowers by color and putting them loosely in the containers. Her southern accent grew thicker. "His mother, bless her heart, hijacked the plans and left me watching from the sidelines. Pretty much the same way her son did with our relationship. I was just watching from the cheap seats."

"But wasn't the wedding ceremony the *beginning* of your life together?"

She shrugged weakly. "You'd think, right? But it didn't feel like Owen cared one way or the other. I'm frankly shocked he cared enough to show up this morning and call me his fiancée." She jabbed the carnations into the buckets with a little more force now. "I mean, he didn't care when I was *there*, so why should he care if I left?" She looked at

Connie, her eyes suddenly bright with unshed tears. *Oh, crap.* They were getting into the dreaded *feelings* zone that Connie usually avoided. But there was something in Lucy's expression that made Connie's heart tighten.

"So you were engaged to a man you didn't really love?"

"I *did* love him, at least at first." A quick smile flitted across her face. "But he was in the Army and deployed, then deployed again, and the closer the wedding got, the less we seemed to…connect. He was all closed up when he came home this last time. It felt like…like he didn't want me to even try to connect." Her eyes hardened. "He actually referred to our wedding day as something we had to *get through*, as if it was some terrible burden he was bearing."

Connie thought about her own wedding day. Danny had been so handsome in his white tux. The bridal party— which included Cecile Manning and a few other members of the Rendezvous Falls book club—had followed the trend of the day, dressed in a rainbow of pastel colors. Like her, the bridesmaids wore wide-brimmed white hats. Memories of Danny usually made her sad, quickly followed by angry. But she couldn't help smiling when she thought of the naughty words he'd whispered in her ear as they headed down the aisle as husband and wife. They'd had a good start.

"A wedding should be a happy day," she conceded. "I mean, marriage is hard work, but the wedding…well… it should be happy. For *both* of you. It's a beginning, like swinging open the door to the rest of your life as a newly formed family unit."

"Pardon the pun, but that's pretty flowery for you, Connie. You had a happy marriage?"

She nodded. "For a while. How about your parents? Did you have a good example for married life, or...?" For someone who didn't care, Connie sure was blurting out a lot of personal information and questions.

Lucy started cutting up the boxes and folding them for the recycling bins. The way she brandished the box cutter after Connie's question made her nervous, but she didn't interfere. Lucy slammed the last box flat and looked up angrily.

"I *thought* I had a good example in my parents' marriage, but they're divorcing. *Divorcing.*" She hit the button that closed up the razor's edge on the box cutter. "I found out the night before my wedding."

The front door bell tinkled softly as the first customer of the day came in. Connie was glad to have a way out of this very personal conversation. She rushed toward the doorway to the shop, patting Lucy's shoulder as she passed her.

"I'll get this if you'll get the cardboard out to the bins. Then we can start planning the weekend." She hesitated. "I hate to tell you this, but we have two weddings this weekend."

Lucy had recovered from her melancholy, and waved Connie off. "I won't hold my antimarriage stance against the bouquets, I promise."

After the customer, Rick Thomas from the college, left with a bundle of yellow rosebuds, Connie rejoined Lucy in the workroom. The conversation stayed in safer territory—small vs. large table arrangements, roses vs. lilies in bridal bouquets, colorful vs. traditional white flowers. They couldn't start making the wedding arrangements yet, but they separated out the stems they'd use into the far end of the cooler. That way they wouldn't accidentally sell flowers they needed for orders. They did have two birthday bouquets to create for the next morning, courtesy of an online floral website. That was when Connie's mood began to sour again.

"Bastards barely give us enough percentage on these orders to pay for the gas we use to deliver them." She flipped open the guidebook to see what the first arrangement was supposed to look like. "But if I didn't accept their orders, they'd have that florist in Watkins Glen delivering to *my* customers."

"Don't you have your own website?"

"Some kid from the college put one together for me a few years ago. It was an extra credit project for him. But I haven't looked at it in ages." Connie had a smart phone and used some social media. She wasn't afraid of technology, but she didn't understand how how the website worked. "The one time I tried to update the website on my own, I removed it from the internet completely and had to call Evie over from the diner to restore it." She hated needing help, and she really hated anyone *knowing* she needed it.

"You don't…look at it?" Lucy tipped her head to the side. "Connie, that's how people find you so they can order right from…" She paused, probably noting Connie's tension. "I'll tell you what—when the shop is quiet, I'll work on updating your website. What platform is it on?" When she didn't get an answer, she rushed ahead. "Never mind. I'll check with Evie. She'll probably remember."

Connie should probably thank her. Instead, she scowled. "I don't care about a damn website. I have enough to keep up with. Besides, it's not like you'll be here to keep it up."

Lucy's eyes went wide. "Why do you say that?"

Connie rolled her eyes. "Please. That man of yours came all this way to sweet talk you right back to North Carolina." The thought made Connie more disappointed than she'd expected. "I'd put money on you being gone by next week."

"He can sweet talk all he wants. It won't change a damn thing." Lucy flipped her hair, looking defiant.

"You say that now, but it wasn't that long ago that you were ready to marry the man. And even after you dumped him, he wants you to go home with him."

"That's just the problem." Lucy pursed her lips. "The problem wasn't just Owen. It's…home. I don't know if I ever want to go back, with or without him." She sighed, looking up at Connie. "But he *has* to go back. His family is depending on him."

"But weren't *you* going to be his family?

"I wouldn't have been as important as the rest of them."

"Well," Connie said, "that's definitely a problem."

CHAPTER SEVEN

LUCY WALKED BACK to the Taggart Inn a few hours later, still annoyed by Connie's conviction that she was going to pack up and run home again. She sniffed. *As if.* Just because she'd bailed on her wedding didn't mean she was some flighty child. Her pace slowed. She could see how other people might think so, though.

She smiled at a young family walking two large dogs and two small children. The parents scurried to grab the leashes, even though the kids were protesting that they could hold on to the dogs. The dad smiled apologetically, but Lucy waved it off and patted the two dogs. This place was a lot like Boone, the town where her grandmother had lived. Rendezvous Falls wasn't a mountain town, of course, but it *was* a tourist town, with a tight-knit base of year-round residents. It was more colorful here, with each Victorian home having a wilder paint combination than the last. Piper told her the history of the place…how it had grown after a famous architect had returned from the Civil War and wanted to bring joy to his hometown with his fairy-tale homes.

Lucy had barely communicated with anyone in North Carolina since her departure. Nikki texted almost daily, and they were working out the logistics of getting the convertible back to her. Her sister, Kris, had checked in a few times, mainly to lay on the guilt about being left to deal with the fallout from Lucy's actions. Her parents had called, but Lucy was too hurt and conflicted to deal with their drama.

"Hi, Luce."

She stopped abruptly at the familiar voice. She hadn't even realized she'd reached the inn. Owen sat on the wooden steps to the wide front porch, one arm resting on his knee, watching her solemnly. He was in cargo shorts and a Rendezvous Falls T-shirt she'd seen for sale at the Spot Diner. So he'd been downtown, right across the street from the flower shop. Her eyes narrowed.

"Have you been following me?"

He sat up sharply. "Jesus, Lucy. This morning you said I could stay. I mean, yes, I followed you to New York, but…" One arm swung up in the universal gesture of *what the hell*

She pointed to his shirt. "So you weren't downtown because of me?"

He sighed and shook his head. "I was downtown looking for *lunch and bought a shirt.* If you were anywhere on Main Street, I swear I didn't know. Look, I don't want us snapping at each other like this. Can we talk?"

They stared at each other like a pair of suspicious cats scoping out a potential rival. Connie's words came back to her.

…you were ready to marry the man…

But she hadn't married him. As much as she wanted to hang on to her anger, the man deserved to know why that happened. She sat on the steps a few feet away from him.

"Did I ever tell you I took piano lessons as a kid?"

"Uh…no. I don't think so." Owen sounded cautious. "I've never seen you play…"

She waved her hand, pushing the memory away. "You haven't. I had to give up my lessons with Mrs. Quakenbush when Kris got sick. Mom and Dad said money was tight and they were so busy with Kris that they couldn't afford the lessons or the time to take me there. They asked me to understand, and of course I did. Anyone would, right?" She watched a beetle work its way across the sidewalk in front of the inn.

"When I was fifteen, my aunt needed help with her flower shop." She turned to face him. He stared at her as if he had no idea what she'd do next. *Join the club.*

"I loved that flower shop. Aunt Shirley said I was a natural. I dreamed that one day she and I would run it together. Even Shirley said it was a great idea." Lucy saw herself, even then, living a life surrounded by flowers. Until it came to an end. "A few years later, Shirley met a man and fell in love and sold the shop. Just like that. She and my new uncle moved to Atlanta. I begged Dad to buy the shop, but he couldn't afford it, and he said I needed to stay in college. And I understood."

She stretched her legs out in front of her. "I was accepted by a couple different schools, but Mom and Dad told me to find somewhere close that they could afford. So I went to App State. I took accounting because Dad said it would give me options. And I understood. I understood *all* of it."

She looked into his eyes, those beautiful golden-brown eyes. His forehead wrinkled slightly, as if he was trying to work some equation that refused to be solved. That equation was her. But at least he was listening—the one thing she'd accused him of not doing. Her voice softened.

"When I met you, I had that job at the tax place in

Wilmington. It was a bore, but I had a part-time job at a florist shop, remember? I was probably the happiest I'd ever been. You met me at my peak, Owen."

His mouth lifted into a smile. "You were something else when we met, Lucy Higgins. You upended my entire life when we met at Topsail Beach."

She nodded. She'd never expected to fall for an oh-so-serious soldier. And he'd called her his *sunshine surprise.* "It was easy for me to fall in love when I felt like I was already living a dream. Then reality came crashing down, asking for my understanding. Again." She stared at the dark red Oriental rug beneath their feet. "Grandma's cancer came back. You were getting ready to deploy, and you said I should go help. That we could wait to get married. That you wanted me to be with family instead of alone on base. So I went home. I understood." She gave a soft laugh, staring out across the parking lot. "That's what I've always been, I guess. An understander."

Owen frowned. "But…your grandmother *did* need you. You stayed and allowed her to live at home. You did the right thing. You're a good person, Lucy."

Then why was she such a mess? She'd stayed at Grandma's double-wide in Boone. Took a job at a tourist shop there. Did what was needed. Put the wedding on hold. Put her life on hold. Just like she had with her piano lessons years before.

"Owen, just when I thought we'd get *our* turn at a life together, making our *own* decisions, you told me you'd decided to extend your service for another year. Without even *discussing* it with me."

"I told you they asked for the extensions because of the

pandemic. Recruitments were down. I had the experience they needed. It was only a year..."

"*Another* year, you mean. After I'd waited years already." She felt that frightening surge of emotion again, and she didn't bother fighting it anymore. The things that led to her fleeing North Carolina were all falling into place, and almost...*almost* making sense. "Then your mom just took over the wedding."

She put her hand over her heart, hot tears burning her eyes. "I felt invisible. And then *you* came back from this tour like a completely different man. All closed up and silent. Short-tempered. Dismissive. I tried so hard to understand. Hell, I should have been good at it by then, right?"

Owen ran his fingers through his air. "I'm so sorry, Luce. I know Mom can be a bulldozer and a wrecking ball all wrapped up in a Southern bow...but you should have told me. I would have..."

She shook her head sharply, refusing to let him off the hook. "Would have *what?* I told you she picked out an eight thousand dollar princess bridal gown with a crystal tiara over the veil. A *tiara.*" Her eyes narrowed. "Do I look like a princess gown and tiara bride to you?"

A smile teased his lips, but he swallowed it fast when he saw her expression. "Well...no... But the guys all said women change when weddings are being planned. They said I should just...go along..." His voice trailed off.

"You took relationship advice from Pete and Marcus? Is *that* why you kept writing me over and over again that everything would be *fine?*" His gaze wouldn't hold on her. "Do you not remember us talking about my dream wedding?"

He hesitated, then gave a quick nod. "You wanted to get married up on Grandfather Mountain. Barefoot, so we could feel the grass in our toes. You didn't want strangers there, just a few people who loved us." The corner of his mouth lifted. "Just you, me and a pastor, with maybe a few eagles flying by as witnesses. I suggested we marry on the beach, but you told me you were a mountain girl."

"Exactly! So why did you think I'd suddenly decide I needed glitz and glam and three hundred people?" He opened his mouth to answer, but she waved him off. "Let me guess…your buddies in the foxholes."

"They don't call them foxholes anymore…"

"Whatever. You didn't pay attention to what I was trying to tell you. How much I hated the dress and the club and that stupid tiara. But I figured you were distracted, being over there, dealing with combat and all. So I freakin' *understood* again." She took a ragged breath, facing up to the worst of it. "And then my *parents*…their marriage was the rock of our family. It was the one thing I wanted for myself someday—a partnership just like theirs. Weathering all the storms. And…and all of a sudden I didn't understand *anything* anymore." The tears overflowed now, and she didn't bother wiping them away. "I've lived my entire life just stuck in the currents of what everyone else needed. What about what *I* need?"

His face had gone pale. He stared for a minute. "So when you left…it wasn't just about me…"

A harsh laugh bubbled up in her throat. "And that's *good* news?"

Now it was his turn to get frustrated. "Well, excuse me for not wanting to be the *only* reason I was left standing in the church foyer wondering where the hell my bride went!" He spread his hands wide. "I know I shut you out. I didn't want to deal with wedding stuff. It felt so unimportant compared to…" His eyes fell closed. "I'm sorry you felt invisible. I'm sorry my mom steamrolled you. I'm damn sure sorry your parents screwed up and then thought they could keep it all some big secret." A flicker of heat returned to his eyes. When he reached over to take her hand in his, she didn't resist. He was hurting, too. "But if it's not all me, if I'm not the only screwup in this, then we've got a chance, babe. We can fix everything else if we do it together. Just come home with me."

She looked at him, wanting so much to believe. And knowing she didn't dare. Greensboro was where their families were waiting. Where his career was waiting. She shook her head sadly.

"I don't think so, Owen. I don't know what I'm going to do, but I don't see returning to North Carolina in the picture. Not for a while anyway." She squeezed his fingers and pulled her hand back. "You should head back tomorrow, after you've rested. Don't stay here and get your hopes up. You know me—the more you push, the further away I'll be."

"That sounds like a challenge." He gestured down at himself. "I've already shown you how determined I can be. Besides, you said you'd give me a month."

She stood and looked down at him, feeling a stab of pity.

...you were ready to marry the man...

She blinked, surprised how much this hurt. She'd loved him. In many ways, she still did. But going back home was not *her* future. So what was the point?

"Do what you want, Owen. But the sooner you go back and start your life without me, the better off you'll be."

OWEN DIDN'T REALIZE how far he'd walked until the sun dipped behind the hills above Rendezvous Falls, casting long shadows. He had no idea where he was. Hardly surprising, since he'd only been in town for twelve hours—

and he'd slept for six of them. He'd been crisscrossing back and forth across town, trying to think through this mess he was in. The streets here were laid out in a neat grid around Main Street, lined with sidewalks, with tall trees arching overhead. In a way, it reminded him of some historic little towns in North Carolina, which might explain why Lucy was so comfortable here. He'd *never* seen so many Victorian homes in one place before now, though. Certainly never so many in such brilliant colors—too bright for genteel Carolina. Purple, green, orange, blue…often all on the same house. They almost looked like cartoons, or fanciful pastries or candies. Too sweet for his taste, that's for sure.

He stopped and looked around, trying to assess his position. He'd gone past the campus of Brady College a little while ago, with the low stone buildings hugging the shore of Seneca Lake. There was a tall conical roof ahead. It was the tower of the dark purple house at the upper end of Main Street. The whole town ran gently uphill from the lake. The town was above the college. Above that the grape vineyards ran to the top of the large hill the sun had fallen behind. He'd come north of town on this final pass, staying closer to the lake, but beyond the town far enough to have left the sidewalks behind. Large houses were on one side, along the water. Some of them were near-mansions. A few were newer, but most were older Victorians, just on a grander scale than in town.

He headed back toward downtown, picking up his pace without breaking a sweat. If he'd been overseas, he'd be carrying fifty pounds or more of weapons and gear right now. This walk, even if it had been a few hours long, was a piece of cake. He groaned. The last thing he needed to be thinking about right now was cake. As much as he was used to walking, he was also used to *eating*. He hadn't had anything since the bagel and egg sandwich he'd had at the Spot Diner that morning. The Army made him hike, but they at least handed out MREs for sustenance.

Sidewalks reappeared in a few minutes, and he made it to Main Street in another ten. It was a weeknight, and most businesses were closed up tight, including the Spot. Great. No fast-food restaurants here—probably against zoning rules in order to keep the town's gingerbread aesthetic untarnished. *Great.* He'd noticed a small grocery store up on Route 12. That was probably his only available option for dinner. Maybe they had an in-store deli or something.

He sensed a car slowing behind him and forced his pace to remain the same. It was instinct to scope out the surrounding area for an escape route or hiding place. In Kabul, you never knew which vehicles were friendlies and which might be carrying the enemy, or worse…the enemy's explosives. Part of his brain was very aware that he was taking an evening stroll in a town proudly declaring it was one of "America's Prettiest Small Towns." But self-preservation wasn't something you just turned off after so much time in dangerous territory.

"Owen? Is that you, man?" Logan Taggart's voice called out. *Stand down, soldier.* Lucy's words came back to him as he took a steadying breath. He turned, then almost stumbled at the sight of Logan in a gigantic old car. Like…an old lady car. A long dark green coupe. Definitely not what he expected from a guy who'd been willing to throw Owen out of the Taggart Inn that morning.

He walked over to the open passenger window, leaning over to look in at Logan. "Uh…is this your car?"

"Seriously?" Logan gestured to himself. "Do I look like a '95 Buick Riviera guy to you? It's my grandmother's, but she hasn't driven it in a few weeks, so I told her I'd give it a run. Where are you headed on foot at this hour?"

Owen looked at his watch. "It's nine o'clock. Do the sidewalks always roll up this early in this town?" He straightened with a groan. "I'm just lookin' for some food."

Logan chuckled. "Get in. I'm headed to the local pub. I'm friends with the owner, so even if the kitchen is closed, I'm sure I can get you a hot meal." He hadn't finished the word *meal* before Owen had the car door open. They pulled into the Purple Shamrock five minutes later. The building was long and low, right off the highway above town. Behind it was an impressive outdoor patio that looked down over the town and Seneca Lake. That's where Logan headed.

As usual, Owen scanned and cataloged his surroundings. There were a few customers out there. Three older women were laughing together by the firepit, drinking wine. A couple sat at a small table, sipping coffee, heads close together. Another couple stood at the back edge of the patio, looking down over the lake. The man stood behind the woman, his arms around her waist and their fingers interlocked over her stomach. Her head was resting back against his chest, her red hair pulled up into some sort of knot.

Cute, but Owen was more concerned that there was no food in sight.

He stopped by the back door to the pub, thinking maybe he'd find some food there. His stomach was growling so loud he was afraid people would hear it. Logan walked over to the standing couple, and they greeted him with smiles.

There was a brief conversation, and the redhead leaned back to look in Owen's direction. He had the strange feeling he was being evaluated. Then the three of them walked his way. The woman patted his arm and kept going, heading inside. Her voice was low and friendly.

"Have a seat. The grill's still hot, so I'll put a plate together for you."

The other man extended a hand. "Finn O'Hearn." There was no mistaking his Irish accent. "Come over and sit. Bridget'll only be a minute. Can't have you starvin' on your first night in town."

Owen introduced himself and sat with Finn and Logan, who was looking amused.

"So it turns out you two have something in common." Logan gestured between Owen and Finn. He directed his explanation to Finn. "Owen here has come to town to grovel and get his girl back. I think you have some experience at that, don't you, Finn?"

Finn smirked and nodded. "More than I'd like, and thanks for reminding me of those dark days, you twat." He looked at Owen. "What did you do to screw up? And who are we talking about? A local lass?"

"No! That's the best part," Logan laughed. "She came here to get away from him, and he's come after her to get her back."

Bridget arrived at the table as those words were spoken. She'd been putting the plate in front of Owen, and *holy hell* it smelled good. But at Logan's comment, her eyes narrowed dangerously and she pulled the plate back.

"Excuse me?" She glared at Owen. "A woman came here to get away from you and you *followed* her?" She shared her glare with the other two men. "And *you* idiots think that's a *good* thing?"

Owen wasn't the only one intimidated by this woman with the sharp green eyes and copper hair. Logan started to stammer. "Bridget, it's not like that. Lucy's staying at the inn, and she assured me she's okay with Owen staying. I saw them talking together on the porch this afternoon."

He winced. That conversation was when Lucy made it clear that in *her* mind, he was wasting his time. Bridget studied him, then set the plate back down. She stepped away, tapping on her phone. She clearly hadn't absolved him yet, but that juicy burger was calling his name. He took a large bite of it and moaned, making Finn laugh.

"Best burger ever, right? She's a treasure."

The *treasure* came back and sat down, seeming a lot less stressed. She slid her phone into her back pocket. "Piper said she thinks you're okay."

Logan sat back in his chair and clutched his hands to his heart. "You didn't believe me?"

"I wanted a woman's sense of things." She accepted a dark beer from a woman waiting tables. "No offense, but…"

Owen nodded, his mouth full of burger. "No offense taken. It's complicated." He looked at Finn. "As for what I did wrong… I have no idea." He had *some* idea, of course. She'd been pestering him about sharing his feelings since he got back to the States. How could he talk about something he couldn't define? Couldn't even face without shuddering?

Bridget's phone buzzed in her pocket, and she pulled it out, then grinned at Owen.

"Piper says your girl is the one who's been working at Connie's florist shop. She's made a big impression already. My grandmother says the arrangements at church the past few weeks have been fantastic. My cousin, Timothy, bought an anniversary bouquet for his wife, and she's been raving about it all week. And my other cousin, Mary, told her husband he'd better order her birthday bouquet from Connie next year."

Owen had no idea who any of those people were. But now he knew where Lucy was working. A flower shop. *Of course.* Finn put his hand over Bridget's, then smiled in his direction.

"Small town plus a big Irish family equals no secrets stay secret for long around here."

He nodded, swallowing another bite of the burger. "Not that different from small southern towns, believe me. Bridget, this burger is fantastic. Thank you."

She gave him a bright grin. "Glad you like it. It's a new one on the menu—angus burger made with sundried tomato paste and special seasonings."

They all had another beer, except Logan, who said he wouldn't manage driving his grandmother's barge of a Buick home with alcohol in his system. Owen did more listening than talking, trying to figure out where everyone fit in the town. Logan's grandmother owned the inn, and he promised to introduce Owen to her. It sounded like she was quite a character. Logan and Piper had been married only a year or so. He'd come here to help his grandmother after she broke her hip, and Piper lived right next door. She'd been running the inn and raising her two kids on her own when she and Logan fell in love.

Finn and Bridget were engaged, with their wedding coming up in the fall. He was a history professor at Brady College, and she owned the pub, which had been in her family for a couple generations. Their wedding was originally planned for the previous year, but they wanted Finn's family from Ireland to attend. The health crisis had made that impossible, so they'd rescheduled. In the meantime, they were remodeling Bridget's Victorian house located across the parking lot—changing it from apartment units back into a single family home.

Owen lost track of the conversation after that. He was glad to have met some people on his first day here, but the person who mattered most wanted nothing to do with him. If Lucy was sitting here right now—if she hadn't dumped him—she'd be laughing along with Bridget and telling her own funny stories. She'd tease Owen about something silly he'd done. He frowned. Something as silly as losing her. Maybe for good.

"I'd better get this guy back to the inn before he starts crying in his beer." Logan pushed his chair back and stood, grinning at Owen. "You need a good night's sleep, pal. Things will look better in the morning when you have a clear head."

Owen wasn't so sure. A clear head might just tell him that Lucy was right. That he should go home without her. And he wasn't ready to do that. Not yet. Not with trying to fix things.

CHAPTER EIGHT

A GOOD NIGHT's sleep *did* clear Owen's head, but things did *not* look any better the next morning. When he went down for breakfast, Lucy was just finishing. She hurriedly put her dishes in the tray on the sideboard, then scooted past him with a mumbled "Good morning." Piper was watching, and gave him a pitying smile when he sat at a small table in the corner of the spacious room. It was bright and cheery in there, with three large windows. The curtain fabric sported large hydrangea blossoms. Lucy's favorite.

"Our special this morning is Logan's roustabout scramble." Piper set a mug of coffee in front of him and put the carafe on the table. She gestured to the chalkboard on the wall, where scrolling cursive letters described the breakfast as having eggs, cheese, sausage, bacon and chopped veggies. "He learned the recipe when he was on the oil rigs. It's definitely hearty, and will get you off to a good start. Or I can make pancakes…"

He shook his head. "The special sounds fine."

"I'll let Logan know—the only time he gets to run the kitchen is when that's on the menu." She was gone and back in a minute. She cleared a table where it looked as though a group of four had eaten.

"Is your breakfast just for guests staying here?" His room had been so quiet he hadn't heard anyone else moving around or talking. But maybe that was because he'd fallen asleep so quickly.

"Yes. I keep telling Logan and his grandmother that technically we're a bed-and-breakfast these days." Piper frowned at a spot on the white tablecloth on the table she'd just cleared, then pulled it off the table. "Iris used to have a small restaurant here, but it's been years since that was open."

"That explains why the room is so big." He could see this being a nice place for dinner.

She flipped a clean linen tablecloth over the table she'd cleared, then straightened and looked around. "We've been talking about dividing the room so it would be a cozier breakfast area, but the extra space sure came in handy when we had to do social distancing."

"How'd you fare during all that?"

She shrugged. "It wasn't easy, but we got through. Once the wineries around here opened back up, tourists were eager for something to do." Logan came in just then, sending his wife a wink. She swatted a dish towel in his direction playfully. "And luckily my husband has a consulting firm. He was gone a lot, but it helped us survive."

Logan set a heaping plate of steaming food in front of Owen. "Talking about the pandemic? Yeah, that was interesting. My gran is eighty-two, so we had to be extra careful about everything."

An elderly woman came into the room just then. "Is it really necessary to announce my age to every guest that comes to this place?" Her words were sharp, but a smile played at the corners of her mouth. She was petite and white-haired, but despite the fancy gold-and-black cane she used, he sensed there was nothing frail about the woman. Particularly her sharp blue eyes, which were currently appraising him where he sat.

Logan stepped to the side. "Gran, this is Owen Cooper. Owen, this is my grandmother, Iris Taggart."

"You used to be Lucy's man, right? The one she dumped?"

Piper winced, and Logan's eyes rolled up toward the ceiling.

"Gran…"

She waved off her grandson's protest. "What? It's the truth, isn't it?" She walked over to Owen's table. She was stylishly dressed, wearing a long blue skirt and a white top trimmed in the same color. He had the feeling this was a woman to be reckoned with. In a way, she reminded him of his mother, but without the hard edges. Her eyes narrowed on him. "So why are you here?"

He choked on his first bite of the breakfast scramble, coughing into his napkin before answering. "I'm here to bring her home." That didn't sound any better this morning than it had yesterday. It made him sound like a caveman. "I mean… I'm here to *convince* her to come home. With me. To me. If that's what she wants."

"And if it's *not* what she wants?"

And there was that very scary question again. The one that opened the door to the Great Unknown. His mother was already furious that he'd chased after Lucy. Apparently, the rift that had grown between his mom and Lucy was bigger than he'd realized. Of course, losing so much money on the canceled wedding and being humiliated in front of her country club friends wasn't helping Mom's mood any. His father told him he was needed at the family business, and could be gone only for a week. Which was odd, since his cousin had been running the nursery and produce side of the landscaping business just fine while Owen was in the Army.

He looked up and realized all three people in the room seemed to be very interested in his answer. Which he hadn't given yet. This felt a lot like last night, when Bridget McKinnon had grilled him before feeding him. He cleared his throat, stalling for more time, then went with the truth.

"I have no idea, but I'm not much of a quitter." He gestured at his plate with his fork, then back to Iris. "And my breakfast is getting cold."

Piper put her hand over her heart. "Oh my God, Owen, I'm so sorry. We're not being at all hospitable, are we?" She moved to shoo her husband and Iris out of the room. "Let the man eat his meal in peace!"

But Iris bristled, tapping her cane on the floor sharply. "Lucy Higgins is a guest, too. Are you sure she's okay with him being here?"

"Yes, Iris. She was very clear about it being okay. She even said good morning to him today when he came in here." Piper pointed to the door. "Leave him alone."

He finished his breakfast after they left. Lucy's "Good morning" may as well have been a "Drop dead," based on her tone. Only a fool would let a woman like Lucy get away, but he'd managed to do it. It might be time for a desperation move. He pulled his phone out and started scrolling through the Dr. Find-Love app until he found the *You Screwed Up?* page. He hadn't been keen on the idea of groveling when Logan mentioned it, but these were desperate times. He opened the article.

Step One: She can't forget you if she keeps seeing you.
Find a way to subtly stay in her orbit without being creepy.

LUCY HAD BEEN working at a frantic pace all day Saturday. She'd been that way since Owen's arrival. There was something about him being at the Taggart Inn this week that put her on edge, and she'd always been one to keep busy when she was uptight. She'd told him there was no reason to stay. And then she'd turned right around and said "but stay if you want to." Why?

She'd been getting up extra early every morning to beat him to breakfast and get out of the inn so she could avoid him. She'd leave right after eating, walking around town and killing time until she was needed at the shop. Fortunately for her, there was plenty of work to be done today, so she'd been able to start early and keep herself distracted.

And speaking of distracted, Connie hadn't been herself that morning. She said she wasn't feeling well, although Lucy suspected there was more to it than that. But she told Connie to sit at the register for walk-in customers, and she'd put her to work on cutting ribbon for the wedding arrangements. Meanwhile, Lucy had finished putting together not one, but *two* large wedding orders for that day. She couldn't imagine how Connie would have managed it without her help, but Connie said she used to farm out large orders to other florists, which cut sharply into her own profits. June was wedding season, and was often a make-or-break time for flower shops. The first wedding order of the day, a relatively simple one in a pastel rainbow theme, had already been delivered to the Methodist church up on the highway.

Lucy had been across the street grabbing a quick lunch from Evie Hudson at the diner when the temporary delivery guy picked it up. Lucy crossed her fingers, hoping everything got there right side up and intact. Connie's usual delivery person when the college wasn't in session, was Greg Charles. But he was off this week to see his new grandchild. She said this new guy was doing some work at her house and offered to help, so she'd hired him for the weekend. All she cared about was that he handled the flowers carefully so her work didn't get ruined.

The second, and much more elaborate order was almost ready for pickup. The wedding planner for this one was a control freak, but that worked out okay for Lucy, because it meant she didn't have to ride along with the driver to help set up the tables at the reception. The planner insisted on doing *everything*. Not very practical, but fine. Anything that kept Lucy out of a wedding hall or church was perfectly fine.

The shop phone rang. She always smiled when that happened, because it was actually a wall phone. With a *cord*. Out front, Connie had a cordless phone, but she snippily insisted there was nothing wrong with the phone in the workroom, so there was no need to replace it. Connie was taking care of a customer, so Lucy answered the call.

"Hey, Lucy. I'm glad I caught you…this is Lucy right? This is Becca up at Rendezvous Falls Methodist." Lucy's heart dropped.

"Hi, Becca," she answered. "Did the wedding flowers arrive all right? They weren't late or anything…?" She'd murder Connie's new driver if he screwed this order up. She'd met the two women getting married when they stopped in last week for a final consultation. They were both happy and funny and so obviously in love with each other.

Becca laughed. "Relax! The flowers were on time and gorgeous. Both brides burst into tears when they saw them—the *good* kind of tears. Everyone's happy. Which is why I'm calling…" Becca explained her sister was getting married that fall and was looking for a florist. She'd sent her photos of today's bridal flowers, and her sister loved them. They set up a planning appointment for the following week. Lucy didn't mention that she might not be in Rendezvous Falls by October, but she could show Connie how to make whatever the bride was looking for. Whether or not Connie would listen was another matter, but she couldn't control that. Becca said something and Lucy realized she hadn't been listening.

"I'm sorry, what?"

"I said thank you for sending that delivery guy."

Lucy frowned. "You want me to thank the delivery guy? Did he do something special?"

"Oh God, don't say anything *to* him. I'd die of embarrassment. Just…thank *you* for hiring him. He is one hot hunk of man."

"Really? I haven't met him yet. Cutie, huh?"

"I don't know if *cute* is the word I'd use. He's not seventy-five-year-old Greg or one of Connie's college kids. He's a man in his prime who's been…well…blessed by God in the looks department."

Lucy laughed. "Well, I'm glad you enjoyed his…delivery."

After the call, she wondered why Connie never mentioned the new guy was a Chippendale look-a-like. Then again, Connie probably hadn't noticed. It wasn't as if Connie was looking for a hot guy. And Lucy wasn't, either.

She put the last of the bright tiger lily boutonnieres in a flat box and covered it in plastic wrap before sliding it back into the cooler. Twenty-one matching centerpieces of orange chrysanthemums, and tiger lilies in dark blue bowls, with two larger arrangements for the bridal table. Five bridesmaids' bouquets of yellow rosebuds and lilies with long streamers of sparkly orange and blue ribbons. And two bridal bouquets—one for the church ceremony and one for tossing. The tossing bouquet was a colorful sphere of orange and blue chrysanthemums, made fluffier with baby's breath. Apparently both bride and groom were avid fans of a college sports team from Syracuse—so much so that the flowers were in the team's blue and orange colors. All except the bride's.

Lucy pulled out the deep plastic-wrapped box holding the bridal bouquet. The bride had apparently drawn the line at walking down the aisle looking like a cheerleader. Her bouquet wasn't sporty at all. It was a decadent waterfall of traditional bridal flowers, from lush white peonies at the top to white roses and then cascading white calla lilies. The bouquet was heavy, but the planner said the bride wouldn't care about that. She may not have wanted to *look* collegiate walking down the aisle, but she'd played basketball for the school for four years. She could handle a heavy bouquet.

The back door opened behind her, and she pushed the box back into the cooler. The delivery guy was right on time. Once this order was out of the shop, she could go back to the inn, sneak up to her room and get some rest. The bridal box stuck for just a heartbeat on the shelf, taking her breath away when it started to tip. She steadied it and stood there, eyes closed in relief. Here she was fretting about a new driver and she'd almost dropped the most important box herself. She really was running out of steam. Connie came into the workroom and greeted the delivery driver.

"Good, you're right on time. The wedding planner is handling all the setup, so you just need to get it inside for her. This is a big order, Owen, and a very expensive one, so I need you to be extra careful…"

Lucy spun on her heel. The cold from the open cooler door behind her was nothing compared to the chill growing in her chest.

"What the hell are *you* doing here?"

He held up his hands in innocence. "This isn't what it looks like. I did a landscaping quote for your boss and she said she was in a bind this weekend."

She couldn't believe this was happening. "How very convenient."

"Honest, Luce. It's only temporary."

Connie looked back and forth between them in confusion, then her eyes went wide.

"Wait…*this* guy is your ex? You left *this*—" she gestured at Owen's admittedly good-looking form "—standing at the altar?" Then she swatted at Owen, earning a startled laugh from Lucy. "And *you*! You made that girl so unhappy that she left the whole damn *state* to get away from you? You took this job under false pretenses. Are you even a landscaper, or did you fib about that, too?"

"I offered to help," Owen protested.

"Whatever." Connie glared at him. "I won't have you harassing my employee. You're fired."

Lucy straightened. Not only did she appreciate Connie coming to her defense, but she'd just called her an *employee*. So maybe that battle was settled.

"Don't fire him on my account, but I hope he told you he's only in Rendezvous Falls for a couple of weeks."

"Actually," he said with another grin, "you gave me a month, remember?" A glint of humor appeared in his eyes. "I have to pay for that room somehow." He looked at Connie. "I didn't mean to upset you, Connie. And I really am a landscaper."

Lucy started to understand what happened. "Is *this* the guy you hired to do work at your house?"

Connie turned to her with regret in her eyes. "Iris Taggart recommended Owen to do some landscaping. I need some shrubs removed and trees trimmed away from the house. When he heard I'd lost my delivery guy for the weekend, he said he'd be happy to help with deliveries."

"Yeah, I'll bet he did." Lucy shook her head. "Iris Taggart, huh?" Lucy thought the older woman had given her a funny look yesterday morning. Sort of a Cheshire cat grin, like she had a delicious secret.

"Does Iris always meddle in her guests' business?"

Connie snorted. "Iris Taggart meddles in *everyone's* business. I should have known there was a reason for her showing up the other day to sing this man's praises. Nothing's random with that woman." She shook her head. "It's too bad, because I really do need to get that work done at the house. I couldn't keep up with it, and my daughter-in-law is using that as evidence of my so-called *decline*."

Lucy cleared her throat. "It's fine. I don't want to keep Owen from employment, even if it is *very* temporary. And he is very good at landscaping." She leveled a look at Owen. "Well, don't just stand there—grab these boxes. The centerpieces can go out first. Then the altar piece and the rest of it. I want the box with the bride's bouquet on the front seat, strapped in safely."

He moved past her to take the boxes she'd pointed to, murmuring a soft but playful "Yes, ma'am."

"This isn't going to work, you know."

"What?" He straightened with two boxes in his arms. "The delivery? Centerpieces first. Then the rest, with the bridal box in the front seat. Strapped in. I got it."

She gestured at the small distance between them. "*This*. Us. Whatever game you think you're playing is not going to work. You can stay at the inn. You can work for Connie. But I'm not going back to Greensboro with you."

He stunned her by just saying "Okay" and giving her a quick kiss on her forehead before turning away for the door. Her mouth dropped open. She didn't think Owen had *ever* kissed her forehead. It was…sweet. Casual. As if he was letting her know that he wasn't there to argue, but he also wasn't giving up. Connie watched him go out the door, a bemused smile on her face.

"Did you just let that man kiss you?"

Lucy rubbed her forehead, suddenly agitated. "On the *forehead*, Connie. That's not a kiss. That's…. something grandparents do to their grandkids."

Connie stared off wistfully. "In our early years, Danny would give me a peck on the forehead whenever he was leaving. It was his silent goodbye-and-I-love-you. His way of saying he couldn't wait to give me a real kiss later on." Her eyes narrowed on Lucy. "There was nothing grand-fatherly about it."

Lucy turned away to pull more boxes out of the cooler. "Whatever. It was weird."

Except…it *wasn't* weird. Unusual, maybe. Unprecedented. But the quiver she'd felt inside when his lips brushed her skin shocked her. That was the heat of desire. And Owen Cooper had lit the spark. If Owen continued to be so charming, it was going to make it much more difficult for her to walk away.

CHAPTER NINE

OWEN PULLED HIS BRONCO into the parking lot of the Purple Shamrock on July Fourth and let out a low whistle at the number of cars already there. Finn O'Hearn told him that after they'd added the big patio behind the pub, the Fourth had been one of their busiest and most profitable days ever. It looked as if this year was going to be a rocking success, too. He found a parking spot and headed toward the sound of music and laughter on the patio.

He'd heard from Piper that Lucy was coming to the Purple Shamrock tonight for the fireworks, so maybe he could make some headway by putting himself in her orbit one more time. If only she'd give him a chance, he could prove how much he loved her. And he *did* love her. Perhaps more than ever. For one thing, she'd stood up to his mother by walking away, which wasn't easy. But he was sensing something in Lucy here in Rendezvous Falls that he hadn't seen in a while—a lightness…a brightness in her walk and her smile.

It was her bubbly, sassy attitude that had attracted him to Lucy in the first place. He felt like a fool for not seeing that was slipping away while he'd been busy playing soldier. And now she had it again…after leaving him. That stung.

He'd been in Rendezvous Falls for a week now, and he had no idea if he'd made any real progress in the Win

Back Lucy campaign. He'd put himself within her orbit by working at the flower shop for a few days, but he'd spent most of his time at Connie's house, trying to salvage the shrubs growing out of control at her slightly neglected lakeside cottage.

But Lucy had given him a month, so he still had some time. Feeling the pressure, we was working his way through the *How to Grovel* suggestions from Dr. Find-Love, just in case one might work.

Go big. Sometimes it takes a really grand gesture to soften her heart. Find something she loves (a place, a song, a movie) and figure out a way to really wow her with it.

It had taken three phone calls, including one with Logan on the line, to convince Nikki Taggart to go along with his grand gesture. It probably didn't hurt that his plan presented a free and painless way for her to get her convertible back, but Nikki never would have agreed if Logan hadn't spoken up on Owen's behalf. How long she'd actually keep the secret from Lucy was anyone's guess, so Owen was doing his best to speed things along. It was taking a whole lotta money, too, but he'd set aside some savings while serving.

"Owen!" Finn O'Hearn shouted his name loudly enough that heads turned. Finn downed the pint of dark beer in his hand. Judging from his slightly sloppy grin, Owen suspected that wasn't Finn's first of the day. The Irishman waved Owen over and slapped him on the back. "How the hell are ya? Come meet my fellow countryman. We Irish have to stick together on yer Independence Day shenanigans, you fekkin' rebels." He introduced Owen to Father Joseph Brennan from St. Vincent's Catholic

Church. The priest was an inch or two shorter than Owen, with a bright smile and a pint of dark brew in his hand.

"Good to meet you, lad!" Father Brennan held out his free hand. "You're the groom chasin' after our runaway bride, right?"

Finn laughed at Owen's expression. "Newsflash— there's nothin' goin' on in this town that the good Father doesn't know about."

Owen blew out a long breath. He wasn't used to so many people being in on his personal business. His mother always insisted that nothing good ever came from sharing news outside the immediate family circle. The people in Rendezvous Falls had different ideas. He did his best to smile at the kind-eyed priest.

"That's right, Father Brennan. If you can send up a prayer or two for me, that'd be great."

"Call me Father Joe, or just Joe if you prefer." Joe waved to a waitress walking by. "Mary, love, bring us a round o' Guinness when you get a chance…" He glanced at Owen. "Unless you prefer somethin' else?"

"I'm more of an ale drinker."

Joe nodded. "No worries. Mary, make it two Guinness and a Smithwicks for Owen here." He gestured toward the tall cafe table behind him. "Come join us, lad. As for the prayer, I'll definitely ask the good Lord to do His will, not mine. I cannot be takin' sides, you understand."

"Of course." Owen wasn't that big a believer in church stuff anyway. War did that to a person sometimes. He didn't expect any religion to provide answers to all the *whys* he carried around inside him. Whenever he'd thought about seeking those answers from some all-knowing entity, all he felt was white-hot anger, so he'd stopped trying a while ago. Better to seal up that emotion for another day. Or forever, if possible.

Finn changed the subject to sports, and that was a subject that felt a whole lot safer for Owen. Baseball season was in full swing . The three men debated the merits and prospects for several teams. Their beers arrived, and Owen approved of the Irish ale Father Joe had ordered for him. When the two Irishmen started talking about the sports of their homeland however, like rugby and something called hurling, Owen only half listened. He was watching the crowd. He told himself he was looking for Lucy, but truth be told, he was also doing his soldier thing again—gauging the perimeter, looking for anything out of place, marking the exits. It was stupid, but old habits were hard to break.

He intended to be out of there before dark, because he and fireworks didn't mix. But Lucy didn't arrive until the sun was settling low on the hills ar. She came with Logan, Piper and their kids, Ethan and Lily. Young Lily was clutching Lucy's hand and giggling about something. Then she spotted Owen and dragged Lucy his way.

"Mr. Owen! I didn't know you were coming tonight! Isn't it fun? Wait until you see the fireworks! They're mag-fis-sent!" He furrowed his brows, trying to decipher the word. The cute kid had proven to have a passion for big words, whether she could pronounce them or not.

"Oh, you mean *magnificent*. Yes, Lily, I'm sure they will be." He hoped to be long gone by then, but it was getting darker by the minute. He was running out of time, but he couldn't leave now that Lucy had just arrived. "It's good to see you, Luce."

She looked straight into his eyes, her face carefully neutral. Her pink hair was tucked behind her ears. He felt as if he was being examined somehow, as if she was looking right into his soul. "It's a *surprise* to see you, but it looks like you've made friends in town already." She nodded at Finn and Father Joe. Her voice dropped. "I know how you like to hang out with your bro-pals."

Was that a jab at how much time he'd spent with the guys in North Carolina after he'd returned? And how little time he'd spent talking with her, despite her begging him to talk about Afghanistan? He deserved it, of course, but he couldn't help getting defensive.

"My *bro-pals* don't tend to leave me high and dry at the altar."

Her face flushed, but before she could speak, Father Joe jumped in.

"Now, now. I'm guessin' there's lots of talkin' to be done between you two, but 'tisn't the time or place."

Logan moved Piper in front of him to shield her from the increasingly large and rowdy crowd. Finn looked around the patio as if suddenly realizing how packed it was, then he stood, pulling his chair out for Lucy.

"Have a seat, love. I'll grab another chair for Mrs. Taggart here, and then I'd better go see if my bride-to-be needs help inside at the bar. The place is getting pretty lively." He patted Owen's shoulder, almost whispering as he passed, "I believe you're supposed t'be groveling, my man, not *snarlin'*."

He nodded in response, staring at the table in silence while Lucy sat with a heavy sigh and the Taggarts pulled chairs in for themselves and the children. The waitress stopped and took their orders for drinks and a few shared appetizers. As she walked away, Owen steadied his voice and leaned toward Lucy.

"Sorry if I was a dick before. But Father Joe's right. We really *should* talk, Luce."

She kept her voice low like his. "Didn't I talk enough the first day you got here? What more is there to say?"

"*You* talked. I didn't. Not really. We haven't had an honest-to-God conversation since the wed…" He paused, grimacing at the truth. "Since well *before* the wedding. Can't we just sit down and…*converse* with each other?"

He heard the whine of the rocket well before the soft *boom* echoed over the lake below them. His brain told him it was a normal practice shot for the fireworks, to check the wind direction. But his body reacted, just for a heartbeat, as if…as if that rocket was incoming. He tensed, looking to the sky. He saw the receding colors of the sunset and the small white puff of smoke from the exploded test shot. Relief flooded his veins, and he sat back, glancing around to see who noticed.

Logan and Piper were laughing over something Ethan had said. Lily was sitting in Father Joe's lap, drinking her lemonade. No one had noticed his mini panic attack. No one except Lucy.

She was staring at him with heavy concern darkening her eyes, and her hand reached out to cover his. Her head tipped to the side and she mouthed a silent question. *You okay?* He swallowed hard, then nodded.

"Yay! Fireworks!" Lily shouted. "But I didn't see it— where did it go?"

"That was just a test, sweetheart." Father Joe was answering Lily, but watching Owen as he spoke. Maybe Lucy wasn't the only one to notice his reaction after all.

"In just a few minutes, we'll have lots of fireworks lighting up the sky. And those big bangs going off. Are you ready?"

Nope. Definitely not ready.

But how could he escape at this point? The crowd had overflowed the patio into the parking lot, with people setting up folding chairs by their cars to watch the show. He was going to have to figure out a way to block out the explosions. Go somewhere else in his mind. Maybe no one else would notice his stony silence while they were oohing and ahhing.

"Oh, my God!" Lucy startled everyone by jumping to her feet. "I forgot something! I forgot…to call my sister. Yes, I *promised* her I'd call today. I have to go…"

Piper frowned. "Can't you call her from here?"

"Oh…uh… I forgot my phone in my room. I need to go back." She grabbed Owen's hand and tugged him out of his chair. "Owen, I saw your Bronco was here. Can you take me back? Right now? We could…um…have that talk."

"But Miss Lucy, you were texting on your phone in the car on the way here. Remember?" Lily looked sad. "If you go now, you'll miss the fireworks."

And *finally*, Owen got it. Lucy was doing this for him. She was coming to his rescue. And he wasn't too proud to accept it. He felt a surge of hope. Lucy stared at Lily, panicked for a second, then she gave the most artificial laugh he'd ever heard.

"Yes, Lily, but that was a *different* phone. I have…two phones…and that one…doesn't…"

He finished for her. "Is that the phone that doesn't have your contacts in it? So you don't have Kris's number?

That number's in the *other* phone, back at the inn, right? I'll take you…"

Lily started to speak, but Father Joe beat her to it. "Sometimes *I* have the wrong phone with me, too. You don't want your sister to worry, Lucy. You two go on. Lily can tell you all about the fireworks later."

Lucy grabbed Owen's hand and pulled him away from the table, calling over her shoulder. "I would *love* that, sweetie. Tell me in the morning, okay? Come on, Owen. The least you can do is give me a ride back to the inn." Another fake laugh. "But don't get any ideas. I'm still not changing my mind about you…"

Logan and Piper looked baffled, but they didn't say anything. Father Joe waved and gave Owen a conspiratorial wink. Good thing he'd given up on his pride tonight, now that both Lucy *and* the good father were feeling sorry for him. They made their escape from the Purple Shamrock parking lot just as the sky lit up orange in the rearview mirror with the first volley. She reached for the radio and cranked up the volume on the Foo Fighters, almost drowning out the thunderous booms over the lake.

He had no idea where he was going. He just drove, going up the hill and away from the fireworks. The silence beneath the pounding music was heavy. He turned onto a side road that still wound upward. It wasn't until he'd nearly crested the top of the hill that he started to relax. He huffed out a soft laugh.

"I have no idea where we are."

And wasn't that the whole damn problem?

"THAT MAKES TWO OF US." Lucy pulled her phone out of her bag. "Let's see if we have a GPS signal up here." She scowled at her screen. "It's not looking good. We can just keep driving and then retrace our route in half an hour or so." The car slowed, and she peered through the darkness to a small sign announcing "Rendezvous Falls County Park—Hike to the Falls—Open Sunrise to Sunset."

She looked over at Owen when he turned onto the narrow gravel road. "I didn't know there was an actual Rendezvous Falls waterfall. Makes sense, I guess. But it's past sunset. It's closed."

"Do you really think the county is patrolling this little park on the Fourth of July? Stopping makes more sense than just blindly driving into the dark in the middle of nowhere." She saw the flash of his grin. She forgot he was a Man with a Plan. Driving aimlessly went against everything he believed in. Getting lost was *not* Owen's idea of a good time. The park had a name. Therefore, if he stopped here, he wasn't lost. She struggled to hold in a grin of her own.

The driveway opened to a small graveled parking area with a lone floodlight on a tall pole in one corner. The light was just enough to show a small open-sided pavilion and a few scattered picnic tables. And no other cars. He parked and turned off the engine. Their hands collided as they both reached to turn down the volume on the radio. He grinned ruefully in the light of the dashboard. "Stopping here makes more sense. Blindly running away isn't really a solution to a prob…"

He caught himself. "I'm talking about me, not you. I didn't mean…" He groaned, half to himself. "I planned on being out of there by the time the fireworks started. Figured I'd sit in my room with my noise-canceling headphones on and be fine. Rather than emasculating myself in front of everyone by freaking out over a loud noise."

"You don't need to explain. I've heard that a lot of combat veterans don't like fireworks." The dash lights faded now that the car was off, leaving only the ghostly gray glow from the parking lot light. They saw a distant burst of green light beyond the trees, and heard a deep boom from the valley. "Do you want me to turn the radio back on?"

"No. It's far enough away now. I don't like it when it's close enough that you feel the thud in your chest, but I can handle this." He turned in the seat to face her. "Thank you, by the way. I don't know what made you do that, but…thanks."

She knew this man well enough to know when he was about to break, and she'd seen it in his eyes back at the Purple Shamrock. He'd been right on the edge, and she had to do something.

"Do you remember that Halloween weekend we spent in New Bern? We took the ghost walk tour, and there was a power failure while we were in the old cemetery? Remember how dark it got?"

Lucy had a horrid fear of the dark, especially in a cemetery.

He chuckled. "I think I still have the scars from where you sank your fingernails into my arm." She swatted at him, which just made him laugh louder. "What? It's the truth! That's when I found out Lucy Higgins is afraid of the dark." He looked out the windshield at the dimly lit lot. "Oh, shit. Does this place bother…?"

"No. I'm fine. As long as that one light stays on." She leaned her head back on the seat. "That night in New Bern, you turned on your phone's flashlight, and called out to people around us asking them to do the same. You told everyone that I had some mysterious vision condition and wouldn't be able to walk without lots of light. No one even questioned you, even though the cemetery didn't have that many lights *before* the power went out." She rolled her head to look at him. "You were a hell of a lot more convincing than I was with my crazy two-phones story just now."

"You did okay. Father Joe helped. But…why did you do it?" Another distant boom rolled through the night. "You're missing the show."

She shrugged. "I've seen fireworks before. And I've owed you a rescue since New Bern. Now we're even."

"I have no idea what we are, Luce, but I don't think it's even at all. I honestly don't know who owes what."

A red glow rose above the trees, followed by a series of explosions. The inside of the car felt suddenly too closed in and warm. Too close…to him. She grabbed the door handle and pushed it open. "Let's check this place out." She hoped he didn't mind going outside, because she couldn't stay there.

"Uh…yeah, sure." He reached into the glove compartment and pulled out a sturdy black flashlight and a bizarre light of some kind attached to straps. He turned on the flashlight, and tossed the strappy thing in her direction. "Put it on your head. I know it looks goofy, but it works. Marcus gave it to me as a gag gift when I left the Army. It's like a miner's light, shining from your forehead." He got out of the car, then walked around to where she stood, trying to untangle the straps. "Here, let me…"

He quickly slid it over her head. The straps were like a helmet, holding the light in place. When he pressed the button, everything in front of her lit up in white light.

"Wow." She turned her head back and forth, sending

the beam of light sweeping across the mowed park lawn. "This thing is awesome!"

"It's supposed to be for working on a car engine and stuff like that, but I've never used it." He tugged the strap tighter around her head, securing it with the Velcro tab. "Looks like it was made just for you." Another burst of fireworks glowed beyond the trees. She reached up to touch his hand, and he smiled. "I'm fine. Distant explosions were normal background noise over there."

"But you're not over there anymore."

CHAPTER TEN

No, HE WASN'T over there anymore. But too many times it felt like *over there* was still inside him. Especially with explosions lighting up the sky.

Lucy looked up at him, nearly blinding him with that wide circle of LED lights on her forehead. She quickly looked away when he winced, mumbling a quick apology. He couldn't see her face past that light. Couldn't read her eyes. But he felt the compassion in her words. His first instinct was to recoil from it, the way he had from that light beam from the headlamp she was wearing. Except... he knew that dodging this topic was one of the things that blew up their wedding. He'd pushed her away the entire two months he'd been home before that, telling himself it would be easier after the wedding was over. After they'd moved in together. After he'd started work at the family business. Always *after*...until all of a sudden she was gone.

She mistook his silence for more of the same, turning away with a defeated sigh. "Let me guess...you don't want to talk about it." Her headlamp lit up a picnic table in front of her and she headed for it. He hurried after her, grabbing her arm and gently turning her. She blinded him again by looking up, then swore and looked away.

"You're right, Luce. I don't *want* to talk about it. But you clearly *need* me to, at least a little. And maybe I need to do it. I don't know." He released her and sat on the edge of the table, rubbing the back of his neck as he tried to figure out what to say. "It's not exactly dinner conversation, you know? And if you haven't been there..." She sat on the seat below him, carefully keeping the headlamp aimed away. Her whole body seemed to be paying attention to him, though. He could sense it in the tightness of her shoulders, the careful tilt of her head. She was letting him talk at his own pace. The woman who'd always waited for everyone and everything was still willing to wait for him. He swallowed hard, determined to give her what she needed.

"You gave me grief about my so-called *bro-pals*, but seriously...the guys I served with are the only ones who *get* it. So it's...easier. I mean... I don't even have to say anything, and they automatically understand." A short burst of explosions echoed below them, and he forced himself to keep talking. "Did you hear that? It sounded like tracer fire, trying to light up one of our drones. That big one? Sounds like an 82 mm mortar, which could have been fired from two miles away. But that one's not coming down close enough to be an immediate threat. If it was any closer...well, then the camp might be under attack." The dark memories threatened to overwhelm him, but Lucy said she wanted to hear this. "If it was, we'd tumble out of our cots and into our gear in the pitch-dark—you'd hate that part—and grab our weapons. Waiting for orders." He paused again. "Each sound brings a heightened sense of... well...everything. It's like wearing one of those shock collars that they make for dogs, but *never* knowing when it was going to go off. No warning beeps. And it goes off so often that you're *always* anticipating it. You never relax, Luce. You can't afford to relax. You can barely afford to sleep most nights. Relaxing gets you killed."

He closed his eyes tightly, thinking about the night the mortar attack hit their camp. How the sky lit up. How his friends died. The smell of sulfur and smoke. The yelling, cursing and cries for help. He was almost lost in the horror again when Lucy spoke, her voice a quiet balm on his shattered nerves.

"I'm so sorry, Owen. I didn't know…" She shook her head, sending a beam of light back and forth on the grass. "I mean… I guess I *did* know. It's war, after all. I know people died, and I know you knew some of them. I was terrified that you would *be* one of them. I was so thankful when you came home in one piece that I put those other realities behind me." She rested her hand on his thigh. Like her voice, it centered him. "It makes sense that you couldn't just put it aside. You *lived* it. But Owen…it can't be healthy to just swallow all your feelings about that. Even if you don't want to talk to me about it, you aren't doing anything to *deal* with it. After this last tour, you came home a stranger to me. I bugged you about it so much because it frightened me."

"You were afraid of me?" The idea made his blood run cold.

"No. I was afraid *for* you. And for *us*." She stood and pulled the lamp off her head, letting the straps wind between her fingers, with the light cast on the ground at their feet. "Remember that word dump I gave you at the inn the day you showed up? When I said I was an understander? Well, I had no way of understanding where the Owen I knew had gone." She moved in front of where he sat, stepping between his legs. "I'd been waiting so long for our life together to finally start, but it was like your body double showed up instead of you."

She was right. He wasn't the guy she'd known before.

There was a bright flash beyond the trees, and a rapid series of explosions followed by more colors lighting up the sky. The finale of the fireworks show. His body tensed at the bombardment of sound and light, no matter how distant. Lucy's hands gripped his biceps. Her forehead touched his. She was trying to stay connected…trying to keep *him* connected to her. To the present, not the past. He rested his hands on her hips, completing the circle.

Neither of them said a word while the finale came to an explosive conclusion. There was a beat of silence after the echoes faded, then the sound of car and boat horns rose, going off as people expressed appreciation for a celebration that had sent him running. And still they stood without moving. He breathed in the soft floral scent of his Lucy, wishing they could stay connected like this forever. Silence fell on the Seneca Valley again, and she made the first move, slowly backing away. Moving out of reach, but not by much. That had to be a good sign, right?

He looked up, unable to see her face with the parking lot light behind her. But he could tell she was waiting for some kind of answer. He was suddenly exhausted from holding on to everything he was carrying, and his shoulders fell in defeat.

"You're right. I didn't come back the same. The last tour…it was so many levels worse than the first two for me. Iraq and Kabul were no picnics, but the last one. The mountains. The weather. The gunfights. We ended up in the thick of things more than once. Fucked up intel. Lousy luck. I don't even know." He stared off into the darkness under the trees. Now that the fireworks had stopped, he could hear the distant whoosh of the waterfall somewhere beyond the woods. Lucy waited quietly for him to return to thoughts he wanted so much to avoid.

"People died before. Even people I knew…sort of. But this time…" His head dropped. "This time some of them died in my arms. *Friends* died in my arms. Friends were in…" He couldn't say the word *pieces* out loud. A strangled sound from Lucy suggested he didn't need to. She was getting the idea. "It makes everything else seem so… unimportant." He rushed to clarify, looking straight at her. "I don't mean it made *you* unimportant. But the wedding plans…the dress…the food…" His hand rose and fell. "I know it was important to *you*, so I should have made more effort, but I truly didn't care." He stopped. "There, I said it."

She considered his words for a moment, swatting at the mosquitoes that had inevitably discovered them and were circling her head.

"Yes, you said it. And I… I respect that, after what happened. But what you didn't hear during those weeks before the wedding was that the problem wasn't in the wedding plans—I never expected you to get excited over choosing daisies or roses for the centerpieces." She stared down at the gently swinging circle of light on the ground from the light she still gripped in her hand. "The problem was that I wanted daisies and I was getting roses. I wanted a simple cotton dress and I was getting a tulle ball gown with a twelve-foot veil. I wanted a small, intimate ceremony and I was getting a country club reception with a full orchestra. The wedding *plans* weren't what I wanted you to care about. My *feelings* about them are what I wanted you to hear."

Silence hung between them again, heavier than before. He blew out a heavy sigh. He'd really screwed things up.

"I'm sorry, Luce. I should have heard that, but I just... I was was trying to hang on, you know? I didn't want any deep dives into feelings. Not mine. Not yours. Your leaving was what jolted me out of my stupor." He thought of that first week he'd spent drinking alone in the apartment. "Eventually, anyway." He pushed himself to his feet, turning her toward the car as he swung his hand at the mosquitoes assembling over them in a low and menacing cloud. "We should head back before we lose all our blood to these assholes." He tried to wind his fingers through hers. She squeezed his hand, then gently tugged hers free.

There had been a shift in the mood between them, though. She may not be angry anymore, but her obvious disappointment in him lingered. He wasn't the enemy. But she wasn't ready to go back with him yet, either. He still had a long way to go on that front. Hopefully Dr. Find-Love had more ideas, because he was fresh out.

LUCY DIDN'T NOTICE Owen in the dining room of the inn the next morning until she turned away from the coffee urn on the sideboard by the windows. She'd been so desperate for caffeine that she'd walked right past him on a beeline for her first cup. He lifted his own coffee to his lips, a corner of his mouth ticking upward.

Any other morning, she'd have scanned the room for him before entering. Maybe last night's conversation had softened her defenses. Maybe she just didn't need defenses at all. Owen had never been her enemy. He hadn't even been the main reason she'd left Greensboro. His coldness had hurt her feelings, but he'd explained away at least some of that. And the explanation had touched her heart more than she cared to admit.

"Are you going to stand there and stare at me all morning, or are you going to sit and have breakfast with me?" He set his coffee mug down and gestured to the empty chair across from him. "Have we declared enough of a truce to be able to share a table peacefully?"

She nodded and pulled out the chair, making a face at him when he tried to scramble up to hold it for her. "Sit. We're not on a first date. You don't need to impress me with your chivalry."

He chuckled. "Were you *ever* impressed with my chivalry?"

Memories of their first few months of dating wound through her head like a newsreel. The magical first week on Topsail Island. Weekend trips to Fayetteville to visit him at Fort Bragg, where she'd stay in a hotel and they'd make plans for dinner or a movie…and then they'd blow off those plans and spend all their time in bed together. He made trips to Greensboro, too, but it was a little more complicated with her living at home. At first he'd get a hotel room, which worked great because she'd sneak out and meet him there. But once her family embraced their relationship—which was pretty fast because Owen charmed them and he was invited to stay at the house. On the pullout sofa in the living room. Where he'd have to tiptoe past her parents' room to get to her bed.

"What are you grinning about?" Owen gave her a curious look.

She unfolded the white linen napkin and spread it on her lap. "Whenever you mention our past, a whole slideshow starts playing in my head. Remember sneaking past Mom and Dad's bedroom at my house?"

He barked out a laugh and she almost jumped. She

hadn't heard a real laugh from him in ages. "Do I *remember*? There was that one stupid floorboard that always creaked, and I swear I stepped on it every damn time, no matter how careful I was. I was always afraid of your dad and that shotgun he liked to remind me he owned."

"I think you were safe. I doubt they really imagined I was a twenty-eight-year-old virgin."

He shook his head. "I don't know. They put me on the sofa bed for a reason. I still say the shotgun was a genuine threat."

"And what about *your* parents? Whenever we stayed at their place, your mother put me in that dungeon of a basement guest room, two whole floors away from you."

"That *dungeon* was a full in-law apartment with a kitchen, but yes—" he winked "—there's a reason we rarely stayed there overnight."

The reason was more than logistics. His mother had never been very welcoming when Lucy visited. Especially after they'd become engaged and the Coopers had agreed to join the Higgins family that following Thanksgiving. Faye Cooper's nose had actually wrinkled when she got out of their luxury sedan in the driveway outside her parents' modest brick ranch.

"Uh-oh." Owen's voice dropped. "What are you seeing on the slideshow now?"

Before she could answer, Piper came in with a tray of blueberry pancakes. She came to an abrupt stop when she saw the two of them sitting together.

"What… I mean…you're together…" She straightened and walked to their table with a bright smile. "I mean *good morning.* I didn't know you were here… I mean…awake, Lucy. Let me get you a plate. There should be enough pancakes and bacon here to get you both started. I'll bring a refill in a few minutes." With nearly every word, Piper's eyes bounced between the two of them, obviously full of questions. Finally, she couldn't take it anymore. "Okay, forget pancakes. What happened last night? You two took off before the fireworks and now you're having breakfast together. Did you make your own fireworks by any chance?"

"No fireworks," Lucy said firmly. "But...conversation. And a truce."

Piper pursed her lips. "So...not engaged but...friends?"

Lucy and Owen stared at each other for a long moment. The corners of his eyes tightened a bit, the way they did when he bit into something sour. He gave her the slightest of nods, and they said the word in unison.

"Friends."

He didn't sound enthusiastic about the idea, but it felt right to her. With Owen in the friend zone, it removed the stress of avoiding him or trying to be angry with him. And it had been an effort. It was beginning to feel like work to stay mad. They ate their pancakes in relatively comfortable silence.

If she was honest with herself, her blowup had been brewing for a long time before the wedding. She kept thinking things would be better *after*, which was exactly what she'd angrily accused Owen of doing. The two of them were quite a pair, just waiting for things to get better without actually *doing* anything about it.

Her phone buzzed in her pocket. She groaned when she saw the screen. Mom. She showed it to Owen as she stood.

"I've been sending most of her calls to voice mail. I think it's time to face the music."

He nodded, chewing his pancakes. "As your friend, I agree."

She rolled her eyes, but with a smile, patting his shoulder as she walked past and answered the call.

"Hi, Mom."

"Oh, you're finally going to talk to me?"

"Well…" Lucy headed up the wide staircase. "You keep calling. Did you *not* want me to answer? Because I'll hang up…"

"No!" her mother shouted. "Of course I want to talk. You just…surprised me."

"I told you I needed time."

"Yeah, well…you've had time. Now you need to come home and start repairing things."

She trotted up the last flight of stairs, phone to her ear.

"You know what, Mom? I don't think so. I mean…what home is there to come back to? Are you and your boyfriend going to get the house? Or will you leave Dad there alone?" Her voice rose with each question. The fact that she and Owen had cleared the air a bit last night seemed to have released *all* of her emotions. "Maybe you can move in with whatever-his-name-is and start a brand-new family, since *our* family wasn't enough for you…"

"That's enough." Mom's voice was sharp. "You're an adult, so start acting like it."

Being addressed this way by her mother was unfamiliar. Mom had always been the steady heart of their home, taking care of Kris when she was sick, putting meals on the table every day, picking up after her daughters and smothering them with hugs when they needed them the most. Mom always knew when they'd screwed up, but they usually got hugs for that, too—after a talk about her disappointment. She'd been the ultimate, down-to-earth mountain mom, right down to the homemade flour sack aprons tied over her mom jeans.

"It's just…" Lucy started, then paused as she let herself into her room and sat on the bed. "Mom, adult or not, I can't help being angry with you. But you're right—my sarcasm isn't helping things, so I'll try to tone that down. No promises, though."

Her mother gave a soft chuckle. "You have always been my build-your-wings-on-the-way-down girl. You jump first, then figure out a way to make things work. I thought you were crazy to want to arrange flowers for a living when you had so much potential for greater things. Not to mention a college degree in accounting you don't want to use."

Lucy chewed the inside of her cheek to keep from objecting to the idea that numbers didn't matter in a flower business just because flowers were involved. Her mother kept going.

"But then you settled in Wilmington on a good career track. You had that little parttime flower job on the side and seemed happy. Until you fell in love. Nothing against Owen, but you left a good accounting job just to take a one with his family's nursery business…"

If she bit her cheek any harder it would be bleeding, so she had to give it up. She did her best to keep her voice level. "Mom, you're revising history again. I left Wilmington because *you* put the guilt trip on me to come help with Grandma."

There was a pause.

"I thought it would be temporary…"

"You mean you thought Grandma Higgins would die sooner rather than later?"

Mom's voice sharpened again. "Don't make it sound

like that's what I *wished* for. I loved her, too. But… I honestly didn't think I was bringing you back home for good, honey. I didn't think you'd take that job with the Coopers."

Lucy stared up at the ceiling for a moment before closing her eyes in frustration.

"I'm confused. You called me to tell me to come home, but you didn't want me to take a job that kept me *near* home?"

"We're getting sidetracked here. I called to ask you to come home to your fiancé and live the life you'd planned before you heard about your father and me. You can't just run away when something makes you unhappy." She paused. "All you're doing is proving that your father and I were right to keep our separation quiet. We were afraid you'd do something impulsive, although I *never* thought you'd abandon your family and friends. Not to mention poor Owen. What were you thinking?"

Mom had a point. It was more than just impulsive to walk out on her own wedding. It was irresponsible. It was also, at the time, the only way Lucy could see to preserve her…if not her *sanity*, at least her sense of who she was.

"My methods weren't the best, but Mom… I had to get away. Staying there and calling off the wedding would have been even more dramatic than this…"

"More dramatic? Or just more uncomfortable for *you*?"

There was compassion in her mother's voice now, even if the words themselves stung with their honesty. Lucy hadn't considered that, but it was, of course, the embarrassing truth. Her mother continued. "Honey, I'd never want you to marry someone you didn't *want* to be married to. Stopping the wedding before you made a mistake isn't what upsets me. It's that you left everyone else to clean up the aftermath. Without so much as an explanation. Or an apology. Or even a goodbye." Her voice cracked on that last point, and Lucy remembered Owen telling her basically the same thing. She looked up from the edge of the bed and stared at her reflection in the mirror on the wall.

For perhaps the first time in the few weeks since she'd bolted, she faced up to her actions without putting the blame on anyone else. Yes, she'd felt pressured from all directions, but it had been *her* choice to leave everything… and everyone…behind. It was time she owned it.

"You're right, Mom. And I'm sorry for pulling a disappearing act the way I did. I felt so desperate and conflicted and angry."

"Angry with me." Her mother didn't say it as a question.

"Yes. Among other people and situations, but…yes. I was very angry with you." She blew out a soft breath. "But that's no excuse. I could have spoken up. Instead… I just left." And running hadn't solved a thing.

"Honey," her mother hesitated. "Your father and I have living separate lives for a while now. We just…let it happen. And then I met someone." Lucy didn't want to hear this, but she stayed silent as her mother continued. "I never planned it. But I was lonely and Jeff actually listened to me, and…"

Lucy stiffened. "Mom, of all the things I'm not ready to deal with right now, the details of my mother's secret affair is at the tippy top of the list."

There was long pause. "Fair enough. The point is, like you, I've made mistakes. Like you, I've hurt people. I'm human. But Lucy, the argument you overheard between your father and I was honestly a fluke. Doing all the pretending for the wedding had us both on edge. But your dad and I are communicating and we're not at each other's throats, I promise. And we both want you to come home."

"To be honest, I thought I'd be back after a few days. I didn't think I was actually *leaving* leaving at the time."

"Well, you've been gone a month now, so I think we can say you've officially left. Is your friend Nikki *ever* going to get her car back?"

That was a good question. It wasn't fair to expect Nikki to drive Lucy's old Volkswagen to New York and then drive the Mustang all the way back home again. That was a fifteen-hundred-mile round trip. But the only other option was for *Lucy* to drive back to North Carolina to get her car. Which meant facing everyone and making all those explanations, apologies and goodbyes that her mother mentioned. It was the responsible thing to do. But she didn't want to. If that made her weak or childish, so be it. Nikki told her to take her time. Said she didn't have time to go cruising in the convertible anyway with her restaurant's new location opening soon. And Nikki had made a good point about Lucy's ancient but beloved Beetle, Buttercup. It probably wasn't up to the long drive to Rendezvous Falls.

"Lucy?" Her mother interrupted her thoughts. "Are you buying that car from Nikki or...?"

"No." She could never afford it, of course. "I'm only putting three miles a day on the Mustang, if that. I can literally walk to work, so it's being driven less than what Nikki would have, so... I'm sort of doing her a favor, right?" She realized her mistake and prayed it would go unnoticed.

"Work?" No such luck. "You have a *job*? Doing what?"

"Don't sound so shocked, Mom. I don't have a bottomless well of money to pay for a room and food. I have a part-time job at a florist shop here. It's not that big a deal."

"A florist shop. Of course. I know you loved your aunt, but you need to…"

Lucy stood with a sigh. "What I need to do is get to work on time this morning. Doing what I *love*. You said you wouldn't want me to marry a man I didn't love, so why do you want me to have a career I don't love?"

She could imagine her mother's face at being cornered—her mouth pinched, her eyes narrowing. Her fingers were probably drumming the kitchen counter right now. And then the deep breath as she decided on a course of action.

"It's not that I don't want you to be happy. I just… I guess I'm applying my standard of happiness to you. Or my expectations. Or something." A pause. "You're the first child in my family to go to college. To you, it's just what's done when everyone turns eighteen. But there was a time when getting a college education was just a dream." There was a serious note to her mother's voice. "When we left you at that campus and I looked back as we drove away, I saw so much ahead for you. You were going to take the world by storm, maybe get a job in Manhattan, or even Paris…" Lucy held her phone away and made a face at it. *Paris?* She'd never once talked about going to Paris. And she'd attended App State, not Harvard. Her mother let out a long sigh. "And I never once asked you what *you* wanted to do after college."

"Mom, you know I wanted a flower shop. I have ever since I was a kid."

"I remember." Her voice was wistful now. "I thought it was a phase…that you'd mixed up the flower business with how much you loved Aunt Shirley. But your dad tried to tell me that once you set your mind on something, you didn't give up. And he was right. You went back to plants and flowers every chance you got. You even got engaged to a guy with a landscaping business. I guess it was a bit more than a phase, wasn't it?"

"I didn't fall in love with Owen because he was in landscaping."

She hadn't even known about the family business until they'd been dating for several months. That's when he told her he was thinking about making a career in the Army, but his parents kept insisting he had to take over the business, which had expanded to multiple locations, with a nursery and produce center. That was the family plan. And as impulsive as Lucy was, Owen was the exact opposite. When there was a plan in place, it had to be followed. He'd often told her that *she* was the only time he'd strayed from his plans.

He was supposed to marry the daughter of his parents' best friends. Monica Sheffly was a younger version of Faye Cooper. She was all about image and hanging out with the country club tennis crowd. Owen explained he and Monica were never more than friends in his mind— they'd gone on a few dates, but he said they weren't *real* dates, because they were always with a group of people. Lucy knew Monica viewed their relationship differently, judging from the barely civil way she'd treated Lucy on the few occasions they'd met at the club or at some family gathering. Owen made it clear that he'd never pulled Monica into the back of his SUV to make love under the stars.

"So you *are* in love with Owen?"

She didn't realize she was smiling until her mother interrupted her thoughts.

"Yes. No! I mean… I don't know." She thought about

the heated look he'd given her last night. The warmth of his hands on her hips. The snap of electricity as they'd stood in that deserted parking lot, foreheads touching. The swell of tenderness she'd felt as he shared some of his experiences overseas. "We're…talking. We had breakfast together. He wants me to come back to Greensboro, but for now we're…friends. I'm still figuring out…"

"You had *breakfast*? Is Owen *there*?"

She winced, closing her eyes tight in regret. She hadn't meant for that to slip out, either. Then again, she'd never really hidden anything from her mom before everything blew up. As angry as Lucy was, it felt good to talk to her mom. "Um…yeah. He just showed up here. I think he thought he was just going to scoop me up and carry me back to Cooper Landscaping, but I set him straight on that. He insisted on staying here for a month to try to *win me back*, whatever that means."

Her mother laughed, and Lucy's heart ached at the sound. She was still furious with her parents for reasons both fair and unfair. But she'd really missed her mom.

"Oh, Lucy-Lou." Her mother chuckled. Lucy blinked. She usually groaned over Mom's pet names, but right now it sounded like love. "That man left his mama—no easy feat after the wedding fiasco—and chased after you? I *knew* I liked him. Tell him I said hi. And tell him I'm on his side."

Lucy's laugh bubbled up from a place that had been closed off for a month or two. "Mom! You're supposed to be on *my* side."

There was a pause.

"I am. That's why I'm rooting for him."

CHAPTER ELEVEN

OWEN WAS HAVING lunch at the Spot Diner when the text came in from Piper Taggart.

Umm...there's a guy here asking for you. Driving a big truck. With a car on it. My husband seems unsurprised. What's going on?

Owen smiled and texted that he'd be there shortly. Then the smile faded, along with his confidence. He and Lucy had been on fairly friendly terms for a few days now. Having breakfast together at the inn. Chatting about innocuous things like the weather or some bridezilla she was working with at the shop. This *supersized grand gesture* had seemed necessary when Lucy wasn't giving him the time of day. But now that they were finally talking, would it seem pushy? Presumptive?

The Dr. Find-Love app said to do something really bold with something the other person adored. Lord knew why, but Lucy loved that damn car of hers, even if it was a rusted hunk of metal with an engine way past its projected lifespan and seats patched together with duct tape. He'd known the 1960s car was getting bad when he went overseas the last time, but he'd been horrified to see its condition when he got home. The fact that Lucy hadn't trusted it to survive the drive to New York proved she knew it needed work.

So…this was a great idea.

Unless…unless it wasn't.

"Did I accidentally put vinegar in your coffee or are you just thinking about how screwed you still are?"

Evie Hudson was standing by his booth. They'd talked a few times in the past week or so. As the co-owner of the townie diner in the heart of Rendezvous Falls, he had a feeling there wasn't much Evie missed. Including the fact that he was trying hard to win back Lucy Higgins. A fact that the sassy woman with a bright red streak in her dark hair seemed to enjoy way too much. He grimaced.

"No vinegar. It's possible I'm even more screwed than before."

"Oh, shit. What did you do?"

"I put a grand gesture in motion that might backfire on me."

Evie's brows shot up on her forehead, and she slid into the seat across from him, propping her chin in her hand and batting her eyelashes at him. "Tell. Me. Everything."

He shook his head, putting a twenty on the table and starting to slide out of the booth. "No time. And too late to stop it anyway." He hesitated. For all her snarkiness, there was nothing but compassion—and maybe a *little* amusement—in Evie's eyes. Owen sighed, and a rush of words followed. "She loves her stupid VW Bug. It was her grandmother's car. But it was a wreck. So I had the thing completely overhauled and painted and trucked it up here." He held up his phone with the text from Piper. "It just arrived."

Evie's mouth dropped open, but no sound came out. She closed it, pressing her lips together tightly, deep in thought. Then she held up her finger, as if trying to work out what she wanted to say. "You took something she loved. And *changed* it. And that's a good thing?"

"I didn't *change* it. I *restored* it. I'm not exaggerating when I say that thing wasn't safe."

She was staring at him as if he'd just morphed into a unicorn in front of her. Her eyes glimmered with amusement and admiration, tempered with a good dose of what looked like pity.

"I can't decide if you're a genius or a fool, Owen Cooper. That move is the wildest combination of over-the-top sweetness and presumptive how-dare-you I've ever heard of. When does Lucy discover what you've done?"

There was something scolding in the way she said *what you've done*, but she was also laughing. At him? At the gesture? Of how Lucy might murder him in the next hour or so? He got up from the booth.

"She'll find out when she gets back to the inn later. Why?"

"Because I need to be there to see this. What's going to happen to the car she has now? That belongs to Nikki Taggart, right?"

"I'm shipping it back to Nikki. That was part of the deal. And she approved...sort of." That had to mean something. Nikki and Lucy were BFFs. So why were his palms starting to sweat?

"And—" Evie looked up at him "—you just made all these decisions...without talking to Lucy about any of it?"

"If I'd talked to her, it wouldn't be a grand gesture, would it? You know what they say—go big or go home."

Evie's laughter rang out as she stood and slapped his shoulder, pushing him toward the door. "Just remember, *go home* is a definite possibility here. But I gotta give you credit…it's a bold move. You're going to have her attention, pal. Don't blow it."

He headed out the door and toward the inn. *Don't blow it* was becoming his theme these days.

"WHY ARE YOU taking pictures of everything this week?" Connie felt like she couldn't turn around without Lucy telling her to step back out of the way, or to hold some flowers and smile. As if.

"It's for the website, remember? Evie gave me the log-on information, and I'm updating the whole thing. The photos on there were all low-res and blurry." She held up an expensive-looking camera. "I borrowed this from Evie's husband, Mark. Not only is he an artist, but he also likes photography. So I'm getting as many candid and mood pictures as I can while I have it. I found a new template for the website specifically designed for florists, and added some widgets so people can order directly. They can even schedule their deliveries online. I've connected a payment system to the business bank account." She pushed her hair off her face. "By next week it should be up and running, and it'll be beautiful."

Sometimes Lucy's energy and enthusiasm made Connie feel even older than she was. And tired.

"I have no idea what any of that means," she said, "but I'll take your word for it. Your pink is almost gone."

"What?" Lucy lowered the camera. "Oh, my hair? Yeah, that was fun, but I'm not sure it's really me." She ran her fingers through the honey blond strands. "I had a *She-Ra* moment after I left North Carolina, and dyed it in a hotel room sink. Along with cutting off about six inches of it. My way of…shedding my old self, I guess."

"You cut off your own hair? And dyed it?"

"Well, I didn't dye the stuff I cut off." Lucy winked. "But yes. It was a statement. To myself, more than anything else."

"But now you regret it." She thought people only cut and dyed their own hair in crime shows, when they were on the run.

"Not at all." Lucy shrugged, setting the camera on the counter so she could move the birthday arrangement for a different angle. "Just because I'm letting the pink wash out doesn't mean I didn't like it at the time. And this length is more my style. It was my almost mother-in-law's idea to let it grow so long—she thought it would be easier to put up for the wedding. But since that's not happening…"

"Are you sure about that? Owen seems pretty determined to win you back." Connie had torn into Iris for sending him work for her without mentioning he was Lucy's ex. But once the dust had settled, the man had proved himself to be more than a pretty face. He was polite, hardworking and honest. And the looks he sent Lucy's way melted even Connie's hardened heart.

Lucy hesitated. "I… I'm sure." Then she nodded briskly, more to herself than Connie. "If I'm going to make a fresh start, I need to leave everything behind. And everyone."

"You don't sound very convincing to me. And leaving all your friends and family behind is a bit drastic. Has it occurred to you that the common denominator in all your troubles is…*you*?" Lucy looked up in surprise. Connie kicked herself. She was caring again, damn it. "I mean…

maybe you need to change something other than your hair if you want to find love. And happiness."

"You're saying it's *my* fault?"

"No!" Connie flinched when the bell over the door chimed, but it was just Cecile. She nodded to her friend before facing Lucy again. "I'm saying you can't hide from your troubles. If things were that bad in North Carolina, then how did they get to that point without you noticing? You didn't just wake up on your wedding day and decide everyone in the world was awful, did you?"

"Ooh…" Cecile grinned as she walked toward Lucy. "Are you getting life advice from Connie Phelps? The woman who's basically made herself into a hermit for the past three years? This oughta be good."

As usual, Cecile was decked out in pink, wearing a neon sundress and pink leopard-print flats. Her hair seemed brighter and fluffier than usual, indicating she'd probably just come from Suzy's Clip & Snip again. Her eyelashes were ridiculously long and seemed to be glittering. No one could deny Cecile had a unique sense of style.

"What the hell are you blathering about?" Connie fixed her so-called friend with a glare. "If anyone knows about unhappiness, it's me. I mean…*dealing* with unhappiness. Like the unhappiness caused by rat fink friends who like to laugh at me."

Cecile just rolled her eyes. "Stop complaining before your face freezes like that. Oh, wait—I think it already has." Lucy made a squeaking sound that was suspiciously close to laughter, and Cecile nudged her with her elbow. "Believe it or not, our lovely Miss Connie here used to *enjoy* laughter. The best New Year's Eve party in town was at the Phelps house, and they used to throw big barbecues every Labor Day. Oh, my God, do you remember the water balloon fights we used to have? We'd get the kids started, but it always ended up as a free-for-all." Cecile leaned her hip against the counter. "And then one day she woke up and decided—" she made air quotes with her fingers "—everyone in the world was awful."

Connie bit the inside of her cheek, trying to cool her rising temper. "We aren't talking about me. We're talking about Lucy."

Lucy threw up her hands. "Oh, hell no. I'd much rather hear about this laughing, fun-loving woman you used to be." She grabbed the birthday arrangement and put it back in the cooler to stay fresh, then turned, wiping her hands on her shorts. "How did you turn into the world's grumpiest florist?"

Conne scowled. It had become the great joke—how grumpy she was. It's not like she'd wanted to be like this. It just…happened. "I don't want to talk about it." Connie grabbed a dust cloth and started wiping the shelves and rearranging the vases on display. It had been quiet for a Saturday. Their only wedding order had been out the door that morning. Neither of the other women spoke, waiting her out until she finally looked up in exasperation. "First, I'm not *that* grumpy." Two pairs of eyebrows rose. "And even if I *am* grumpy, I've earned the right." She pointed at Cecile first. "You forget that you still *have* a husband." Then Lucy. "And you *could* have had one, but you ran out on him." She ignored the hurt expression on Lucy's face. "My husband *left* me for some young chickie. The two of them are off in Florida driving their little golf cart around their village full of gray-haired old people. I didn't make the choice to be alone, sick and handling everything here by myself—it was made for me."

Cecile's eyes softened, but her words didn't. "That *young chickie* was sixty-two at the time. Sandy's only a few years younger than you and Dan. He didn't leave you because you were old. He left you because he was convinced *he* was getting old, and he'd grown to be a vain, self-centered dolt who thought he could beat back the drums of time." Cecile walked toward Connie. "It's been three years. I get why you were angry, but you don't have to stay that way forever. You don't have to be alone, either. You don't want to hear it, but *you* made that decision when you kept refusing help from everybody." Cecile reached out and wrapped her fingers around Connie's arm. "Lucy here made a decision to be happier. Maybe you should take a lesson from her. Haven't you been angry at the world long enough? Aren't you tired of it?"

She hissed in a sharp breath, ready to tell Cecile to get out of her store and stop lying to her. But the words refused to come out the way she'd planned.

"How...how dare... I..." She let that breath back out with a whoosh, and her shoulders sagged under the effort. It had become such an effort to maintain her rage, which was basically there only because she didn't know what she'd do without it. Her eyes began to sting, making her blink. "I don't wake up in the morning and think of all the ways I can be grumpy that day. It's not something I work on..."

Cecile chuckled. "You're saying you're just a natural at it?"

Connie nodded with a wry grin. "Maybe so." She looked up at Lucy. "She's right. I'm no one to be giving advice, girl. Or criticism. I'm sorry." She glanced at the clock above the window. "It's almost closing time. Why don't you head back to the inn for the night? I'll lock up."

Cecile squeezed her arm. "I'll help."

Lucy stared at the two of them, as if she sensed something relatively momentous had just happened.

Cecile grinned. "Lucy, I think you and Connie have a lot to teach each other. Running from your troubles may not be the best choice, but neither is wallowing in them."

Lucy reached behind the counter for her purse. "Sounds like we have some interesting conversations ahead. I'll admit there's some truth in what Connie said about me being a common denominator in my own drama." She stopped next to Connie and arched a brow at her. "But it sounds like I'm not the only one." She waved and went out the door with her usual energetic stride, gone from sight in an instant.

"I like her," Cecile said.

Connie pressed her lips together, then nodded.

"I like her more than I like *you* at the moment."

Cecile laughed out loud.

"You love me and you know it."

"Maybe." She hit the light switch and turned off the Open sign in the window. "But right now I don't like you that much. You're a pain in my ass."

"That's what she said!"

And Connie couldn't help it. She laughed at—no— *with* her best friend. And realized for the first time in a long while that she didn't have it all that bad. She had a business, even if it was draining her. She had a family, even if they hovered too much. And she had friends. Annoying, bad-joke-telling friends who'd never once given up on her. Maybe it was time to start listening to them.

CHAPTER TWELVE

LUCY COULDN'T COMPREHEND what she was looking at. The first thing she'd spotted after walking back to the inn after a busy day at the shop was Nikki's convertible on a flatbed tow truck. Her heart stopped—had something happened to the car? Was Nikki taking it back? But no—they'd just talked last week and Nikki hadn't said anything about it. Lucy knew she'd been pushing the limits of friendship by keeping the car so long. But it *was* Nikki's second car. And she fully intended to either find another vehicle or figure a way to get Buttercup to New York.

Maybe someone had hit the Mustang in the parking lot? But from this angle, there didn't seem to be a scratch on it. She blinked a few times and looked around, noticing a small crowd gathered on the wide porch of the inn. Logan and Piper. Iris Taggart and a few of her friends from the book club Connie had talked about. They'd all stopped by the flower shop the previous week to check out Lucy…at least that how it felt when the seniors had come in en masse and insisted she come out front so they could meet her. She already knew Iris, of course. And Cecile, who was next to a tall gentleman…she was pretty sure his name was Rick. The well-dressed woman with the perfectly coiffed champagne hair. Lucy frowned… Vickie something. And there was Bridget McKinnon from the

Purple Shamrock, sitting at a table with her grandmother, Maura. Maybe there was a book club meeting here today.

But Lucy was quite sure Evie Hudson wasn't part of the book club, yet there she was, walking up the sidewalk toward the inn arm in arm with her husband, Mark. She still had the red streak in her hair from Independence Day. Evie waved at Lucy. In fact…everyone seemed to have their eyes on Lucy. She straightened and headed for the tow truck, pulling her phone out to call Nikki if needed.

That's when she spotted Owen. He wasn't facing her, but she could tell from the slant of his head that he was watching her from the corner of his eye. Oh, God…was he trying to force her to go back to North Carolina by taking her car? She started to bristle, but…that didn't make sense. A unilateral move like that wasn't Owen's style. Besides, they'd been reasonably friendly since the Fourth of July.

But whatever was happening here had *something* to do with Owen. He was standing near a vintage yellow VW that reminded her of Buttercup, but was *much* nicer. This one had been fully restored. It was gleaming, with shiny new tires with wheels that looked like daisies—yellow in the center and white "petals" as spokes.

Wait…she'd *seen* those wheels. In a catalog. And she'd shown them to Owen over a year ago, laughing about how cute they'd look on Buttercup. He'd pointed out at the time—accurately—that anything so bright and new would look goofy on a rusted old car like hers. She walked toward the car. It *couldn't* be Buttercup, but it looked like it was from the same year…1966. The car had been Grandma's pride and joy.

As she got closer, she saw the maroon-and-white graduation cap tassel hanging from the rearview mirror, with a tiny brass "66" charm on it. *Grandma's* tassel. Her heart warmed as memories of her free-spirited grandmother—an original flower child—washed over her. She turned toward Owen. Had he replaced Grandma's car with a nicer version? Did he think she'd want any car other than Buttercup? She pointed at the car.

"What have you done?"

Owen chewed his lower lip before answering, carefully avoiding her face and the faces of the audience they'd attracted.

"Lucy, I know how much you loved your car…" His words sounded as if he was reciting a speech. "I wanted to show you that I…uh…" His eyes narrowed in concentration, then he looked up at her. His cheeks were ruddy. If she didn't know better, she'd swear he was blushing. "This is a gesture of love, and an acknowledgment that you have things you…love…aw shit, I'm not saying this right. It's a gesture of how much I know you…"

She held up her hand. "You think finding a car that looks something like mine but fancier means you *know* me? How did you get my grandmother's tassel? And why is Nikki's car on that tow truck?"

Owen swallowed hard. "This is a gesture of…" His face twisted in frustration. "Oh, forget the script, I did this for *you*. I wanted you to know how much I care. I know I've made mistakes, and I thought this might…"

"You thought someone else's car would make me feel better?"

"It's not someone else's car, damn it. It's *your* car."

She took a step back in surprise, turning back to the little yellow car. No rust. No dents. No bald tires. She looked inside—no torn seats kept together with duct tape.

"It…it doesn't look like my car…" She remembered back when the car wasn't a complete wreck, of course. In her childhood, it sat in Grandma's garage, looking so bright and cheery. That's when she'd first fallen in love with it. Lucy had declared right then that Buttercup would be *her* car someday, and Grandma agreed.

Owen's voice was soft. "You may have loved the car the way it was, but it wasn't safe. Now it is." He opened the driver's door. "Think of it this way—now it looks like the same car your grandmother fell in love with back in the sixties."

Lucy stared at him, her vision suddenly blurred with tears. Her first thought was that he'd taken something away from her, but that wasn't true. His words made her think of an old Polaroid photo tacked to Grandma's sewing room bulletin board. It was of Grandma standing proudly in front of the shiny new Beetle. She was wearing bell-bottom jeans and a halter top, her hair in long braids and a beaded leather band wrapped around her head. Grandma would have loved to see the car look like that again. But it must have cost a fortune…

"Okay, it looks new." She fixed him with a hard stare. "But you basically stole my car and did all of this without even asking me. And *paid* for it. What were you thinking?"

"I didn't ask you because it's supposed to be a surprise."

"Mission accomplished. I'm surprised. But Owen… we're not together…we agreed to be friends…"

"You *suggested* we be just friends. I love you. I want *us* back, Luce."

"And you think a car will do that? How did you even accomplish this?"

"It's meant to be a…a gesture. A big one. You love your car…" He rubbed the back of his neck. "To be honest, I was going to do this as a wedding gift and surprise you with it when we got back from the Bahamas. I have a friend with a body shop so the cost wasn't as high as it could have been…"

She wanted to be angry, but she couldn't hide the incredulous laughter that was trying to bubble up. She looked up at the Mustang and her laughter faded. "Does Nikki know you're doing this? What are you doing with *her* car?"

"Nikki knows and she eventually approved." He winked, which made her heart do something funny. "I think it helped that I'm paying for her car to be returned without putting any more miles on it."

"She didn't say anything to me."

"Um…surprise, remember?"

Lucy's eyes narrowed. "A surprise from the fiancé *she* helped me dump at the altar. You must be quite the charmer, Owen Cooper."

He gestured toward their audience on the porch—pointing to the Taggart family specifically. "Logan helped convince her my intentions were honorable. The reason her car is still here is because she insisted you have the choice to turn me down. If you don't want the VW…"

"It's *my* car!" She couldn't help laughing again. The man was just unbelievable. "What are you going to do if I don't accept it? Peel the paint off, bang it up with a hammer and put the old tires back on?"

A grin twisted his mouth in the most attractive way. So attractive that she was tempted to kiss it. "I made sure those old tires got tossed. But if you prefer it dinged up,

I guess I could manage that." He looked over at Logan again, who had five-year-old Lily on his shoulders. "Think Lily might help me hammer some dents in this car?"

Lily clapped her hands enthusiastically. "Yes! I'll help! Let me down, Dad…" Logan obliged, and the little girl dashed down the stairs. Lucy instinctively stepped in front of the Beetle and spread her hands.

"No!" Everyone laughed now, and her cheeks heated. "No one is putting a mark on this car."

Owen's eyes brightened with relief. "So you *do* like it?"

"Oh, please." She waved him off, looking at the car, still trying to wrap her head around what was happening. "What's not to like? But Owen—" she stepped closer to him "—there can't be any strings attached…"

"There aren't."

"I mean it. I don't want you getting your hopes up about sweeping me and my adorable car back to Greensboro. I'm not in a place where I can make that decision. I may never be…"

He took her hands in his. "Hope is all I have. But I swear to you there are no strings attached to the car. I just want you to be safe. And happy." He shocked her by cupping her cheek with his hand. "I was stupid not to see how unhappy you were before, but I promise I'll be paying better attention from now on. Because I never want to be the cause of your unhappiness again."

His warm brown eyes were focused tight on hers. His face was just inches away. She could almost feel his breath on her skin. It reminded her of their first kiss. That was in a parking lot, too. The parking lot of Bluebeard's Beachfront Bar and Grill. Owen had ditched his noisy friends and taken her for a moonlight walk on the beach. But instead of kissing her where the soft waves brushed onto the sand, he'd waited until they were in the parking lot, standing next to his Bronco. And then...*finally*...he'd pulled her close and kissed her. And damn if she didn't want him to do it again. Right now. Right here. Where it was the two of them in this little bubble...

"Kiss the woman already!" someone hollered from the porch. It must have been that Rick guy from the book club, because Cecile whacked him in the stomach with her purse, making him double over. The moment was broken, and Owen dropped his hand to his side. But that twisty, playful, sexy grin returned.

"You were thinking about Bluebeard's just now, weren't you?"

She chewed on her lip. She gave a quick nod, then turned toward the car. Away from the tractor-beam pull of his eyes. Away from the heat she'd seen there.

"Thank you for doing this." She peered inside the car. It smelled brand-new. "It was very...clever. And generous. Not everyone gets a wedding gift after ditching the wedding."

"Not a wedding gift. A friendship gift."

She looked up at him over her shoulder.

"That makes you a pretty good friend."

THANK YOU, DR. FIND-LOVE.

There was something about Lucy's voice when she said *good friend* that gave Owen all the hope she'd warned him against. A gravity...a heaviness that wasn't somber. It was more like the weight of some deep emotion. An emotion that might mean she was moving him out of the friend zone and into something...better.

It was touch-and-go for a few minutes there, but in the end, she liked the car. She was sitting in Buttercup now, showing it off to Piper and Evie, who stood at the open door. Lily had crawled into the tiny back seat. They didn't even look up as the truck pulled out with Nikki's car and headed south. The driver had family in Pennsylvania, and was headed there for a day or two before delivering the car to Nikki.

Logan Taggart stepped up next to Owen.

"I just texted my sister a shot of that." He nodded at the women crowded around the little car. "She wanted to know two things. Is she in trouble with Lucy, and are you still in one piece?"

Owen grinned. "Tell her I think we're *both* safe. Lucy and I are officially at the *good friend* stage now, which is a solid step up from last week." It felt like he'd turned a corner with her.

"So what's next on your Magic 8-Ball app?"

He grimaced. "Keep it down, man. No one's supposed to know about that, remember?" He glanced back at the porch, but everyone seemed too busy talking among themselves to have overheard. "If she thinks I'm playing some kind of game with her, I'm screwed. She barely trusts me as it is."

Logan held his hands up in innocence. "She won't hear it from me. I want to see how this app of yours is going to play out, so I won't interfere. And hey—it's working so far. Didn't you say this counted as two steps?"

He nodded. "That's what I'm telling myself. This is what they call a *supersized grand gesture*—something really big and over-the-top to show how much you care. And it's also *Know what she loves.* I'm supposed to show her that I know the things that matter to her, and her grand-mother's car is one of her favorite things in the world. It could probably count for *Be her hero*, too, since I made it safe to drive."

The book club members were coming down off the porch now to check out Lucy's car, and the two men stepped onto the grass to let them by. Owen was catching lots of side-eye from the ladies. Especially Logan's grandmother. Iris was a tough old broad, and her steely glare had him on the defense all of a sudden. He gestured toward Lucy and the car.

"Why are you giving me that look? She's *happy*!"

He'd never realized people could actually *harrumph* in real life until Iris did it. She narrowed her eyes at him.

"It's a *stunt*. Stunts don't work long-term."

Logan started to laugh. "That's rich, Gran, coming from the woman who engineered a way for me and Piper's family to be forced together to decorate her Christmas tree so we could reconcile, *after* you and your posse had that come-to-Jesus talk with Piper's former mother-in-law."

Iris, a diminutive octogenarian, shook her finger in Logan's face, forcing her grandson to take a step backward. "I was just seeding the ground so there was a chance for something to grow. You-all did the work on your own."

"To be fair, Mrs. Taggart," Owen argued, "that's all I'm trying to do. Thaw the ice enough that Lucy will give me a chance."

"A chance at what? To do what *you* want her to do?"

He opened his mouth to answer, then stopped. Was this a trick question?

She waved her hand and turned to follow her friends. "That's what I thought. Figure your shit out, Mr. Cooper.

Decide your endgame before you do any more grandstanding. Don't get that chance you say you want, then
not know what to do with it."

He blinked a few times as she walked away, her ebony
cane clicking on the concrete. Logan rested his hand on
Owen's shoulder.

"Gran's a take-no-prisoners sort. But she's also an-
noyingly right about most things. What *is* your endgame
with Lucy? Back to what you both had planned? A fresh
start somewhere else? I think that might make a big difference in her reactions."

Lucy scrambled out the car, gesturing toward the daisy
wheels and giggling with Piper about something. She
seemed lighter. Happier. Not just because of the car. She'd
been that way since he'd arrived in Rendezvous Falls. As if
walking away from their wedding plans had freed her. The
sound of her laughter washed over him again. Maybe…just
maybe…the chance to hear that sound every day would
be worth making a few changes in his life.

"A picnic."

Logan pulled his head back and frowned at Owen.
"What?"

"That's next on the list." He shrugged. "There technically isn't any order to the tips. Dr. Find-Love says to
play it by ear. But *picnic* is up next. Says they're romantic, but casual. The woman's guard will be down…" He
gritted his teeth. "Damn it, I wish these ideas didn't have
that tinge of creepy-stalker-dude whenever I say them out
loud. There are actually tips on each step to make sure
you *don't* act like someone who needs a restraining order
filed against him."

"Good." Logan slid his hands into his pockets, rocking back on his heels. "Because that *did* sound creepy as shit. But I think I have an idea for you, if Piper approves."

"What's that?"

"We're going up to the winery Monday for a vineyard boxed lunch. It's something Whitney and Evie want to try. They want to experiment with a few guinea pigs first, and we have an invitation. They're going to have tables scattered through the vineyard, and they'll hand out boxed lunches that Evie will bring from the diner. Whitney and Luke will serve some of their wines, in small portions in some sort of covered wineglass people can take with them. Sort of an outdoor tasting? I don't know—winemaking is *not* my thing. But Piper and I are going, and I'm sure they wouldn't mind another couple joining in."

Lucy didn't work on Mondays, so maybe…

"You said you need Piper's approval?"

Logan chuckled. "Not on everything I do, but getting involved in whatever you two are up to? And the way she and Lucy are becoming attached at the hip? Yeah, I need her blessing. Hang on…" Before Owen could object, Logan was gone, tugging his wife aside with a kiss for her and an apology to Lucy. They talked away from the crowd, which was beginning to disperse. The show was over, apparently.

Piper's lips pursed and her brows gathered as she listened. Then her eyes went wide and she looked at Owen— who did his best not to look desperate—then at Lucy, still talking to Evie. He wasn't sure, but it seemed as if the corner of her mouth ticked up a notch. She said something to her husband, and he laughed before he pulled her in for a surprisingly hot kiss in a parking lot still fairly full of people.

Iris smacked her cane on the asphalt twice, scowling. "That's enough of that. It's still broad daylight, for heaven's sake, and you're a married couple. Have some dignity."

Rick Thomas gave Iris a mocking nudge. "You're just jealous, old woman."

"Bullshit. You think I need an afternoon quickie at my age? Been there. Done that."

Piper put her hands to her cheeks. "Oh my God, it was a kiss, not a quickie." She held up her hand. "And no, I don't want to hear about your quickie conquests, Iris." She walked back to Piper's side, but not before sending Owen what seemed to be a promising wink.

Logan joined him again. "Easier than I thought. Lucy's already planning to go. Evie invited her a couple weeks ago when they were at the tattoo studio."

"Oh, good," Owen started to nod, then froze. What had Logan just said? "Did you say *tattoo studio*? Lucy was just there to hold Evie's hand, right?" She'd always said her parents would have a hissy fit if she ever got a tattoo. The body was a temple or something like that.

Logan snorted. "Does Evie look like she needs hand-holding when she's getting a tattoo?"

He had a point. The bubbly brunette had a lot of ink. Evie didn't look like she needed any moral support while getting a tattoo.

"I'm pretty sure it's supposed to be a secret," Logan said, following Owen's gaze. "But I think your runaway bride got ink. And that's all I'm sayin'."

Owen had some tats. A celtic band around one bicep. The name of his Army division on his back shoulder, with his deployment dates under it. Logan had a lot of ink himself, with a colorful ocean scene—above and below the water—covering one arm and up under his shirt.

But *Lucy* with a tat? Owen would have bet a thousand dollars that would *never* happen. Now he'd pay ten times that just to see it. Artwork, with her beautiful skin as the canvas. Was it big? Small? And most importantly…

"But…where?"

"Uh-uh. I value my family jewels right where they are, thank you very much. Piper would kill me, or worse, if she knew I was even talking about this. You'll have to find out the rest on your own." Logan was enjoying Owen's distress. "Anyway…the good news is Piper thinks it will be fine if you join us. Dr. Find-Love wants you on a casual picnic? You got it."

Logan stepped away to assist his grandmother up the steps and into the inn. Owen was anchored to the ground, unable to move. He watched as Lucy locked up the Bug and waved goodbye to Evie. She saw him staring and tipped her head in curiosity, but before she could do more, little Lily Montgomery was tugging at her hand, pulling her away to look at something. He watched the two go across the parking lot toward the pink Victorian house.

If only he had X-ray vision so he could find if she really had a tattoo under her clothing. He had a feeling he wouldn't get a peaceful night's rest until he knew what—and where—it was.

CHAPTER THIRTEEN

LUCY KNEW OWEN was going to be at Falls Legend Winery for lunch. Piper had asked her the night before if it was okay with her. As if he needed Lucy's permission. But at least she was prepared to see him. Or so she thought.

She'd driven her "new" car up the hill to the winery, picking up Piper's friend Chantese on the way. Chantese loved Buttercup, and Lucy had to admit it was a really sweet ride now. She was pretty sure the old version of Buttercup would never have been able to climb this hill. Owen hadn't been that far off when he'd called it a deathtrap.

Evie Hudson and her husband, Mark, were stacking white boxes on a table just outside the tasting room and wine store. Each box was wrapped with a wide burgundy ribbon tied into a bow.

"The winery store is a miniature of the house!" Lucy hadn't been up here before, and she was instantly charmed. The house—a Victorian like everything else in Rendezvous Falls—was painted in a cheery combination of green, ivory and dark red. A round tower graced one corner, and a wide porch wrapped around the house, with hanging baskets of red and white geraniums. The two-story wine shop was across the gravel parking lot from the house, and looked like a mirror reflection—same tower, same colors, same flowers on the porch. Just smaller. Chantese nodded, the beads in her tiny braids clicking together softly.

"Helen Russo's late husband converted the old carriage house into their wine shop ages ago." They got out of the car in front of the store. "Whitney's accounting office is upstairs."

"Do they live here with Helen?" She'd met Helen Russo at the flower shop last week when she came in looking for a centerpiece for a book club meeting she was hosting. Helen had tried to convince Connie to go, but she'd refused. Helen struck her as a kind soul with a warm smile.

"Yes," Chantese answered. "I'm sorry, I forget that you're not a local. Helen is Whitney's aunt. She has a downstairs suite and Luke and Whitney have the upstairs. Of course, they had to convert one room into a nursery for their new baby, Anthony. But that house is plenty big enough for everyone. Oh, there's Whitney up in the vineyard..." Chantese laughed. "And she's got that baby strapped to her chest. I'm beginning to think she never puts the kid down."

The rows of vines marched up the hill like rungs of a ladder, thick with wide leaves and enormous bunches of grapes. She could see people moving back and forth in the rows. One by one, colorful picnic table umbrellas popped open. From what she understood, the idea was to have a "Lunch in the Vineyard" event one day a month in the nice weather. Customers could purchase a boxed lunch and dine outside. They'd found a company that sold plastic wineglasses with snap on covers, so customers could try a small serving of Falls Legend wine with their lunch. For nondrinkers and children, they had glasses filled with white grape juice.

There was a soft breeze blowing, and Lucy had to hold her hair back from covering her face completely. The view from the winery was beautiful, looking down the hill where Seneca Lake could be seen shining bright blue beyond the trees, stretching north to south in the narrow valley. A few more cars pulled in and parked. Helen Russo was greeting people as they arrived.

Logan Taggart's large SUV came up the driveway, parking next to Buttercup and dwarfing it. Chantese laughed at the sight, saying Logan had originally arrived in Rendezvous Falls on a motorcycle, which wasn't exactly practical as a family or work vehicle. She said he still had the bike for fun, but had purchased the SUV last summer as his everyday transportation.

Logan gave the women a quick wave as he hopped out to help Lily escape her booster seat in the back. Piper stepped out on the other side, with Owen doing the same from the back seat. He was talking with teenage Ethan about some baseball game. The two walked over to Luke and Mark in front of the tasting room, and soon the men were all animatedly talking about sports. Owen was in dark shorts, canvas sneakers and a green polo shirt that had a logo she recognized from the Purple Shamrock. He clearly hadn't packed for a month-long stay, and had been adding to his wardrobe around town. He draped his arm over Ethan's shoulders and said something to the boy that made him burst out laughing. She couldn't help smiling. Owen was beginning to relax…and smile…again. She was beginning to see more of the man she'd fallen in love with.

"Lucy! Chantese!" Lily ran over to clasp them each in one of her precious bear hugs. "I didn't know you were coming, Miss Lucy! Why didn't you ride with us? Lift me up!"

Lucy did as commanded, propping Lily on her hip with

a groan. "Whoa, I think you're getting too big for this, kiddo. And your car looked pretty full. That's why I picked up Miss Chantese and met you here." Plus she didn't trust herself being scrunched tight next to Owen in the backseat. "Are you excited about lunch?"

"Yes! It's a picnic and I get to drink wine from grapes."

"No, you don't." Piper joined them. "You get to drink grape *juice* from a wineglass. Not the same thing. Get down before you break Miss Lucy's hip, you horse." Lily wriggled and Lucy leaned over so the girl could dash off to greet everyone else. Piper sighed. "I swear if I had half her energy I could rule the world."

Another car pulled in, and several of the book club members got out. Cecile was there, along with Rick Thomas and Vickie Pendergast. A tall, elegant Black woman was the last to emerge, talking rapidly on her phone.

"I don't care when the client *wants* the pottery, I'm telling you I can't *complete* the pottery until next week." Her lips thinned in annoyance. "Remind the client that I'm not the one who kept making change after change to the order. This is why I don't like commissioned work. It's not *art*, it's just aggravation." She ended the call and slid the phone in her pocket, looking up to catch Lucy's eye. "Sorry. I swear I love everything about my business *except* the people I have to deal with." Her expression softened. "You're Lucy, right? I'm Lena Fox. I know Connie at the flower shop from way back. I've heard all about the Runaway Bride of Rendezvous Falls."

Gold and silver bangles slid up and down her arm musically as she moved, contrasting against her dark skin. There were rings on her fingers and thumbs, and huge hoop earrings dangled from her ears. A long cotton skirt with bright tribal designs swirled around her legs.

Piper visibly cringed at Lena's title for Lucy, but Lucy didn't mind. It hadn't been said meanly, but more as a matter of fact. And she could hardly argue—she *was* a runaway bride. One whose jilted fiancé had followed her all the way to Rendezvous Falls. She imagined she and Owen were probably the talk of the town by now.

"Nice to meet you, Lena." She shook the older woman's hand.

Before Lena could say more, Whitney Rutledge clapped her hands, standing near the lunch table. Tall and willowy, with dark hair cut into a shoulder-length bob that was tucked behind her ears, she called out to get everyone's attention. Her infant son, sound asleep in the carrier in front of her, didn't flinch.

"Okay, everyone, it's time to do this!" Whitney said, gesturing toward the box lunches. "Thank you for being part of our trial run for Lunch in the Vineyard. We want to make sure this will work the way we intended, and that it will be something people will enjoy. You have a choice of lunch between roast beef sandwiches with horseradish or turkey sandwiches with cranberry mayonnaise. Each box also has chips, a small bottle of water and one of my aunt's famous homemade cookies. For vegetarians, there are some boxes with large salads and no sandwiches." She took a deep breath, glancing over at Evie with a wink. "Today's lunches are provided by the Spot Diner. Luke will give you a choice of red or white wines—today's picks are chardonnay or pinot noir. Once you have your lunches, you can walk up to the vineyard and find a table and chairs to enjoy your meal right among the grapes."

She held up a finger. "But please…no touching of the grapevines. That's our livelihood, and for today they are for atmosphere only."

Luke Rutledge nodded behind her. "I'll second that. My biggest concern with this whole idea is that someone will get handsy with the vines, but we'll be wandering around keeping an eye on things. We really want to know what you guys think of this, so don't be shy about telling us what works and what doesn't. The larger tables are up the center, off to the sides and in the wider swaths between grape varieties. But there are more intimate tables located in some rows, with room for just two if that's what you want." He cleared his throat. "So without further delay, please come up and select a lunch and a beverage."

Lucy fell into line with Chantese and Piper, but as people headed up the hill, families and couples started breaking into groups. The Taggarts, with Chantese joining them, filled a table on their own. Lucy waved off Piper's invitation and turned to see if there was another group she could join. Maybe the book club? She sensed someone behind her and turned to find Owen. He held up his box with a tentative smile.

"Join me for lunch?"

The temptation to say yes surprised her, but she caught herself.

"Bad idea, Owen."

"It's only lunch, Luce. In broad daylight. With people all around us."

"*I* know that, but I'm worried *you* don't." She shook her head. "I don't want you getting your hopes up that things are going to change."

The lines around his eyes tightened a notch, as if she'd stung him. She gave a heavy sigh.

"You see? That's what I mean!"

"What?" He straightened.

"That kicked-puppy expression of yours just now. I don't want to be the bad guy. I don't want to hurt you any more than I already have…"

"Hey…" He stepped closer, his voice dropping. "You're not the bad guy. You never were." He started walking up the hill. There didn't seem to be anyone else dining this high up in the vineyard. He looked over his shoulder to make sure she was following. "We both did our share of causing pain, and I think we've agreed neither of us intended to do that, right?"

"Right." He turned between two rows of grapevines, toward a tiny table with two chairs. There was no umbrella over it, so you'd never know it was there unless… she narrowed her eyes at his back. "You set this up, didn't you? This table, way far away from anyone else. Owen…"

She stopped, but he kept walking, setting his lunch and wine on the table, then taking hers from her hands and doing the same. He held out the closer chair and looked at her expectantly.

"Set up isn't the right word," he answered. "They did say we might find tables for two up here." He glanced at the chair, then back to her. "It's still just lunch. In broad daylight. With our friends nearby.

"If you want to go sit with the Taggarts or someone, that's fine. I get it. I just thought this would give us a chance to talk more. AS friends." He paused. "Please."

Lucy stared at the table, then gave in and sat down. He was right—it's not like he'd invited her to join him for some private, romantic candlelit dinner or anything like that. It was a boxed lunch and wine. Outdoors. He moved to the other side of the table and sat. The grape leaves on the vines brushed his shoulders. He looked from side to side and grinned.

"This reminds me of those old TV shows I used to watch where the stars always ended up stuck in a room with mechanized walls that closed in on them and threatened to crush them."

She laughed. "Right? And they'd stop the walls with a chair or something silly so they could miraculously escape. Everything was easy in those old shows. All problems solved in sixty minutes or less." She'd opened her box as she talked, pulling out her turkey sandwich and unwrapping it. She folded the paper napkin on her lap, then looked up when she realized Owen hadn't spoken.

He was staring at her, his smile gone.

"What is it?"

"I wish our problems could be solved that easily."

She shook her head emphatically. "No sad puppy eyes, remember? We're friends, and friends don't play the guilt card over lunch."

He straightened with a nod. "You're right. Sorry." He uncovered both wineglasses and handed her chardonnay to her. He lifted his pinot for a toast. "Here's to friendship." They clinked their glasses together. "But don't hate your friend for hoping for more."

"Owen…"

"I know, I know." He held up his hand. I promise I'm not going to try to convince you of anything today. I'm just saying… He leaned forward. "Tell me the door is still open, even if just a little bit."

He was so earnest that she found herself starting to believe in this hope he was clinging to. Maybe whatever she needed to leave behind didn't include Owen? But he had a job waiting for him at home.

"Let's just say the door isn't locked." Her words surprised her as much as it did him. "It may not even be latched. But it's not open by much, so please…"

He sat back, his eyes warm and…slightly eager. She could tell he was trying to stay cool. He finally smiled. "Say no more. Let's eat. As friends. Tell me how the flower shop is doing. Are you having as much fun there as it looks?"

A soft breeze ruffled through the vines, making the leaves roll like a stadium crowd doing the wave in a stadium. Owen seemed genuinely interested, and she relaxed at last.

"I am. I mean…you know I love working with flowers, so that's a natural fit. But it's been fun trying to drag Connie kicking and screaming into the twenty-first century. She fusses a lot, but she's actually more open to change than I would have thought. She's letting me build her a new website and…"

They both took a bite of their sandwiches, and moaned in unison at the flavor. She told him about the small wedding coming up that weekend, where the bride and groom didn't agree on anything, including the flowers. The original order was pretty basic, probably because that's all Connie wanted to offer. In the prewedding consult, Lucy noticed the disappointment in the couple's eyes. She'd suggested a few changes. Adding her favorite hydrangeas to the bride's bouquet for dimension, and putting the bright orange lilies the groom wanted—what *was* it with

upstate New York and orange?—in the centerpieces instead of the bridal bouquets. They'd left the appointment
with smiles, and even Connie had approved, telling her
she'd *handled it well*.

Owen chuckled. "That's high praise from Connie. She's
not easily impressed. Don't you find her a little prickly
to work with?"

She thought for a moment, not wanting to mention Connie's physical challenges. "I think she's had a lot to deal
with since her husband left. Then the pandemic hit her
business hard—she lost dozens of wedding orders last
year. Stress hits everyone differently…"

"Then add dealing with Parkinson's."

Lucy looked up from her sandwich in surprise. "She
told you that?"

His mouth slanted into a grin. "No, you did. Just now.
But I was pretty sure that's why her hand trembles so
much. Plus she told me she'd moved her bedroom downstairs at her house, and she's not that old that she shouldn't
be able to go up and down stairs." He took a sip of his
wine and grimaced. He'd always been more of a beer guy.
"My uncle had it, remember? He was younger than Connie when it started, but the tremor was the same."

"I know Connie can be…prickly." She reached over
and rescued the wine from Owen. He opened his water
instead. "But I think her temper is a coping mechanism."

"Can't help with winning over customers, though."

They both smiled over that undeniable fact.

"No, but I'm hoping I can help her with that."

He finished his sandwich and unwrapped the cookie.
"Sounds like you plan on being here awhile." He'd said

it calmly, but she could feel the tension right below the surface of his words.

"Maybe. I honestly don't know."

Staying in Rendezvous Falls as a part-time florist didn't seem like a very practical career plan. And yet…it was tempting for some reason. Owen had the cookie almost to his mouth, but he lowered it without taking a bite.

"You…you're really thinking of *staying*?"

She didn't answer right away. Laughter rose up from the other tables on the slope below. It seemed the trial run was a success. She wondered if there was a way to get the flower shop involved. Tiny floral bundles for the ladies to take with them? It would be a good promotion for the shop. She bit into her white chocolate and macadamia nut cookie. If she was thinking of the future of Rendezvous Blooms, she was thinking of *her* future, too.

"Like I keep telling you, Owen, I don't know." Was it fantasy to think she might want both him *and* a life in Rendezvous Falls? He frowned, then his face smoothed. His smile seemed just a little bit forced. "I'm just saying… there are flowers in Greensboro, too."

Not according to your mother… Lucy had tried to convince Ed and Faye to let her have just a corner of the nursery for loose flower arrangements, but Faye always had some excuse not to do it.

"Hey, you two!" Whitney Rutledge walked down the row toward them. Her son had woken, and she had him resting on her hip. His chubby hands were playing in her hair, and she winced as he tugged on a strand. "Easy there, tiger." She peeked into their empty boxes. "Looks like you enjoyed your lunches. What do you think of our little experiment?"

Lucy stood. She was suddenly feeling restless…pressured by her own conflicted feelings about staying or going, not to mention Owen's obvious opinions about it. She finished off the last of Owen's wine—hers was long gone—then turned to Whitney with a bright smile.

"The lunch was great, and if you can guarantee weather like this, people will really enjoy dining in the vineyard. I think it's a great plan."

Owen also stood, gathering their boxes and glasses into a stack. "I agree. It was a very nice lunch."

Whitney looked back and forth between them, and Lucy had a feeling more Rendezvous Falls meddling was on its way.

"Did you think it was a *romantic* lunch?"

Owen answered before Lucy could. "Absolutely."

Lucy shot him a warning look. "It definitely *could* be. Our lunch was…friendly. Pleasant."

"Ouch." Whitney chuckled, looking at Owen. "*Pleasant*? What did you do to earn such an underwhelming description?"

"That *was* sort of harsh." He grinned. "But we are just friends…for now."

Lucy was beginning to wonder if they'd ever been just friends. They had a history. And a chemistry. Even now, after everything that had happened, Owen's smile had the power to send a rush of heat through her. Reminding her why she'd fallen in love with him in the first place.

CHAPTER FOURTEEN

OWEN KNEW HE WAS pushing his luck with those last two words, but Lucy didn't object. She hadn't slammed that door in his face yet, despite him pushing the envelope a few times. Lucy pointed to a small white sign near the trees at the end of their row.

"What does that sign say over there?"

Whitney squinted, holding one hand over her eyes as she followed where Lucy was pointing. "Oh! That's the trail to the falls. We'll probably have to take that down, because our insurance guy had a fit when I inquired about letting customers use the path."

"To the falls? Rendezvous Falls?" Owen asked. "So the county park is on the other side?"

"I'm surprised you've even heard about that little park, but yes. That's on the far side of the creek, and my aunt's property is on this side. Have either of you been to the falls? I think our view is prettier, but the park has steps to the top of the falls, so that's nice. But our land is closer to the rock the legend revolves around."

"We haven't been…" He cleared his throat. "I…uh… drove by the park but…it was nighttime." Lucy's cheeks went pink, but she stayed silent.

"Be careful driving up here at night if you don't know where you're going. There are a lot of weird curves and drop-offs, and wildlife that likes to just stand in middle of the road for some reason. Piper went off our road once in the wintertime and scared Logan half to death until he found her." She caught the pacifier her son dropped in midair and returned it to his mouth without skipping a beat. "I keep telling Luke there should be more street-lights around here, but he reminds me that would be light pollution and that this is the countryside, not downtown Chicago. He's not wrong."

"Wait…" Lucy finally joined the conversation. "Did you say there was a legend?"

Whitney gave them a big wink. "That's where the win-ery got its name—Falls Legend. My uncle used to tell me the story all the time. This is Iroquois country, or used to be. The confederacy of different indigenous tribes had been living in upstate New York in peace for generations before white people arrived. The Revolutionary War divided the tribes between the British and the colonists. The legend says that two star-crossed lovers from suddenly warring tribes met at the falls…" She wiggled her eyebrows. "And had a *rendezvous* there to declare their undying love for each other, even though it meant they'd be killed if discovered. An Iroquois goddess saw them, and turned them into a stag and doe so they could run away together. Some people say they can hear them singing in the water."

She cooed at the baby as the boy snuggled against her neck and closed his eyes. Her voice lowered. "There's a flat boulder in the water, not far from our side, and the legend says that's where the couple stood. And that any couple who stands on the rock and declares their love will be together forever."

Owen could see that Lucy was captivated by the story,

but he couldn't resist adding, "Hopefully without turning into deer."

Whitney laughed, then caught herself when Anthony made an annoyed grumble. "That's exactly what my Uncle Tony used to say. Hey, you two should go check it out." Lucy's eyes went wide and Whitney rushed to explain. "Not standing on the rock, silly. But go see the falls. The path is right there, and it's only a five minute walk." She reached out. "I can carry your boxes back down the hill for you."

Owen was eager to take her up on the suggestion, but he hesitated when he realized she already had an armful with her son. She laughed and gestured for him to give her the boxes.

"I can handle it. I did taxes for half the town with this sweet boy in my lap this spring, and I've been working the vineyard all summer with him in his carrier or in my arms. I'll be a weight lifter by the time this kid starts walking."

"Come on," Owen said, "we couldn't see the falls during the fireworks show. Let's go check it out. As friends, of course."

She studied him, then gave in and joined him in walking toward the rustic sign that read Waterfalls, with a small arrow. He took her hand, and she didn't pull away. *Progress.*

They went into the trees, and it felt as if they were suddenly sheltered from everything. No sounds of laughter. No traffic sounds. No wind. Just coolness and quiet... other than the soft gurgling sound of moving water ahead, splashing on rocks and continuing down the hill toward Seneca Lake.

It wasn't Niagara or anything, but the stream tumbled

over large outcroppings from high above, splashing and swishing its way to the shallow, swirling pool at its base.

"That must be the legendary rock." Lucy pointed at a large boulder a few feet from shore, smoothed by centuries of flowing water. Its surface was just a few inches above the water, and he imagined in the springtime it would be submerged. He opened his mouth to answer, but she raised her hand to stop him. "Do not even *think* about asking me if I want to go stand on it. There will be no open air declarations of love to goddesses or anyone else."

They stood and listened to the soothing sounds of moving water, their hands still clasped together. Her fingers were warm and soft. He'd missed this. Finally, he just had to say it.

"My first declaration of love to *you* was in the open air."

They'd driven out to their favorite little motel on the Outer Banks. They'd discovered Pelican Place by accident, laughing when they saw the two-story pink-and-green motel and its big, faded roadside sign with a neon pelican. Owen had pulled into the parking lot of the 1950s throwback, and, because it was the off-season, they'd been able to get a room for that weekend. He'd canceled the much nicer room he already had booked at the Hilton down the road. Everything about Pelican Place made Lucy laugh, and her laughter had always been his favorite sound.

At the time, he'd been getting ready to head out for a few months of training out in California. He was determined to soak up every minute of Lucy's laughter he could get before he left. It was a balm to all the stress he was feeling between the Army wanting him to reup and make it a career, and his parents chafing for him to get out and come home to run Cooper Landscaping and Nurseries, so they could retire to their country club life.

Lucy was his one happy spot. With her, he had no stress. Nothing but smiles and silliness and world-rocking sex. She'd been the one thing offering him hope and clarity in a world of hard decisions to be made. And that first night at Pelican Place, walking the beach hand-in-hand, he'd told her he loved her for the first time.

She made a soft sound at his side. It was somewhere between a laugh, a scoff, and…something warmer. "I was going to say something sarcastic like 'look how well that turned out' but…" She looked up at him. "That was a special night."

That acknowledgment made him feel like she'd opened that door just a little bit farther. He swallowed hard, not wanting to ruin the moment.

"Not all our memories are bad, Luce. We had good times, too. Loving times." His hand cupped her cheek. And miracles of miracles, she closed her eyes and turned her head to lean into his palm. He was both terrified and thrilled. It was like capturing a frightened bird. He was afraid to make the wrong move. Her shoulders rose and fell with a sigh…sad or content? He couldn't tell. Her eyes opened and met his gaze.

"They weren't all bad. That weekend was pretty great." The corner of her mouth twitched. "I mean, it's not like you didn't take me to the classiest places."

The Pelican Place Motel was clean…mostly. But the rooms hadn't been updated since approximately 1962. Beige paneling on the walls. Orange curtains. Green carpets. Framed artwork he was pretty sure were paint-by-numbers kits that perhaps someone's child—or grandmother—had painted. In one of the rooms they'd used, because of course they'd gone back after that first week-end, there was a framed jigsaw puzzle of a ballerina that someone had put together. Nothing but the best at Pelican Place. He chuckled.

"It wasn't fancy, but we damn sure had some fun at that place. I even proposed there…" He stopped. He should never have brought up the wedding that wasn't. She didn't recoil in rage, but she did move away from his touch. He cursed under his breath. "That was dumb. Sorry."

"It's okay. I remember that day. It was crazy windy on the beach. It was right before a hurricane brushed the coast, right?"

At least she was speaking of it with some fondness. He'd been about to leave on that last deployment—the one that ended up being extended, but they didn't know that would happen. He was determined to marry her the min-ute he got back home and left the Army. Being with Lucy calmed the tension that kept ebbing and flowing inside of him after his previous tour. She was the one thing in his life that felt…right. As if she belonged there in his heart.

"Best decision I ever made." His voice broke, and he cleared his throat again, blinking rapidly. *Focus, soldier.* "I didn't follow it up with the best decisions, but I don't regret proposing to you for a minute. Tell me you feel the same…" She started to protest, but he clarified. "Not that you want to marry me right this instant, because I know we have some hurts that need to be mended. But tell me that day…that moment…tell me you don't regret saying yes in that moment. Not knowing what would happen. Tell me you loved me that day."

Lucy's mouth fell open. Her lower lip trembled, and

she bit it to keep it steady. He waited. He was going to be really good at this waiting business by the end of his month in Rendezvous Falls. A month that was speeding by. Her deep blue eyes never wavered. She held his gaze and finally answered him.

"I loved you that day. I loved you a lot of days."

Thank Christ for that. He put his hands on her waist and gently moved her closer. She didn't resist, stepping so close her ruffled cotton blouse brushed against his shirt.

"I want you to love me again." His voice was raspy in his own ears. "I want to *deserve* your love again."

She looked toward the falls, and he had to lower his head to hear her.

"It wasn't just you I ran from. You were the one who was left standing there, but I was running from other things. Running from not being heard. Running from other people's expectations. Running from…disappointment. In my parents. And yes, in you." She looked up again, her blue eyes cautious beneath her long lashes. "Everytime we're together, though, I remember the good times. The beaches. The mountains. The silly motels. The romantic dinners." She grinned. "The back of your Bronco."

His fingers tightened on her hips involuntarily. They'd had some great times in that Bronco. They'd had some great times, period. And it sounded as if he wasn't the only one who thought so. She slid her hands up to his shoulders, then behind his neck and up into his hair. Again, he waited. Afraid to move. Afraid to breathe.

"Half the reason I was so mad at you was because I *missed* you. The you of those fun times. The you who laughed, who loved me. It probably wasn't fair, because I should have known you'd gone through stuff over there. I should have understood…"

He had to stop her there. "No. You *tried*, Luce. You begged me to talk to you. You knew there was something eating at me, and you tried to get me to share it with you. I refused. That's on me, not you."

Her fingers moved slowly and lightly through his hair. He wondered if she even knew she was doing it. She didn't seem convinced of his words.

"But if we loved each other, I shouldn't have had to…" She sighed. "And I did love you. I think I *still* love you….." His pulse jumped. It wasn't exactly a ringing endorsement, but it wasn't a shutdown, either. "I just need…time to sort this all out. My frustrations with everyone have spilled onto you, and I can't separate it in my mind. I look at you, and I see *your* parents and *my* parents and the business and…"

"Then don't look."

"What?"

"Don't look. *Feel.* Close your eyes and let your heart feel what's right or wrong." She stared at him as if he'd started speaking Portuguese. This moment wasn't anywhere in Dr. Find-Love's app. He hadn't planned it. But it felt right, and he was going with it. "Close your eyes, Lucy."

She did, and he pulled her in, wrapping his arms around her waist. He breathed the words against her neck, her skin silky soft on his lips.

"Keep them closed and feel. You can stop me any-time you want, but…give it a chance. Give us a chance." His mouth traced slowly along the line of her jaw, and he felt her tremble before pressing herself against him. He was instantly hard, but he forced himself not to move his hips. This was about *feelings*, not physical chemistry. Even though his physical chemistry felt combustible at the moment.

His mouth brushed the corner of hers, and her head turned ever so slightly to meet him. Her eyes were still tightly closed, but her hands were pulling his head down, lost in the moment. Owen had to be careful. One misstep and the moment…and maybe all hope…would be lost. He barely kissed her—more like a brief meeting of mouths before he pulled away. That's when Lucy took control. Her fingers tightened, twisting in his hair and tugging him down to meet her lips. Just before they crashed together, she murmured something so softly he almost didn't hear her command.

Kiss me.

As a soldier, he sure as hell knew how to obey an order. They connected so quickly their teeth clicked together before his tongue pushed forward and she surrendered with a moan that shot straight to his groin. His hands lowered to cup her bottom and hold it against him. Patience and self-control be damned. Their heads turned and twisted, but their mouths didn't part. He just wanted to taste her— his sweet, sweet Lucy. He didn't want to stop, and clearly neither did she, considering the way her leg hooked around his as if she wanted to climb him. *Yes, please.*

Owen grabbed her thighs and lifted her so she could wrap her legs around him. He turned and braced her against a tree trunk, pressing in against her and wondering just how far this little experiment of his was going to go. He lifted his head to fill his lungs, and barely had time to do even that as she pulled him back down to her kiss. Things were burning hot. Just the way they used to be. Just the way he liked it. Her legs tightened, and his fingers moved up under her flowy little skirt. Brushed against her panties. His brain was yelling at him to slow down, but his heart and his dick were telling him something *very* different.

Lucy groaned and dropped her head to kiss his neck, gasping for breath as she whispered his name.

"Owen...yes..."

He was just lifting the hem of her dress when he heard another voice. A child's voice.

"Mommy, what are they doing over there?"

Shit, shit, *shit*!

The opposite side of the waterfall was a park. A *public* park. A *family friendly* public park. And here he was, basically humping Lucy against a tree trunk. Maybe he should have listened to his brain after all.

Lucy heard the boy's voice, too, and her whole body went still for a beat, then her hands pushed frantically on his chest. He'd already lowered her feet to the ground, and he slid them both around to the other side of the tree. She buried her face against his chest, hiding from whoever it was who'd appeared across the stream.

"What did you see, sweetie?" A woman's voice. A woman who luckily hadn't seen their display of animal instinct. But her little boy had. Owen rested his cheek on Lucy's head as they listened.

"A man was carrying a lady and they were *kissing*!"

The kid sounded disgusted. His mother's laughter was wry, but not angry. "Well, this is a popular place for... that. Your aunt and uncle got caught up here once, kissing and...stuff. In fact, there's a very gushy, romantic legend about the waterfall. Do you want me to tell you about it?"

"Ew! Gross! No!" The little boy sounded horrified,

which was probably exactly what his mother intended. She chuckled, and he heard them walking away. Had he and Lucy managed to stay hidden from view?

The woman spoke again. "That's what I thought. Come on, Eric, let's go up the trail to the top of the falls." Her volume increased. "By the time we get up there, I bet there won't be anyone kissing, or doing anything else, behind that tree over there."

The woman knew they were there, and was telling them to scram. He glanced around the tree and saw mother and son disappear into the trees. He and Lucy got the message loud and clear. They hurried down the trail toward the vineyard. They were deep into the trees when Lucy stopped, covering her face, her shoulders shaking. Owen's heart fell.

"Damn, I'm sorry. I don't know what I was thinking…"

She lifted her head in surprise. There were tears on her pink cheeks, but her wide eyes sparkled with laughter. The relief almost made his knees buckle.

"We both had a hand in whatever that was." She giggled and reached up to smooth his hair. "And it *was a* mistake." She waggled her finger in front of his face. "That will *not* happen again. Especially in public!" She laughed again, then started tugging at her clothes, which were a lot more rumpled than before. "I can't believe we got caught. I mean, I *can* believe it because it's a lovely summer day and that's a public park, but what were we thinking?"

Owen nodded, helping her straighten her skirt. His brain was stuck on *especially in public.* Did that mean she *wasn't* opposed to doing that in private? Kissing her could have slammed the door shut on hope completely, but maybe…just maybe…it had done the opposite.

She swatted his hand away and shoved him. "Get back. I don't want anyone seeing us together and knowing about that…that…"

"That smokin' hot kiss? The way you crawled right up my body to get more of it? My fingers brushing against your…"

"Stop!" She punched him in the shoulder, but she was still laughing. "I was there. I don't need a play-by-play. How do I look? Normal?"

He chuckled, plucking a leaf from her fading pink hair.

"Lucy Higgins, you have *never* looked normal in my eyes. You've always looked special. Unique. Wild. Beautiful. Hotter than hell." She was staring at him now, her mouth soft and slack. "But *normal*? No way, babe. Normal is boring. And you have never been that. It's why I love you."

Lucy was the only unplanned thing in his life. And he'd never been able to resist her, right from the moment they'd met. She'd bewitched him with her laughter. She'd made him imagine a different, happier future with her at his side. His parents said it was impossible, but for the first time ever, he'd defied them. For Lucy. He swooped in for a quick kiss on those inviting lips. She returned it for a moment, then stepped back, waving her hand in front of his face.

"No more kissing! You're not playing fair." She gestured at him from head to toe. "And no more of that sweet talk, either. You've never been a sweet talker. A *dirty* talker, yes. But flowery prose is not your style and you're…you're confusing me." She stepped back again. "And don't stand so close. I don't want anyone to see us and get any ideas." Her eyes narrowed. "Especially *you*. What happened back there was not what friends do, and we agreed to be…" Her voice trailed off. She'd already admitted it wasn't just him who'd gotten hot and heavy in the first place.

"I think…" His voice grew serious. "We can both agree that what happened means we're not just friends anymore. Let's not kid ourselves. No one needs to know. I get that, and I respect it. But *we* know. And we're going to have to talk about what that means sooner or later. That kiss… that heat…there's something between us that's worth saving. Admit that much to me."

She licked her bottom lip, then pressed her tongue against it. Her eyebrows drew together as she stared at the ground between them. Eventually her shoulders fell and she let out a long breath.

"You might be right. But I'm not ready." She glanced up in time to see his brief smile, and she returned it. "Yes, I know I seemed *very* ready just then. But Owen… I walked out on our wedding. I need to deal with that. With what made me do it. With what I do next. With what other people are going to do about it…" Her smile deepened. "I'm pretty sure your mom plans on suing me. Part of me still loves you. But for now, I really need you to be my friend. Not my lover. That wouldn't be fair to either of us until we know what our plans are going to be. And that?" She pointed back toward the falls. "That doesn't help me. It just muddles things even more."

His chest felt lighter. Hope. She was giving him hope.

"I hear you, and I understand. But remember…you gave me thirty days, so if I seem anxious, it's because there's a clock ticking in my head. Louder every day. But I'll behave. No kisses unless you beg me for them."

She scoffed as she turned to walk away. "In your dreams."

Yup. That's exactly where that kiss was going to live. In his dreams, every time he closed his eyes.

CHAPTER FIFTEEN

CONNIE WATCHED LUCY wipe down the counter in the shop. Or more accurately, wipe one particular spot on the counter. Over and over again. While smiling and staring off into space. Lucy could be bubbly. Unpredictable. Strong-willed. But dreamy-eyed was a new side of her. Connie closed the cooler door and arched her brow.

"If I didn't know better, I'd say you were downright swooning over something. Or somebody." Lucy looked up in surprise, as if she hadn't even noticed that Connie had walked right in front of her to get to the cooler and back again to stand in front of her.

"What? What do you mean?" She scrubbed with a bit more energy, still on that one spot next to the computer monitor.

Connie nodded. "Ah…that's what it is, isn't it? Some-*one*. Is that fiancé of yours finally making some progress?" Lucy's blush deepened. *Nailed it.* "Well, isn't that interesting. Does this have anything to do with the picnic at the winery the other day?"

She'd barely gotten the last word out before Lucy jumped to deny it.

"No! Why would a picnic change anything? Besides, there was a whole group there. It's not like it was a romantic tryst…"

Well. That was an interesting choice of words.

"I never said anything about romantic trysts, but now you have me curious." She leaned her hip against the counter. "Helen said the two of you were at a private table near the top of the hill. And Cecile saw you walking into the woods together."

Lucy's cheeks were flaming now. Bingo. Something *had* happened.

"Oh, my God. The gossip in this town is worse than down South, and I didn't think that was possible. Owen and I walked over to see the waterfall. That's all Cecile saw. And we only took that table because the others were full. Nothing happened."

"I call bullshit on that."

Lucy's mouth fell open. "I beg your pardon?" Her Southern accent deepened. She stared as if she expected Connie to back down and apologize, which was not about to happen.

"Look, *darlin'*." Lucy's eyes narrowed dangerously at the mockery, but Connie kept right on talking. "You were staring so far off into space just now that you didn't even see me putting flowers in the cooler. And you've been wiping the same exact spot on that counter for ten minutes. I've been around the block a few times, girl, and I know a besotted expression when I see one. There's no one else you'd look that way for except for Owen Cooper. My guess is you're beginning to regret leaving him at the altar."

It was as if she'd pushed a button that collapsed Lucy like one of those floppy dolls they sold at the fair. She was still standing, but all the air was let out of her, and…there were *tears* in her eyes. Lucy hadn't come close to shedding a tear in front of Connie before now.

"Oh, shit." This was what happened when she started

caring about people. She had to deal with waterworks. "Come on in back. I'll get you some water." She took Lucy's elbow and led her back to the worktable, where Lucy sat on a stool and buried her face in her hands. Connie kicked herself. She'd really done it now. Emotions. Emotions were flowing all over her workroom, and she didn't know how to stop it. She awkwardly patted Lucy's shoulder as she cried silently. She'd misread this completely. Owen must have done something stupid. She fetched a bottle of water. She checked the front of the shop to make sure no one was there. Then she sat at Lucy's side.

"Look…men can be jerks. They're born idiots and aging doesn't help them one bit. Whatever Owen did…"

Lucy wiped her cheeks with the back of her hand.

"He kissed me."

Connie sat back, trying to figure out where the tears were coming from.

"Without your permission?"

Lucy shook her head emphatically. "No, nothing like that. I kissed him, too. In fact, I think I kissed him first."

"I see. That bastard."

A bubble of laughter came up through Lucy's tears. "Right? I'm so confused. I mean… I *left* him. And he picked me up, put me against a tree and kissed me like nothing had ever happened. And it was…it was…"

"Earth-shattering?"

She wiped her face again, then took a drink of water.

"Something like that, yeah. I thought we were done. We had to be done, right?" She turned to face Connie. "Why wouldn't we be done after I dumped him? Isn't that the definition of dumping a guy? That you're done? But then…"

"Then he kissed you. Against a tree."

"Yes. He kissed me. Against a tree. And said he loved me. And I…said I might love him, too. But that makes no sense!"

Connie put her hand over Lucy's.

"This may come as a shock to you, but love rarely makes sense."

The room was silent for a few minutes. Lucy sniffled, her tears finally coming to an end.

"Tell me about your husband."

"Where did *that* come from?" Connie yanked her hand away. "What does my marriage have to do with you and Owen?"

"You mentioned love as if you loved your husband once. But you never talk about him."

She was now well and truly bristling, her voice sharp. "I don't *have* to talk about him. He left me. You know that, right?"

"Yes, but that doesn't mean you didn't love him once." Lucy's eyes went soft.

Connie started organizing ribbons and beads, trying to ignore the welling up of emotion inside of her. "I did, right up until he left me here alone and took off with that Sandy woman. I never saw it coming. That wasn't the deal. It wasn't the plan…" She sighed, remembering the absolute shock of the day she'd found Danny packing his suitcase. "I guess it isn't fair to say I didn't see it coming. I knew *something* was wrong. We'd settled into different lives. Him with his real estate business and me with the shop. Our son was grown and gone, and we had to find a new life just for the two of us. But Dan went out and found a new life that didn't include me at all.

"And yes… I loved him for a long time. Even more importantly, I *liked* him. We had fun together. Like Cecile said, we threw some wild parties and laughed all the time. But once our nest was empty, I guess I wasn't enough for him anymore. Maybe it was my health worries. Maybe it was male menopause or whatever they call it." She tried to smile. "I guess I wouldn't be this angry with him if I hadn't loved him so much. Like I said…love doesn't make sense. But he betrayed me. He betrayed our vows. He betrayed all the plans we'd made together."

"I'm really am sorry." Lucy tipped her head to the side. "You sound like Owen with all of your focus on *plans.* He doesn't like having plans derailed, either."

"He doesn't mind derailing your plans to leave him."

"Ha! That's true." Lucy's forehead wrinkled. "I wonder why. He's always said meeting me was never in his plans, but now he won't let me go. I can't figure out if it's because he really cares about me, or because I disrupted The Plan. And since The Plan is based in Greensboro, that's not going to happen."

"You talk about Greensboro like it kicked your dog. Greensboro is a dot on a map. What is it that *really* chased you all the way to the Finger Lakes?"

Lucy was silent. Her tears had stopped. *Thank God.* She looked around the workroom. The coolers were full of assembled bouquets for weekend orders. Connie had a feeling Lucy wanted to be busy with something, but the work was done for the day.

"I like it here." Lucy said the words softly, almost to herself.

"In Rendezvous Falls?" Connie asked. "That's understandable, I guess. Even an old crank like me can see it has its qualities."

Lucy shook her head. "No, I mean I like it *here*. In the shop. Doing this work. It's what I've always wanted. No one ever listened when I tried to tell them that." She blew her nose and sat straighter. "I could tell you all the things that chased me away from Greensboro, but it comes down to just…not being happy there. Not being heard. By anyone. I let it go on for years, waiting for things to change. I guess I finally realized that nothing would change if *I* didn't make it change." She smiled at Connie. "Maybe running away wasn't the best way to make that happen, but it ended up showing me what I want. I want…this." She gestured around the workroom.

"You want *my* business?"

"Well, I'm not claiming it by eminent domain or anything." Lucy laughed. "But if you're ever looking for a partner…"

Connie's eyes widened. A *partner*? She'd never considered that as an option. She'd thought her choices were *sell* or *keep*. She hated the idea of selling, regardless of how much pressure her son and daughter-in-law put on her. Or maybe *because* of all that pressure. Lord knew she could be too stubborn for her own good. But a partner…that might be a happy medium. Someone to share the workload.

"That's an interesting proposal." She picked up her water glass, then set it down sharply. "This conversation requires something stronger than water." Instead of going for the chilled wine she kept in the cooler, she went to the corner cabinet and pulled out the good stuff—a bottle of Courvoisier. Dumping the water from their glasses, she splashed the cognac in its place, then sat back down.

The task gave her time to think beyond the immediate appeal of a talented young partner who knew the business. She liked Lucy. But...

"I've only known you for a minute, Lucy Higgins. And one of the things I do know about you is that you took off and left a lot of people hanging back in North Carolina. Regardless of your reasons, it doesn't look great on a résumé." She sipped her drink, watching Lucy over the top of her glass. "And I can't help but wonder if you have some secret stash of investment money you haven't mentioned yet. I'm not just gifting you half of my business."

Lucy frowned into her drink, her mouth pressed into a thin straight line. She stayed like that for a moment before swallowing hard and meeting Connie's gaze. "Fair enough. I'd have to work my way into full partnership. But you know I've got the skills and the energy to do it. As far as my recent history...that's an...aberration..."

"Really? Tell me your work history before that."

She chewed her lip before answering. "I had a job in Wilmington after college. For a tax preparation company." She brightened. "But I worked part-time for a florist in town. On weekends and before the big flower holidays."

"For how many years?"

"Uh...a few.... The only reason I left was that I had to go home to the mountains to care for my grandmother. She had cancer and needed live-in help."

"And you have training in home health care as well as accounting and flowers?"

Lucy paled. "No, but she was my grandmother. My parents didn't want some stranger living with her, so they asked me to come home."

Connie narrowed her eyes at her. "You just dropped everything and left Wilmington? I'm sensing a pattern."

LUCY WANTED TO ARGUE, but what could she say? Becoming Connie's partner had been barely the whisper of an idea. She hadn't thought it through. Just blurted it out.

"I don't think that's fair, Connie. Yes, I left Wilmington, but it was to help my family. You can't hold *that* against me. And I didn't leave everything—I met Owen when I was in Wilmington. I kept him."

Connie took another sip of her drink. "For a while, maybe. Were you the only family member who could care for her? Even though it meant giving up your job and moving across the state?"

"I was very close to my grandmother." She closed her eyes. There was no point in denying the truth. "I've always been the one to give up things, Connie. It's just how it was. My older sister was sick as a child—leukemia. I gave up music classes. I gave up school activities. But she was sick and…my parents needed me."

"Ah, I see," Connie said. "I had you pegged as a feisty one, but you're really a people pleaser, aren't you?"

"That's me." Lucy lifted her glass in a mock toast. "Although I think Owen's mom would argue about me pleasing *anyone*."

"So you were a people pleaser right up until your wedding day?"

"Something like that." *Exactly* like that. "I just couldn't do it anymore." She gave herself a mental shake. "But we're drifting from the subject of a partnership. Is that really something you'd consider?"

"Are you serious about the offer?"

"Yes. I haven't thought through all the details of making it work, but yes." She looked around the cozy-but-efficient workroom. "I know it's fast, but I'm interested. I meant it when I said I love this place. And Rendezvous Falls feels like…"

"Home? After a month?"

"It feels like it could be, yes."

"And Owen?

Her face heated. "What about him?"

"Don't play coy, Lucy." Connie's brows drew together. "I don't want to start making business plans and wake up to find you've packed up and left for North Carolina with him. You have the right to do what you want, of course, but I don't want to be left dangling in the wind."

"Owen is *not* going to get me back to North Carolina." She held up her hand. "And yes, I know Greensboro is just a dot on a map, but it represents more than that to me. It's where our families are, and if I go back…"

"You're afraid you'll fall back into your old patterns of making everyone happy but yourself?"

Lucy chuckled. "You're pretty smart, Connie."

That was exactly it. She wanted Owen, but she didn't want Greensboro. And she couldn't imagine Owen turning his back on his parents' plans for him.

"Maybe," Connie answered with a soft smile. "But what's going to stop you from trying to please everyone here in Rendezvous Falls?" The older woman's voice sharpened. "What if I have a bad spell with the Parkinson's and I say you have to do everything for the shop? What if I ask you to move into my house and take care of *me*? Would you turn into Florence Nightingale all over again? Or would you run?"

Lucy pursed her lips, trying to decide how serious Connie was. And trying to decide the answers to the questions. It wasn't a bad thing to care about other people, was it?

"Is your Parkinson's getting worse? Have you had trouble at home?"

"Of course not. She'll outlive us all and laugh about it." Cecile Manning stood in the doorway. "What brought on *this* morbid conversation? You two didn't even hear us come in."

"Us?" Lucy stood. "A customer?"

"No, it's just Maura and Vickie."

"Oh, thanks a lot." Lucy recognized Maura McKinnon's voice, although she couldn't see her. She'd met her one morning at the diner, having breakfast with her granddaughter Bridget. They'd been working on wedding plans for Bridget's upcoming marriage to Finn. "But she's right, dear." Maura called out. "There's no hurry. Just picking up Bridget's order for the bachelorette party she's catering at the pub tonight, but we're early. Vickie is in a roaring hurry today."

Vickie Pendergast muttered something they couldn't hear, but Lucy was pretty sure it rhymed with *witch*.

Cecile leaned farther into the workroom, barely whispering as she pointed between Connie and Lucy. "I want to hear more about this later."

Connie grabbed Lucy's hand as she stepped away.

"For the record, I'm fine. The new meds seem to be working, actually. I was just trying to make a point."

"I… I'm glad you're doing well. But you scared me." She patted Connie's shoulder. "And you also gave me something to think about. But I'd still like you to think about…" She glanced at Cecile, and noticed Vickie's silver-blond hair right behind her. Connie had mentioned Vickie could be a busybody. "About what we discussed."

Cecile and Vickie both gave her a curious look when she walked out to the front of the shop, but she just flashed them a cheerful grin as if she hadn't just been drinking cognac with her boss in the middle of the afternoon.

As if she hadn't just floated the idea of becoming a partner in Rendezvous Blooms.

CHAPTER SIXTEEN

"TIMBER!"

Luke Rutledge called out as a huge limb from a maple tree along the side of the vineyard came down with a crash. Logan Taggart was on the far side of Luke, where he'd been holding a rope to keep the limb from falling on the rows of grapevines. Luke nudged Owen's arm, then called up to the guy in the tree, who'd turned off his chain saw and let it swing from the strap over his shoulder.

"As long as you're up there, let's get that other low-hanging limb out of there. Can you reach it?"

"Hell yeah, I can reach it. Let me just adjust my harness hookup." Burly and bearded, Zayne Taggart easily maneuvered himself to the other side of the tree, bracing one foot on the stump of the limb he'd just cut, and fastening his safety strap around a larger one above him. On the ground he moved with a noticeable limp, but you'd never know it watching him up in that tree. Owen looked at Luke and shook his head with a laugh.

"Your brother is a beast!"

"Tell me about it. He's unstoppable." Luke looked down the treeline. "That storm last winter damaged a lot of our trees. I'm glad we're getting them trimmed. Thanks for helping. I don't imagine you have much experience with winter storms."

He waited as Zayne made quick work of the other tree

limb with the chain saw. "Guess again, pal. I've seen my share of snow." Just thinking about it made his body tense.

Logan walked over after watching Zayne come down the ladder and out of the tree. "Give me a break. I've lived in the South, man, and what you call snow is not what *we* call snow."

"Yeah? *You* ever been to Kabul in January, or up in the Hindu Kush mountains when the temps are below zero *before* the winds starts howling and the avalanches start breaking free?" He didn't realize how much his voice had raised until he stopped for a breath. He jammed his fingers through his hair, turning away from the men who'd been nothing but generous with him the past few weeks. A hand rested on his shoulder. It was Logan.

"That was stupid of me. I don't know how I forgot that you'd served over there."

"Yeah." Luke's voice was filled with regret. "Sorry, Owen."

Owen nodded. "It's okay." He blew out a long breath, trying to slow his adrenaline. He'd been so focused on fixing things with Lucy that sometimes he forgot about what happened over there. It was always a jolt when the memories hit.

Zayne moved in front of him, leaning over and looking up, waiting for Owen to open his eyes. The other man stared hard at him, frowning. Then he straightened with a sorrowful shake of his head.

"I know we just met pal, but you are *not* okay."

He stood tall and did his best to smile. "I'm good. It's not a happy memory, that's all."

"When did you get out?" Zayne didn't look like he'd served. There was a certain way military people carried themselves, and this guy didn't have it. But he did have that limp.

"I was out in March. You?"

"Never got the chance. Car accident messed up my leg when I was young. But I volunteer at the VA clinic up in Auburn. I drive veterans to their appointments and help them get settled and fill out their forms and stuff. I got to know a lot of the guys. And women." He shifted his weight. "Especially the ones going to group therapy. They tell me it helps to talk."

There was a beat of silence among the four men. Luke finally gave his brother a shove. "How many times have I told you to employ that filter of yours?" He turned to Owen. "Zayne spent ten years or so as a hermit, and his social skills are rusty."

Owen held his hand up. "It's cool. I got the message." He looked at Zayne, who didn't look at all sorry. Owen respected that. "You're not the first one to suggest therapy, but I don't think it's for me."

Zayne shrugged. "I didn't think it was for me, either, but hey... I'm not a hermit anymore, and I haven't had a drink in five years, so it seems like maybe it worked."

"I thought you said you weren't a vet?"

"I'm not. But my doc has a private practice as well as working the clinic. He's the one who suggested volunteering to get me out my own head and thinking about other people." He pulled off his leather work gloves and fished his wallet out of his pocket. He handed Owen a card. "If you change your mind, Dr. Curtis is good at helping you sort through those memories. Especially the not happy ones."

Instead of smacking at his brother, Luke pulled him

into a bear hug. "I don't tell you often enough how proud I am of you."

Logan caught Owen's eye, looking bemused. "I'm pretty sure I heard something about drinking wine after we played lumberjack."

Luke and Zayne stepped apart, but it was clear that there was a lot going on between them still. Owen clapped his hands, eager to move past all this unexpected emotioning.

"I hope there's some beer in this place. Wine is really not my thing."

Luke clasped his hands to his chest dramatically. "You do realize you're in *wine country* here, right? That you're standing in a vineyard? At a winery?" He turned to head down the hill. "And yes, I have beer. My pal has a micro-brewery between here and Watkins Glen, and I always have some in the cooler."

The men headed down to the winery…a Victorian miniature of the main house on the opposite side of the parking lot. Before they went inside, Owen glanced back up the hill, toward where he and Lucy had lunched before strolling into the trees. Where they'd kissed. Now *that* was a happy memory he didn't mind hanging on to.

Zayne stopped at the door, looking back at Owen. "You good, man?"

Surely that kiss had changed things between him and Lucy. Surely she'd give him a chance now.

"Yeah, I'm good."

Lucy stood on the sidewalk just past Piper and Logan's pink house and looked at the very similar home right next door. Same lacy gingerbread trim. Same covered front porch. Same long, narrow footprint, with a garage behind the house. Instead of the cotton candy pink of the Taggart house with all its heart-shaped trim, this house was many shades of yellow and gold. The trim around the windows was almost orange. She rolled her eyes. Who was she kidding—it *was* orange. There weren't any hearts in sight, but there were wooden designs under the upstairs windows that were shaped like tulips.

"What do you think?" Piper stepped off her front porch, carrying two bottles of water. It was hot and humid that afternoon, and there were storms in the forecast later that week. She handed one bottle to Lucy. "It's cute, right?"

"Cute is one word for it." Lucy shielded her face with one hand. "Sunny would be another."

"The Three Sisters are famous in Rendezvous Falls!" Piper laughed, gesturing toward the third house, which was shades of mint green, with leaf-shaped details.

"Three Sisters?"

"Iris told me that back in the 1800s, the guy who had the inn built wanted to build housing for his staff. He only got as far as these three houses. The floor plans are almost identical. People started calling them the Three Sisters, with the inn as the momma." She shook a key ring in front of her. "Wanna take a look inside?"

"You really think I can afford to rent a whole house?" They walked past the For Sale sign and up to the porch and Piper unlocked the door.

"The owners have about a dozen of these vacation rentals between the Glen and Lake Ontario. They're trying to sell some of them, including the yellow Sister. But in the meantime, they don't mind doing rentals." She stepped inside and Lucy followed. "Especially when they think you might be a buyer…"

"What? I can't afford to buy a *house*. I don't even think I can afford to *rent* one."

"I didn't promise them anything. I just told them you were a friend who was thinking of moving here. They loved the idea of a nice single lady, whom I vouched for, renting long-term, instead of having revolving vacationers in and out every week while the place is on the market." Piper pulled open the heavy drapes on the trio of large front windows. "Besides, even with your friends-and-family discount at the inn, the monthly rent here will be less than our nightly room rate. And it's fully furnished!" She swung her arm around at the living room, and Lucy started to laugh.

"Yeah…like a funeral parlor." It wasn't ugly, just very… Victorian. A large tufted sofa sat in front of the windows, upholstered in burgundy velvet. The walls were sage green, and the curtains were dark gold brocade, with tasseled ropes holding them back. There were a few wingback chairs and ornate little marble-top tables. The wall opposite the sofa was covered with portraits of Victorian men and women— some were photographs and some were painted.

Piper grimaced. "I know. They went a little overboard with the Rendezvous Falls historical theme. But the kitchen is fully updated—it's fancier than mine next door. And when I say the place is fully furnished, I mean dishes, cookware, linens…the works. There's even a cute little deck out back with a wrought-iron table and chairs. I could walk over and have an evening glass of wine with you."

They walked down the short hall to the kitchen, which really was lovely. Antiqued ivory cupboards, marble countertops, a large island as well as a cozy breakfast table for two by the side window. The upstairs was more Victorian frilliness, but functional and cozy, with three bedrooms and one bathroom. Lucy raised a brow at that.

"Yeah…luckily my house had been remodeled before I bought it, so I have a small master bath plus the other bathroom. But you do have a half bath downstairs, so no one has to come up here except you and—" she gave her a wink "—anyone else you want to invite."

There would be no invitations offered to the upstairs bedrooms. Or to the house, for that matter. The place was nice enough—and cheap enough—to make a comfortable home base while she was figuring out her next step in Rendezvous Falls. But she had no plans for entertaining guests. Especially the guest Piper was referring to. Now that a few days had passed, that wild kiss in the woods seemed more and more like a mistake. She'd been just as willing a participant as Owen had been, but that didn't mean it was a good idea. It just made things more confusing, and she was confused enough these days.

She told Piper she'd take the house, and Piper gave a little squeal of happiness.

"We'll be neighbors!"

Piper went downstairs to call the home's owners as Lucy continued to explore. The house would save her some money, and would also give her some distance from Owen. Less temptation. Having her own place to escape to would help set boundaries. And that's just what she needed.

The truth was, she thought about Owen all the time. She looked forward to seeing him, which was a mistake. His time in Rendezvous Falls was almost up. And she wasn't going to go home with him. It wasn't fair to let him think she might. So…a little distance was good for both of them.

FOUR DAYS LATER, she was moved in. It wasn't like it took much effort—just bundle up her clothes and walk down the sidewalk and into the sunny yellow house. The middle Sister. With all the curtains and shades opened, the place had less of a funeral home vibe in the daylight. The cooking supplies, dishes and glasses were a mismatched hodgepodge, but she'd never been one to care about that stuff anyway. The owners promised the Realtor would provide twenty-four-hours' notice if a potential buyer wanted to come through, and she'd have at least thirty days to vacate if it sold. They were happy the place wasn't sitting empty, and she had a haven all to herself. It was a win-win.

Telling Owen the day before hadn't been easy. It's not like she needed his permission, but she knew he might read a dozen different things into her moving into an entire *house* here in Rendezvous Falls. It was a big step…in the opposite direction of where Owen wanted her to go. He'd taken it well after his initial surprise. He'd simply blinked a few times, and repeated the words "a house?" a few times, then he'd shrugged, as if trying to appear casual about it. And failing.

"If that's what you want, then I support your decision."

That felt odd, coming from him. She'd appreciated the sentiment, but the sentence seemed rehearsed or something. Almost robotic, and definitely said without enthusiasm. Or sincerity. But he hadn't said anymore about it. In fact, he'd offered to help her move, but she'd declined as gently as possible. She didn't want him getting the wrong idea about them. She didn't want to risk lowering her defenses. It would only hurt them both to start something, then have him leave.

Then he'd surprised her by taking her hand in his. "I called a VA clinic not too far from here. I'm going to try a group thing…talking…with guys who've seen what I've seen. Like you suggested. See? I'm listening. I'm *trying*."

She'd pulled her hand back, but not before giving his fingers a tender squeeze. He'd called the VA. He *was* trying. She'd almost kissed him right then. The man still owned a big part of her heart. Hell…he owned all of it.

"I'm really glad to hear that. But I still need to figure *me* out before I figure *us* out. Does that make sense?"

He'd agreed, reluctantly. He'd made sure she knew she could call him if she needed anything repaired at the house, but she reminded him she had a landlord for that. He'd watched from the porch of the Taggart Inn when she'd started her yellow Volkswagen and pulled out of her parking spot with a wave to drive a few hundred feet to the yellow house that was waiting for her.

She put a pot of water on the stove. That was another advantage of living somewhere other than a bed-and-breakfast. She could cook her own food. Well…she glanced at the jar of prepared pasta sauce on the counter. She could *heat up* her own food, at least. Cooking had never been her strong suit, although Grandma had tried her best to teach her. Lucy was better at baking things than cooking meals. And even then, it was hit or miss. Her phone buzzed on the counter. She poured the pasta into the boiling water and grabbed it. *Mom.*

She'd reached a tentative truce with her father, who'd repeatedly reassured Lucy that he was doing *just fine*, but Mom had been much more challenging. One day she'd call trying to play loving mother and friend, and then the next she'd be accusing Lucy of being childish for "overreacting" and leaving. She could have let the call go to voice mail. But if she was really going to embrace this new and improved Lucy, she had to start facing challenges instead of running from them. She grabbed the phone just before the third ringtone ended.

"Hey, Mom."

"Hi, sweetie!" Maybe today would be a good call. Mom's voice was all singsong and cheery. "Kris told me you rented a *house* there in New York. She says you're staying there for good, but I told her that was ridiculous. First, you'd have told me something like that. And second, you'd never go Yankee on us…right?"

Or maybe it wouldn't be such a great call after all.

"Mom, I tried to tell you about the house the other day, but you hung up on me, remember?"

There was a pause. "I didn't hang up on you. I said goodbye first, so it wasn't a hangup. You were just asking so many questions about Jeff, and I didn't want to talk about it."

Lucy sighed, stirring the pasta. "You don't want to talk about the guy you left my father for? A couple weeks ago you couldn't wait to talk about the guy."

"He's part of my life, but I know that upsets you, Lucy. But don't worry, your dad and I are being very civil about everything."

"Mom, I love you both, and I'm doing my best to keep my distance, but *God*, you're leaving Dad for another man. So yeah… I have questions." She put the phone on speaker and set it on the counter while she searched for the colander she knew she'd seen somewhere. Ah, there it was. She set it in the sink and took the pot off the stove, speaking louder so her mother would hear her. "And yes, I rented a house. I'm cooking myself dinner in it right now. And yes, I might just become a Yankee on you, Momma. Because what y'all got going on down there is more than I can handle right now."

She leaned away from the steam rising from the water she'd poured out.

"Lucy Higgins, you can handle more than you think. You've always been stronger than me." Mom's voice softened. "This isn't a conversation for a phone call. Come home and talk to me in person." Another pause. "Honey, I miss having you around to talk to. Come home and we'll sit on my little balcony and drink wine together."

"Your little balcony?"

"Oh…uh…yeah. I have an apartment now."

Kris had told her their mother was going to leave the house—and their father—to move into an apartment. With her lover.

"You mean…*we* have an apartment. You're with Jeff, right?"

"Yes."

She poured the pasta back in the pan and added the sauce she'd heated in the microwave. She scooped some into a bowl, taking phone and bowl to the little kitchen table.

"Mom, I'm just sitting down to eat…"

"It sounds like I'm not the only one setting up house with someone. I saw Vivian Locke yesterday at the grocery store." Vivian was Owen's aunt. Her daughter, Kelli, had been one of her bridesmaids. Lucy barely knew either of the women. It had been Faye Cooper who'd insisted on Kelli being in the wedding. Her mother went on. "She told me Owen *still* hasn't come home. His mother is having an absolute fit about it. Is he still in New York? Is that why you bought a house?"

"I didn't buy a house, I'm renting it. And Owen has nothing to do with it. He sure as hell isn't living here."

"He *left* New York? Where'd he go?"

"He's still in town. I agreed to give him a month, but it's almost up. And when it is, he'll be back in Greensboro, running the family business." She thought that was what she wanted. But it made her feel unexpectedly sad.

"Is that man still trying to win your heart? And you haven't caved yet? Not even a little?" Lucy thought of that wild kiss in the woods.

"Not even a little." *Liar.* "Mom, my dinner's getting cold."

Another pause.

"If you're tempted…even just a little…to love Owen…" Her mother's voice cracked. "Don't let him get away. A chance at happiness…"

"Are you saying you were never happy with Dad? With us?"

"Oh, honey. Of course I was. I love you and Kris with all my heart—you're my world."

"And Dad?"

Silence. Then her mother let out a sigh big enough to sound like a gust of wind across the phone.

"We were…friends…when we married. High school sweethearts, but not the kind where we got all starry-eyed and knew we were soul mates. We were pals. We hung out in the same circles. I was a cheerleader. He played football. It made sense for us to date each other, and everyone seemed to expect it. We were homecoming king and queen. So… we got married after we graduated. And we started a family together. We made a life. We had some fun." Lucy knew the story, of course, but had always viewed it through rosier glasses than what her mother was describing.

"You never loved him?" She pushed the bowl of pasta away, no longer hungry.

"I… I loved him, but not that Hollywood movie sort of love, you know? I cared about him. He was a terrific guy. He *is* a terrific guy. It sounds cliché but we just grew

apart. We were roommates more than lovers, and that's
not a good thing for a marriage. But we had you girls and
we both loved you and wanted the best for you. Always."

"And then Krissie got sick."

"That was hard. We were a gret team, so it brought us
together that way. But your dad and I became…business
partners. We managed the business of Kris's treatment
and recovery, and we never bothered to break out of that
setup once she was better. Whatever personal connection
we'd had between us had disappeared. We resented each
other. We started living separate lives. Your dad played
poker with the guys, and I… I started talking to Jeff at
work, and then over coffee, and then over dinner. He was
someone to talk to, and your father wasn't there for me."
She rushed over her next words, as if she knew Lucy was
about to have something to say about it. "And it wasn't
your father's fault. But…it wasn't all mine, either." She
hesitated. "We should have divorced years ago. We knew
it was over, but we stayed together because it was easier.
For you girls. And for us, because we didn't have to deal
with the logistics of selling the house and making new
starts. We were lazy, I guess. Cowardly. But none of it
was malicious."

Her father kept insisting the same thing when he called.
He didn't hate her mother. He even understood why she'd
found someone else. In fact, Dad had found a new…*friend*,
too. As much as it stung as a daughter, her parents had a
right to be happy.

"I know you heard us arguing," her mom continued, "but
honestly…that didn't happen very often. The wedding had
everyone on edge, and we were confronting the finality of
a thirty-five-year marriage in the middle of it all, and we

just…snapped. What you clearly didn't hear was that we apologized to each other a few minutes later. You father and I don't hate each other. We just don't love each other, and we *deserve* a chance to be loved by someone. Your father deserves that as much as I do. And you deserve it, too."

"Mom…" Lucy was surprised to feel damp tears on her cheeks. She'd been clinging to her anger at her parents so tightly that she'd never taken the time to see them as people who wanted…who *deserved*…to be loved.

"I'm just going to say one more thing before I go." Mom sounded as if she was crying, too. "If I'd taken off on your father before our wedding day, he would *not* have chased me across the country to bring me home. If Owen is sincere in wanting you—so much so that he's defied his family and stayed away from his job for almost a month now—then you have to at least think about your feelings for him. If you don't love him anymore, fine. But if you're punishing *him* for the mistakes your father and I made, or what Owen's mother did to your wedding, or for whatever Owen went through in the military…" A pause. "Try to see things clearly before you do something you'll regret. You've always been a puzzle to me. Equally responsible *and* impulsive. Don't let your impulsive side push away the love of your life."

"But what if he wants me to go to Greensboro to be his *partner* in life, like you and dad? Or what if he gives up his parents' plans for him and then ends up regretting it? Resenting me?"

"Well, that's what you need to figure out. But you can't figure anything out if you're not letting the man in."

CHAPTER SEVENTEEN

"I'M HITTING A WALL, man." Owen pulled a bag of mulch from the back of his Bronco, and Logan Taggart was right behind him, taking the last bag and following Logan to the front of Connie's house.

Logan watched him slice open a bag. "Seriously? It's only noon."

"No, I don't mean that kind of wall." He spread the mulch and Logan grabbed the nearby rake and started spreading it. Over the past three weeks, he'd pulled out a lot of overgrown shrubbery and trimmed the ones that were left. He'd added new hydrangea plants on either side of the wide stairs leading to the front porch of the lake-side cottage. It was Victorian, but on a smaller and simpler scale than the big houses in town. There was gingerbread trim, but only in the corners of the porch and at the peak of the roof. Even the colors were more subtle than the so-called Painted Ladies of Rendezvous Falls. The house was a soft gray, with ivory and dark blue trim. Now that the foundation landscaping was back under control, the whole place looked neat and tidy.

"Then what wall did you hit?"

"With Lucy."

Logan grunted. "Her moving out of the inn this week didn't help your cause any, did it?"

"Nope." They were both raking now, spreading the

mulch evenly under the shrubs. He missed his breakfasts with Lucy. Missed bumping into her in the lobby, or sitting with her on the porch in the evenings. It was hard to follow Dr. Find-Love's tip to *stay in her orbit* when her orbit had moved down the road. She clearly wanted space, and he wanted to give it to her, but still. "I told my folks I'd be here a month, and that's almost up. I managed to get us from enemies to friends, but that next step just isn't happening."

Logan leaned on his rake and stared at Owen. The guy had spent years working on oil rigs, and he looked every massive inch like an oil rig worker. He tipped his head to the side. "Do you *want* to go back to Greensboro? I've seen at least three people walk over here this week and give you their numbers for landscaping work after seeing what you did with Connie's place."

"I already have a job waiting there. My dad wants to retire." He hadn't really heard his dad complaining about that as much as his mother had. "The plan has always been for me to take over when I was out of the Army."

"Who's been doing the work while you were *in* the Army?" Logan started picking up the empty mulch bags. They'd had a truckload of loose mulch delivered earlier in the week, but it hadn't been quite enough, so Owen had enlisted Logan's help to finish up.

"My cousin. And my parents, of course. But Lori's been doing a great job. She's the one who had the vision to expand into selling plants and trees and flowers and produce…it's a whole different company than when I left it."

"And do you want the job of running this whole new business that your cousin's already running?"

"Nope." He straightened, surprised at himself for saying that out loud. "I mean…uh…sure. It's just going to be an adjustment, you know? I'm more of a hands-on guy." He gestured at the work they were doing. "I like the actual work of landscaping. And hardscaping, too. I enjoyed building patios and retaining walls and stuff like that. Selling magnolia trees for other people to plant? Not so much. Same with tomato plants. I don't know a beef-steak from a plum. It's not my thing." He shrugged. "But I guess it's going to be."

"Even if you end up doing it without Lucy?"

Shit.

"I don't want that to happen. But like I said, I've hit a wall with her. She wants time, and it's the one thing I'm running out of."

"What does Dr. Find-Love say? Maybe it's time for another grand gesture…although she already has a car now, thanks to you."

"And the car almost backfired on me…no pun in-tended."

Logan laughed. "Intended or not, that was funny. How do you figure?"

"She was uncomfortable with me going behind her back, not to mention secretly involving you and your sis-ter."

"But she liked the car, right?"

He nodded as he helped clean up. Yeah, she'd liked it. She'd told him on their picnic lunch that Buttercup drove like a brand-new car now, and that her grandmother would have loved it. Especially the daisy wheels.

Logan picked up the rakes and shovels off the lawn.

"And she liked the picnic. I saw you two go strolling into the woods afterward."

Owen nodded again. The picnic had led to a scorching hot kiss. He'd thought he'd made a real breakthrough, until she told him it was a mistake and moved out of the inn.

"So... Dr. Find-Love worked," Logan said. "What's next?"

Owen rolled his eyes, but he pulled his phone out of his pocket and opened the app. He scrolled down the list, looking for something he hadn't tried.

When all else fails, puppies and kittens almost always work! No woman can resist a baby animal. Soften her heart with a small ball of fluff that signifies unconditional love.

He turned the phone so Logan could see the photo of an adorable puppy and the accompanying tip. Logan really started laughing then.

"All I can say is my wife was *not* impressed when her former in-laws gave a puppy to the kids for Christmas. She was a cute ball of fluff, but she was also a terror that peed and pooped on everything for a month. Piper adores Rosie now, but as a puppy? You don't have enough time in town to get past that housebreaking curve." Logan looked thoughtful for a minute. "But a kitten could work. Lily's been begging us for a cat, and the Martins up on Hill Road near the winery have a litter of them. I know this because Lily heard about it from the Martins' granddaughter at church camp, and Lily mentions it to Piper and I at least five times a day."

Owen sat on the back of the Bronco and brushed mulch and dirt from his sneakers. "Are you seriously suggesting I give Lucy a kitten?"

"Hey—something cute and fluffu was Dr. Find-Love's idea, not mine. But...you could call it a housewarming gift." Logan pulled his own phone out and pulled up a picture. "And they are pretty damn cute. Unfortunately for Piper and I, the Martins' granddaughter has her own phone...she's eight...and has been sending kitten pictures to all the kids at church camp. She has a bright future as a marketing genius."

The photo was of several balls of golden fluff with round eyes and long hair. Damn. They really were cute. And if *he* thought so, Lucy might think so, too. A kitten just might be a way to open that door of opportunity a bit more while he still had a week or so to win her heart. He ignored Logan's laughter as he got the phone number and directions to the Martins' farm, just a mile or so beyond Falls Legend Winery.

By three o'clock, he'd showered, changed and driven to the farm. There was a For Sale sign at the end of the long driveway, and the elderly couple explained they were moving to Florida to escape the New York winters. The home was more farmhouse style than Victorian, although they had painted it bright blue with white shutters and trim, so it was still cheery. There was an enormous old red barn behind the house, and a tall metal pole barn beside that. Mr. Martin used to be a long-distance truck driver, and had built the pole barn to house his truck. It was a nice setup, but he could see how it was probably too much for them to maintain any longer.

The kittens were so freakin' cute that he was tempted to scoop up all six of them, but four were spoken for already. Besides, handing Lucy an entire basket full of kittens to care for didn't seem like a very good idea. So he'd selected the smallest because she had the most interesting features, with four white socks and white tips to her ears and tail. As if her extremities had been dipped in white frosting.

And now she was mewing inside the soft-sided carrier he'd picked up at the pet store, along with dishes, kitten food and a litter box. He wasn't just giving Lucy a kitten, he was giving her a kitten kit. He glanced at the cat carrier on his passenger seat. This was a bold move that could backfire. But a kitten would give Lucy some company in that house she'd rented. And every time she looked at the cute cat, she'd think of him. *That was pretty brilliant.*

He parked in front of Rendezvous Blooms and grabbed the carrier. The supplies could wait. Maybe he'd even get an invitation to deliver them to her house personally tonight. This kitten was the best idea ever.

She looked up when the bell rang over his head. She was behind the counter, and he stayed on the opposite side of the display shelves, wanting to hide the surprise. Lucy's eyes widened.

"She rubbed her nose, but she had a small smile on her face. "Doing deliveries for Connie again?"

"Not today. Connie hired Mack Dennis's son from the hardware store to cover whenever Greg couldn't do it."

She rubbed her nose again, and coughed, frowning as she answered. "You're sounding like a local, Owen. You know all the news." She sneezed. "Excuse me!"

"Bless you." He waited as she pulled tissues out of the box under the counter. "Summer cold?"

She shook her head, sneezing again and blowing her nose. "I was fine this morning." She sneezed again, then rubbed her hand on her chest absently. "What brings you in?"

"I haven't seen you much this week, and wanted to see how you were doing. How's the house?"

"It's…it's fine." She sneezed twice in rapid sequence, swallowing hard before continuing. "It's nice to have the space and privacy and…" Another sneeze. "The ability to cook for myself and operate on my own schedule."

Connie walked out front from the workroom, with Cecile Manning close behind.

"Is that you having a sneezing fit out here?" Connie asked Lucy.

"Yes…" She sneezed again. Owen realized this might be the perfect time to spring the kitten on her. With an audience of two cooing older women who would surely love the kitten, Lucy wouldn't be able to resist. The women talked while he set the carrier down and pulled out the kitten, who was wide-eyed and clinging to his hand with needle-sharp claws.

"Are you feverish? Your face is red…" Connie put her hand on Lucy's forehead. Lucy coughed, her hand at the base of her throat.

Cecile frowned. "It's not red, it's blotchy. Like hives…"

Owen stepped around the display unit, holding the golden kitten in the air like it was the Lion King. "Surprise!"

Cecile gave a big grin. "Oh my God, look at that adorable little thing!"

Yes. This was just the enthusiasm he'd hoped for from the ladies. Lucy was coughing again, and waving her hand back and forth. Waving at the kitten? At him? Waving them away? He brought the kitten to his chest and focused—really focused—on Lucy. She sneezed again, and her eyes were puffy and red. Had she been crying earlier and he hadn't noticed? She took a deep breath, and he heard a wheezing sound. He stepped closer, holding the kitten with one hand as he reached out with the other.

"Lucy? What…"

"Get back! Get away!" Lucy cried, swatting the air between them as her tears fell. He took another step, instinctively wanting to help. It was Connie who finally put the clues together.

"It's the cat! Get out of here with that thing!" Connie put her hands on Lucy's shoulders, her voice leveling. "Come in back, away from that damn cat and your idiot fiancé"

Owen groaned. Allergies. Lucy had allergies. He *knew* that. He just didn't know one of them was *cats*. What in the hell had he done?

Connie rushed Lucy into the backroom and out of sight. He was going to follow, but Cecile disabused him of that thought in a hurry, stepping in front of him. There was accusation in every word she spoke.

"You knew she was allergic and you brought her a kitten?" Cecile was usually a bubbly bastion of pink. She'd told Owen she was on his side, but that didn't seem to be the case right now. "What kind of person *does* that? Did you think you could make her ill and then rescue her somehow? What sick kind of trick are you pulling?"

"I didn't know!" he shouted. "I knew she had some allergies, but I didn't know she was allergic to cats. Is she okay?"

There was silence from the back. Had she passed out? Was she still breathing? Cecile glared at him, then walked to the doorway and checked. Her shoulders eased, and her anger faded when she came back.

"Looks like she's fine. Connie's got her sitting by the

open door." She looked at the kitten he was still clutching to his chest and her expression softened. "You didn't kill *Lucy*, but I'm a little concerned about that cat."

"The cat's fine." But he relaxed his grip anyway, and the kitten mewed its thanks.

"The cat needs to leave. And frankly, I think you do, too."

He put the carrier on the counter as Cecile watched, and slid the protesting cat inside. Looked like he was going to have to check the Taggart Inn's policy toward pets. He headed for the door, but Cecile stopped him.

"You *really* didn't know Lucy was allergic to cats?"

He searched his memory, trying to think if the subject had ever come up. "If she ever told me, I don't remember it. I know she has mild asthma, but… It's not my fault if she never told me, right?"

Cecile looked both sympathetic and sad. "The fact that you were about to marry that girl and don't know basic information like severe allergies makes me wonder what else you two don't know about each other."

He rubbed the back of his neck in frustration. He didn't know how to answer the question. Through the doorway, he could see Lucy and Connie sitting by the back door, which was propped open. Lucy's face wasn't as red anymore. Her body looked relaxed. Or maybe exhausted was a better word for it. But she wasn't in distress anymore. He called out to her.

"I'm so sorry, Luce! I didn't know…"

Connie glared at him, and even from one room away, he felt her scorn. "Stop thinking of yourself and get that damn cat out of here!"

Lucy met his gaze, but her emotions were harder to

read than Connie's. She didn't speak, just stared. Not with anger, but...disappointment? Connie cleared her throat pointedly, and Owen turned to go, cat carrier in hand.

He could have handled Lucy's anger better than the resignation he saw in her face. His time was almost up, and he'd made a huge blunder. Maybe Dr. Find-Love wasn't all that wise after all.

CONNIE GOT LUCY settled at the worktable with a bottle of water and some cookies from the box Helen Russo had delivered the other day. Frankly, Connie needed the cookies as much as Lucy. The girl had scared her half to death. Helen was the best cookie baker in Rendezvous Falls... probably the whole Seneca Valley for that matter. This box was a mix of Italian sweets, including some pastry cookies folded over a rich chocolate filling. It was good enough to move Lucy out of her melancholy. She held the cookie up after one bite.

"Whoa. This is amazing. I need this recipe."

Cecile joined them with a chuckle, grabbing a cookie for herself.

"Someone's feeling better?"

Lucy nodded. "Yes, thanks. The fresh air helped. Sorry for scaring you."

Cecile waved her off. "Please. My Charlie is allergic to shellfish, so I know all about it. If I'd thought you needed an EpiPen, I had one in my bag."

Lucy took another cookie. "I don't have a lot of allergies, but cats are the worst. Dogs aren't quite as bad, but cat dander just slays me." She sat back in her chair, the corner of her mouth lifting. "That thing *was* adorable, though."

"The kitten or Owen?" Cecile asked.

Before Connie could scold her, the bell rang out front. Lucy started to stand, but Connie put her hand on her shoulder and shook her head. They'd have to air out the front of the shop before she'd trust Lucy out there.

"You sit and relax. I've got it." She fixed a hard look on Cecile. "And *you* stop talking about how cute Owen was. The man almost killed her."

"Not exactly…" Lucy started, but Connie walked out front to take care of her customer. She stopped abruptly when she saw the younger couple walking through the shop, pointing at Lucy's latest window display—a large cardboard cutout of the sun behind rustic metal pails filled with miniature sunflowers, with a few full-size sunflower blossoms she'd picked up from a farm near Geneva. The display created so much interest that a photo of it had landed on the front page of the local weekly paper.

But this pair wasn't here to admire the window display. Her son and daughter-in-law turned at the same time and spotted her. David's face lit up with a warm smile. His wife? Not so much. Typical. Ever since Connies husband left, she had the distinct feeling her daughter-in-law, Susan, was firmly on his side of things. She loved telling Connie how great Dan's Florida place was—the one he shared with Sandy. The one big enough for Susan and David to visit every winter for a free vacay.

"Mom!" David came over and kissed her cheek. "I saw a picture of your window on my social media timeline, and I told Susan we had to come down and see it for ourselves." He looked from Connie to Susan. "I thought we'd surprise you and maybe take you out to an early dinner."

Susan spoke up behind him. "Unless you have other plans, of course. We know this is last minute."

In other words, Susan had no desire for the three of them to dine together. And if going to dinner with them would annoy Susan…

"I'd *love* that, David. What a lovely surprise. Let me just tell Lucy…she can close for me."

"Lucy? Oh, is that the part-time girl you hired?" David tried to look into the back.

"She's not a girl, and she's no longer part-time. She's the one who did the famous window. She's thinking about becoming my partner in the business." The shock on her son's face was worth the tiny white lie. The partnership idea was Lucy's, not hers, but David didn't need to know that. . Connie hadn't been thrilled at the idea originally, but its appeal was growing. Especially when she saw the disapproval in Susan's eyes.

"Partner? When did *that* happen? I thought we'd agreed that you were selling the shop and moving to Syracuse."

"I never agreed to any such thing."

"Mom…your Parkinson's…you know you can't keep the business… or the house…"

Cecile came into the shop from the workroom. She'd been listening, of course. Cecile gave Connie a bright smile and a conspiratorial wink before answering for her.

"Hi, David! Hi, Sue!" Connie bit back a laugh. Cecile knew darn well that Susan hated being called Sue. "Did you know that lots of people have Parkinson's *and* manage to still do their jobs? Your mother's latest medication mix has her feeling great. And with her new…partner—" Cecile gave Connie some amused side-eye "—her workload and stress are both reduced, which helps with the disease progression. Isn't that right, Connie?"

"Not that I need a spokesperson…" She raised her eyebrows at her friend. "But yes, it's true. I'm feeling better. I'm not sure if I can credit the meds or having help in the shop, but I'm definitely better."

"Mom, you know Parkinson's can come and go. You might just be having a little remission now, but eventually…"

"And when exactly is *eventually*, son? Is it next year? Or is it ten years from now? You don't know how much time I have to live independently any more than I do." She pulled her shoulders back, silently thankful that she barely had any tremor in her hand that afternoon. "Do you want me dreading the future, or living it day by day for as long as I can?"

"I… Mom…of course I want you to be happy. I just… worry."

Susan coughed softly from behind him. "But can she still maintain that house all by herself?"

To Connie's surprise, David beat everyone else to the punch. "Susan, knock it off. Everyone knows you like the lake house, but I'm not going to let you force my mother out of it. Has it ever occurred to you that we'd get invited to enjoy it a lot more often if you'd lay off the constant hints?" He turned back to Connie without giving his wife a chance to answer. "And Mom, *you* need to ease up, too, and accept some help. I've offered to trim up the trees for you and mow the lawn, and you always say no."

Cecile crossed her arms. "*Really?*"

"Oh shush, you." Connie glared at her, which, as usual, didn't faze Cecile one bit. It was true that she'd turned down David's offer to help more than once, but only because she figured there was some other motive behind it.

It was possible…just maybe…that she'd been wrong.

She looked at her son, and silently forgave him for reminding her so much of his father. Her emotions had been in knots since Dan left, and she'd pushed David away in the process.

Susan stepped up next to David. "I'm confused." She pointed at her husband. "Don't yell at me—I'm being honest. I thought the plan was for Connie to move closer to us? And yes, we'd keep the lake house for weekends, but I'm not suggesting we steal it out from under her." She looked at Connie, and there was a surprising hint of warmth in her eyes. "If I got ahead of myself, I'm sorry. I do that sometimes. I'm just…tasky. If there's a goal, I'll figure out a plan to get there."

Connie had always known how driven her daughter-in-law was. Susan was a high level executive at a major pharmaceutical company.

David smiled at his wife and shrugged. "I thought moving was what was best for Mom." He glanced at Connie. "You were so depressed after Dad left, Mom. Then you got sick, and…well…you *are* getting older. It would be nice to have you a little closer to us if something happens, but only if that's what you want." He looked at Cecile. "You have people here who support you."

Susan took a deep breath, and Connie could almost hear the wheels grinding to a halt and changing direction.

"I mention the house so much because I miss it."

Susan's confession surprised Connie. "It's still right where it always was."

David gave her a sad smile. "When's the last time we were invited, Mom?"

Cecile muttered "Oh, touché" from near the counter. Lucy had come out of the workroom and was standing with her.

Connie stammered for a moment. "I...well...you're family. You're always welcome."

"You hate drop-in guests, Mom. Family or not." David chuckled. "I think what Susan is saying is that we used to have cookouts and go boating and spend whole weekends with you and Dad. And then..."

"Your dad left." And everything had stopped for Connie.

"Yeah. And I get why you shut down for a while, but... we miss the old days. And Dad doesn't need to be there for us to have fun."

Connie looked back and forth between her son and his wife. It seemed everyone had been making assumptions. "I thought... I thought you were on your father's side."

"There aren't any *sides*." David threw his hands up. "I want you both happy. He is. You're..." He paused. "I was going to say you're *not*, but you seem different. Like maybe you could be happy again."

"I think..." Connie shook her head in disbelief. "I think I could be. I also think it's time the three of us sat down and had an honest conversation. Like...over dinner?"

"I'd like that," David said with a smile.

"Good." She winked in Lucy's direction. "But first, let me introduce you to my new business partner..."

CHAPTER EIGHTEEN

"OWEN COOPER, GET IN HERE right this minute!"

Owen stopped in the hallway and dropped his chin to his chest. Iris Taggart had called out in her best don't-ignore-me-boy voice, which was intimidating enough. But he knew she wasn't sitting in the library alone. He'd seen her book club biddies arriving at the inn an hour ago, including Connie Phelps. After the Great Kitten Debacle yesterday at the shop, he had a feeling he was in for a lecture by a room full of old folks. It was one he probably deserved, but still...

"Don't make me come out to get you—I know you're hiding out there."

He stepped into the doorway, putting on his best Southern gentleman smile. And accent.

"Not hiding, Miss Iris. Just preparin' myself to face this room full of beauties..." He noticed Rick Thomas sitting in one of the armchairs near the fireplace. "And esteemed gentleman." Rick was a professor at the college. He mouthed the word *wow* at Owen, who did his best to ignore him as he continued. "What can I help y'all with today?"

Iris's eyes narrowed at him. She was seated in a tall wingback chair near the fireplace, looking every inch like a dowager queen. "First, you can lay off that Southern charm nonsense. I've seen you turn that accent off as eas-

ily as you turn it on." She gestured to an empty chair between her and…he thought the well-dressed woman with
perfectly arranged hair was named Vickie. Connie was
across the room, on a bench next to Helen Russo from the
Falls Legend Winery. Cecile was in the far corner, whispering something to Bridget McKinnon's grandmother,
Maura. Iris cleared her throat when he took the seat as
she requested. "I overheard something this morning that
I need you to clarify. Are you actually using some computer app-thingy to come up with these schemes to win
Lucy over?"

His eyes fell closed. She must have overheard him talking to Logan in the kitchen that morning, trying to figure
out how to recover from the kitten backfire.

"Uh…yes." He looked over at Connie and rushed to
apologize. "Please don't tell Lucy. It's just that I—"

"Thank the good Lord!" Iris exclaimed, sitting back
in relief.

"What?" Why would she be *happy* about him using that
stupid app that had caused so much trouble?

"For a while there I thought you were a complete and
total idiot. But at least now I know those crazy ideas
weren't actually *yours*."

A few of the women snickered, and Rick let out a snort
of laughter. Owen felt his face heating.

"I…um…thank you? I'm not sure if that's a compliment or…?"

Iris's mouth slanted into a grin. "Well, it may not be a
compliment, because trusting some computer wizardry to
fix a broken heart is *not* very bright, but…" She winked
at him, and he couldn't help thinking she must have been
a real knockout in her younger days with those silver-

blue eyes and sharp mind. "You've given me hope that you might take some *good* advice from *real* people. Assuming you want to actually get that woman back to the altar with you."

"I do."

Everyone chuckled at the wedding pun, including Owen. Maybe instead of a lecture, he was going to get some advice. Or maybe a little of both.

"I don't know you well enough to smack you across the back of the head, but if I did, I would." Iris shook her head. "What kind of doofus thinks some generic internet list is the way to go?"

"Dr. Find-Love has a four-star rating in the app store…"

Rick's head fell back as he started laughing loudly, wiping his eyes and wheezing as he started to speak. "I'm sorry, did you just say you paid someone called *Dr. Find-Love* actual money to win back the love of your life? No wonder you don't want Lucy to know." He straightened. "And they only had a four-star rating? Out of five? For something this important, that's…not great."

The professor had a point. "A friend put me onto the site."

Rick tried to calm his laughter. "And this friend found love using the app?"

Pete Lamphear was happily single. Owen let out a groan.

"In my defense, I was drunk and desperate at the time."

"And are you still drunk and desperate?" Rick's brow rose sharply.

Owen grinned. "I am not drunk."

Connie raised her hand with a laugh. "I can attest to the fact that he is very desperate!"

Laughter went around the room again. Helen's smile softened.

"I've seen the two of you together, and there's definitely something charming there. But there's a wall between you that needs to come down. And I don't think these big showy acts are going to do the trick."

"The problem is they all *feel* like tricks to Lucy." Connie leaned forward. "You're turning this into a game, and that's not what love is about. There can't be a winner and a loser. Your gestures are so superficial." He started to argue that the expense of refurbishing her car hadn't been superficial, but he thought better of it.

"And how could you *not* know she's allergic to *cats*?" Iris demanded. "Haven't you been engaged for years?"

"Well...yeah, but..." His shoulders fell. "I was deployed a few months after we met. And even when I came back, I was still full-time Army—going to training exercises and trying to get into the Rangers. Then Lucy's grandmother got sick, and I was going to deploy again, so she moved back to Boone to take care of her grandma. I asked her to marry me right before I left."

"In other words," Helen said, her voice gentle, "you've spent more time apart than you have together."

"Probably."

"Oh, Lord," Connie tsked. "No wonder you two are such a train wreck. You barely know each other."

"But I *love* her."

"Why?" Iris's question was so sharp he almost felt the word hit his skin.

"What do you mean, *why?* I just...do. That's all. I love her." He thought about that first week at the beach. "The minute we met... I knew she was something special. I haven't had a lot of unexpected things happen in my life—I grew up knowing my parents' expectations for me. I went into the Army and followed orders there, too. I'm a guy who follows the plan, you know?"

Owen looked around the room. He could swear that was pity he was seeing in the faces looking back at him. The kind of pity people had for a fool. He straightened.

"Lucy blew my plans out of the water. She was funny and sweet and sexy all rolled up in one woman. She didn't care about convention or expectations. She cared about *people*, of course. In fact, she cared about other people more than she cared about herself. And she made *me* care. When I was with Lucy, I wasn't thinking about the landscaping business I was going to run someday or the next tour of duty. She made me feel…lighter. More in the moment. Happier."

There was a moment of silence before Iris spoke.

"In other words, what you loved was the way she made *you* feel." The older woman fixed him with a warm, but firm, gaze. "That's a whole lot different than loving *her*. Maybe if you'd gotten to actually know Lucy, you wouldn't have been blindsided when she dumped you. You'd have known what she needed."

He blew out a long breath. "She tried to tell me. But my last tour was…rough. I had a lot of things on my mind. Stuff I had to deal with emotionally. I'm *still* dealing with it."

Maura McKinnon nodded. "That's why you left the Shamrock when the fireworks started."

"Yes. And Lucy knew that. She covered for me. Took care of me, because that's who she is." He let out a soft, humorless laugh. "She was paying attention, which is more than I can say. I just… I thought we'd have time to get to know each other after the wedding. I thought things would calm down once I found my role in the family business and then she and I would figure stuff out, you know? She'd taken on the wedding plans…until my mother hijacked them. But…the wedding was only one day in our lives. We'd have time to…"

Vickie held up her hand, her mouth a thin, flat line.

"Excuse me, but did you really just say your wedding was *only one day in your lives?* Your *wedding.* The day you commit to love someone for the rest of your life is just a day? No wonder she left you at the altar, you dolt."

Owen blinked a few times, trying to find a defense and failing.

"Vickie, dear," Rick started, smoothing the front of his linen shirt. "I know you have more experience at weddings than anyone else in the room, but considering you've been through three husbands, do you really think you should be the one lecturing on the sanctity of marriage?"

"Fuck off, Rick. I *buried* two of those husbands and you know it. Frankly, I *am* the expert on weddings here. And *none* of my ceremonies were 'just another day.'" She made air quotes with her fingers. "Each one was special, whether it was in the church, in my backyard, or up at the winery. Maura, Iris, Lena and Helen were at every one of them, and they'll tell you the same. They were *special,* damn it."

Lena Fox, who'd been silent this whole time, rose to her feet with grace, lifting her large leather bag and setting the row of gold bangles jangling on her wrist. "I need to get back to the studio. But I have to say, I think we're sidetracking the real issue here." She turned to Owen.

"The real issue isn't that you're an idiot. It's that you're a coward."

Oh, hell no. His head started shaking immediately. "I can assure you, ma'am, I am not a coward. I fought battles that—"

"I don't give a damn about that." She seemed to catch herself, her tone softening. "I mean, of course I appreciate your service and sacrifice, and I'm sure you were a fine, brave soldier. But when it comes to life…" She tipped her head to the side, as if considering her next words carefully. "When it comes to life, you'd rather wait and hope your problems go away instead of dealing with them. You're a self-absorbed coward, Owen Cooper."

His jaw was still tight with anger, but there was a soft whisper in his head suggesting she might be right.

"How do you figure that?"

Lena was tall and attractive—Piper mentioned she'd won a modeling contest for seniors and he could believe it. Especially when she struck a pose with one lean leg in front of the other, a long-fingered hand resting on her hip, and the other gesturing in his direction.

"You talk about your parents' plan for your life, but I haven't heard you once mention *your* plan for your life. But I *have* heard you talk a lot about waiting until *after* something happens. After the Army. After the wedding. After you take over the family business—which you don't sound very keen on. You're a *someday* person. You're a Scarlett O'Hara. You'll think about your problems *tomorrah*." The others laughed when Lena held the back of hand to her forehead dramatically and drawled the last word in a thick Southern accent, mimicking the famous movie scene. She narrowed her eyes on Owen. "Scarlett said that after the only man who'd ever loved her had walked away. And you're just as ridiculous as she was. You're avoiding anything that might make you uncomfortable…"

"Right now," Owen chuckled, "this whole conversation is making me uncomfortable."

"Good." Lena stepped closer. "I like Lucy. She deserves a man who cares about *her* more than he cares about how *he* feels when he's around her. A man who doesn't expect her to wait until he's ready to deal with what she needs. Is that man you?"

He swallowed hard. "It…it can be… I mean…it *is*. Yes, damn it. It is. I love her."

She raised her chin. "Then prove it. Prove it to *Lucy*. Instead of all this gamesmanship, just show her you're the man she deserves. Right now. Not later." She turned toward the door, tossing the last line over her shoulder. "And for God's sake, get to *know* the woman. At the very least, know her allergies so you don't kill her."

LUCY WAS JUST finishing up the shop's only wedding order for the week when Connie and Cecile came back into the shop. She'd enjoyed having a few quiet hours to create the *something special* the bride had requested. The opulent combination of white roses, hydrangeas and lilies, with palm fronds to give a fresh green contrast, would probably do the trick. She peeked over the top of the massive centerpiece for the bridal table and raised a brow at Connie's expression.

"If I didn't know better, I'd say that was almost a smile, Miss Connie. What have you been up to?"

Connie didn't answer right away, but her cheeks went pink as she watched Lucy. That grin kept teasing the corners of her mouth. Like someone with a secret. Cecile started giggling and Connie shushed her.

"Cecile dragged me to a book club meeting, and it was…" Oh, yeah, that was definitely a smile. "It was surprisingly entertaining."

"Wow, that must have been some book. You ladies aren't reading Shades of Fifty or whatever, are you?"

Cecile rolled her eyes. "That book is ten years old, and painfully inaccurate about BDSM."

"I…um…didn't realize that…" Lucy was dying to know how *Cecile* knew that. Connie said once that there was more to her best friend than ruffles and curls. "So what book *were* you reading?"

They struck a matching pose, with mouths open and deer-in-the-headlights expressions. Lucy put her hand on her hip. "If I didn't know better, I'd swear you two have been up to no good. Is this one of those so-called book clubs that's more about drinking wine that actually reading anything?"

Cecile straightened. "Oh, we usually have a book to discuss, but sometimes we get sidetracked. Sometimes we have…surprise guests."

"Really? Who?" Was there an author living in Rendezvous Falls?

Connie swatted at Cecile, who started to stammer.

"Ow! Uh…no one! Nope. No guests today." She held up a warning finger at Connie, who was threatening to smack her again. "We just got distracted with…local gossip." Cecile stepped closer to the table. "Look at those flowers! Who are they for? Anyone I know? Is it a wedding? Show me what else you've done…"

Lucy knew a subject change when she saw one, but she

decided to let the women keep their secret. As long as it
didn't involve her, they could have their fun. She opened
the cooler and pulled out the bridal bouquet, which was
primarily hydrangeas in white and blush pink. Her boss
and the boss's best friend approved enthusiastically, and
she put everything back in the cooler until morning.

Cecile pulled out a seat at the worktable, and Connie
joined her—after pulling out her "secret" bottle of wine
from the far corner of the cooler. Lucy had discovered
it her first week as she was rearranging the storage. She
lifted what should have been an empty flower bucket and
discovered a bottle of chardonnay inside. Without saying
a word, Lucy took three plastic glasses from the shelf and
joined them.

Connie poured. "Did Owen find a home for that kitten?"

Lucy grimaced. "Yes, thank goodness. Piper's daughter
Lily had been begging for a pet, so Logan took the kitten
off Owen's hands. They have that big dog, of course, but
she sleeps with Ethan up in the attic bedroom. I guess Lily
has been complaining about it. I got a text this morning
saying Lily *adored* the kitten and has already named her
Snowball." She shrugged. "Perfect name for a golden kitten, right? It means I'll need to take a big dose of antihis-
tamines if I visit my neighbor, but I'm happy that adorable
little ball of fluffy allergens found a good home."

Cecile's head tipped slightly. "Did you ever tell Owen
how allergic you were?"

She had to think for a moment. "I'm sure I did at some
point, but I don't know if we ever had a specific conversation about pets and allergies. If he'd ever said he wanted
a dog or cat, I would have made it very clear that we had

to be careful. But I don't remember him wanting animals of any kind."

"What *did* you talk about? Ow!" Cecile leaned away from the smack Connie had given her. "What? I'm just wondering how these two almost got married and know so little about each other after years together. And yes…" She glared at Connie. "I know it's none of my business, but I'm curious. If Lucy doesn't want to answer me, that's her choice."

"The key words there," Connie huffed, "are 'none of your business.'"

"It's okay, Connie." Lucy held up her hand. "It's a fair question. I think Owen and I made a lot of assumptions about each other. He spent a lot of time deployed or away for training, I ended up busy caring for my grandmother. I think we both mentally filled in the blanks for all those mundane questions." She took a sip of her wine, thinking perhaps she should lock up the shop if they were going to drink. "Then we got to our wedding day and realized we didn't know each other very well."

"You mean *you* realized it." Connie lifted one shoulder. "It sounds like Owen was oblivious to everything."

"But he said he lo…oof!" Cecile reacted to what seemed to have been a hard kick under the table from Connie. These two were acting awfully shady. Cecile straightened, reaching up to fluff her bright blond curls. "I mean…you *must* have loved each other, right?"

Lucy stared at the table, its surface crisscrossed with years of cutting marks and stains. "We fell for each other fast and hard. In a weird way, being forced to be apart so much was a bit of a thrill. We were always looking forward to seeing each other again—we were in a constant state of anticipation." She smiled, tracing her fingers along one long scratch on the table. "But now I wonder if that was just me being in love with the anticipation."

That didn't ring true, even as she said it. She'd loved Owen's quiet calm in contrast to her frenetic energy. He settled her with all of his confident planning and his devotion to familial and military duty. He'd been her rock, saving her when she felt like she was ping-ponging between jobs and towns and dreams. She'd loved him. She *still* loved him, but what difference did it make when he'd be going back to Greensboro in a week?

"And the sexy times were good?" Cecile asked, this time avoiding Connie's swat with a fast duck to the side. "Hey, if the sex is good, you can build off that as a foundation. Charlie and I started as what they call *friends with benefits*, and look where we are now—happily married for almost forty years and madly in love. And let me tell you, the sexy times are *still* good. Never better, as a matter of fact."

Lucy's face was hot, and she couldn't stop the embarrassed laugh that bubbled up. Maybe all those opinions the woman had about BDSM romance novels were based on personal experience? It was hard to believe, with Cecile's overall pastel fluffiness. And it was definitely something Lucy didn't want to try imagining.

"Oh, for God's sake, woman." Connie drained her glass. "Everyone knows you and Charlie are horny toads. You don't need to fill poor Lucy's brain with that image."

"But...*were* your sexy times good?" Cecile persisted.

"Yeah. The sexy times were good. Really good." Lucy giggled. "Our first time was in the back of that old Bronco of his. Parked on the beach with nothing but the moon and stars over us. And every time we got together after a separation of any sort…even if it was just a week." She sat back with a sigh. "We came together and…pow. Fireworks and big brass bands. Every damn time."

Cecile's smile softened. She reached over and put her hand on Lucy's.

"Brass bands every time? Yeah, that's something to build on, for sure. Big brass band sex doesn't come around often, and you don't want to give that up, honey."

"I can't marry a man just because the sex is good. Marriage has to be more than that," she spoke to herself as much as to the two women with her. "Then again, what do I know about marriage? I thought my parents were happily married, and look at them. Lying. Cheating. For *years*. And I had no clue."

That was another sentence that didn't quite ring true. If she was honest with herself, she'd known things weren't as they seemed on the surface with her parents. She just hadn't poked at it, not wanting to admit the Higgins family might not be the true love ideal she'd wanted it to be. But then again, as a family, they'd been good. She grew up in a loving home, even if her parents' attention was often on her big sister more than her. She'd still never wanted for anything. They didn't understand her love of flower arranging, but other than insisting she have a backup plan with that accounting degree, they'd been supportive of the choices she'd made. She frowned. It was less confusing when she'd been flat-out angry with them. Time was softening her anger and making her see she may have been too hasty the night before her wedding.

But no. The problems were real, even if her response was…drastic. Her dream wedding had turned into a nightmare. She'd felt powerless. Just as she'd felt powerless when trying to get Owen to support her. Just as she'd felt powerless when she overheard her parents discussing divorce. Or when Owen had taken that extension of duty without even discussing it with her. And she was tired of feeling powerless in her own life. Her spine stiffened. She was *done* being powerless. But was any of that Owen's fault?

"Do you miss being in Owen's arms?" Cecile's words echoed Lucy's thoughts. She *did* miss him. His touch still had the ability to send shivers of desire across her skin. That afternoon kiss at the falls had proven that their chemistry was alive and well. She nodded in answer to the question.

"I do. When I left, I felt cornered. Like I had to fight or…lose myself." She sighed. "But yes. I miss his touch. I miss the man he was before his last tour. I've seen glimpses of that man here in Rendezvous Falls, but… even if he does manage to fix things between us…what then? He's not going to leave the family business and move *here?* Of course not. He made them a promise, and if there's one thing I know, Owen is a man who honors his promises."

Cecile leaned forward. "But what if he did stay here?"

Lucy's pulse jumped. But no. "He'd never forgive me for forcing him to make that choice."

Now it was Connie's turn to sigh. Loudly. And with a fair measure of disgust.

"You two are a hot mess. You deserve each other." Connie pointed a finger at Lucy across the table. "You're both chicken. And foolish. Here I've been angry with him for bringing you that damn cat, but I bet you don't know *his* allergies either. Have the two of you ever done anything other than screw in the back of his Bronco?"

"Easy, girl." Cecile patted Connie's shoulder with an amused grin.

"Bah! What I mean is—have you ever sat and made plans *together*? How do you know what he'd resent or not? Don't you two ever talk?" She turned to glare at Cecile again. "You see? This is what happens when you base a relationship on big brass bands. They've never talked about what comes *after* the band marches off the field!"

Lucy gripped the edge of the table and stood. She was pretty sure the annoyance she felt was because Connie had struck perilously close to the truth.

"Okay, this conversation about my sex life and brass bands is over, ladies. All you're doing is reinforcing the fact that I made the right decision. I almost married a guy who makes my toes curl when he kisses me, but doesn't know my allergies. If I'm going to marry someone, it should be someone who knows *everything* about me."

Cecile finished her wine with a shrug, fixing Lucy with a steady gaze as she lowered the glass. "A medical bracelet can tell him your allergies, honey. But it damn sure won't keep you warm at night. My vote is for marrying the guy who makes your toes curl."

CHAPTER NINETEEN

OWEN GRABBED CHINESE takeout from a little place near the college campus and walked back to the inn. The restaurant didn't look like much—a tiny storefront with faded gingham curtains strung on twine, and a flickering neon sign identifying it as "Hunan City Chinese Takeout." It reminded him of the divey little joints and food trucks clustered near the base in North Carolina, catering to soldiers too lazy—or too broke—to cook for themselves or go to a *real* restaurant. It had been hit-or-miss around Fort Bragg. Some had decent food—that Mexican food truck had better food than any restaurant he'd been to. But the Chinese place there had been…less than great.

Hunan's, on the other hand, had proved to be a pleasant surprise. The takeout was served steaming hot and the wonton soup was delicious. He started with that when he got back to his room, setting up his Saturday meal on the side table near the window as usual. Once in a while he joined the Taggarts for a meal if invited, but most nights had found him either at this table or sitting on a bench near the lake, eating his dinner from a paper bag. His mother would have been horrified.

He opened the bag of crab rangoons and groaned when the tempting scent filled the room. Piping hot and crispy… damn, he could make a meal of these alone. But he knew the sesame chicken would be just as good, so he opened that, too. There was a rumble off in the distance. It was loud enough to make him freeze for a second until he identified it as thunder. He'd heard there was rain in the forecast. Thunder wasn't his favorite thing, but it didn't bother him as much as it bothered some of the other guys he'd served with. Once he knew what it was, he could dismiss it as something natural, therefore not to be feared. Certainly not worth letting his food get cold.

He'd spoken with his mother again that morning. It hadn't gone well. As usual on their weekly calls, she'd launched into a laundry list of reasons why he needed to come home right away. His month was almost up, He was wasting his time "chasing" Lucy. He was shirking his duties at the business. He was letting his father down. He was embarrassing his mother. Making the family a laughingstock. Acting like a moon-eyed teenager. Being irresponsible. Blah, blah, blah.

Usually he just let her rattle on without saying much, but he'd run out of patience. He snapped at her to please stop talking. Her stunned silence on the line almost made him laugh. Shocking Mom was a new skill set for him, and it was kind of fun. He filled the silence with a pointed question.

"Did you ever listen to Lucy when she told you what kind of wedding she wanted?"

"Why?" Mom's voice had turned suddenly cautious. "What did she tell you?"

"Never mind that. Answer the question."

There was a hesitation, then her voice hardened.

"If you're referring to her nonsense about wanting some hippie wedding on a mountaintop, the answer is no. Of course I didn't listen. You were coming home from military service to take over Cooper Landscaping and be the public face of our company. I wasn't about to let you traipse off to some barefoot woo-woo ceremony with ten people in attendance. I explained to Lucy that it wouldn't be appropriate, and she was fine with it."

"She dumped me the day of the wedding, Mom. I think it's a safe bet that she was *not* fine with it. And it's also a safe bet that you knew that."

"Knew what? That she'd humiliate us all? Of course not! If she had any objections to my plans, she should have said so."

Had Lucy given in because his mother had suggested her dream wedding in the mountains would be bad for *him*? He was beginning to understand what Lucy meant when she said she'd spent her whole life doing what was good for *other* people. He'd ended the call with a terse acknowledgment that yes, he knew he was almost through the four weeks they'd agreed to. And guess what? He might need a couple more. He'd hung up before waiting for her response.

Connie's book club friends were right. He'd been coasting along, not paying any real attention to what Lucy needed. He'd been focused on his own needs. And that's exactly what Lucy had been focused on, too. Damn it to hell—he was such an idiot.

...show her you're the man she deserves...

What Lucy deserved was a man who knew—who *cared*—about every tiny detail about her. He took the last bite of sesame chicken. And he was going to be that man. No crazy grandstanding this time. No more Dr. Find-Love. Straight from the heart.

It had grown dark outside the window, with occasional

flickers of lightning. His ears were well-trained in determining direction, and this was coming from the north. Moving fast down the valley toward town. A sharper clap of thunder echoed over the lake, and the wind started moving the trees in the backyard of the inn. Looked like Rendezvous Falls was about to get a summer storm. Being from North Carolina, he knew all about summer storms—they happened on a near-daily basis in the sultry months of July and August.

Owen grinned as he piled his food containers into a plastic bag to dispose of them. He may not know as much as he should about Lucy, but she was a North Carolina girl. Storms wouldn't phase her, either. He headed to the door as raindrops began to hit the windows. Just because he liked eating in the quiet of his room didn't mean he wanted it to smell like a fast-food joint when he woke up in the morning. He always took his containers down the hall to the kitchen trash can when he was finished. Logan was coming out of the kitchen as he approached.

"Late night snack attack?" Owen nodded toward the tray Logan carried, which was loaded with chocolate chip cookies. Logan chuckled.

"Not for me. The women up in room 8 got the munchies, and my wife was foolish enough to tell them to text her if they needed *anything*. And they did. At nine o'clock at night."

"I didn't know you had room service in this place."

"We don't." Logan put a hand on his chest. "That's why *I'm* delivering their order instead of Piper. She's too much of a softie. I'll set them straight that this is a one-time thing. Nicely, of course."

Owen chuckled. "Of course."

Thunder boomed outside, and a hard gust of wind rattled the windows. The hallway lights flickered. Both men hesitated, waiting to see if they'd stay on, and they did. For about a minute. Then they flickered again, and Logan swore under his breath. Off. On. Off. Then they stayed off. Darkness and silence fell over the inn. And on the entire town, judging from the lack of light from outside.

Owen automatically reached for the phone in his pocket, punching up the flashlight. Logan set the plate on a sideboard and did the same, but his phone rang before he could go anywhere.

"Piper? Everything okay at the house?" Logan walked to the front lobby, guided by an emergency light over the door. "No lights anywhere outside. Looks like the whole town is out. From the way it flickered, I'm guessing a tree limb hit a wire somewhere. Or maybe a whole freakin' tree." There was a pause, and Owen let out a long sigh. "Yes, I know there are LED lanterns in the closets in all the rooms… Yes, I'll knock on doors and make sure everyone finds them and is okay… Ethan's checking on Gran? Perfect…no, you stay there if Lily's asleep. I'll put lanterns, cookies and some bottled ice tea and water in the dining room if anyone wants to come downstairs… Yes, I know where everything is… Piper, I got this… Love you, too."

By the time Logan ended the call, Owen was the one swearing under his breath. His friend's brows rose. "What's wrong with you?"

"Lucy. She's afraid of the dark. Like…*really* afraid. Got any extra lights?"

"Are you kidding?" Logan clapped his hand on Owen's shoulder. "My wife makes plans for her plans, and then plans for twenty contingencies after that. There's a couple lanterns behind the reception desk. Take them both, because she has at least a dozen more stored in the laundry room."

Owen grabbed the lanterns, pulling the top up on one to turn it on. He waved to Logan and dashed out the front door. He couldn't remember *why* Lucy hated the dark, but he knew she did. Their conversation in the parking lot at the falls on the Fourth confirmed it was still true. And right now she was alone in a strange house in a blackout. He took the steps two at a time to her front porch, opened the wooden screen door and knocked more sharply than intended.

"Who's there?" Lucy's voice had a high, frightened pitch to it. He'd probably just scared the daylights out of her. *Smooth move, Cooper.*

"It's Owen. Are you okay?"

The door swung open, and he was immediately blinded by a bright flashlight aimed straight at his face. He held his hand up to shield his eyes.

"Jesus! Get that out of my face, will ya?"

"Oh…sorry." She was breathless, turning her head away "What are you doing here?"

"Checking on you…damn it!" The light shone in his eyes again, but not before he realized what the source was. "Are you wearing that headlamp I gave you?"

"Shit…" The beam of light moved to their feet. "Yes. I keep forgetting and trying to look at your face." She didn't move to let him in, keeping her head down. "Are those lanterns?"

"I thought you might want some light. I forgot I gave you the headlamp. Good thinking."

A gust of wind shook the screen door, but the storm was moving off to the south just as quickly as it had arrived. The rain was letting up, but not until after he'd gotten a good soaking running to her place. He pushed wet hair off his forehead, and the movement caught her attention. Which meant she looked up...blinding him again in the process. He muttered and reached out, grabbing the headlamp off her head.

"Okay, clearly you do not know how to operate this thing in public." He handed her the lit lantern and opened the second one. "These might be a little more guest friendly."

She laughed, finally moving aside and gesturing for him to come in. "They're a little more Lucy friendly, too. The headlamp light moved so fast when I moved around that I kept seeing creepy shadows that looked like *they* were moving." She set her lantern on an end table, sending soft light around the small living room at the front of the house. "That was right about the time you tried to break my door down like a soldier on a search mission. You almost gave me a heart attack."

"Sorry about that. I'd run all the way here and let the adrenaline get to me."

She tipped her head to the side, a smile playing at the corners of her mouth. "You ran over just to check on me? And bring me light?"

He was going to say something brilliant like *it's no big deal* or that he'd *do that for anyone*. But he thought better of it. As his mother had made clear that morning, he didn't have a lot of time to fix things, and he'd set his progress back substantially with that damn kitten. Time to put it all on the table. He stepped closer, taking her hand in his.

"There are *some* things I know about you, Lucy Higgins. And one of them is that you're afraid of the dark. So yes, I brought you light." He tugged her closer, and she didn't resist. "I also know you still think we're through... even after that kiss at the falls. But I'm not giving up on us. Not until you *really* give me a chance." He cupped her cheek with his hand. Did she just quiver at his touch? A flicker of hope lit in his heart. "So...tell me what I need to know—what I need to *do*—to get you to trust me. Give me a chance. Give *us* a chance."

The only sound was the softening shush of wind through the trees outside, and the distant roll of thunder. Everything outside the circle of light cast by the lanterns was pitch-dark. She didn't move, but he could sense she wanted to. Maybe that was just him seeing what he was wishing for, but he could almost feel her struggling.

What was the right move for him now? Scoop her up in his arms and kiss her, like some Hollywood hero would do? That's probably what Dr. Find-Love would advise, especially since he already had her face cupped in the classic Hollywood pre-kiss move. Instead of pulling her in, though, he took his hand from her cheek and rested it lightly on her shoulder.

The old ladies told him to use his heart, not his head. Not Dr. Find-Love. And his heart was telling him to wait. Be patient...let her deal with her struggle on her own terms, not his. No games. No pressure. He'd stated his case. The next move was up to her. She stared up at him, her forehead furrowed in confusion.

"That's it? No more begging? No more grandstanding?"

"Not unless that's what you want from me."

"No. Definitely not." She chuckled, her hand still in his. She squeezed his fingers. "But I can't help imagining myself answering your request by filling out a spreadsheet so you'll know all about me."

He'd just started to answer when there was a large thump outside, as if something had hit the back of the house, and the sound of breaking glass. Owen looked over his shoulder and down the dark hallway in the direction the sound came from. Lucy…well… Lucy leaped into his arms with so much force she knocked him backward a few steps. While screaming. He gripped her around the waist, laughing in surprise as he turned toward the hall, swinging her with him. He really had no choice, since her arms were locked around his neck.

"What the hell was that?" Her words came in a rush. "No! Don't go down the hall without a light!"

He was reaching for his cell phone light, ready to tell her he figured a hallway was a straight, safe path, even in the dark. But he stopped when he heard the pure panic in her voice.

"Hey…" He rubbed her back with his hand to sooth her. "Relax, babe. Everything is okay." He moved away from the hall, toward the table where the lantern sat. "It was probably just a tree branch or something coming loose from the storm. You stay here and…"

"No! Don't leave me alone." She buried her head in his neck and he froze. He was holding Lucy Higgins in his arms again. He brushed her hair with his mouth, knowing he couldn't take advantage of her fear. No matter how tempting.

"Babe, it's okay. Open your eyes. The lantern's on. You're not in the dark. But I need to go check what happened. If that was a window that broke, the rain will get in." She hesitated, then her grip slowly loosened on his neck. He slowly set her feet on the floor. "You can stay right here where it's safe, or you can come with me and bring the lantern. Which is also safe. Your choice."

She stepped back, one hand firmly wrapped around his forearm. She blinked and looked around the softly lit room. "I can't stay here alone."

"Okay. You grab that lantern and I'll take this one. Plenty of light. Hold my hand…thatta girl. Where does this hall lead?"

"Um…to the kitchen, and then the staircase. Past that is the back door to the deck and yard."

"So pretty much a straight line. I'll lead the way." They moved down the hall, with Lucy so close she almost tripped him a few times. They passed a dining room on the left, then a spacious kitchen with ivory cabinets and marble counters. The lanterns cast weird shadows around them, especially as they moved past the open stairway leading up to what he assumed were the bedrooms. His fingers were losing circulation from her tight grip. They were going to have a good long talk after this. This was no average *I don't like the dark* sort of fear.

He held his lantern higher as they came to the back, looking for the sparkle of broken glass on the floor. He didn't see any, but it occurred to him at that moment that he didn't think Lucy was wearing shoes. A glance downward confirmed it. He stopped abruptly, and she bumped into him with a gasp.

"What is it? What do you see?"

"What I see is that you're barefoot, and there might be broken glass back here. Stay put, and let me check it out." She started to protest, but he shook his head firmly. "Not negotiable. Stand right there. We already know no one's in the house but us." He swung the lantern toward the windows, which were all intact and closed. "The door's locked. And seriously, Luce—you know I'd never ask you to do anything dangerous."

Lucy hesitated, then nodded…a bit reluctantly, but in agreement. "You're right. Of course. You're *right*. I'll stay here. Just…hurry, okay?"

He slid her hand off his arm and lifted it to his lips, kissing her fingertips. "I'll be right back."

As soon as he stepped outside to the deck, he saw the cause of all that noise. A large limb had fallen from the maple tree behind the house. It looked as if it had rested on the support for the pergola overhead at first, then fell to the decking, taking a section of railing with it. A narrow wrought-iron table had been knocked over, and something must have been on top of it. There was a planter broken at his feet, and shattered purple glass all over the deck. A mess, but nothing that couldn't be fixed. Other than the planter and the glass object, of course. He went back inside, locking the door behind him. True to her word, she hadn't moved. Her eyes were wide and dark. He slid his arm around her waist and turned her around, heading back toward the front of the house.

"A tree limb broke the railing and knocked over a metal table. Looked like there was a planter and something glass that broke when it fell."

"Aw… I'd just put some pansies in that planter. It was full of weeds when I moved in. The glass must have been the oil lamp I put out there. It didn't have any oil in it, though. I found it in a closet—I'm sure it was a reproduction. At least, I *hope* it was, since I'll have to replace it now. It was purple and matched the pansies so nicely. I used museum putty to anchor it to the table so it was safe from wind, but if the table went over..."

She was babbling, probably a result of the adrenaline rush she'd just had. As they got back to the living room, he turned her to face him.

"What happened in your head when we heard the glass break? Why are you so afraid of the dark?" He brushed her hair over her shoulder and tucked it behind her ear. The pink was almost gone now, except for the very tips. "I know you don't like the dark. But I never knew why, and after tonight, I think I need to."

She stepped back, leading him to the front of the house and the huge Victorian sofa by the front window. In the muted lantern light, he couldn't be sure of the color, but it was something dark. It was long and low, and the back was deeply tufted. He sat near the center of it, expecting a stiff horsehair cushion, but was surprised at how comfortable it was.

He looked around the room, taking in the heavily carved furniture and about a dozen old paintings and photographs filling one wall. Most were portraits of people in Victorian garb, with dark, heavy frames. There was a nice Persian rug on the floor, and heavy brocade curtains pulled back with golden tassels on the tall windows. Lucy liked things clean and simple. This room was *not* that.

"This place doesn't strike me as your style."

She gave a soft laugh. "It's definitely not. It was furnished as a vacation rental property. It's mostly reproduction stuff, like this sofa, with an occasional real antique thrown in for atmosphere. I'm pretty sure a lot of it came from garage sales." She looked at the lace-covered tea table in the corner. "Rendezvous Falls is famous for its Victorian houses, so they leaned heavily into that for the decor. But the kitchen is updated and nice, and the upstairs bathroom has a really cool claw-foot tub *and* a walk-in shower." She was still talking fast, but this time he had a hunch she was doing it to avoid his original question. Lucy noticed his expression and her words trailed off. "But you didn't ask for a history of the house's decor, did you?"

"Nope. I want to know how you got so scared of the dark." He looked at the artwork across from them. "Although I can understand why having all those grim faces looking at you could freak you out. This place isn't haunted, is it?"

She settled back on the sofa, looking at the portraits with a shudder. "Don't joke about ghosts! But no, I don't have the sense there are spirits wandering the rooms here." She paused, glancing around nervously. "At least, I don't *think* there are. But one never knows. And that's the problem, isn't it? I don't *know* for sure what's here. Especially with the lights out."

"Are you saying you're genuinely afraid of ghosts?" He had a hard time believing she was afraid of anything, but...*ghosts*?

"Well... I *believe* in ghosts. Not that I've ever seen one." She shook a finger playfully at the portrait wall, talking to the pictures. "And I don't *want* to see one, either!" Her other hand was still in his, and she squeezed his fingers. "It all started with my horrid cousin Barbara."

"Have I met her?" He'd met plenty of the extended Higgins family, but the name didn't ring a bell.

"Hopefully you never will," Lucy said firmly. "She's actually a second cousin once removed or something. Her father was my dad's cousin, I think. Anyway, she's a nasty piece of work. The last time I saw her—at Grandma's funeral—she hadn't changed. She's that worst sort of Southern belle, who smiles at you like you're her best friend while she gleefully stabs you in the back." Her voice had grown harder with each sentence, making her dislike crystal clear.

"O-kay. How did this evil Barbie make you afraid of the dark?"

Lucy barked out a laugh. "Oh, God, she *hates* to be called Barbie. Promise me if you ever do meet her that you'll call her that." Whether she'd intended to or not, she'd just suggested a future where he would still be a part of her life. That door was opening more all the time.

"I promise. Tell me what Barbie did."

She leaned toward him. She was close enough now that he could smell her perfume. It smelled like the flowers she loved so much, with just an edge of something spicy. He remembered a food truck he and Lucy went to in Wilmington. They sold cupcakes, including a dark chocolate version with a hint of jalapeño. Unexpected. Delicious. Just like Lucy. He waited, knowing she was trying to get her courage up. Or was she thinking of happier times, too?

She stared at him for a long, highly charged moment before she started the story. As much as he wanted to hear it, he was disappointed the brief, intimate moment had been broken.

"When Kris first got sick, Mom and Dad were constantly going back and forth to the hospital in Durham, and they stayed overnight a lot. I was eleven, and I got pawned off to friends and relatives who offered to watch me. Some were more enthusiastic about it than others. Barb's parents were nice enough, but she did *not* want me hogging her spotlight as the precious only child." One shoulder lifted slightly. "She was the ultimate mean girl. Had the adults all convinced she was an angel with her sweet smile and all those pretty dark curls and pouty lips. But she and her nasty little friends were nothing but bullies."

She stopped, her brows drawing together as she frowned at a memory. Without thinking, he released her hand and slid his arm around her shoulders. She didn't resist, moving closer yet before she continued the story.

"She had a thing for scary movies. Her parents didn't know that's what she was watching down in their basement." A shudder went through her. "Ugh...basements. Hers was one of the few houses I'd been in with a basement, and I've hated them ever since. Theirs was partially finished, but half of it, the part outside the so-called playroom, still had the original stone foundation and dirt floor. And cobwebs." She shuddered again. "Anyway... after Kris's first round of treatments, I ended up staying at Barb's house for a whole week. She made my life hell, all while putting her prettiest smile on for her parents. One night she and her minions had a movie night." She stared at the rug, lost in a childhood memory.

"Her folks thought we were watching Disney, so they went to a neighbor's for drinks. Barb showed *The Blair Witch Project*. You know, the movie that was shot in the dark woods, with that wobbly flashlight? I was already traumatized from the movie, and then they convinced me to play a so-called *game* afterward. We had to go into the old part of the basement and find clues or something. All I know is we all went in there with the lights on and started searching. But as soon as I was in the farthest corner, they ran out, locked the door and turned off the lights."

"Shit. How old were you again?"

"Eleven." She pressed her body to his side. The warmth and familiarity of having Lucy cuddled against him made tears burn unexpectedly in his eyes. He cleared his throat and focused on the horrific story she was telling.

"What happened?"

"Everything you'd expect. I couldn't see anything, so I bumped into boxes and tripped over things so much that I finally just froze, swinging my hands out in front of me and spinning around. I convinced myself that things were coming *at* me instead of me running into them, which was silly, but…"

"It wasn't silly for an eleven-year-old kid. How long did those bitch…little girls leave you in there?"

"It felt like hours, but it was probably ten or fifteen minutes. Maybe even less than that. They went upstairs to get soda and chips, and took their sweet time about it. Oh, and they stomped around whatever room was over my head, shaking dust down on me, screaming and generally sending me into a catatonic state. I ended up in a ball on the floor, crying my eyes out." She looked up at him. "I think a couple of the girls felt guilty when they found me like that. They cleaned me up and gave me cookies. Barbara just laughed." She put her head against his chest again with a sigh. Christ, no wonder she panicked in the dark.

"My dad stopped by to check on me the next afternoon, and I jumped into his arms and started bawling. I didn't tell him what happened—I never told anyone other than my sister, and that was years later. I just sobbed and wailed and begged him to take me home. Barb wasn't there, and her parents were so embarrassed. I think they were afraid Dad would think *they'd* done something wrong. I wasn't letting him leave that house without me, so he took me to Grandma's. He assumed it was the trauma of my big sister being so sick…and that may have added to my…vulnerability." She looked up again, a soft smile on her face. "And that's the story of why Lucy is afraid of the dark to this very day. Like I said…silly."

"And like *I* said, not silly for a little girl."

"I'm not a little girl anymore, though. I'm a grown woman."

"Yeah, you are. You're a kick-ass woman with one little chink in her armor thanks to some nasty cousins. But it's a very small chink…nothing that diminishes who you are. And now you won't have to add it to that spreadsheet. Now I know."

"Oh, God—I'd forgotten about the spreadsheet1 Dodged a bullet on that one." She smiled. "What else do you need to know?"

She reached up and brushed her fingers into his hair, barely touching his scalp. Setting off electrical currents that shot across his skin and ended somewhere below his belt. Her eyes went wide, as if she'd felt the same thing. Her pupils were already huge because it was so dark, and the effect made them look like mirrors. Or maybe like doors…ones he wanted to enter.

"Luce…" Her name came off his lips in a breath, the most natural—and most desperate—thing in the world at this moment. "I'd rather explore the things I *do* know. How you feel in my arms. How soft your lips are. How you moan when I kiss you."

She inhaled sharply, then did the exact thing he needed. She tightened her fingers in his hair and kissed him.

CHAPTER TWENTY

It wasn't a decision for Lucy. Kissing him was just…what needed to happen. What *she* needed. And sure enough, she let out a soft moan when their mouths met. His arm tightened around her, the other hand cupping the back of her head as he pushed his tongue inside her mouth. She moaned again. Was this a mistake? Maybe. Probably. But he'd come to her rescue. He hadn't laughed at her fear. He'd listened to her story—hell, he'd *asked* to hear it. Maybe he really was trying to change. Her tongue met his, pushing and turning. Maybe they both needed to sex away all their distractions.

She straddled his lap on the sofa, and this time he was the one who moaned. Or was that a growl? Owen's guttural sound of desperation flipped a switch inside her, and there were no more distractions. There was just Owen. And her. And the heat of desire enveloping them both. She rose up on her knees above him, holding his face between her hands and kissing him, pushing her tongue into mouth this time. His hands fell to his sides in surrender, letting her take the lead in whatever was happening. Their mouths moved in perfect rhythmwhile her hips rubbed up and down his body. He finally growled and grabbed her waist with both hands, pulling her down against the erection she could feel growing against the zipper of his shorts. He arched up against her as he held her, and the erection went rock hard. That little voice of doubt tried to whisper one more time…this is a mistake…

Shut up, voice.

This kiss was deep. Intense. Dizzying. And unstoppable. Their lips didn't part when she started tugging at his shirt, finally yanking it so hard the buttons went flying across the hardwood floor. Didn't part when she tugged at his belt, unbuttoning and unzipping his shorts. He froze for a heartbeat when she wrapped her hand around his now-exposed erection. Their mouths moved against each other again. More slowly now, but no less intense.

There was a momentary separation when he flipped her onto her back on the sofa, but he claimed her mouth again immediately. On top and in charge, his hands made quick work of her shorts and panties, working them down her legs until she could kick free of them. Somewhere along the way, he'd shed his clothes, too, including the now-buttonless shirt. His hands slid up under her top and cupped her breasts over her bra. She reached for him, eager for him to make love to her. To be inside of her. But he'd stopped moving. Her eyes flew open to meet his somber ones.

"I want you so bad right now my brain feels like it's melting, but I need to know we're on the same page. Before we go any further, are you sure this what you want?"

Her only answer was a groan that sounded a little like *well…duh* as she lifted her head to try to kiss him again. But he pulled up and away.

"Not another move until I hear words, Lucy. Tell me what you want. Not just what your body wants…*you*. Are we doing a heavy make-out session here, or…?"

Was he for real right now? She finally managed to form words, and they were tinged with laughter.

"We're both basically naked, so I think we passed *making out* a while ago."

His erection was heavy and warm on her abdomen, and she felt him twitch against her skin.

"Tell me what you want." His voice was like sandpaper across her heart, rough and exciting. But tender, too. He *was* for real with his question. He wanted to know her thoughts. Her needs. Just like that devil-guy in her favorite TV show, he wanted to know what she most desired.

And right there, lying on her back on a tufted sofa in a house cloaked in the dark of a blackout…she finally knew what she wanted. And her doubts had not only shut up— they'd vanished completely.

"What I want," she started, her voice low but steady, "is for you to make love to me, Owen Cooper." She smiled when his erection quivered on her belly again. "I want you to remind me why I ever climbed into the back of a Ford Bronco with you in the first place. You made me feel like a goddess that night. Make me feel that way again."

His head dropped and he kissed her hard and fast before speaking.

"And tomorrow?"

The question should have made her pause. It would have at any other time. But not tonight.

"Tomorrow is tomorrow's problem. You asked what I wanted, and I told you. Even if we decide there's not a lot of tomorrows for us, right now I want you to screw me into oblivion for one night." She kissed his jaw, tracing her tongue along the strong line of it and on down his neck. His whole body practically convulsed, making her feel powerful. Desired. And sassy. "Take it or leave it, big guy."

"Are you kidding? Hell yeah, I'll take it. Your wish is my command, madam." He took her hands from his shoulders and pressed them over her head on the sofa, rocking against her as he slowly lowered himself to settle between her legs, teasing her with a press against her wetness. He kissed her lips, slow and soft this time.

"Condom?"

She winced. They'd stopped using condoms years ago, secure in their commitment to each other. "I hate to say it, but…we'd better. I stopped taking my pills when I… you know."

"Left me? I get it. Luckily I'm prepared."

"Why are you prepared? Have you been…"

"Sleeping with anyone but my fiancée? No. Not a chance in hell, which I think you know."

She nodded. If there was one thing Owen was, it was true blue loyal. But still… He answered before she could press the issue.

"I bought them after that kiss at the picnic. Just in case. Hoping…and wanting to be ready if you had any concerns." He scooped his shorts up off the floor, pulling his wallet out before tossing his shorts again. "And since it was a nice new box, I grabbed more than one." He waved the connected packets over her face, making her giggle.

"Hope springs eternal?"

"Always be prepared."

"Here, let me."

She took the condom and slowly rolled it onto him, feeling a little thrill at the way he trembled at her touch. Then he settled over her again. Touching her once. Twice.

Teasing. Entering a little, then out. She bit her lower lip in frustration. He did it again. And she bit *his* lower lip. A sexy laugh rumbled up from his chest. And then he was in her all the way. Like…*all* the way. She let out a cry and arched against him. He started moving, and she wrapped her arms around his neck, pulling him down until his sweating chest was against hers.

This. *This* was what she truly desired.

They moved together as one gasping, moaning, biting, kissing, scratching unit. She didn't know where she ended and where he began. And she didn't care. They just let go of everything and…moved. He growled her name and the sound made her close her eyes tightly as she dug her fingers into his back. She didn't need to see. Or speak. Or think. She just needed to feel. She surrendered all to him, basking in the sensations. The intensity built until he nipped her neck with his teeth, surprising her enough to open her eyes again.

"I want to see you when you go," he said, sounding winded. "Ready?"

"God, yes!"

They went together, each giving a cry at the same instant, tightening their holds on each other as he pumped a few more times and she lifted her hips to keep him there. At last, when there was no steam left—no *air* left—he collapsed on her.

"Damn, Lucy Higgins. You just destroyed me. *Destroyed.* I can't… I can't even think right now. I sure as *hell* can't move. Are you…?"

She patted the back of his head absently, struggling to focus. "Shhhh…"

His head lifted, and she opened one eye just enough to see his amusement. "Woman, did you just shush me?"

"You can sing my praises later, big boy. When I can think rationally and appreciate it. Right now, just shush and hold me."

"Yes, ma'am." His voice was huskier now, and he shifted to the side so her back was against the back of the sofa. It was wide enough to hold them comfortably, but definitely cozy. He pulled her against him, kissing her softly on the temple. "Go to sleep baby. I got you."

She wanted to answer him. Thank him. Say…something…that would describe her appreciation of what they'd just done. But between the warmth of his body and the heavy, sated feeling still glowing inside of her, all she could manage was a mumbled version of his name before everything went still and silent.

OWEN DIDN'T WANT to leave this dream. He was floating, warm and happy, on clouds of…something. If he thought about it too much, the dream would disappear. So he floated. And smiled.

Until someone smacked him hard on the shoulder. He tried to shrug it off, not wanting to leave the dream, but a voice started hissing in his ear.

"Owen! Wake up! Owen!" He finally opened his eyes. And damn, *this* dream was even better than the last. Lucy was naked in his arms, staring at him in…alarm. Well *that* wasn't good. He blinked a few times and shook his head.

"What?" It wasn't a brilliant response, but his brain hadn't quite kicked into gear yet.

"All the lights are on! The power's back!" She was hissing her words as if someone would overhear. But she was right. He hadn't even noticed that the lamps were on around the room, and the hallway light was glowing, too. Now he could see the walls in here were painted a sage green, and the tufted sofa they were on was dark red. Lucy's skin was alabaster tinged with pink. Her eyes were royal blue and…sharp. She was annoyed with him.

"So?" he said. "Turn the lights off and let's go back to sleep. Unless you'd rather…?" He waggled his eyebrows at her and she groaned, staring up at the ceiling as she counted backward from ten. He stopped her at six. "Okay, what am I not understanding here? What time is it?" It was still pitch-dark outside the big windows.

"It's quarter after eleven," she said, as if stating the obvious. "The lights are on. We're naked. And none of the drapes are closed. This house sits about twenty feet from the sidewalk. Anyone walking by can see right into the house!"

"Okay, okay. I'm catching up with you now." He looked over his shoulder to the floor, where their clothing was scattered. "No problem. I'm a soldier, remember?"

He reluctantly released her and slid off the cushion and onto the green-and-gold rug. She had a point—the tall old windows came down to about a foot off the floor. And damn if he could hear voices outside. Probably neighbors out to check storm damage now that the power—and the streetlights—was back on. He did his best belly crawl across the floor, tossing pieces of fabric over his shoulder toward the sofa as he went. Shirts. Shorts. Lace panties. He flopped onto his back like a fish and pulled on his own boxer briefs and shorts. That's when he noticed Lucy wasn't panicked anymore. She was laughing.

He laid his head back on the floor and watched as she

wiggled into her shorts while still on her back on the sofa. She playfully tucked her panties into her pocket. His sweet mountain girl was commando. Did that mean she was planning on shedding those shorts again soon? She held up his shirt, now minus most of its buttons thanks to her, and her cheeks reddened. Then she gave him a saucy look and pulled the shirt on, without wearing anything else on top. She pulled the shirttails together and tied them under her breasts. The neckline plunged open down to the knot. It was sexy as hell. He started going hard just looking at her. She noticed.

"None of that, mister." She sat up, then stood, turning off the light closest to the sofa. She tugged on one end of the tassel holding the front curtains, and the heavy drapes fell across that half of the windows. She did the same on the other side, then walked around taking care of windows and lights until the only light was coming from the hallway and they were in privacy once again. Her words… *none of that*…had taken care of his erection in record time. He'd known there was a chance tonight's sofa sex was an aberration, but he'd been hoping for another round somewhere more comfortable. Like her bed upstairs.

None of that.

He stood, heading for the door and grabbing the lanterns. She turned, her brow arching.

"I locked the door earlier."

"He nodded. "I know. Lock it again behind me, okay?" If the night was over, best for all concerned if he made a fast exit. Like yanking off a Band-Aid.

Lucy's face fell. "You're leaving?"

Why did she sound so surprised?

"I thought that's what you wanted. You said *none of that*, so…"

Relief filled her soft gaze. "I meant right at that moment. None of *that* with people outside, the lights on and windows open. I'm not an exhibitionist." She held out her hand, and he didn't hesitate to walk over and take it. "I didn't mean it couldn't happen somewhere else."

He followed her down the hall like an eager puppy. *Somewhere else* sounded promising. Hell, he'd take *anywhere* else if it meant he was staying the night. There were lights on in the kitchen, too. Owen smiled to himself—she'd made sure she wasn't in the dark in any room… until the power went off. Lucy stopped so quickly in front of him he almost ran into her. She looked back with an apologetic smile.

"Would it be a total mood killer if I said I was hungry?"

He put his hand on his bare chest. "It would shatter my manly pride, unless…" He winked at her. "Unless you told me it's because our lovemaking took so much energy out of you that you need to replenish."

She laughed. "That wouldn't be far from the truth. I only had a salad with tuna fish for dinner, and we *were* pretty…athletic."

"I could use a midnight snack myself." He kissed her forehead. "After all that athleticism."

"Grilled cheese sandwich?" She gestured for him to sit at the island, which was topped with an unusual oval-shaped slab of unpolished gray marble. He nodded and sat down.

"For all the froufrou frilliness of the living room, this kitchen is pretty modern."

Lucy was reaching for something in the refrigerator, and answered over her shoulder.

"I guess it's a vacation rental thing. People want all that fun atmosphere stuff everywhere else, but they'll pay more if there's a fancy kitchen." She took the cheese and butter to the counter and started putting the sandwiches together as the pan heated. "Would you like a slice of tomato in yours?"

"Sure." He spotted a wine rack and stood. "How about I pour some wine?"

"Glasses are in the cupboard right above the wine." The pan sizzled as she set the sandwiches in. "I've only been here a few days, but I like this house. Other than that wall of dead people portraits in the living room. They need to go."

"Are you allowed to redecorate?" He chose a red wine, but before he opened it, he turned to face her. "You like pinot noir, right?"

She grinned. "Yes. And to answer your first question, I don't think they'd want me redecorating while I'm renting, but it's for sale."

He started pouring. "What's for sale?"

"The house. The owners have put a few of their rental properties up for sale. Including this one." She flipped the sandwiches. "It's a great house, right?"

"Um…yeah. I guess." He didn't think much about it as he put the wine on the island and found some plates, setting them near the stove. He was too distracted by how good his shirt looked on his woman. "You know you've left me half-naked by stealing my shirt, right? I don't think any of your tops will fit me."

Her hesitation was so brief he wasn't sure he'd seen it.

She put the grilled sandwiches on the plates and handed him one, flashing a quick smile. "First, you look good half-naked. Second... I have an idea, but..." She gave him a hip bump as she walked past him with the food. "We don't have to worry about that until morning."

They sat and ate. They really had worked up an appetite. Or they both wanted to get to whatever was coming next. She was almost finished with the second half of her sandwich and sipping her wine before she spoke again.

"Oh, this wine is good." She sat back, swirling the dark liquid in her glass. "And one less thing for me to have to put on that spreadsheet. You know what wine I like. Maybe you know me better than either of us thought."

Owen's smile faded. "I don't know *enough*. I told you I'd do better, and I will. We have a lot of talking to do after tonight, don't we?"

"Yes, we do. And tonight doesn't..."

"Tonight is tonight. I get it." He knew one night wasn't going to set everything right between them. "At least now I know you didn't dump me because the sex was bad."

She barked out a laugh, almost choking on her last bite of grilled cheese. "No, I didn't. One more thing I don't have to put on that spreadsheet—you definitely know how to please me sexually. And tonight was exceptional."

"It was. And it's not over yet."

"Nope. Why don't we head upstairs. Where the beds are." She put their dishes in the sink, then surprised him by refilling the wineglasses and handing his to him before heading to the stairs.

Something was bugging him about all her spreadsheet talk. If she was ready to share, he knew he had to do the same. He tried to avoid being hypnotized by her butt moving back and forth ahead of him on the stairs. "You know, this whole learning about each other thing goes both ways—I'll have to do a spreadsheet for you, too."

"What don't I know about you?" She seemed genuinely surprised. And interested. His behavior on the Fourth of July had hinted at the darkness that enveloped his last overseas tour. But that was something that happened *to* him. Around him. He had a feeling he needed to share something deeper. He blurted out the first truth that came to mind.

"I stayed in the Army to avoid taking over the business."

Lucy stumbled on the top step. "I'm sorry...*what*?"

He got to the landing and looked her straight in the eye. "That extension I took had nothing to do with you or us or the wedding. I wanted to avoid dealing with the business and my parents and..." His shoulders dropped. "I didn't know how to *say* any of that to you. Or them. When the Army offered extensions, I took one."

"Okay... I need to sit down." She led him into the back bedroom and hit the light switch. The walls were soft blue in here, with ivory drapes and a small fireplace that was blocked with an ornate iron cover. The carved four-poster, fitting the Victorian theme, had a lacy canopy and skirting, with a colorful quilt over the sheets. Lucy sat, patting the mattress for him to join her, but he hesitated. *Sitting* wasn't what he'd had in mind for that bed. Better to keep his distance until they got this conversation over with. Lucy looked up at him as he leaned against the bedpost. "You don't want to run Cooper Landscaping? I mean...since *when*?"

He stared past her to the headboard, with its floral

carvings and a center arch that had to be nearly eight feet tall.

"Owen?"

He stared over at the fireplace now, wishing he'd never opened this can of worms. Not now. But Lena's words came back to him. *Be the man she deserves...*

"The past few years...since I met you, actually..."

She held up a hand and laughed. "Do *not* blame this on me!"

"I'm not. But the truth is you...you changed me, Luce." He wasn't avoiding looking at her anymore. He needed her to hear him. "You weren't part of the plan—mine or my parents. Meeting you knocked me off the train track I was *very* firmly on. You derailed me." She started to object, but he pushed on. "I'm not *blaming* you. I'm *crediting* you. I had doubts about taking over the business because I didn't even *know* the business anymore. When I went into the Army after college, it was a landscaping business. Planting stuff, building patios, maybe a firepit or retaining wall. Then they added the nursery and the produce market and a second location and..." He pushed his fingers through his hair. "It became more of a retail operation, which was never what I wanted. But how could I tell my parents I don't want what they built? My entire life they'd made it clear that was my *legacy*..." He formed air quotes with his fingers. "Whatever that means. I didn't know how to start that conversation, so..."

"So you decided the answer was to just avoid the topic...avoid *them*...as long as possible? You put yourself in harm's way, just to avoid a *conversation*. What were you planning to do when you and I got home from our honeymoon?"

He felt like a fool, but he had to come clean here. Even

if it didn't exactly enhance her opinion of him. "I didn't say I had a plan, much less a *good* plan. I convinced myself that I had no choice but to just...do it and it would work out somehow. That having you there would make it better." He sat on the edge of the bed and dropped his head into his hands. "And now that I've said that out loud I realize how stupid it sounds."

Her hand touched his shoulder. "Poor Owen. You've always been such a rule follower. Such a straight arrow. You do what people expect you to do. That's why you loved the Army so much. They told you what to do and you did it." He winced. Was that a compliment? It didn't feel like one. She tapped her fingers against his skin, bringing him out of his own head. "But you're *not* stupid. You just...do stupid things once in a while."

"Gee, thanks."

"You're a good man. A caring man. A responsible man." He lifted his head and turned to look at her. "You ran over here in a storm to bring me lights. I mean...you may go to extremes to avoid certain difficult conversations, but..."

"Jesus, Luce. You start out making me sound great, then the more you talk..." He straightened a bit, not taking his eyes from hers. Even in the dim light, he could see they were shining with something. Was it pity, or was it warmth? She shook her head with a soft smile.

"I was going to *marry* you. You must have done something right."

"But you didn't." His voice dropped. "You didn't marry me."

Her tongue traced along her upper lip. She was killing him.

"No. But that wasn't all on you. Yes, you were being

distant. Unengaged." He started to draw back, but her fingers gripped his shoulder, holding him there. "But that was just one piece of what made me throw that bomb into everyone's lives. I could have dealt with you. I loved you, and we could have figured it out." She sighed. "But it was like playing Jenga—the tower can stand if you pull one piece out. Then two pieces. But more and more pieces get pulled out until there are so many holes the tower can't support itself anymore. That's how I felt the day of the wedding. There was nothing holding me up anymore. I hurt you more than anyone else, and you didn't deserve it."

But there was only one word echoing in his mind… *loved*. She'd said it in the past tense. *I loved you.*

"Do you think you could ever love me again?"

"What?"

"You said you loved me…past tense. Could you love me again? I mean…*really* love me?"

"I… I could. Let's face it, I still do love you in so many ways. But is that enough? We've both made such huge mistakes…" She didn't look away. Her mouth slanted up on one side. "Maybe that spreadsheet would help. Maybe we need to know each other better so we know if we're really right for each other."

"I don't need any damn spreadsheet to tell me that." His voice was rough in his own ears. "Yeah, we screwed up. But I never once stopped loving you."

"And yet you never saw that I was struggling."

It wasn't said as an accusation. Her voice was steady… tender. Which didn't do a thing to blunt the pain he felt. Did he not know what *love* meant? There was something about this moment, sitting so close—when did she get this close?—in this frilly Victorian bedroom, that felt pivotal. Make or break.

"Is it possible for both to be true?" he asked. "Is it possible that I love you and still screwed up and hurt you? Is it possible you loved me and left me…but still love me?"

Her soft huff of laughter sent warm air across his cheek. "As if I wasn't already confused! To answer the question that I *think* you're asking… I don't know. I guess anything's possible." Did she just move closer still? "I can't really criticize you for avoiding big conversations. That exactly what I did when I left North Carolina. I ran instead of facing the music."

Owen didn't want to agree and hurt her feelings, but… yeah. They'd both made some big mistakes. She nudged his shoulder. "There are definitely things I miss about us. Like what we just did on the sofa—I've missed that. But does great sex solve anything? Or are we just letting the physical take over the logical?"

She was pressed up against him now, and he had a feeling she didn't even know she'd done it. He hadn't moved, but she was right there, with desire—and hope?—written on her face.

He slid his arm behind her and pressed her back against the colorful quilt. Talking could wait.

"I think we should find out."

CHAPTER TWENTY-ONE

LUCY DIDN'T EVEN think about objecting to the suggestion. He untied her shirt—correction, *his* shirt—and let it fall open. His arm was still under her back, and he slid her toward the head of the bed while crawling on his knees to stay above her. His eyes were dark with desire. His expression alone was enough to make her body arch and tremble, her core growing heavy and hot.

Downstairs in the dark, they'd been quick. Fevered. Frantic. It was a passion bomb going off. But she could already tell this time was going to be different. He was just as intense, but it was contained.

His hands slowly unfastened her shorts, sliding them down her legs and folding them carefully before setting them on the nightstand next to the lamp. He stood and worked his own shorts off, folding them along with his boxer briefs and setting them on top of hers before crawling back into bed. He produced the other two condoms from his pocket, and the entire time his eyes never left hers. She started to slip off the open shirt but Owen gave a slight shake of his head.

"You look too good in that shirt. Keep it."

"Okay…" She flipped the tails of the shirt out to the side playfully, but he didn't smile. Instead, his mouth fell open, as if in awe. That thought made her feel good, but it was unlikely…

"Christ, Lucy. You look like an angel. You're so beautiful that I'm afraid to touch you…"

"Oh, you're gonna touch me, mister." She reached out to grab his hand, tugging until he moved over her. But he still held himself above her, his gaze sweeping down her body.

"Yeah, I am going to touch you." He slowly lowered himself onto her, running his fingers through her hair and kissing her. "I'm going to touch every last inch of you. And I'm going to take my time. And I'm going to make sure you enjoy it. A lot. Sound good?"

"That sounds very good. You leaving the light on?"

He glanced over at the fancy lamp with its lacy shade, then back to her. "Do you mind it on?"

"No. But it's not like you haven't seen all this before."

She knew the words were a mistake as soon as she said them. It was an unwelcome reminder that they weren't new lovers discovering each other. They were lovers who'd almost married. Who'd definitely made love through the years—when he wasn't deployed. Had even made love the week before the almost-wedding. It had been slightly awkward and subdued, but she'd blamed it on them both being exhausted. Truth be told, Owen hadn't really been engaged in anything 100 percent since leaving the Army. Until now.

His face flinched for a moment before he looked at her with nothing but kindness and understanding in his eyes.

"That's true. I've seen you from pretty much every angle known to man and woman." His mouth slid into a slow, sexy smile. "But this is different. This is us being grown-ups. This is us getting to know each other on a whole different level. This is me begging for a second chance. It's you giving me one." His hands slid across her shoulder, grazed her breast—and stopped for a quick pinch that made her gasp—before moving down her ribs and between her legs.

"This is me looking at you and not missing one thing. Not taking one single thing for granted. Not ever again, but damn sure not tonight." He kissed her lips, pressing his fingers against her warmth until she moaned against his mouth. "Downstairs was hot and heavy. That was you and me in the Bronco that first night. Better. But not...not like this." He stroked her again and her head fell back as she gave herself up to sensation. His touch. His voice. His tender words spoken in a gravelly voice. "If we've got all night, then I'm taking it. So lay back and relax, baby. I got you."

I got you.

How many times had he said those three words lately? Every time she stumbled, physically or emotionally, he kept reassuring her.

I got you.

His fingers gained entry and her hips rose off the bed as she gave a whimper of need. He captured the whimper with his kisses, then trailed his mouth down her jaw. Down her neck. Down her chest. Like his hands, he paused at her breast just long enough to pull and nip before continuing the journey across her belly to hit the same spot his fingers were moving against. The combination was lethal, and she cried out his name. She forced her eyes open, determined to watch him. At the same moment, his lashes swept up and he caught her gaze. He held it as his mouth found its target and he went to work. She wanted to close her eyes and scream in need, frustration and pure carnal delight. But she couldn't take her eyes off him.

They stared at each other as he brought her closer and closer to the precipice, his tongue and his fingers working together like a very efficient team. She reached for his head, twisting her fingers in his hair. He made a deep, guttural sound but didn't slow down. Why was she resisting? She could just let go…she was ready. But she held on, denying herself and absorbing the sensations rocketing through her body. She held on until she couldn't anymore, letting go with a cry as he cupped her buttocks in his hands and pressed on until she thought she'd lose consciousness. She gasped his name and somehow he understood. He slowed until she settled back onto the mattress, then he traced tiny kisses around her quivering heat and down each thigh.

She forced her eyes open again when he stopped. He'd lifted his head and was smiling up at her. It was a very satisfied smile. She knew the feeling, and was probably returning that slightly goofy grin. He gave a last kiss to her thigh and started moving back up her body, dropping more kisses along the way. When his mouth finally reached hers, his hands were cupping her breasts, kneading them slowly, flicking her nipples.

He kissed her deep and hard, tasting of sex and love. Then he lowered his head close to her ear and breathed, "As good as we've been, that look on your face right now… that's something I've never seen before."

The rest of the night was more of the same. Him on top. Her on top. Him between her legs, her between his. Kissing. Sucking. Nipping. Sighing. Tangling and teasing until neither of them knew who was *where* anymore. Both of the remaining condoms were put to very good use, and neither of them got any sleep until nearly dawn. He had to gather the sheets and blankets up off the floor, pulling them up as she burrowed into his arms. So tired. So happy.

OWEN HEARD MUSIC in his dream. That made perfect sense, since he was dreaming about Lucy and flowers and butterflies and lots of naked skin. Music was a natural fit, but there was something...off. The music was too loud. There was scrambling movement next to him. And cursing.

"Shit, shit *shit*!" He opened his eyes at the sound of Lucy hissing. She crabwalked across the bed, his rumpled shirt still covering her back, and fished her phone out of the shorts he'd folded on her nightstand. "That's my alarm. It's morning. Daylight morning. Shit..."

Owen sat up and reached for her waist, pulling her down next to him while she continued stabbing at her phone until the noise stopped. "Okay...when did you become the start-the-day-cursing sort of morning person? Especially on a Sunday? Because I do not remember this side of you."

"You spent the night!" Her eyes were wide with panic, and maybe confusion. "This is...this wasn't supposed to..."

He stopped her with a kiss. After a brief freeze-up, she melted into him. He ran his fingers up her spine and he was pretty sure she purred in response. She kissed him back, long and hard. She finally pulled back, calmer but still looking baffled. Her hair was wild around her face. Her lips were kiss-swollen and pink. He didn't think she'd ever looked more beautiful. Her head went back and forth slowly.

"What have we done?"

What, indeed? There'd been no promises of having more than one night. But the fact that she was this uncertain meant he wasn't the only one who felt it was much more than that. Something had fallen between them, leaving them...exposed. Vulnerable. On a precipice of a miracle. Or a disaster. He did his best to sound composed and confident.

"What we've done is spend the night together. Having the best sex of our lives. Talking about things neither of us had talked about before. Not to each other, anyway." He tugged her into his lap. "What we've done is…maybe… turned a corner?"

Lucy rested her head against his chest, soft and warm in his arms. She nodded against him. "We did all of that. But what's around the corner we just turned? Is that daylight in the distance or an oncoming freight train?"

"Whatever it is, let's make a deal to face it together. Luce, you're going to have to start trusting again. You're going to have to trust me. Trust us."

She sighed. "I know. But Owen… I'm not going back to Greensboro. I know that for sure."

"Okay." He kissed her hair. "That's okay. We'll figure something out. I'll talk to my family and we'll figure something out."

"Like what, exactly?"

He chuckled. Because he had no clue.

"I don't know. But I do know it's something we don't have to solve right this minute. Not when we're in bed together and…" His hand moved up her leg, but she stopped him. *Damn. So close.*

"And I need to get ready for work. I convinced Connie we should do a complete inventory of the shop today. I can't be late for my own idea." She looked up at him with a playful grin. He was glad to see her relaxing again. "But hold that thought for later, okay?" She stood with a groan, and he almost groaned with her.

"You are so beautiful."

She laughed, pushing her hair up off her neck and looking into the mirror before glancing back at him over her shoulder.

"I look like a mess."

"A beautiful, sexy mess." Then he remembered something. "Hey… I heard a rumor you got a tattoo? I didn't see any last night. Where…?"

She rolled her eyes. "The rumor mill in this town is unbelievable! I went to the studio with Evie, but I decided that was one step *too* wild. The needles were a no-go for me."

He crawled out of bed and pulled her in for one last squeeze and kiss. "I love you, Lucy Higgins. Every messy, non-inked inch of you."

She looked deep into his eyes. Into his soul. Testing him. Still doubting his words. That was okay. He could be patient.

"I know you do. Lord knows, I've given you a laundry list of reasons why you shouldn't." She put her hand to his cheek. "But your family is *not* going to approve. They're not going to let you just walk away from the grand plan without a fight. And even if they do, that means you have no job. We have no home if this place sells. We can't just live at the Taggart Inn. I don't know if Connie wants a partner or not. What if she sells the shop instead? What if—"

"Hey." He covered her hand with his. "Don't spin out on me. The only thing that matters right this minute is that we're together. I love you. You love me, too, even if you don't want to admit it. That's all that matters. The rest will fall into place. Or it won't." He shrugged. "The only grand plan I'm concerned with right now is us being together. I tuned out on us once. I won't do it again. Whatever you need is what I'll give. We'll figure it out together. And we'll talk, the way we did last night. No assuming. No secrets."

He mentally crossed his fingers when he said those words. He was pretty sure telling her about using the Dr. Find-Love app was a bad idea. She might think it was funny, but she might not. She'd accused him once of acting like this was a game. No sense giving her any ammunition.

She hesitated, then her mouth slowly slid into a smile. "Together. No assumptions. No secrets." She went on tiptoe to kiss him, then turned away. "I really do need to shower and go to work."

"I'll cook you breakfast." He found his boxer briefs and shorts, and pulled them on. Lucy *still* wore his buttonless shirt. As if reading his mind, she went to the dresser and pulled out something that looked familiar. It was an olive green T-shirt, well-worn and faded. He laughed when she tossed it at him. "You kept my old shirt from Fort Bragg?"

She headed into the bathroom, talking to him through the open door as she turned on the shower. "I've used that as a nightshirt for years, but you can borrow it back for today. It'll save you from walking around bare-chested."

He pulled it over his head. "I wouldn't be bare-chested if someone hadn't destroyed my shirt last night."

"It's not my fault you decided to play hero and come running to my rescue. How was I supposed to resist a move like that?" She came to the door and started to close it, giving him a quick wink before she did. "It's like someone scripted your way to my heart, Mr. Big Brave Soldier."

He headed downstairs, whistling to himself. She thought he was irresistible. He frowned. She thought it could have been scripted. It wasn't. Last night had nothing to do with that dumb app on his phone. But *Be her hero was on the list.* Intentional or not, that's what he'd done. And it had worked. He had a hunch Lucy wouldn't see that as a good thing.

CHAPTER TWENTY-TWO

"Gu-u-r-r-l..." Piper scanned Lucy from head to toe. "Hot sex with your ex looks good on you."

Piper and Lucy were in the lobby of the Taggart Inn, waiting on Logan and Owen, who were checking on Piper's kids one last time. Teenage Ethan was babysitting, and Logan wanted to make sure the boy knew there'd be consequences if any of his pals showed up to play video games.

The two couples were headed up to Falls Legend Winery for a cookout. Lucy made a face, but she turned toward the big antique mirror anyway.

"I don't think I look any different than I did a few weeks ago. Just less pink." Her hair was less choppy, too, thanks to a trip to Suzy's Clip & Snip. It fell in soft layers to her shoulders. She'd lost a few stress pounds since her arrival in Rendezvous Falls, but they were beginning to come back now that she had Owen preparing meals every night. That had happened as naturally as the sun rising and setting. He'd spent every night at her house since the storm. It felt so...easy. Like when they first fell in love. They laughed. They talked about everything. Except the future.

She studied her reflection. She was wearing a short yellow sundress and flat sandals. Nothing special. And yet…she *did* look different. More at peace. More confident. Like a woman in love.

Piper's reflection appeared in the mirror behind her. "I guess I technically can't call it 'hot sex with an ex' if that ex is living with you. Pretty sure that means he's no longer an ex." Piper winked. "But still—hot sex looks good on you."

"Hell yeah it does." Owen's deep voice came from the doorway.

Lucy covered her face with her hands with a squeal of horror.

"Hey, mister—" Piper pointed a finger at him "—no eavesdropping! You men have big enough egos."

He walked over to Lucy, pulling her hands down from her face to give her a swift kiss. "Have you been telling your friends about our hot sex, baby? Do you want *me* to fill them in?"

"No!" She swatted his shoulder. His rock-solid shoulder. Her skin began to heat. Damn if that didn't happen every time the man got close. The chemistry wasn't complicated. Match. Flint. Fire.

In the past ten days that formula had proven to be very reliable. All he had to do was touch her. Or laugh at something. Or walk by on his way out the door to go for a run. Spontaneous combustion. They'd managed to christen every room in the house, except maybe the downstairs bathroom…no, that wasn't true. He'd pulled her in there the other afternoon, while Connie, Cecile and Iris were sitting on the back deck after having lunch with them. The older ladies were laughing over tea while Owen had set her on the sink and dropped to his knees on the bathroom floor…

His fingers brushed her cheeks. "Why are you blushing, Lucy?" His voice was teasing and suggestive.

"Okay, that's enough!" Piper pushed both of them toward the door. "Logan's waiting in the car and we need to go."

THE FIVE COUPLES—Luke and Whitney, Evie and Mark, Finn and Bridget, Logan and Piper and Owen and Lucy—gathered their chairs around the fire pit after an amazing meal of grilled steaks and potatoes baked in foil right on the coals of the grill. After they'd cleared the outdoor tables and shut down the grill, Whitney brought out slices of rum cake that her aunt, Helen, had made for them. The wine and beer had flowed as easily as the conversation had, but the drivers in the group were now sipping glasses of iced coffee or cider. Soft music played from a Bluetooth speaker on the porch behind them.

Owen reached over and took her hand.

"This is nice."

She nodded, her heart suddenly too full of emotion to speak. She glanced around at their friends, who were laughing and talking over each other as they shared stories and argued and gestured with their hands. It was chaos. And it was home. They were *part* of something—part of this circle of people.

"We've never really had this." She'd leaned toward him, her words low. His forehead wrinkled in confusion, so she explained. "Think about it. You had your Army pals, and once in a while we hung out with them, but they were yours. I had a few friends, and you knew them, but they were mine. We each had our families, for better or worse." He nodded at that. "But these people are...ours."

He looked around the fire and nodded. "They're good people."

She was quiet, her head almost hurting from the feeling of answers falling into place. Then she sat up abruptly, turning to face him.

"We were always each other's escape. Think about it—we both had so many obligations and people relying on us that we had to steal time together. When we spent a weekend at the beach, we were both so relieved to be away from our families and our jobs."

He was frowning again now. "Is that a bad thing?"

"I don't know, but I think…maybe? What we had in common was our desire to escape. Maybe that's why we didn't have a full connection with each other. Half our mind was always on what we were getting *away from* instead of being fully…us."

Before he could respond, Whitney called over to them. "Hey, hey, hey. No serious talk tonight. And no canoodling, either."

Evie laughed. "Definitely no canoodling at the firepit. That's a rule, right?"

Several glasses were raised in agreement. But Owen ignored them all, leaning closer and staring straight into her eyes.

"You're saying we're fully us here? Now?"

She nodded.

"And it's good? You like that?"

She nodded again.

"And you want it to continue…just like this?"

She knew what he was asking. She still had doubts about trusting the future, but those doubts had suddenly taken a big step backward.

"Yes. I love you, Owen." Their friends had fallen silent, watching the conversation play out. "Let's try to make this work."

He reached over to hold the back of her head as he kissed her. Their friends let out playful groans as if they were children.

"Oh, gross—they're kissing!"

"Ew!"

"My eyes! My eyes!"

Owen smiled against her mouth before kissing her even harder.

"Our new friends are jerks."

"Luce, you know I have to go back to settle things."

He'd been trying to have this conversation with her ever since the cookout three days ago. He was right, of course. If their life was going to be in Rendezvous Falls, then things needed to be…dealt with. She slowly lowered her coffee mug to the table. Every time the topic came up, her panic threatened to overwhelm her. Owen's voice softened.

"Babe… I told them I'd be gone a month. This is week *six*. There's a family business to be handled. I can't just walk away like you…" He stopped, but not soon enough.

"Like *I* did?" Lucy pushed her chair away from the table and stood, taking her breakfast bowl to the sink. "I get it—I'm the infamous Runaway Bride, and that's probably how our family in North Carolina will always think of me. But…" She turned, unable to keep the panic from her voice. "But if you go back…"

Owen started to roll his eyes, then caught himself as he pushed to his feet. Again…too late. She raised her finger to scold him, but he spoke first. "We're past that now. It's just that…there's nothing inherently *bad* about the state of North Carolina or either one of our families. They're not specters waiting to entrap us if we have contact with them." His gaze caught hers. "But that's how you're acting. As if I won't be able to resist their evil powers or something. Are you really planning on staying away from there—from *them*—for the rest of your life?"

She started to pout, but he had a point. Maybe that's what annoyed her so much. "I never said I wouldn't go back ever. But right now, Rendezvous Falls feels like where I need to be." The way his gaze flickered away to some invisible spot over her shoulder confirmed her worst fears. Her heart fell. "Oh, my God. Did you still think I might move back to Greensboro with you?"

Owen jammed his fingers through his hair, staring up at the ceiling for a long moment.

"I can't say it doesn't cross my mind once in a while." He looked back to her and held his hands up. "Before you get mad, I know it won't happen. And that's okay. But you have to admit it would be a lot less complicated logistically. I thought the *wedding* was a mess to clean up, but this…*us*…staying here…" His hands dropped to his sides. "This is going to blow up a lot of plans people have made. Big plans. Life plans. Business plans. I have to go back and deal with that, and you should, too. It's the responsible thing to do."

She tried not to react to his implication that she had been irresponsible. She didn't think that's what he was saying intentionally, but that's the message she'd received. He was her straight arrow plan follower, and she was trying hard to understand what he was saying. But she couldn't shake her fear that once he left their little Rendezvous Falls bubble, things would change. She took a deep, steadying breath.

"I know you need to deal with the business. I know you have a responsibility there, and I understand…or at least, I'm *trying* to. I'm just…" She tried to come up with the right word. "I'm scared." Her voice was almost a whisper. They'd promised to be honest. "I'm afraid you'll get back there and get sucked back into the life that was planned for you. That you'll decide following the plan is more important than…us."

He walked to her, cupping her face in his hands tenderly, his nose almost touching hers. So close that looking into his eyes was like looking into a pot of molten gold. He was so sure and so much more confident that she could possibly be right now.

"Lucy, I *love* you. Yes, I came here to convince you to come back home with me, but I can see how you've blossomed—pardon the pun—in Rendezvous Falls. Your happiness is *everything* to me."

"And if my happiness hinges on you doing something that might make you unhappy?"

His hesitation was so brief…no more than a heartbeat. But that half second of silence made her shudder. He must have felt it, because he moved even closer, resting his forehead on hers and closing his eyes.

"I can't be unhappy as long as I'm with you. We'll make this work." His eyes opened again, darker than before. "I'll call my parents and tell them I need one more week. But after that… I have a lot of decisions to deal with. The business. My employment options. The apartment. And yes, my family. I know I've asked you to wait for me too

many times since we've met, and I know you don't want
to do it again, but haven't I always come back to you?"

It made sense. But then again, it had *always* made sense
when someone wanted her to put her life on hold. That
didn't make it easy to swallow.

"You have." She rested her hands on his shoulders,
then slid them behind his neck. "Maybe I'm being childish. Maybe I'm being paranoid. Maybe I need a shrink.
But Owen, I'm *so* scared. I can't even rationalize it to
myself, much less to you, but this fear inside of me is…
overwhelming."

He chewed his lower lip and looked away.

Lucy narrowed her eyes. "What?"

He blew out a breath, as if he needed to brace himself.
Against her? He took her hands in his. "You know how
you…uh…*suggested* I talk to someone at the VA?"

She smiled, understanding his emphasis on *suggested*
meant she'd done a lot more than suggest. And to his
credit, he'd done it. And it seemed to have helped him
shrug off the darkest of his nightmares. She nodded and
he continued.

"Well…have you thought about…about *you* talking
to someone?"

Her mouth fell open. "You mean…you think I *do* need
a shrink?"

"I don't know if *need* is the right word…but maybe it
would help?" He squeezed her hands and rushed ahead
before she could speak. "Babe, you've been talking about
how frustrated you've been, how ignored you felt before
the wedding, how upset you are about your parents' divorce, your resentment about being taken for granted…"

She tugged her hands away, her spine stiffening. "And

you think those feelings mean there's something wrong with *me* instead of everyone who made me feel that way?"

"No!" He spread his hands in innocence. "I'm saying that talking to someone professional might help you sort those feelings out and figure out how to deal with them. Babe, you're carrying around all this…this *stuff* inside you. And you have to know it's not North Carolina's fault. Avoiding your home state forever isn't the answer."

Tears suddenly burned Lucy's eyes. Connie and Iris had said virtually the same thing. *There's a big difference between running away and moving forward…* But a therapist? Would talking to some stranger really help? Shouldn't she be able to sort this out on her own? She'd always taken care of her own problems. Except…she hadn't really taken care of anything, had she? She'd just left them behind.

I thought the wedding was a mess to clean up…

She swallowed hard, nodding as much to herself as to him. "Maybe you're right. Not about going back…at least not for now. But about talking to someone. I don't really want to be a runaway *anything* anymore. But can we… can we just…wait? A little longer?" She shook her head hard enough to send her hair back and forth across her face, as if that would help her think better. "Give me time to…just a little more time to…make decisions. I know I should have thought about it all before now, but I didn't. And now that we're together again, well…it complicates things, doesn't it?"

Owen's forehead furrowed. "I'd like to argue with you on that, but you might be right. Instead of an ending and moving on, we have to start all over in a lot of ways." He lifted one shoulder. "We can't keep putting it off, but I think one more week will be fine. The business has been running along without me, just like it did when I was deployed." He smiled. "And the idea of one more week of just us, without any family interference, is pretty damn tempting."

She knew they were just delaying the inevitable, but let him pull her into his arms. They'd switched roles. He was finally ready to face some hard facts, and she was trying to hold him back from doing it. He kissed her, sliding his hands under her knit top and up her back to unhook her bra.

Those facts could wait a little bit longer.

CHAPTER TWENTY-THREE

CONNIE WAS JUST paying her bill at the Spot Diner when Father Joe Brennan came in. He waved at her in the booth, but chose to sit next to Owen at the counter.

"Mind if I join you, lad?" The priest gave a bright smile to Evie behind the counter. "I know it's after the breakfast rush, but could you spare a cup of coffee, darlin'?"

Evie laughed as she reached for the pot. "Father Joe, it's a diner. There's always coffee brewing. Owen, you want another?" He nodded and she set them up with two coffees, then set a plate between them with a pile of chocolate chip cookies. "Free samples. We're trying a new bakery. These have dark chocolate chunks and walnuts. Tell me what you think." She looked at Connie. "Come up and try them—they're amazing." Evie gave Owen a pointed look. "You look like you need sugar as much as you do caffeine."

Connie sat on the other side of Owen, opposite Father Joe. Owen had just grunted in reply to Evie's comment. Between him and Lucy keeping themselves busy at night, and him working so much at Connie's place during the day, he probably wasn't getting a lot of sleep.

It was good to stay busy. But as Connie kept telling Lucy, eventually the two of them were going to have to face the music. Of course, Lucy had just given her a pointed look and reminded her that it had taken over three years for Connie to start fixing things after her husband left.

Lucy had a point. Connie had wallowed in her anger and loneliness for too long, allowing things to happen around her instead being a part of the action again. She wasn't punishing Dan by being unhappy. She was only punishing herself. It had taken Lucy's arrival to make her see she had options.

When Connie, David and Susan had dinner together, they'd started planning a big Labor Day cookout at the house. It was a month away, so she had plenty of time to get the house ready. And she'd put Owen to work in the backyard and the waterfront, making sure the place would look as nice as it used to. David had taken one look at her old grill and said he'd buy her a new one and call it an early Christmas present. It felt good to have something to look forward to again.

Owen grabbed a cookie and bit off half of it.

"You're attackin' that wee cookie like it kicked your best friend." Father Joe was watching Owen over the top of his coffee cup. "Anything you want to talk about?"

Evie was wiping the counter near them and snorted. "I'm guessing he has a whole lot of things he *should* talk about, but he probably won't."

Owen straightened. "What does *that* mean?"

She set her hand, still gripping the damp rag, on her hip and stared straight at him. "Dude. You're besotted with Lucy. She's your kryptonite. And you have no freakin' idea what to do with her."

Connie snorted, but Owen just shook his head with a bemused grin. "I spend every night at Lucy's place and trust me—we have no problems knowing what to do…"

He glanced at Connie, then at the priest sitting on his other side. "I mean…well…the point is, we're together. We're happy."

Evie pierced right brow rose high. "Happy in the *sack*, maybe." She pointed at him, clearly not worried about having this conversation in front of her priest. "But you two need to figure some shit out, and you know it."

By the time Owen started to answer, Evie was gone. The doors to the kitchen swung back and forth in her wake. Owen scrubbed his hand down his face with a heavy sigh.

"*Women*, right?" Then he realized who he was saying that to. "Oh…uh…sorry, Connie."

She took a sip of the coffee she'd brought from her table. "Your talent for digging holes extends way beyond planting trees, my friend."

Owen laughed. "I think you're right. And I'm sorry to you, too, Father Joe. I didn't mean to imply you knew anything about… I mean…"

The older man's eyes were twinkling. No wonder everyone called him a leprechaun.

"More than half my parishioners are of the female persuasion, so I understand. And don't assume I didn't learn a thing or two about women before I became a priest." He winked, making Owen and Connie laugh. "One thing I've learned about the ladies, though, is that they're often right. And they *know* it, which is probably why it bothers men so much, don't you think?"

"It can be irritating, yes." Owen shook his head while reaching for another cookie. "But I don't think of Lucy as my kryptonite. I mean, that's what destroyed Superman's powers, right? And Lucy would never…"

"Didn't she leave you at the altar?" Connie asked pointedly. "And haven't you been here trying to fix everything she blew up that day?"

"Fair enough," Owen said. "But it wasn't just her. I contributed to what happened, too."

"But *she's* the one who ran." Joe sipped his coffee thoughtfully, glancing out the window toward the flower shop, then giving Connie a wink before turning back to Owen. "Then again, so did you."

"Me? I didn't run... I *chased*, and that's different."

There was a long pause before Joe replied.

"Is it?"

Oh, Connie thought, *this priest is good.* Those two short words had clearly poked a tender spot in Owen, and he started defending himself.

"She came to Rendezvous Falls to *escape* something." To escape being married to *him*, but Connie thought it would be cruel to point that out now. "And I came here to..."

"To win her back," Joe finished. "With the help of a phone app, if I heard correctly."

"At first, yeah. But I won her back on my own. The night the power went off. We...uh..."

"I understand what happens in blackouts," Joe held his hand up with a mischievous grin. "I'm sure I'll be baptizing a few extra babies in nine months' time from that storm."

Connie laughed in agreement. "Without a doubt! I think what the good Father is trying to say is that Lucy isn't the only reason you ended up in Rendezvous Falls, Owen."

"Connie, you of all people know I came here for Lucy."

Father Joe set down his coffee cup and wiped his mouth

with his napkin before standing. He looked at Owen with what seemed to be…sorrow.

"I know what Lucy was running from. But what are *you* running from?"

"Nothing!" Owen looked between Joe and Connie, pleading his case. "I came here for *her*."

"And now you have her, or so you say. But you're still here. You haven't left. So what are *you* running from?"

"Well, I can't leave without her." Owen was clearly frustrated.

Joe tipped his head to the side with an impish grin. "I didn't say you had to leave."

"But…" Owen straightened, trying to unravel the riddle. "I'm here because Lucy's here."

The priest shook his head. "Maybe. I'm guessing you'll have to work that out for yourself."

Joe waved and left the diner, leaving Owen staring into his coffee with a scowl. Connie grabbed a cookie and patted Owen on the shoulder before she headed to the shop. The poor guy still didn't get it, and Connie could relate. She'd refused to admit the truth for a long time, too. Hopefully Owen would realize that he had to face the music as much as Lucy did. Those two lovebirds weren't in the clear yet. They both had work to do.

THREE DAYS LATER, Father Joe's question still echoed in Owen's mind. *What are* you *running from?*

He was scrubbing the grill behind Lucy's bright yellow house. He'd picked up a couple of steaks that afternoon. They'd sat at the ornate iron table on the patio and laughed together over rare steaks and red wine. They'd talked about inconsequential things like whether the burgers were better at the Spot or at the marina restaurant on the waterfront. They talked about the floral order Lucy was working on for the McKinnon family. The flowers were for Maura McKinnon's surprise birthday party, and they'd insisted on green, white and orange centerpieces to honor her Irish heritage. Lucy had ordered tiny Irish flags for each arrangement, and little potted shamrocks for each place setting.

The evening felt so…normal. Relaxed. Perfect.

And still, as soon as Lucy went inside with the dishes, Joe's question popped up again. Owen closed the grill. Okay, maybe he had never been wild about taking over the family business. But it was still what his parents expected. Cooper Landscaping had been built for him. They'd been telling him that his entire life. He'd been ten when they'd held the big ribbon-cutting ceremony when the nursery side of the business opened. Dad had handed him the weird giant scissors and said point-blank, "This will all be yours, son." From the moment he'd cut that thick red ribbon, he'd felt the weight settling on his shoulders. The weight of his future. It was a lot for a ten-year-old. It was a lot now. He walked inside, carrying the last of the dishes and condiments.

Lucy stood at the sink, her hair pulled up in a short, messy ponytail. She tossed him a bright smile over her shoulder. In her shorts and snug tee, she looked like a queen. His queen.

What are you running from?

He dismissed the annoying question once and for all. He'd been running *to* something. He'd come running for Lucy Higgins. And her smile was his prize.

"What?" She laughed. "Do I have salad in my teeth or something?"

He walked over and slid his arms around her waist from behind, tugging her back against him. "No salad in your teeth, silly. Just a bright shining light in my world." He kissed her neck, feeling her continued laughter. "Okay, that was over the top But you are beautiful, Lucy. Irresistible. Like a flame draws a…" She spun in his arms, shaking her finger in his face.

"I swear if you refer to yourself as a moth, I'm going to slap you. How many glasses of wine have you had tonight?"

"Enough to make me drunk on…" He stopped again. What had gotten into him?

Lucy's eyes went wide, and she patted his chest playfully.

"No more wine for you, Casanova. But if you're feeling this…um…amorous…maybe I could meet you upstairs when I'm done with the dishes?"

His heart thumped hard in his chest directly under her palm. This was why he'd come to Rendezvous Falls. This feeling. This woman. He'd been right when he spoke with Father Joe. He hadn't been running from anything. He'd been running to this.

"Well?"

He shook off his stupor. The woman he loved wanted sex. Who was he to disappoint?

"I think if you want to make love, then…that's exactly what we should do." He kissed her lips lightly. "I smell like the grill, so I'm gonna hop in the shower first. I'll meet you in bed?"

She grinned and returned the kiss. "Sounds like a plan.

I'll finish cleaning up and meet you upstairs. It won't take me long, so you'd better shower fast, mister."

Didn't have to tell him twice. He took the steps two at a time. The shower was quick, and he pulled on his cargo shorts without bothering with underwear. He was just going to be peeling them right off anyway. He sat on the edge of the bed, looking around the room as he waited for Lucy. This whole house was too frilly for his taste, and the bedroom was no exception, with its lacy canopy bed and brocade wallpapered walls. But they'd been having a damn good time in this frilly little room. He glanced at his watch and frowned. She was taking a long time to clean up. He finally decided to go get her himself.

On his way out the bedroom door, he saw the head-lamp he'd given her hanging on the back of a chair. That might make for some fun later. He grabbed it and jogged down the stairs.

"Hey, Luce?"

"Owen…" Her voice was coming from the living room, so he headed that way, slipping the headlamp over his head and turning it on.

"I figured out a great little game we can play after dark." He jogged down the hallway. "I'll be the big bad mine owner." The light from the headlamp bounced on the hall walls. "And you can be the damsel in dis…"

He came to a sharp halt as soon as he reached the end of the hallway. He found his voice after a long beat of stunned silence, speaking to the two people standing next to Lucy.

"Mom? Dad?"

Owen's brain had stalled and was trying to restart, but without success. He knew he looked just as shocked as he felt—eyes wide, mouth open, probably pale as a ghost. His parents. Edward and Faye Cooper. Standing in his... in Lucy's living room. In New York. His father seemed to be mirroring Owen's emotions, frozen in place like a deer in the headlights. His mother was equally immobile, but the waves of disapproval were rolling off her and across the room, engulfing both Owen and Lucy. He blinked and looked at Lucy, standing so close to the dangerous rage building in his mother's expression. He should help her, but his damn brain still wasn't cooperating.

Lucy was...*laughing*? Not out loud, but he could see it in the smile that kept flirting with her lips, and the amusement shining in her eyes. Her cheeks had high spots of color, and both brows were raised as if to say *Can you believe this?* She almost smiled again, and put her tongue on her upper lip to control it. Of all of them, she was the first to move, raising her hand to the top of her head and nodding his way. She was trying to tell him something... his hair? *Oh, shit!* He was still wearing the freakin' headlamp! He snatched it off his head, turned it off and threw it onto a chair like it was a bomb.

The sudden movement seemed to kick-start his ability to function. He took a quick inventory of the situation. He at least had shorts on, even if he was going commando underneath. He had briefly thought of coming downstairs undressed and ready for action. Thank Christ he hadn't. But there was no escaping the fact that he'd come running down the hallway half-naked, wearing a headlamp and suggesting a naughty role-play game. He straightened and fastened the button on his shorts, touching the zipper to make sure it was closed and cleared his throat loudly.

"Uh…what a surprise. What are you guys doing here? How did you even know…?"

"Were we not supposed to know where you were?" Ice fell from his mother's words.

"No! I mean…yes. I told you what town I was going to. But this house…"

Her brow arched sharply. "You mean the one you're using for playacting? This house you acquired for your ex-fiancée?"

Lucy's shoulders went back. "He didn't *acquire* anything. I rented this house myself."

Faye Cooper's head turned slowly, like a tank turret about to take aim.

"With *what*?"

"Mom…"

Lucy waved him off. "Not that it's any of your business, Faye, but I have a job here. As a florist." His mother stared at Lucy, her eyes narrowed. It was the look that usually sent him running as a boy, but Lucy was unmoved. She raised her chin. "I'm building a new life." Her expression softened, gazing inward now. "The old one wasn't working for me."

She glanced at Owen, and he could see the worry. And a flash of defiance.

"Now that we've established whose home we're in, I'll give you some privacy. I'm guessing you three have a lot to discuss." She brushed past him and down the hallway without slowing. "I need a nice long walk."

Owen hesitated. Should he chase after her? Or deal with his parents? His mother =moved to the sofa—the one in front of the windows—and sat with a heavy sigh. His dad joined her. If only they knew what had happened on that sofa on a fairly regular basis over the past few weeks. Probably best if they didn't. Mom looked up at him expectantly, nodding toward the armchair in a silent command for him to sit for his inquisition. She expected obedience. But she didn't get it.

"I'll be right back." He turned and hurried into the kitchen. Lucy hadn't left yet. She was at the coffee maker. "Luce, I had no idea…"

"I know that." She scooped coffee into the basket, and he waited. Her shoulders slumped as she gave up the pretense of playing happy hostess. She turned to face him. "Like you've said before, this talk needed to happen. I kept you from going to them, so they came to you. So… it's time to decide what you really want."

"I want you." He rubbed the back of his neck. "I want to honor my responsibilities, too. People are depending on me…"

Her lower lip trembled once…twice…then she bit it and regained control. "I get it. You're the responsible one. The good son. Go talk to your parents."

"Luce…" Instead of stalling, his brain was now spinning into overdrive…more like hyperdrive. Bouncing all over between the expectations different people had of him. How could he possibly make everyone happy?

She shook her head slowly, pushing the button on the coffee maker before heading to the door. She stopped by his side, looking deep into his eyes. Making him feel emotionally naked. Exposed. Vulnerable.

"You need to figure this out, Owen. Once and for all. Talk to them, but make the decision for yourself." She patted his arm and walked to the door.

"Where are you going?"

"Right now? For a walk. I'll give you-all some time."

"And after right now? Where are you going, Lucy?"

Her eyes were shining a little too brightly.

"I'm going nowhere, Owen. I've reached my destination, and it's right here." She opened the door and headed out. "With or without you."

He watched her stride purposefully away down the sidewalk and blew out a long breath before joining his parents in the living room. His mother started to say something, but he raised his hand to stop her as he settled into the chair.

"I told you I needed another week."

"Right," she scoffed. "Just like you told us you'd be gone a week. And then you needed a month. And now you're tacking on more weeks one at a time. Can't you see she's manipulating you?"

He huffed out a humorless laugh. "Manipulating me? You think she left me at the altar as part of some great conspiracy to get me to the Finger Lakes? You think she *needs* me in her life at all anymore?" He leaned forward, resting his forearms on his knees and looking hard at his parents. "Because she doesn't."

"Then why are you even here?" His mother gestured around. "Good Lord, I never knew how bad Lucy's decorating taste was."

"It's a furnished vacation rental, Mom."

"Well, it's dreadful." She met his eyes again. "*She's* dreadful. Why can't you see that? Even now, after humiliating us at the wedding…at the nonwedding…she has you nipping at her heels. What is her power over you?"

"She makes me happy."

"Oh, please…"

Edward Cooper put his hand on his wife's knee to silence her, finally joining the conversation.

"Tell me what that means, son." Dad's voice was level, his curiosity genuine. But Mom wasn't finished.

"Oh, please, Ed. Isn't it obvious? They play sex games together. That's the only hold she has on him. *Sex.*"

Owen was still leaning forward, probably looking more relaxed than he felt. There was no sense jumping into the argument his mother was clearly spoiling for. His hands clenched against his legs. Tightening and releasing. Until he could control his voice almost to his father's level.

"Yes, the sex is good." He ignored his mother's feigned shock, since she was the one who brought up the subject. "But that isn't what makes me happy. It's the other way around—the good sex is a result of how happy we are. We're in love, Mom. Isn't that what you want for me?"

She pressed her lips tightly together and inhaled sharply. "Every mother wants her children…especially her *only* child…to be happy. But I told you when you brought that girl home the first time that she was too… *wild* for you. You were a bad match, and I should have put a stop to it right then."

Owen shook his head. "And how do you think you would have done that?"

His father raised a finger and opened his mouth, but never got the chance to speak.

"I don't know. God knows I wanted to stop it, but I knew if I'd tried it would just drive you further into her arms I thought she'd just be a butterfly you chased for a while before you got bored." His father started to speak, but she talked right over him again. "Even after you got engaged, I never really thought it would happen. And then it *was* happening, so I tried to help. I brought her into the business. I guided her through the wedding planning…"

"Mom, get real. You bulldozed her into the exact type of wedding she told you she didn't want."

Dad made another move to interject, but Mom was on a roll. "Don't be ridiculous. She has a mind of her own— she proved that when she ran off and embarrassed us all. It's not *my* fault she didn't speak up. And now she has you chasing her all over the country like a plaything on a string. Don't tell me she's not capable of making decisions. It's her *decisions* that got us into this mess, and she knew exactly how to take you away from us."

"She didn't take me anywhere. She left me behind. She didn't want me here…"

"If she didn't want you, why didn't you turn around and come home?"

"Because I wanted *her.* And I was willing to fight for her."

"Well that's just… I don't know. I don't want to say it's weak, but…"

Owen buried his face in his hands. "I'm *weak* because I decided to fight for what I wanted? How does that work, Mom?"

His father leaned forward, but was shut down again when Faye Cooper replied.

"What makes you weak is *chasing* some girl and ignoring your responsibilities at home. It's bad enough the Army made you stay away longer than expected…"

"I volunteered, Mom."

"They gave you no choice, I'm sure."

"Mom, I had a choice. I *chose* not to come home."

But she refused to listen. Her nose wrinkled. "Nonsense." Owen met his father's eyes, and the older man gave a slight shrug as she continued.

"My point is we deserve to be able to retire, and you need to step up and take over the business. You don't need a wife to do that, and even if you did, there are many fine young women in Greensboro. Women who aren't... flighty."

"Mom, Lucy isn't flighty. She's the most grounded person I know. And the strongest."

"Oh, please. She left on her wedding day. We'll never outlive the humiliation of that. And if you think I'll let you marry her after doing that to us..."

He sat up straight. "That's enough. You're talking about the woman—*not* a girl—who invited you into her home and then left so we could talk. In *her* house. She's apologized to you. To me. She sent apology notes to all the guests. And *I'm* the one who was left on my wedding day, not you. So knock it off." He pointed at her, and she sat back, looking surprised. "You've never once asked *why* she left, or if she's okay. Just like you never once asked if *I* was okay when I got home from overseas."

Her face paled, and her mouth opened and closed a few times without forming words. His father started to answer.

"Son, I think I'm beginning to—"

But Mom interrupted. "Your father built that busin—"

"God*damn* it, Faye!" His father erupted in a rare show of temper. "His father is sitting right here and can speak for himself, if you'd give me a chance. We came to New York to talk to Owen. That's what you wanted. That's why we flew up here. But you never told me you didn't intend to give *him* a chance to talk. You're not even *trying* to listen to the man. You just want to talk about *you*. And you are nowhere near as fascinating a topic as you may think."

Mom's mouth snapped shut, her eyes narrowing to slits. "I beg your pardon?"

Now it was Dad's turn to wave *her* off. He turned to Owen.

"What is it about Lucy Higgins that makes you so happy, son?"

He took a deep breath, trying to compose an answer that held all the reasons he loved her.

"I feel lighter when I'm around her. I laugh more. I..."

He remembered Lena's words from the bookclub meeting. That love wasn't about how Lucy made him feel. It was about who she was. He cleared his throat and started again.

"She's smart. And funny. And she cares more than any person I've ever met. I mean...she *cares* right from the bottom of her toes. All in. For family. For friends. For total strangers. She'd literally give you the shirt off her back if she thought you needed it. Hell, she knows how much you resent her, Mom, and she *still* let us have this conversation in her living room. She's all in with her caring, which is why she had to leave."

There weren't enough pieces left to hold me up...

"She cared so much she had to humiliate us?"

"Be *quiet*, Faye. Let the man speak." Owen's father nodded to him to continue, while his mother's face grew more red.

"She cared so much about what *other* people wanted, needed, expected...that she forgot to care about what *she* wanted and needed. She got lost, Mom, and none of us saw it. Not even me." He scrubbed his hands down his face. "Not even me, and I *loved* her. Or…thought I did."

His mother pounced on that. "*Thought* you did? What…?"

"I loved her, Mom. But not as the way I should have. As a friend pointed out recently, I loved how I felt around her, without actually loving *her*." His eyes suddenly began to burn at the truth of what he was saying. "And all that time, she was trying so damn hard to love me, no matter how messed up I was. Until she just couldn't do it anymore." He looked at his parents. "And now I've had to earn her love all over again. But she never stopped caring, even when she didn't want to."

"I don't understand any of that," his mother said. "You were never *messed up*, Owen."

"That's the thing, Mom. I *was*. I *am*. And Lucy saw it. She was helped convince me to get help."

There was a beat of silence, and it was his father who broke it.

"The VA?"

Owen nodded.

"And did that…did it help?"

"It's a process, Dad, but yeah, it's helping."

His father's jaw worked back and forth. He'd always been a man of few words, only loosening up on the rare occasions he'd had a few drinks. Even now, with so much he clearly wanted to say, he managed just one word.

"Good."

His mother let out a dramatic sigh, apparently frustrated to no longer be the center of attention. "Oh, for heaven's sake. None of this means anything."

Thanks, Mom.

"What it all comes down to is that we need you at home. You took time to recover from the wedding fiasco, and that's fine. You needed…closure, or whatever, so you came here to talk to her. Fine. You've done that." She swept her gaze up his nearly naked body. "You've had some fun. But it's time to come home."

"And if I told you I'm already home?"

His mother went very still.

"*If* you told me that, I'd say you're being irresponsible. Disrespectful. Foolish…"

She would have gladly kept going, but he held up a hand in surrender. "I get the idea, Mom. But I'm telling you that anyway."

"Are you…are you seriously saying you might move *here*? To New *York*?" Her accent grew ever thicker. "I've never heard anything so…so…"

"Romantic?" He gave her a lopsided smile. There was a spark of amusement in his father's expression, but *not* his mother's. "Look, Mom. I came here to bring Lucy home. That was always the plan. But…plans change. I'm still trying to figure out how to make everything work." He was trying to break it to his parents as gently as possible, giving them a glimmer of hope and tying himself in verbal knots in the process. "Lucy loves this place right now. Maybe it's a fluke. Maybe she'll forgive her parents. Maybe she'll forgive *you*. Maybe she'll get homesick. You shouldn't give up hope…"

"Oh, yes, you really should." Lucy stood in the hallway entrance. She must have come in from the kitchen. Her expression was flat. Cold. And she was looking straight at him. "*You* should give up hope."

She held up his phone, and even from six feet away he

could see it was open to the Dr. Find-Love app. Of course she knew the passcode for his phone—they'd both used the same code. The day they'd met. And of course, he'd put the app on his home screen page. Front and center. He scrambled to his feet, but she held the phone back and warned him off with a furious glare.

"I can explain that…"

"Really? You can explain *Make her laugh?* Or maybe you can explain *When all else fails, puppies and kittens almost always work?* Oh, here's a good one—*Try a picnic lunch with friends to break the ice.*" Her voice had somehow managed to grow colder with each tip she read. So cold that it cracked on the next one. "But we both know the winner, don't we? *Be her hero—look for opportunities to come to the rescue.* When you showed up that night during the storm, it wasn't out of concern for me. It was because you saw an opportunity to play on my emotions. To take advantage of me…of my fears…"

"No! I wasn't even using the app by then. Everyone convinced me it was a bad idea. That I needed to follow my heart if I wanted you back…"

"*Everyone?* Who else knew you were just roleplaying this whole time?"

"That's not what I meant… I wasn't role-playing…"

"What is going on?" He'd forgotten his parents were there until his mother stood, indignation dripping off every word. "Did that girl go snooping through your phone? And *this* is what you want to build a marriage on?"

"I didn't *snoop*. I grabbed his phone by mistake and didn't realize it until I opened it to make a call and saw…" She stopped as soon as she heard the tremor in her own voice. A tremor that gutted him. Unintentional or not, he'd hurt her badly. Again. She bit her lower lip.

"You should go." There was no tremor in Lucy's voice now. She was calm. Deadly calm.

Best idea ever. He and she needed to talk this through. Owen started nodding. "Yes. Mom, Dad, you should go to the inn and we'll talk in the..."

"You too, Owen."

"What?"

Lucy blew out a slow breath. "I want you all to leave. I want you *all* to just leave me the hell alone."

"No...babe, you don't understand." Panic rose in Owen's chest. "I was desperate when you left, and so afraid of screwing up. I didn't know what to do. I needed to win you back. I wanted to do it right, and the guys convinced me this stupid app might work." He gestured to the phone gripped tightly in her hand. "I just needed you to give me a chance, and I thought if I followed a plan I'd have better odds..."

Her eyes narrowed. "Better *odds*? *Win* me back? My God, this really was just a game to you, wasn't it? What's the rest of the plan? Soften me up until I agree to go back to Greensboro with you? To follow *your* plans instead of mine? So you can be the winner?" She gestured angrily at his parents, both standing now. His dad had his hand on his mother's shoulder. "Or should I say so *they* can be the winners? After all, their plans have always been more important than mine, haven't they?"

Owen had no words. He barely had a pulse.

His mother straightened, shoulders straighter than any soldier. "If you think bringing the woman who humiliated us back into our lives is part of anyone's plans, you are sadly mistak—"

Her husband's fingers gripped her shoulder tightly. "Be quiet, Faye. This isn't our fight."

"The hell it isn't!" Faye bristled. "She just brought us into it."

Edward Cooper closed his eyes, shaking his head. "Only because we're standing right here in *her* living room, and because you can't let our son solve his own problems." His father looked at Owen solemnly. "I think it's time we listened to him and let him make his own choices about his own damned life."

There was something in his father's steady gaze that made Owen stand taller. The warmth in Dad's slow smile made him feel as if he'd been…heard. He swallowed hard. That's what Lucy told him *she'd* needed. To be heard. In this instant, he realized what she'd meant. She hadn't wanted the literal sound of her voice to be heard. She'd wanted someone to *listen*. To understand. To respect. To support.

There had been a shift in his father's view of him. He was the man's son, but he was no longer a child, held to some long ago promise made before Owen had a chance to truly live his life and find his own purpose. That shift in perspective made Owen feel…free. He turned back to Lucy, still wrapped up in the steely coldness of her hurt and anger.

"I've made my choice, Dad. My choice is to love this woman the way she deserves to be loved." Lucy started to protest, but he talked over her. "And that means listening to what she wants. It means being the man she deserves. And a man she can trust." He held out his hand for his phone. "The only way I can win that trust is by respecting her boundaries. Which means we're all leaving. Right now." He took his phone from her, feeling the snap of heat from her fingertips when they grazed his palm. "But I need you to know this, Lucy Higgins—when I use words like *winning*, it's not because this is a game. It's because you are a treasure, and having you by my side would be the greatest achievement…the greatest win…of my life."

She didn't answer, but he could see in her shining eyes that she *wanted* to believe him, which gave him hope. And hope was good enough for now. One of his shirts was hanging on the back of a chair, and pulled it over his head. His dad directed his mother out the door without giving her a chance to do more than bluster a few words about how "she'd *never*!"

Owen stopped in the doorway, capturing Lucy's watery gaze. No doubt tears would be falling as soon as he left. She was still chewing on her lip. He wanted to stay and comfort her, but staying right now and fighting it out was not what *she* wanted. And he was done trying to bend her will to his. She needed to be in charge here, and he needed to step back. Even if it meant losing her.

"Luce… I get why you're mad. I know how it looks. But how it looks isn't the whole story. I hope you'll give me a chance to explain. I hope you'll think back on the past couple weeks and know that none of my words were scripted. Especially the ones about loving you." She winced, but he couldn't tell if it was defensiveness, or acknowledging the truth of what he was saying. "I'll go back to the inn because you asked me to. But I'm not *going* anywhere."

She gave a low, humorless laugh. "That's not what your mother thinks. They came here to take you home."

"You don't get it, babe. I *am* home. Wherever you are is home for me."

CHAPTER TWENTY-FOUR

LUCY WATCHED OWEN walk out the door, feeling both angry and confused. He'd left. Because she'd told him to leave. She felt like a balloon with a slow leak, deflating from her white-hot anger and trying to wrap her mind around what had just happened.

Seeing that ridiculous app on his phone really had been an accident. She'd been so stunned by his parents' arrival, and so eager to escape, that she'd grabbed his phone off the kitchen island without remembering that hers was on the charger. So there she was, stalking angrily down the sidewalk, when she realized she needed someone to talk to. Someone to vent to. She'd whipped the phone out of her pocket to call Piper, then muttered when it wouldn't open on facial recognition. Still suspecting nothing, she'd tapped in the unlock code—the date she and Owen had met. That's when she finally realized it wasn't her phone. It opened, but the apps were all wrong on the home screen.

Realizing her mistake, she'd started to turn back when one app—with a big red cupid's heart on it—popped up in the middle of the screen. *Dr. Find-Love?* Technically, it wasn't her phone. And it wasn't her place to open apps. But it wasn't as if she'd opened his text history or anything. It was an app. And she was curious about what kind of love Owen was trying to find.

It opened right up to what she assumed was the last

page he'd used on it—*Here's How to Win Her Back*. It was funny at first. Leave it to Owen to use some online planner in order to reach his goal. But as she started reading through the list of tips on winning back a woman, her blood had run cold. She recognized every single one.

Stay in her orbit. He'd done that by taking the job with Connie.

Show her you know what she likes. It was tough to narrow that one down, but she couldn't help thinking of him referring to making a spreadsheet. Or had she mentioned that? It didn't matter. He'd claimed he wanted to know her. Because Dr. Find-Love told him it was a good idea.

Sometimes it takes a really grand gesture to soften her heart. Buttercup had clearly been his grand gesture. You couldn't get much more personal than her grandmother's car, and he'd definitely gone big with that move. And she'd fallen for it.

Instead of an intimate dinner, start with a casual picnic lunch. She wouldn't put it past him to have arranged the entire Falls Legend al fresco luncheon just to woo her. He must have really patted himself on the back after that kiss they'd shared at the waterfall.

Be her hero—look for opportunities to come to her rescue. Tears had stung her eyes reading that. The night he came with the lanterns, so very concerned for her safety. The night they'd made love on the sofa by lantern light. It was just a…a trick. She felt used.

When all else fails, puppies and kittens almost always work! Yeah, that kitten had broken the ice, all right. And nearly sent her into anaphylactic shock. She'd wondered what had possessed him to bring her a kitten. Now she knew. A five-dollar app on his phone. The thought made her feel used. Betrayed.

That's when she'd hurried back to the house and thrown the Coopers out. All of them. Even Owen. *Especially* Owen. She had every right to be angry. He'd played games at a time when her trust was at its lowest. She was offended. And hurt. And mad. She stomped her way into the kitchen and pulled a bottle of wine from the rack. A Finger Lakes pinot noir Owen had brought home. Because he knew it was her favorite. She stared at the bottle, trying in vain to keep her anger burning.

...none of my words were scripted. Especially the ones about loving you...

She was mad at Owen, damn it. So why was she still hearing his arguments in her head? And why had he sounded so...believable? She opened the bottle, filling a wineglass with the ruby red wine. He'd used an *app*. He'd trusted someone called *Dr. Find-Love*. Who does that?

I thought if I followed a plan I'd have better odds...

She sat in a kitchen chair with a deep sigh, taking a drink of her wine. That was definitely believable. There was a reason she called him her Man with a Plan. He was lost when things veered off-course, and a wedding being canceled at the last minute was about as off-course as things got. So he'd panicked.

A breeze made the wind chimes on the back deck tinkle merrily. Owen had bought the chimes as a gift for her last week. He said it reminded him of her because it had butterflies on it. Like her tattoo. She folded her arms on the table and dropped her head on them. Did that mean he cared, or was he just following the *Show her you know what she likes* tip from Dr. Find-Love? Her phone buzzed on the counter, but she ignored it. How was she ever going to be able to trust his words again? It probably didn't matter, as he'd probably be following his parents back to North Carolina.

Wherever you are is home for me...

That sounded pretty, but he'd told her over and over that he had a life waiting for him in Greensboro. A business to run, whether he wanted to run it or not.

"Oh, boy, this is even worse than I feared..."

Piper's voice in Lucy's kitchen made her jump. Piper stood inside the side door.

"What...what are you doing here?"

"I knocked on the front door and got nothing. I called the shop and Connie said you had the day off. I called your phone and got nothing. The side door was open, so I figured I'd better do a wellness check."

Lucy wiped her face quickly with the back of her hand, trying to gather herself together when she felt like she was falling apart. She started to smile and realized very quickly that it was a bad idea. Her mouth trembled, but she still tried to sound something close to normal.

"What made you think I needed a wellness check?"

Piper grabbed a wineglass for herself and filled it, then pulled out a chair and sat across from Lucy at the small breakfast table. "Well, a very pissed-off older woman came into the inn to claim her reserved room. She was accompanied by a subdued older gentleman. And Owen. In cargo shorts and a rumpled T-shirt. Barefoot." Piper shook her head. "He looked...ravaged. Shattered. Devastated."

Lucy lifted her hand. "Okay, I get the picture."

"He told me he needed a room, and then introduced those people as his *parents*, and... I knew *something* had happened. So I came to check on you." She took another sip of her wine. "Plus Owen pulled me aside and told me to get over here. What happened?"

"His mother clearly hates me, but I already knew that. But Owen…"

"No way he's going back with them?"

"Well, he might *now*. After I told him to leave." She ran her fingertip slowly around the top of her glass. "This whole time, with all his fancy wooing and courting and kittens and getting me to love him again…did you know he was just following some stupid phone app? None of it was real!" She paused, looking up at Piper. "Wait…*did* you know?" Piper's white face told the story.

Everyone convinced me it was a bad idea…

"You *knew*."

Piper held up her hands. "I didn't know all the details, but yes, I knew he originally started out using something he found online. Logan knew about it, and so did Iris and the book club. Those old ladies gave him *hell* about it, and he promised to stop using it."

"The book club knew?" No wonder Owen used the word *everyone.* It seemed everyone in Rendezvous Falls had known about Dr. Find-Love except Lucy. "And if the book club knew, then… Connie knew?"

This was a replay of the wedding weekend—everyone knew about her parents but her. Piper's hands shook slightly as she lifted her glass. "I honestly don't know that. Look, when Logan told me Owen was using an app, I didn't believe it. I figured he'd misunderstood or something. I mean…an *app*? Who would do that?"

"Well, I think you know the answer to that question."
I was desperate…

"If I'd thought he was that deep into this stupid app, I swear I would have told you. But after the kitten disaster—which ended great for Lily, by the way—Iris and the book club yelled at him and he stopped. And then you guys were together, and happy. I forgot all about the app." Piper's eyes went wide. "Oh, no…was that kitten a suggestion from…?"

"From Dr. Find-Love? Yup."

Piper snort-laughed so hard she started coughing on her wine.

"Did you just say Dr. Find-Love? No way that was really the name, right?"

Lucy raised her hand in the air. "Hand to God. He *paid* for advice from someone called Dr. Find-Love." Both women chuckled, but Lucy's laughter trailed off. "It makes me feel like such a fool, Piper. Like I was…"

"Manipulated."

"Exactly."

Piper shook her head, lost in thought for a moment. "Okay. I get that. But did you feel manipulated before you found out about the app? You couldn't have known, but did anything feel…off…about Owen's feelings for you?"

"Well, for one thing, I *could* have known if my friends had warned me." Piper's face went pink. "But no. It felt sincere, even if it surprised me. I never expected him to come after me when I bolted. I had a lot of doubts about how sincere he was, but I never thought he was playing me."

"Just because he used an app doesn't mean he was playing you. It was stupid, but it doesn't mean his intentions were bad." Piper reached over to put her hand on Lucy's.

"You know I love you, but you're awfully quick to cut and run. Why are you so sure everyone's motives are suspect?"

Lucy winced at Piper's words, but she couldn't argue with them. It was a fair observation, and a fair question.

"I haven't always been the cut-and-run type," she said softly. "I was the do-what-people-wanted type, right up until the minute that… I wasn't. And I can't seem to find any middle ground, where I trust myself, much less trust anyone else."

The windows were open, and a soft, warm breeze pushed into the kitchen, ruffling the edges of their napkins. Lucy stared at her wineglass, replaying the past two months in her mind.

"I panicked before the wedding. I'd been pushed and pushed and pushed and I kept giving in and giving in and… I was *sick* of it. Maybe I should have spoken up sooner, but that's not how I was raised. My parents…" She laughed bitterly. "My shining example of suppressed emotions…they raised me to be considerate. Don't be rude. Don't cause a scene. I don't think I ever saw them argue. They just drifted along, ignoring their own unhappiness for thirty-some years." She paused, thinking of all the times tension had wafted through the air at home, but had never manifested. All those years her parents had wasted feeling unhappy and alone.

"I don't want that, you know? I don't want to live like that—doing what's expected instead of what brings me joy." She looked up with a shrug. "I panicked when I saw that was where I was headed. Instead of fighting, I ran. Maybe I'm confrontation-phobic."

"Maybe," Piper agreed. "If so, you know that one of the most common cures for phobias is conditioning yourself to face whatever scares you. Like those classes for people afraid to fly, where they end up taking a flight in a plane. Maybe you need to go back to North Carolina to face what sent you running. You might find out it's not so bad."

Lucy shook her head vehemently. "I can't go back. Besides, I like it here."

"Do you? Or do you just like that it's not Greensboro?"

She thought of Connie's questions a while back. Would Lucy get upset about something and leave Rendezvous Falls the same way she'd left North Carolina? If she spent her life running from things that upset her, how was that any different from her parents staying together while ignoring the things that eventually tore them apart? Both ways of living were more like hiding.

"You think I should go home."

Piper took a sip of her wine before answering.

"I think you should confront your fears. You keep saying you panicked. The people and circumstances that pushed you to that panic point are *there*. Other than Owen, of course. And yes—" Piper patted her hand before releasing it "—Owen was a dumbass about a lot of things. He brushed off your worries before the wedding, but you know a lot of that was due to what he was dealing with after being overseas. But Logan says Owen's in a veteran's group now and he's dealing with it. He apologized. He patiently wooed you." They both chuckled at that. "Okay, maybe not patiently, but…with determination. And even if he used Dr. Find-Love to do it, it was for a good cause. He wants you back. I truly believe he loves you, Lucy."

"You don't know how much that man loves a plan. And the plan is for him and I to run the Cooper Landscaping empire in Greensboro. And now his parents are here to press their case. He talked to them like it was still a possibility. Even if he stays here, won't he resent me eventually? I can't get past this feeling that if we try to make that work, we'll be my parents all over again. My mom said they became more like management partners than lovers. I don't want that."

"Since Owen came up here, have you ever felt like he was looking for a business partner instead of a lover?"

"No." She didn't even have to think about that answer. "For all his foolishness, he hasn't made me feel that way. But…"

"But you're still afraid. Of something that happened to someone else. Maybe your fears are making things look a lot worse than they are."

Lucy sat back in her chair, her path suddenly clear.

"I need to go home and face the music."

"SHE'S NOT THERE." Logan called over from his front porch to where Owen stood at Lucy's door.

Those three words hit a lot heavier than they should have. There were several places in town that Lucy could be, but Owen had a feeling she was a lot farther away.

"How do you know?"

Logan walked to the edge of his porch, only twenty feet from Owen. His face was solemn.

"Piper took her to the airport in Syracuse before dawn this morning."

Owen blinked a few times, not sure how to respond. She'd run away. Again.

"Where'd she go this time?" He didn't bother hiding the bitterness in his voice. She'd just up and left, without saying a word.

"Greensboro."

"She went *home*?" That didn't make sense. She said she'd never go back.

"Something about 'facing the music.'"

"Is she coming back?"

Logan held up his hands at Owen's demanding tone. "I have no idea, but I do know she only took a small overnight case with her."

"And you know that because…"

"Because I put it in the car before they left at four this morning. I wanted to make sure they were set before driving all that way."

"You didn't think I should know my fiancée was leaving?"

"You keep using that word, but I haven't seen a ring on her finger. Lucy didn't want you to know until after she was gone." He turned to go back into the house. "But I'm telling you now."

Owen swore, tempted to kick at the locked door in front of him. Instead, he spun on his heel and walked away, barely grunting when Logan waved and went inside. She was *gone*. After everything. Just…up and left again. He kept walking, oblivious to his surroundings, with no destination in mind. He was marching, actually. Stomping his way down the sidewalk. Just when he thought the universe was righting itself, now everything was blowing up all over again. What was he supposed to do about it?

He looked up a few minutes—or maybe longer—later and realized he'd been going in circles, marching around a four block area around the Taggart Inn. He cursed to himself. It was a perfect metaphor to his life. Marching in fucking circles and getting nowhere.

He was surprised to see his parents sitting on the wide

front porch of the inn. At the table next to them was Iris Taggart and three of her book club pals, including Connie Phelps, along with Father Joe Brennan. Connie was saying something to Owen's mom, but Mom's body language screamed that she was *not* being very receptive. His father, however, was leaning forward and listening.

All six people turned and watched with a great deal of interest when Owen came up the stairs. Iris Taggart gave a little smirk to her tablemates.

"Well…speak of the devil and the devil appears."

His mother bristled.

"My son is *not* the devil in all of this. He's the one who got dumped, remember?"

Iris shrugged, one of the few people fearless in the face of his mother's fury.

"And why was that exactly? I think it had something to do with someone thinking their son's wedding was about *her* instead of the bride and groom."

Owen leaned against the porch post and crossed his arms waiting for his mom's response. She puffed up in outrage, glaring at Iris, but when she saw that had no effect at all, she turned on her silent husband.

"Are you just going to sit there and let them insult me like this?"

Edward Cooper gave a low chuckle, and Owen sucked in a surprised breath. Laughing at his mother was something even Owen never dared. His dad looked at his wife, then to the people gathered at the next table.

"If you think I'm stepping in between you and these ladies and the good Father, Faye, you are mistaken. I'm not stupid. Besides—" his dad took a sip of the coffee in front of him "—they have a point."

If his mother puffed up anymore she'd explode.

"I *beg* your pardon?"

"Faye, it's time for you to get off this high horse you've been on and listen to people." His father seemed very calm for a man walking into battle with a dragon. To Owen's surprise, though, the dragon sat back in silence, blinking at her husband as if seeing him for the first time. His father set his cup down on the table. "You've been acting like this for too long. I thought it was a phase. I thought it was menopause…" That made his mother stiffen, but the other ladies snickered among themselves. "I thought you'd calm down after the wedding, but now I see I should have stepped in a long time ago."

"Stepped in? As if you have a right to tell me what to do?"

Dad shook his head, and Owen realized his calm demeanor had a touch of steel to it. "Nope. But I should have offered some…guidance. Given you my opinion to consider. Maybe it would have prevented some of this." Before Mom could say a word, he pushed on. "You've been so determined to have your way that you've lost sight of the big picture. You want me to retire, but what if I don't want to? You want Owen to take over a business our niece is running very well, so what if Owen doesn't want to do that? What if Lori doesn't want to give it up?"

"But…but…that business is ours!"

"Ours as in yours and mine? My brother and I started that landscaping business straight out of high school. He ran it while I went to college, remember? Butch is gone now, but his daughter is doing a great job expanding the business and managing it. We've got two locations, with another set to open. I know we all expected Owen to take over, but so what if he doesn't? Why can't Lori run it?"

"Dad…" Owen pushed away from the post, stunned at what he was hearing. His father turned to face him.

"Son, do you *want* to run the nursery and business?"

"No." He didn't have to think twice. "I love the work of landscaping, but I want to get my hands dirty, not run an empire."

"Then why the hell didn't you say so?" His father stood, looking annoyed. "Don't answer that. I know why. We never let you think it was an option, did we?" Dad gestured between his wife and himself.

"Uh…" Owen swallowed hard. "Frankly, sir…no, you didn't."

Faye Cooper found her voice at last. But it was cracking a bit.

"But… we had a plan…the condo in Palm Beach… retirement…"

"Sweetheart, *you* had a plan. You had a spot for everyone to fill and that made you comfortable. You've always been a driven one. But… I don't want to retire." Her eyes went wide, but he kept talking. "Cut back some, sure. Go to a beach somewhere in the winter, sure. But I *enjoy* my job. I can't tell you what to do, but damn it, you can't tell other people what to do, either."

His mother's mouth snapped shut, her face pale. An off balance Faye Cooper was not a common sight. Owen didn't get any satisfaction from it, because he could see the hurt and—was that fear?—in her silver-blue eyes. In group session the other day, the leader said sometimes the people who seem to have it the most together are the ones falling apart inside. He said to be careful about envying or resenting those people, but some were just really good actors, and keeping up that façade was exhausting.

And just like that, a lot of puzzle pieces fell into place. Lucy had pretended to be okay with everyone else's plans, when she was quietly letting her resentments eat her up inside. His mother had turned more and more aggressive in getting her way over the past few years.

He knelt on one knee by his mother's chair. Her eyes were shining with unshed tears. Her lips trembled.

"Mom...what are you afraid of?"

Her hand went to her throat, and she made a strangled sound as she swallowed a sob.

"I...nothing... I'm not..." She looked up to her husband, standing silently by her side with his hand on her shoulder. "I'm afraid of losing you. Of losing...what we planned... I mean...what will happen...?"

It was Helen Russo who leaned over from her nearby seat and put her hand on his mother's other shoulder.

"I know exactly what you mean, Faye. I lost my husband much too soon, and I was *so* angry at the world. But what you're feeling...the fear about plans changing...you're afraid of something that hasn't happened yet. Think of all the energy you're wasting over something you can't control."

"But I *can* control it!" His mother's mouth was hard and thin. "All I need to do is get Owen home and away from that girl..."

Connie sat up straight. "That *girl* is a lovely, talented, caring woman that any family would be lucky to have. And I'm pretty sure your son, however misguided his methods have been, is in love with her. Do you really want him to walk away from the woman he loves?"

"You mean the woman who's left him twice now?" His mother sniffed. "You told me yourself she flew to Greensboro this morning. Whenever things get too hot, she takes off. My son deserves better."

"Your son won't find any better." Father Joe joined the conversation. "And Helen was right. You're wasting whatever life you have left by tryin' to control it. That's not how life works. The more you try to shape the future, the more elusive it becomes. What's the saying? Man plans and God laughs?" Joe lifted a shoulder. "Not to be cruel, but if that's true, God could be laughin' at you, Mrs. Cooper. Your efforts are wasted on trying to change whatever He has in store. Far better to enjoy what happiness you can share with those you love in the here and now than fret over what might happen tomorrow."

Iris tapped her cane on the porch floor next to her chair. "Hear, hear, Father Joe. You think I planned on being a single mother with a money pit of an inn to run all those years ago? And here I am, happy as a clam."

Cecile Manning giggled. "As happy as a clam about to be steamed and eaten, maybe." She rolled her eyes when Iris flipped her middle finger in Cecile's direction. "I get your point, Iris. You survived and thrived. Just like Connie did."

Connie thought for a moment before answering. "I think I'm just getting to the thriving part, but yes." She gave Owen's mother a meaningful look. "Thanks to Lucy and Owen. Lucy got my business back on track and forced me out of my…melancholy." Cecile did a fake cough and said what sounded like *bitchiness*. Connie ignored her. "And Owen got my house looking nice again. He helped me feel in control of my own life."

Helen patted Faye Cooper's shoulder again before sitting back. "That's the only thing we *can* control."

His mother didn't answer, but he had a feeling she'd listened to at least some of it. He didn't expect her to change her stripes after one brief conversation It was up to her to decide if she was going to take any of the advice she'd been given.

Meanwhile, all this talk of *here and now* had him thinking of his own dilemma. Keeping Lucy in his life. Right now, she was in North Carolina. So what was he doing sitting here?

"I need to go after Lucy."

It seemed so logical. To his surprise, he was the only one who thought so. Everyone else cried out "No!"

He looked around the faces in confusion. He knew why his mother didn't want him to go, but…he looked at Connie.

"I thought you said we belonged together? Don't you want her back?"

The older woman's eyes narrowed on him. "And how are you going to make that happen? You going to drag her back to Rendezvous Falls single-handedly? Were you not listening just now?"

Cecile nodded. "You can't control her or persuade her to be where she doesn't want to be or love who she doesn't want to love." She gave him a soft look. "To be clear, I'm quite sure she loves you. But it's not up to you to *win* her. She has to choose her own life. You just…" She paused, and Iris finished the sentence.

"You just have to do what Lena told you a few weeks ago. Be the man she deserves."

Father Joe added his thoughts. "And be patient, lad. Trust the future instead of tryin' so hard to bend it t'your will."

CHAPTER TWENTY-FIVE

"Okay, this is weird." Nikki Taggart held her glass up for the bartender to refill. "Am I the only one who thinks this is weird?"

Lucy didn't answer, but her sister, Kris, didn't hesitate. "It's a little weird. This is where it started. Or ended. Which was it, Luce?"

The three women were sitting at the same bar where Lucy's bachelorette party had happened. It was much quieter tonight. For one thing, it was a weeknight. And there was no music playing. Instead, there were groups of people gathered at tables in the far corner playing trivia.

"Maybe both?" Lucy finally answered. "Something ended. Something started."

"The funny thing is, it was the same thing." Nikki held up her glass. "You and Owen ended. And now you and Owen are starting."

Lucy arched a brow at her friend. "Oh, are we?"

"Give me a break. You know you are. That man, dumbass though he may be, loves you. You complete him." Nikki leaned forward, hand over her heart. "And you love him, too. He had you at hello."

Kris shook her head. "I don't think it was at hello, but not long after. There's something just a little caveman about him chasing after you, but in the hottest possible way. It's like something out of one of those bodice rippers Mom reads."

Nikki straightened, taking offense. "Bodice rippers? Excuse me, but they aren't called that anymore. They're romance novels, and cavemen alphas are not the norm anymore. But Owen was so sweet about it…he's more of a cinnamon roll hero."

"You read that stuff?" Kris shrugged. "I couldn't get past all the heaving and gasping and swollen manhoods."

The bartender, a young man in his early twenties, moved quickly to the far end of the bar. Lucy bumped her sister's shoulder. "Nice work, Kris. You scared the bartender."

"*Scarred* is more like it," Nikki snorted. "Poor kid has never heard that word, because it's from some 1990s romance novel. Remind me to send you something more current to read, Kris. You don't know what you're missing. A cinnamon roll is a guy who might be a little crusty on the outside—like a hardened military veteran, but he's all sweet and soft on the inside. Like a man who'd download a phone app in order to win the heart of the woman he loves."

"But he didn't chase me back to North Carolina." She wasn't sure how she felt about that.

"Please," Kris said. "You've only been here two days, and you're going back north tomorrow. Do you really expect him to trail you everywhere you go?" She shook her head. "Creeper alert."

"No, but…" She had expected to turn around and see Owen after she got here. Instead, he'd sent a quick text saying he hoped she accomplished whatever she needed to in Greensboro. That he was there if she wanted to talk.

There. Not here. "His parents came home. I figured he'd be with them."

She'd seen his parents yesterday at the nursery. She'd stopped by to talk to his cousin Lori. The Coopers pulled in just as she was leaving. Faye had given a reluctant wave and gone inside, but Edward had walked over to greet her warmly.

"Owen drove us to the airport last night." He'd watched for her reaction, but she stayed silent. "He showed me around Rendezvous Falls while we were there. It's a nice little town." She'd only nodded. "He says there was an opportunity for a landscaping business there. I'm always open to expansion."

"What? A landscaping business in New York?"

"It was just something he mentioned. As we were driving around looking at…places."

She'd tried to get him to tell her more, but he was playfully coy. Two words she never dreamed she'd use in relation to Ed Cooper.

The bartender approached the three women cautiously, probably trying to determine the topic of conversation first. Lucy covered her glass as a sign she was finished. She was driving the other two, so she'd stop with this one. She pointed to the menu and ordered a plate of nachos.

When the plate arrived, Kris scooped up a pile of toppings on a chip.

"Mom said you had a good talk this morning."

"Yeah, I guess. The most important thing is we talked. I met Jeff What's-his-name and managed to carry on a few minutes of civil conversation with my mother's lover."

"Ew. Don't call him that." Kris grimaced. "Even if it's true, it's gross. He's not a bad guy."

"He had an affair with a married woman." Lucy pointed out. "He's no saint."

"I never crowned him with sainthood. Or Mom, for that matter. But what's done is done. He adores Mom and she seems happy." Kris flipped her hair back. "You have to admit she laughs more now."

"Hmm." Lucy took a bite of the nachos. "What about Dad's happiness?"

Kris shrugged. "To be honest, he was more upset about *you* leaving than he was about Mom leaving."

That's what her father had told her two days ago. He said he'd been bracing for a divorce for a few years now, but he'd never once expected his daughter to be a runaway bride. But he'd told her he was proud of her. *Proud.* He said she'd been right to demand what she deserved, even if she *had* waited until the last minute.

Nikki gave Lucy's shoulder a nudge. "So have you completed your apology tour?"

"That's not…" She grimaced. "Yeah, I guess that is what I'm doing. I didn't talk to Owen's mom, but I think that can wait. Considering she didn't convince him to come back with her, she's probably not too happy right now."

"You have to admit," Nikki said, "it's ironic that you're here and he's in New York."

Kris leaned forward to see Nikki. "But they'll both be in New York tomorrow afternoon. *Then* we'll find out what's going to happen. Or not happen. But I'm guessing it's gonna happen."

Nikki agreed. "My grandmother says he's planning something big." She clapped her hand over her mouth. "Oh, hell… I don't think I was supposed to say anything!"

"Bigger than rebuilding my car? Bigger than almost killing me with a cat?"

Bigger than making her fall in love with him all over again?

Nikki's smile faded. "I honestly don't know, but act surprised." She quickly changed the subject. "So did you find the closure you needed here?"

"Yes. If nothing else, I'm not just a *runaway* anymore. I left. But I came back and faced the music." She started ticking things off on her fingers. "Apologized to everyone. Offered to pay for the bridesmaids' dresses." Luckily for her wallet, no one had taken her up on the offer. "Made peace with Mom and Dad. Met Mom's friend, What's-His-Name…"

"Jeff!" Kris groaned. "His name is Jeff."

"I talked to the Coopers. At least with one of them. Not my fault Faye walked away. I apologized to the church pastor. So I guess that's closure. My friend Piper…"

Nikki raised her glass in a toast. "That's my sister-in-law!"

"Yes. And she's great. She told me I needed to face down my fears. Owen sort of told me the same thing. That's why I have an appointment with a therapist next week. I might need a little help on that front." She sat back, knowing she was finally *doing* something instead of fretting about doing something. "The funny thing is, once I got back here I realized I didn't fear anyone as much as I'd feared my own complacency. I'm the one who let myself get pushed around. I just waited too long to do something about it."

"Part of that is my fault." Kris frowned. "You were just a kid when I got sick. You grew up thinking your job was to make everyone else's life easier." She grabbed Lucy's hand. "And you did, sweetie. You were really good at taking care of us. But now it's your turn. Claim your time, sis."

The two sisters stared at each other for a moment. Lucy smiled, her mouth trembling.

"Claim my time. I like the sound of that."

PIPER PICKED UP LUCY from the airport, but she'd been steadfast during the drive back to Rendezvous Falls that she was not talking about whatever Owen might have planned. Instead, she talked about the happy news that Evie Hudson was pregnant. Mark and Evie were going to move in with his grandmother in her large lakefront home, not far from Connie's less grand cottage. Piper said Connie and her friends, and even her son David, thought that between Lucy working at the shop and someone helping maintain her home, Connie would be able to stay in her cottage for a lot longer.

Owen was waiting for her on the front porch of the yellow house when Piper dropped her off. He stood when she got out of the car, watching silently as she walked toward him. She stopped at the bottom of the steps.

"You're still here," she said to him, her mind blank of anything more clever to say.

He leaned his hip on the porch rail, his arms folded on his chest.

"Where else would I be?"

"Home in Greensboro?"

"My home's not in Greensboro."

She started to smile, and he returned it. She wasn't feeling as cautious anymore. She'd spent the whole flight home thinking about what *claiming her time* would look like.

"My home's not there, either. So…what do we do now?"

"Maybe build a home together?"

She tipped her head and propped her hand under her chin in mocking thoughtfulness. "That's an interesting idea." She looked up at him coyly. "Do you think there's an app that would tell us how to do that?"

Owen put his hands on his chest and staggered back. "Ouch. That hurt." Then he grew serious. "You forgive me for that?"

She walked up the steps and moved into the embrace he offered, laying her head against his solid chest.

"I don't know if I'll ever stop wondering why you'd trust anyone who calls themselves Dr. Find-Love for relationship advice. But I believe your intentions were good. And let's face it, I made mistakes, too. I was as big a fool as you were, not trusting anyone. At least *you* trusted Dr. Find-Love." They stood silently, his head resting on hers. This was where she belonged. "I forgive you, Owen. And I love you."

His arms tightened briefly, his lips brushed her hair.

"Good." He took a deep breath and released it slowly, his body relaxing against hers as if he'd just heard the best news of his life. She smiled and snuggled closer. His hand slid under her top, brushing against the small of her back.

"I missed you, Luce. Did you do what you needed to do in Greensboro?"

"Yes."

"I thought about following you."

She hesitated. "I think you've done enough of that, don't you?"

He put two fingers under her chin and lifted it until she was looking straight at him.

"If you understand only one thing in your life, Lucy—understand this." His eyes were dark with emotion. "I would follow you to the ends of the earth and back if I had to. If that's what it takes to keep you in my life, I will follow you forever…" The corner of his mouth twitched. "But, as Dr. Find-Love says, not in a creepy way." She laughed, and he continued. "The only reason I didn't follow you this time was that some very smart people told me to trust the future. I knew in my heart that you'd be back."

"Is that your grand gesture? That you're staying in Rendezvous Falls? I think I'd already guessed that."

He chuckled. "Someone squealed on me." He released her and led her back down the steps, away from the house. "I'm not so vain to think me staying here is the greatest gift I could give you."

"It's a pretty big deal, Owen." It was everything. He was staying. "Your parents are okay with it?"

He shrugged. "Dad is. Mom…not so much. But she'll adjust. Or not. Her choice." He looked back at her. "That sounded bad. I want Mom to be okay with it. I hope she will be. But it really is up to her. Dad says he's going to work on her. After all, he needs to keep his newest business partner happy."

"Your cousin Lori?"

"Nope. Me."

They were almost to his Bronco. She dug in her heels and pulled her hand out of his. Her first thought was that meant Owen was going back to Greensboro. But no. He said he was staying. She remembered what Edward Cooper hinted at.

"*You're* his partner? How will *that* work?"

Owen opened the passenger door. "So whoever gave

up that I had a surprise for you didn't know what it was, eh? Hop in. I want to show you something."

He turned up Main Street and on up the hill toward Luke and Whitney's place. A surprise party? No, that didn't sound like Owen. His expression was that of a little boy who'd just done something fabulous and couldn't wait to show it off. She half expected him to shout "look at this big bug I found in the mud!"

But he didn't say a word. Not even when he drove *past* the entrance to the winery. After another mile or so, he slowed the truck. There was a farm on the hillside, with a cheerful blue farmhouse with white shutters and a broad front porch. The house overlooked a small pond. Beyond the house was an old red barn and some other outbuildings. The whole place was tidy and pretty, especially with the afternoon sunshine hitting it. She had no idea why Owen was slowing down for it. Was he proving he couldn't get lost in Rendezvous Falls? Or was he lost now?

Owen pulled into the long driveway and stopped next to the For Sale sign. He turned off the ignition.

"Okay…" Lucy looked around. "I'm trying to see what this is, but…"

Owen rested his hands on the steering wheel, then rested his chin on his hands. "What this is…is a farm. It's where I got that damn kitten."

She chuckled. "Please tell me you're not giving me another cat."

"Nope."

"Then what…"

"See that metal pole barn?" He nodded toward it. "I figure I can keep a couple pieces of equipment in there. Backhoes. Bobcats. Mowers." He nodded at the big barn.

"That will be great storage for mulch and gardening soil."
He looked toward her. "And maybe even a horse or two.
Some goats. Chickens. Whatever you want and aren't al-
lergic to."

"What *I* want?" She looked at the farm. It was pretty.
She could imagine baskets of flowers hanging on the
porch. Children running in the yard. Whoa…was this
some magical place that allowed people to see the future? She blinked, and it was just a well-kept farm again.
A farm that was for sale. A grand gesture.

"Oh, God, Owen. Tell me you didn't buy this place."

"Not yet. I'd never do that without talking to you first.
But…" He sat back in the seat and turned toward her. "It
would be a great base for the newest Cooper Landscaping location."

Her mouth fell open. "I… I don't… I think it's time for
you to stop the mysterious act and just tell me straight out
what you're thinking."

He slid his arm over her shoulders and unhooked her
seat belt with his other so she could slide closer to him.
"My dad and I had a long talk. I told him the part of the
business I enjoyed was the dirty part. Working with my
hands. Actual landscaping instead of selling plants for
other people to plant. The guys here think there's a real
opportunity for a good landscaping business. So Dad's
investing the seed money to get it started. The New York
division of the family empire." He kissed the tip of her
nose. "This place would be great, but if you don't like it,
we'll keep looking. Nothing happens from this day forward that you and I don't both agree on."

"So the job is your grand gesture? Bringing Cooper
Landscaping here? Turn this into commercial property?"

"Well…yes about the job. But I want this place to be more than a business. The house is really nice, Luce. And look at that pond! Imagine having our coffee together in the mornings out on that porch, looking down over the valley and the lake. You'd almost be a mountain girl again."

She *could* imagine it. She could *see* it as real as if she was right there living it. They'd be happy here in that big blue house and that big red barn.

He pointed at the top of the hill above the farm. "And guess what? There's a trail that runs along the ridge and right behind the Luke and Whitney's vineyard. Right down to Rendezvous Falls. We can walk there any time we want."

"Sounds perfect."

"*You're* perfect, Lucy. You're what makes *everything* perfect. I love you." He started to laugh softly. "God help me, I still want to marry you. But this time you and I make every decision together. No one else."

"No one else," she echoed. "I love you, Owen."

They kissed, in the Bronco, next to the For Sale sign. Overlooking the farm that would become their home. The kiss lasted a long, long time. After the kiss, he held her close to his chest. Safe. Warm. Loved.

She smiled up at him. "It would be a short drive to the flower shop from here."

Relief filled his eyes as he nodded. "It would. Although it might be more challenging in the winter." He kissed her. "I think little Buttercup will have to live in the barn in the winter. We'll get you something a little more robust for the cold months."

"Yes," she agreed. "Look at us. Making plans…together."

His gaze went solemn and warm.

"It's about time, don't you think?"

"I do. Together is a good thing."

He kissed her again.

"You and I are a very good thing, Lucy. And we're going to stay that way."

She dropped her head back down to his chest, looking out the windshield at the farm. She gave a soft, contented sigh.

"I know exactly where I want our real wedding to be."

He brushed his fingers through her hair.

"Let me guess…standing on a rock at the bottom of a waterfall?"

"Wow…you really *do* know me, Owen Cooper." She sat up, flashing him a bright smile. "Can we go look at the house?"

He started the ignition. "Yes, ma'am. I told the Martins you might want to check it out."

He drove toward the farmhouse. Lucy gave herself a little hug, and he raised a questioning brow in her direction.

"We're going to be happy here," she explained. Owen nodded.

"I believe you're right. We will be."

He twined his fingers through hers when they got out of the Bronco, and gave her a boyishly bright grin as they walked up the steps and into their future together.

EPILOGUE

"IF I FALL in this mud, I will totally blame you, Owen Cooper."

"Oh no you don't!" Owen laughed, grabbing Lucy's hand as they walked the path from their house to the vineyard. He'd warned her the trail would be slippery after three days of rain. He'd offered to drive her to the waterfall. Lucy had given him a lengthy explanation of the "symbolism" of walking the path to the falls, like the original couple in the legend had done.

He'd promised her she'd have exactly the wedding she wanted, and if she wanted them to walk to meet everyone else at the wedding site, then that's what he'd do.

She was using her free hand to clutch her cotton skirt up around her waist to keep it clean as they walked. After a dreary week of cold and rain, the weekend had arrived sunny and relatively warm. They started down the hill, and he slid his arm around her waist to be sure she didn't slip. He couldn't resist reminding her.

"This was *your* idea."

"Getting married? You asked me, remember?"

"You know, that was so long ago I can hardly…"

"Oh, be quiet, you." She giggled. She'd been doing a lot of that lately—bright, sparkling giggles. Throughout the exhausting move into their farmhouse, repainting almost every room in the place and trying to make it their own…giggles. Sometimes he'd hear her giggling to herself in a room as he walked by, as if she was so happy she couldn't contain it. He knew the feeling. He'd been close to giddy himself more than once. It was hard to believe they could both be so happy. But that's what love did. She was his sunshine surprise every day.

Cooper Landscaping was off to a busy start in Rendezvous Falls, although the winter months would slow things down a bit. But Lucy was now co-owner of Rendezvous Blooms with Connie, and the winter months would be fairly busy with *that* business over the holidays and Valentine's Day. Their incomes would balance out between the two jobs.

"Stop!" Lucy hissed, and he did, looking at her in confusion.

"What's wrong?"

"Shush!" She released his hand. "We're almost there. Give me the bag!"

They were at the edge of the woods now, and the ground wasn't as muddy. Lucy let her skirt drop, brushing her hands down the front to smooth it. She looked like an Earth goddess in the long ivory eyelet dress. The design was simple, but it suited her, with the hemline swishing around her ankles. A ring of fresh flowers in fall colors rested on her head—she and Connie had put it together last night at the house with flowers from the shop. Long beaded ribbons fell from the back of the flower crown. She was *his* goddess. He still couldn't believe it. And he'd almost lost her.

He handed her the bag he'd been carrying. She pulled off her shoes and gasped at the cold of the ground under her toes. She dropped the muddy shoes in the bag and held it up, brows raised.

"Is this really necessary?" He grumbled the question

but tugged his shoes off before waiting for a reply. And damn, the ground *was* cold. He could only imagine how cold the water in the stream was going to be. He looked at Lucy, and she giggled again.

Hell, if she'd asked him to stand directly *under* the freezing waterfall, he'd say yes...just to hear that laughter again. He rolled up his pants, hoping the rain hadn't made the water too deep for wading.

"Come on," Lucy grabbed his hand, her face shining with happiness. She tugged him to follow her. "They're waiting!"

THE LEGENDARY ROCK was dry on top, but still slippery under their bare, wet feet. More than once, Lucy thought she and Owen would end up sitting in the cold water. But they got through the ceremony—a civil one blessed by Father Brennan—while staying relatively dry.

The officiants and the guests had stayed on the shore. But Lucy was determined that, barring a downpour, she and Owen were going to stand on this legendary rock and take their vows, sealing them with a kiss that would guarantee they'd be together forever. After the first wedding fiasco, she wanted *everyone* to be sure about one thing—this marriage was forever.

Owen stepped off the rock into the water, grimacing from the cold before smiling up at her. Instead of taking her hand, he swept her off the rock and cradled her in his arms, high and dry as the freezing cold water swirled around his legs.

"Hello, wife," he sai, his eyes gleaming with love.

"Hi, husband." Her arms wrapped around his neck.

"I love you."

"I know. I love you, too."

"That's good." He kissed her softly. "Between the justice of the peace, Father Joe's blessing, and the legend, there's no way we're turning back now."

She giggled. "Not to mention we have two businesses and a mortgage together. We're in this for the long haul, mister."

He tipped his head back and laughed.

She'd married a man with the best laugh in the world.

He walked to the shore and set her down, keeping her in the circle of his arms. They were surrounded by a small group of their closest friends and family. Another group of people, those who didn't want to deal with hiking and October weather, were waiting at the warm, dry Taggart Inn for a wedding luncheon catered by Nikki.

"Can we put our shoes on now?" Owen asked, making her laugh.

"Yes! My feet are freezing!"

Piper Taggart handed them their shoes, as well as two fluffy towels to dry off with. They sat on a large rock near the water, and she bumped her shoulder against Owen's. "Thank you for giving me my barefoot wedding."

He straightened. "Haven't you figured it out yet?"

"What?"

"I'd give you the moon if you wanted it, Lucy Hig..." He caught himself and chuckled. "Lucy *Cooper*. I like the sound of that."

"I like it, too. But you can leave the moon where it is. As long as I have you, I'm good."

Owen leaned in and kissed her, and she knew she'd never walk away from this man again. He was hers... forever.

* * * * *

"So, why are you here?" The question again, whispered this time.

She might as well just dive in. "I…need your help."

He frowned again. "What do you want?"

Her heart stuttered. Now that the time was here, she didn't know
what to say. Or how to say it. Or anything.

Danny's lips tweaked into a sad smile. "You're procrastinating,
Lizzie. You never procrastinate unless it's something bad."

Her expression must have given something away because he
paled.

"Are you okay? Are you sick?"

She shook her head. "I'm fine. But it's…" She trailed off.

Danny pinned her with a sharp look. "What is it you want to tell
me?"

She took a deep breath. "About that last fight we had—all those
years ago."

"What about it?" His tone was tight.

Right. "The one where you told me you didn't want marriage or children." She met his gaze as bravely as she could. "Well, I was pregnant."

Lizzie's words hit Danny like a tidal wave. All kinds of emotions swamped him, so many that he couldn't separate them, couldn't make sense of them. Couldn't…anything.

He stared at her. "Pregnant?" The moment passed in a sizzle of silence. She pulled out her phone. He didn't understand the move at first, but then she turned it to him and he saw.

It was a picture of an adorable cherub with a heart-shaped face, bright brown eyes and a toss of dark curls. The dent in her chin even matched his. She was a perfect and exquisite mix of the two of them. There was no doubt about that. Danny's heart thudded as he stared at the image.

His daughter. This was his daughter.

He had a child.

Some strange and great elation rolled through him at the sight of her. It made him giddy and filled with joy. What a pity it was quickly followed by dread and fury as the facts clicked into place. "Why didn't you tell me?"

Don't miss
Accidental Homecoming
by New York Times *bestselling author Sabrina York,*
available August 2021 wherever
Harlequin Special Edition books and ebooks are sold.

Harlequin.com

Don't miss the next funny and heart-tugging romance in the Rendezvous Falls series by

JO McNALLY

Falling in love with your friend can be trouble...

"Readers will be charmed by this sweet, no-nonsense Christmas romance full of genuine emotion."
—*Publishers Weekly* on *Stealing Kisses in the Snow*

Pick up your copy today!